Now the War is Over

ANNIE MURRAY was born in Berkshire and read English at St John's College, Oxford. Her first 'Birmingham' story, *Birmingham Rose*, hit *The Times* bestseller list when it was published in 1995. She has subsequently written many other successful novels, including the bestselling *Chocolate Girls* and *War Babies*. *Now the War is Over* is Annie's twentieth novel. She has four children and lives near Reading.

PRAISE FOR ANNIE MURRAY

Soldier Girl

'This heart-warming story is a gripping read, full of drama, love and compassion' *Take a Break*

Chocolate Girls

'This epic saga will have you gripped from start to finish' *Birmingham Evening Mail*

Birmingham Rose

'An exceptional first novel' *Chronicle*

Birmingham Friends

'A meaty family saga with just the right mix of mystery and nostalgia' *Parents' Magazine*

Birmingham Blitz

'A tale of passion and empathy which will keep you hooked' *Woman's Own*

ANNIE MURRAY

Now the War is Over

PAN BOOKS

First published 2016 by Pan Books
an imprint of Pan Macmillan
20 New Wharf Road, London N1 9RR
Associated companies throughout the world
www.panmacmillan.com

ISBN 978-1-4472-8630-1

1 3 5 7 9 8 6 4 2

A CIP catalogue record for this book is available from the British Library.

Typeset by Ellipsis Digital Limited, Glasgow
Printed and bound by CPI Group (UK) Ltd, Croydon, CR0 4YY

Visit **www.panmacmillan.com** to read more about all our books
and to buy them. You will also find features, author interviews and
news of any author events, and you can sign up for e-newsletters
so that you're always first to hear about our new releases.

For our Rachel xx

March 1961, Selly Oak Hospital

'Nurse! Student Nurse Booker – what on earth has got into you? You never, *ever*—'

The remainder of Sister Anderson's admonitions about what student nurses must never, *ever* do faded into a bewildered silence as she stood in the doorway of the ward sluice.

Melly felt the glower of Sister Anderson's eyes drilling through her as she leaned over the sink, her clammy hands locked to its cool whiteness. She knew that the senior staff usually saw her as an intelligent student who was eager to please. She wanted to be the best nurse you could ever be but she had just rushed off in the middle of the Sister's showing her a procedure, in a quite disgraceful manner.

Melly hung her head, with its neatly fastened mouse-brown hair and nurse's cap. She was trembling so violently that she was afraid her legs might give way. Her heart felt as if it was about to pound right out through the front of her chest.

'Nurse?' Sister Anderson tried again, though her voice was a fraction less harsh now.

Melly simply could not turn round. How could she explain to Sister that every day had become a nightmare to her, of exhaustion after lying awake, her mind churning;

1

that she could no longer concentrate on anything, that she felt as if she was going mad? And even worse, that when Sister had requested her to remove that drip from Mr Brzezinski's arm, she had seen that bead of blood, round and shiny as a ladybird in the crook of his elbow . . . And while she knew this was normal and that the platelets would make the blood solidify into a scab, in her mind the blood forced its way out, gushing, pumping . . . She had actually seen it: the bedclothes dyed red, the pulsing tide of it coming and coming, unstoppable . . . And that was when she ran . . .

'I –' she gulped, trying to find words, desperate for anything on which she could hang a normal thought. For days now, everything had felt so grey, so full of fear and panic, it was as if she was locked in this prison alone and no one could hear her.

She heard Sister's footsteps moving closer and her body shook even harder, as if in the face of great danger. Sister Anderson was in her forties, a sturdily built woman with pink cheeks and grey eyes, her brown hair always in the neatest bun under her frilled cap. She was stern, though usually fair: an excellent nurse, everyone said so.

Melly could feel Sister Anderson standing just behind her.

'What is the meaning of this, Nurse Booker?'

'I don't know,' she managed to say. 'I just can't . . .' She held out her hands. 'I can't stop shaking.'

'Nurse –' The Sister's tone was gentler now, but there was still a tough firmness to it. 'I understand that recent events have been difficult for you. We have all been aware of the . . . circumstances. But shocking and upsetting things happen. It's in the nature of the work. A nurse has to be able to face such events and not be borne down by them. You have to keep going and do your best for your patients. And you never, *ever* dash about like that on the ward.'

Melly hung her head. She knew nothing now, except the leaden, joyless feeling that filled her, the panic that rose in her however hard she tried to stifle it.

'I do understand,' Sister Anderson went on. 'But you must also realize that this situation cannot continue. We do not expect displays of emotion from our nurses. If you cannot control yourself, your nursing career will be at an end. You will have to think of withdrawing from—'

'No!' Melly whirled round. 'No, please! I want to be a nurse. It's all I've *ever* wanted.' Her usually sweet and cheerful face looked pale and strained. 'Please, Sister – just give me a few moments. I'll try, I really will!'

'Very well. Take a short break now. I shall expect you back on the ward in twenty minutes. In command of yourself.'

'Yes, Sister,' Melly whispered. Looking down, she could see Sister's solid black shoes move away, leaving her alone.

She tried to do as she was bidden. But she still could not move. She sank down, leaning against the wall next to the sink, and wrapped her arms around her knees.

I

1951

One

March 1951, Aston, Birmingham

All Melly had wanted to do that terrible Saturday morning was to give Mom a surprise. The baby was due any
day now and her mother, Rachel, was sickly and
exhausted.

'You'll have to go down to the shops again for me
later, Melly.'

Rachel Booker stood, holding on to the back of a chair
for support as the children finished their bit of breakfast.
Her face was pale, twisted with nausea. 'We've no lard –
we need cheese ... bread ...' She was talking half to
herself but Melly was taking it all in. 'You can go later.
Mind Tommy and Kev for me while I lie down for a bit,
there's a good girl. I must've overdone it yesterday. Oh
– I'll be glad when it's over.'

Clutching her belly she crawled off upstairs.

Melanie Booker, nine years old, looked about the
cramped room, the only downstairs living space of a
back-to-back house. There was a gas stove, the table and
chairs, a stool and armchair, and a sideboard where they
kept the crocks and cutlery. The most impressive feature
was the old iron range, which they only lit in the winter.
A door opened to a tiny scullery with a sink, though
there was no running water in the house. It had to be carried from the tap in the yard. Dad and Auntie had done

the house up last summer. They stoved the house yet again to get rid of the bugs and papered the walls with a green-on-white pattern of trees and country scenes. Auntie Gladys was proud of her house and kept it nice, even though it was a running battle against damp and vermin in all these back-to-backs on yards which clung round the heart of Birmingham, pressed in tight between factories and warehouses.

The room was crowded enough now, but soon there would be a pram in there again . . . Mom was forever cursing the place, saying it was a 'flaming rathole'. But so far as Melly was concerned, it was home.

Melly was used to being in charge of her brothers. Two-and-a-half-year-old Kev, a wiry, active little lad, was on the floor, a crust in one hand, which he was posting absent-mindedly into his mouth along with a ration of snot. With the other hand he was scraping a tin lorry back and forth along the lino. He was brown-haired, with thin, dark arcs of eyebrows which made him look both innocent and quizzical. Tommy, who was seven and darker in looks than Melly and Kev, was in his special chair, still eating his breakfast too. He could feed himself well enough with his good right hand, but the muscles of his tongue gave him trouble. It took him a long, laboured time to eat his food.

'Right, Kev – eat up now,' Melly bossed him. 'You'll get muck all over it, else. And keep out of my way while I do the washing-up.'

She dragged a chair over to the gas stove. Clambering up, she lifted the heavy kettle down with sturdy movements, to pour hot water into the enamel bowl she had placed on the floor. She had to get on the chair again to put the kettle back. Then, narrowing her eyes against the steam clouding from the bowl, she carried it carefully to

8

the table, added some cold and washed up the breakfast things, leaving them overturned to dry. Wielding the heavy broom, she swept out the room, working round Kev, chasing scraps of crust from under the table to cheat the mice.

She wanted to please her mother – to do everything so that Mom would not have to work while she was feeling so poorly. Dad and Auntie had already gone out, because they worked at the Rag Market on Saturdays, so it was up to her to help around the house.

A daring idea came to her. She would go and do the bits of shopping now. This was nothing new – she was always popping up and down the road for Mom. But this time she would take Tommy with her!

'You finished, Tommy?'

Tommy nodded and said, 'Yes,' with his usual side-ways mouth movement. They'd thought Tommy would not be able to walk or talk – but he could do a bit of both, in his own fashion.

Melly wiped his mouth and hands and made sure he was strapped into the chair contraption that their neigh-bour, Mo Morrison, had rigged up for him. Mo had adapted Tommy's first chair for him when he was very small. This was the next size up. Mo had taken another wooden chair as Tommy grew and modified it. He fixed arms on and a high headrest. There was a bar across the front that you could swing round to stop him falling out. This one had better wheels than the last – with rubber on – so it was easier to push along. Mom had always been determined that Tommy should not be shut away.

Melly went to the mantle and rattled the jug where her mother kept the ration books and bits of loose change. She wrapped the coins in a rag and pushed it into her pocket. Then she went and scooped Kev up into her arms and carried him out into the yard. He roared with annoyance.

'Shurrup, our Kev,' Melly said as she carried him. 'You're going to see Auntie Dolly.'

Theirs was one of five houses built round a brick yard, accessed through a narrow entry on to the street. Three of the houses – or half houses – backed on three others which faced on to the street, sharing a roof with them. The other two were built up against the wall that divided their yard from the one next door. The far end was bounded by the blank, sooty wall of a wire-spinning firm called Taplin & May's. The Booker family lived at number three on the yard with Melly's dad's auntie, Gladys Poulter. Melly carried Kev to number one and knocked on the door.

'What's up, bab?' Dolly Morrison, a pretty woman with dark Italian looks came to the door wiping her hands on her apron. 'You all right – yer mother's not started . . . ?'

'No,' Melly panted. Kev was a slender child, but heavy enough and he was wriggling like a fish on a hook. 'Can I leave him with you for a tick? Mom's having a lie-down and I said I'd go up the shops . . .'

'Course you can, bab. Here, give me him. Donna'll be all over him.'

Mo and Dolly had six children – five boys, all blonde, before Donna, their adored little girl, had come along with her brown eyes and black curls.

'Ta,' Melly said. She ran back to Tommy. 'Come on then – we're going to the shops for our mom.'

Melly had pushed the wheelchair before, short distances. It was hard, but she was determined. Getting it out over the step was the first problem. As she struggled to shove it over the door frame and into the yard, Ethel

Jackman, the bad-tempered woman from number two next door, saw her.

'What d'yer think you're doing?' she said, crossing the yard, shoulders draped in washing. Ethel was in her fifties and had lost her only son in the war so they made allowances, even though she'd been almost as crabby before.

'What's it look like she'm doing?' Irene Sutton from number four came breezing over. 'Want a hand with that, bab?' Peroxide blonde, heavyset, aggressive, Irene was never usually this helpful but she was more than happy to oblige if it annoyed Ethel Jackman. Melly shrank from her. Irene's youngest daughter, poor little Evie, was the same age as Tommy. Everyone in the yard looked out for Evie because Irene had taken against her at birth. What with this and Irene's loud, Black Country ways – 'that yowm-yowm' they called her because of her accent – her drunken husband and squalid pit of a house, she filled Melly with dread. Mom said Irene was like a big child herself. But Melly did need help and it was clearly not coming from Ethel Jackman. She nodded.

'There yer go –' Irene tensed her brawny arms and hauled the chair out for her.

'Ta,' Melly whispered.

'Mind how yer go . . .' Irene said, unctuously amiable.

Melly pushed Tommy across the yard's uneven blue bricks and along the entry to the street. Her muscles were already beginning to tremble with the effort of balancing the chair, which she could hardly see past, and keeping it moving forwards. She managed to turn out on to Alma Street.

Many of the houses along the busy road were small business premises. They were a mixture of metal bashers – drop forgers, metal stampers and piercers, motor-spring makers, wire makers – and other little businesses. There were shops selling furniture, coffee shops, the pawn-brokers, grocers, painters and confectioners and little hucksters' shops which sold almost everything. The place was full of sounds: metallic hammering and bashing from behind the walls of the various works, vehicles coming and going, bicycles whisking along, shouts and conversations, a dog barking somewhere. The gritty air was full of smells of glue and metal mingled with the whiff of freshly baked bread and beer as they passed one of several pubs along the street.

At this moment Melly could smell more than she could see. She kept her head down, pushing Tommy, only her own feet in her scuffed brown T-bar shoes visible to her on the mucky blue brick pavement. It was hard work keeping it in a straight line and her arms ached. She only just steered the chair round a heap of galvanized buckets, narrowly missing them. Every few yards she had to stop for a rest. But Mom would be so pleased – she'd taken Tommy out!

The grocer's where Mom usually did her shopping seemed much further away than usual, but at last she stopped outside it and weighed up what to do. It dawned on her then that Mom only took Tommy to the shops if she or Dad were there. Now she could see why her mother didn't go alone. It looked impossible to get Tommy's chair in through the door and even if she did, it would take up most of the space inside. But she was reluctant just to leave him outside on his own.

'I'm gonna have to put you here while I go in,' she said to Tommy. 'You stop here – all right?'

Tommy nodded silently. She could not tell what he was thinking.

Just as she was moving the chair sideways, to rest

against the grimy bricks of the front, she heard a woman say:

'Oh, dear – look at that. Fancy bringing that thing out for everyone to see. Shouldn't be allowed.'

She didn't trouble herself to keep her voice down. Melly could see she was talking about Tommy.

'Ugh,' her friend said. 'Cripples make me feel bad. Come on, Josie – let's get past. I don't like to see it.'

Melly hung her head until the women had passed, her cheeks raging hot. She was trembling with embarrassment and hurt, hearing their cruel words. Once they had passed she looked up to see the backs of two middle-aged women belted into neat little macs, with shopping bags over their arms, talking with their heads close together. She felt like running after them, shouting at them . . . She was already close to tears. She shouldn't have brought Tommy out! She knew people could be unkind but now she was here with him on her own it felt as if it was all her fault.

'Just going to get a few things,' she said brightly to Tommy. He must have heard the women. There was nothing wrong with his hearing even if nasty people like that behaved as if he was deaf. But Tommy showed no sign of being upset. She patted his leg. 'Won't be a tick.'

Melly fidgeted in the gossiping queue inside the little shop, everyone holding their ration books, grumbling about the way there were more queues and less food now than during the war. The tiny shop was crammed with things and smelt of fire-lighters and salty bacon and cheese. It seemed to take forever for the other women to finish their bits of shopping. She kept glancing out of the window at Tommy. She could see the side of his head, the dark curve of hair over his ear as he sat waiting.

Mrs Bracken who ran the shop looked a little startled to see Melly on her own.

'Not with your mother today then?' she asked. She was a widow, thin but cheerful and kindly. Lowering her voice, she said, 'Has she had it yet?'

'No, not yet,' Melly said. 'But she's a bit poorly.' She pulled the ration books out of her pocket and asked for their groceries – a loaf, some lard, bacon, tea and cheese. The lady was cutting cheese in her deliberate way when a commotion began outside.

'Oh, Lord love us, what's that?' Mrs Bracken said, looking up, the cheese wire poised in her hand.

Melly could see the boys outside and she rushed to the door. After those horrible ladies her senses were alert for trouble. The group of lads had gathered right up close to the shop now and they were all round Tommy, jeering and elbowing each other.

Melly froze on the shop step. There were three boys, but to her they felt like a huge crowd. They were bigger than her, older, twelve or thirteen, and she did not recognize them – one ginger, two mouse-haired – nothing special about them. They were egging each other on, shouting and braying. Two of them had hold of the chair.

'Look at this cripple carriage! It's a go-kart! Come on, let's see how fast it goes!'

'Want a ride, do yer?' the third shouted right in Tommy's face. They grabbed the arms of the chair and jostled it away from the wall. Melly saw Tommy's face. His pale, usually sweet features were frozen in helpless terror.

'Race yer. Look at 'im – 'e can't even talk!'

Melly felt as if she was going to explode. There was no time to think, she just started shouting. 'Stop it! *Stop it* – that's my brother. Gerroff him – you're hurting him!'

They were shaking the chair, rocking it from side to side. Tommy was spluttering, trying to say something and struggling in the chair. She could see he was terrified that they were going to charge down the street with it and tip him out. His eyes were dark and enormous. She ran round the boys, shouting and trying to get hold of the chair. One of them elbowed her viciously. Winded, a sharp pain in her chest, she reeled away, her rubber shoes slipping on the cobbles so that she almost fell.

'Help!' she shouted, crying now. 'They're hurting my brother!'

People began to take in what was happening: the boys' jeering, their nasty expressions, the way they had pulled the chair away from the wall, fighting between each other to have control over it. Melly saw a man set out across the street towards them, an arm raised.

But before he could get there, another figure hurled itself into the fray, someone who appeared to Melly like a rushing whirlwind of salvation. A blonde-haired lad, bigger than any of the three bullies, flung himself at them.

'Get off of 'im!' he bawled. He hauled them back from Tommy's chair, giving one of them such a shove that he landed on his backside in the gutter, face gurning with pain. 'You get off – leave 'im alone! What's 'e ever done to you, yer cowing little buggers?'

This avenging lightning streak, Melly now saw to her amazement, was Dolly's third son Reggie Morrison. Reggie was nearly seven years older than her and she remembered him playing with her when they were much smaller, pushing her about in a little cart when she could barely walk, and playing marbles. But Reggie was so grown up now at the grand age of sixteen that he had nothing to do with her these days.

The third boy attempted to fight back, but Reggie

seized him by the shoulders and shoved him up against the wall.

'Wanna fight me, do yer?' he demanded, pushing his face close up to him. The boy shook his head. The second lad, having been pushed away, hovered about, looking as if he was considering running away.

'Hey – lads, lads!' The man from across the road had now reached them, still holding his arm up as if directing the traffic.

Reggie stood, hands on hips, panting. He was usually the quietest of the Morrison boys, the one you didn't notice. But he seemed taller now, wirily strong, his blue eyes fierce, eyebrows pulled into the frown of a man who meant serious business.

'Calm down,' the older bloke said, putting a hand on Reggie's shoulder. But Reggie shook him off as if to say, look, it's me that's done the *work* around here. He wiped his arm across his forehead and glanced at his right hand which he seemed to have grazed.

'You lot,' the man shouted at the already fleeing group of boys. 'You just clear off!'

Melly, still trembling with the shock of it all, went to Tommy, who had started to let out big gulping sobs. Tommy didn't cry often. When he did he found it hard to breathe.

'Tommy?' She put a hand on his shoulder, close to tears herself. She wanted to thank Reggie Morrison but she couldn't seem to bring out a word.

Reggie was still standing in front of Tommy, elbows jutting out, hands on his waist.

'You're all right, mate,' he told him. 'They've gone now. They won't be coming back.'

Tommy looked at him, his little face straining and wet with tears, in too much of a state to say anything back.

'You're all right, Tommy – no need to blart,' Reggie said again, sounding like a man. Turning, he adjusted his shoulders and took off up the road.

Melly watched him in wonder: the strong set of him, his straight back, the wide shoulders and confident stride. She saw Reggie as if for the first time; saw what *a man* meant. Something soft and yearning budded inside her. Reggie. She tried the name in her head. Reggie Morrison.

Melly was crying so much herself by the time she got the chair back into the yard that she hardly had the strength to push it inside the house. Tommy was still bawling and the commotion brought their mother groggily down-stairs. She stood clutching the ends of her cardigan round her.

'What the hell's the matter with the pair of you?'

It was a while before Melly could get the words out. It was her fault. All of it. She spilled out the story.

'I wanted to help,' she wept. 'I went to get the bread and rations and . . .' A terrible thought struck her. She'd forgotten the shopping! What if someone else had taken it – there was hardly any food to be had, Mom was always saying so! Panic rattled around in her head.

'Well, where is it?' Rachel asked.

'I never . . . I mean, there were these boys and they were going for Tommy – trying to turn his chair over and I ran out and . . . and then Reggie . . .'

Rachel drew a chair from the table to sit down, her face hardening with fury. 'Who – who were they?

'I d-don't know. They weren't from up this end. . . Reggie came and stopped them but I never went back to get the things from Mrs Bra – acken.' The last word was interrupted by a hiccough.

'Never mind Mrs Bracken – she'll keep it for us. But those lads – the rotten little sods – if I ever get hold of them . . . C'm'ere, Tommy. It's all right, babby. No one's going to hurt you.'

Melly watched as her mother leaned in and unstrapped Tommy. Even though he was seven now, she pulled him on to her lap, cuddling her distraught little boy. Melly wished Mom would cuddle her as well.

'I never meant—' she said.

'I know you never *meant*,' Rachel said harshly. She sounded so furious and unforgiving that Melly shrank inside. It was as if she had committed a crime. 'But you should never've taken him. Oh, God . . .' Rachel was speaking as if to herself, her face raised towards the cracked ceiling. 'What're we going to do?' After a moment she turned to Melly.

'Well, go on.' There was no softness in her voice. 'You'll have to go back and get the bits from Mrs Bracken, won't you?'

Melly slunk out into the yard, pulling her sleeves across her eyes. She didn't feel like crying now. Leaving Mom cuddling Tommy she went along the entry, frozen with misery. Reggie had saved them! Mom didn't seem interested in that. But she couldn't stop thinking about Reggie and those blazing blue eyes of his. She thought Reggie was amazing.

After that, Tommy refused to be taken out anywhere. He was content to go into the yard where everyone knew him. But if Rachel said she was going to take him out, his little body would start to sway this way and that like a sapling in the wind and he'd get all worked up.

'No!' he would mouth, getting more and more panic-stricken. 'Not going – no – stay here!'

Melly could not rid herself of a heavy feeling of

wrongdoing. It was all her fault – she had taken Tommy out and this had happened. She had been trying to do something good and it had all gone wrong. She took it completely to heart. As Tommy's big sister, she had always been the one to teach him and to look after him, ever since he was tiny. Mom relied on her – she always had. Looking after Tommy, she had come to believe, was what she was *for*.

Two

'I saw this little lad with his arse hanging out of his trousers,' Rachel would relate, a mischievous but fond twinkle in her eye. 'You could hear him right across the market, yelling his flaming head off, selling his comics. Some of them were so old they almost fell to bits in your hand! That was your dad – always up to something. I fell in love with him there and then.'

Melly knew that her mom and dad, Rachel and Danny, had fallen in love very young. They often told the story of how they had met on the Rag Market when Nanna Peggy, Rachel's mother, had a pitch there.

Whenever Mom told this story, when they were sitting round having Sunday tea or some such, Auntie Gladys would shift a bit in her chair, pulling her shawl round her, making her face at Dad which meant she was pretending to be hard done by and say, 'That was before I was landed with him day in, day out, the cheeky little sod. Heaven knows what I did to deserve that.'

A boyish grin would stretch across Dad's face and he'd look from one to the other of them, tweak his cigarette from his mouth between the V of his fingers, blow out a lungful of smoke and say, 'Clapping eyes on me was the best day of both your lives, weren't it?'

Melly and her brothers had all grown up living with their mom, dad and auntie Gladys. Gladys, a widow, had lived in the yard for over twenty years. She was a strong, striking-looking woman in her fifties with a blade-like nose and piercing blue eyes. She had worked on the city's Rag Market for years as a 'wardrobe dealer' selling second-hand clothes. Although she could tease him about it now, Danny had come to be in her care for very sad reasons. When Gladys's sister, Danny's mother, died, Danny's father couldn't – and didn't want to – cope with his four children. He delivered Danny and his sisters into separate orphanages. Gladys tried to find out where they were, but she never did know where they had gone and as there was no love lost between her and Danny's father, he wouldn't tell her. It was only when Danny reached fourteen years of age and was able to work that he got out and came to find Gladys, who took him in. Though he found two of his sisters later, they were never really a family again and they had made their own lives outside the city. Rachel and Danny had married young and had lived with Gladys in her tiny, but spick-and-span, house ever since.

Melly had never lived anywhere other than this yard, down an entry off Alma Street in Aston. She heard people talking about what a state the place was in, thanks to Hitler and his bombs. But she was born just as the worst of the blitz on Birmingham began. She could not remember it any other way than it was now.

Hitler had certainly done his part and the district was pocked with damage, bomb pecks and water-filled craters, gaps along the rows of houses and factories, still full of rubble and now strewn with weeds. Some of these made cut-throughs from street to street. Children played in them, hunting for shrapnel, mimicking spies, and shooting at each other with pretend guns. But even before Hitler, Aston was an old, tightly packed industrial area of factories and warrens of leaking houses, their very brickwork eaten away by the industrial effluvia in the air and black with soot from thousands of chimneys.

Everyone in Aston knew the smells – the hoppy blasts from Ansell's brewery, the sour tang of vinegar from the HP Sauce factory when you walked near Aston Cross, depending on which way the wind was blowing. You might get a sniff of Windsor Street gasworks, of factory chemicals, of mouth-watering vinegary chips from one of the fried-fish shops, or the sweet inviting smell from the corner shop where the lady churned her own ice cream.

Melly knew these streets behind which were cramped yards of back-to-back houses: two houses under one roof. And most of all she knew the one court, or yard, where she had grown up.

Melly had become aware as she got a bit older that Nanna Peggy, Rachel's mother, had never approved of the match between her mom and dad. Nanna, a proud, neat little woman, very preoccupied with her clothes and appearance, lived in Hay Mills over the haberdasher's shop she ran with her second husband, Fred Horton. With them lived their daughter Cissy, Rachel's much younger half-sister, who was born the day war broke out in 1939.

Peggy thought she had gone up in the world since marrying Fred and didn't like to be reminded that she had once worked on the Rag Market as well. Nanna Peggy could be very snobby. 'Tuppence looks down on a halfpenny,' as Gladys said. Melly was angry with Nanna for the way she talked about Tommy, as if he didn't matter, almost as if he wasn't a person. In fact it was her grandmother who had first made her feel an enraged sense of protection towards Tommy. She talked about him being a 'spastic' or a 'cripple', about having Tommy 'put away' somewhere. Melly had never forgiven Nanna Peggy for that. None of them went to see her very often these days.

When Melly looked after Tommy and helped Mom, everyone said she was a good girl. Looking after people was the thing you were supposed to do. Tommy was a 'cripple' – as some people said – who needed looking after. He needed his big sister to teach him things and help him. And Melly had seen close up what it meant when people didn't look after each other. She had seen Evie Sutton who lived across the yard.

Evie was born just after Tommy in 1943. Irene, her mother, wanted a boy. Ray, her husband, threatened to leave if she didn't give him a boy. Lo and behold, she had a girl. Ray didn't leave – he stayed and got drunk as usual. Although Irene already had two daughters, she couldn't seem to stand the sight of Evie. Sometime after Evie was born, Melly overheard, in the yard gossip, that Irene had been very poorly and 'had it all taken away'. Melly had no idea what this meant except that there was not, apparently, going to be any boy to follow Evie – or any girl either.

Melly knew her mother kept an eye out for Evie – everyone did. Evie was an odd child. You'd come across her at the end of the yard somewhere, pulling a worm out of a patch of rough ground and muttering to it. She was very pretty, blonde like her mother with huge blue eyes. But the other children, even though they felt sorry for her, also found her smelly and annoying. Her sisters were mean to her. She was never clean, always a whiff about her. And she was always, always after something, wanting to play your games, come into your house, sit on your

23

knee or whatever it was but it was always too much and people ended up shooing her away.

'That's enough now, Evie – go on, stop mithering me – buzz off.'

But the glimpses Melly had had of the inside of Irene and Ray's house, the bare walls, the dirt, the miserable-looking table with spilt milk and crumbs all over it, the scuttling bugs, gave her the shivers. Auntie Gladys's house was jerry-built just the same, but she worked hard to make sure it was decorated and clean inside.

Gladys had been a rock in all their lives. Melly thought of her as her other grandmother even though everyone called her Auntie. And Dolly and Mo and their family at number one had shown Gladys the staunchest of support through good times and bad. Their boys were part of the scenery, of all that was familiar. As were the other neighbours, sour Ethel Jackman with her silent husband, and dear old Lil Gittins at number five, caring for her shell-shocked husband Stanley. Melly felt happy to live in this yard, amid these streets with their factories, their neighbourliness, their grime, their harshness. It would never have occurred to her to think of living anywhere else. Her school was just along the road, all the family she most cared about were here. It was Alma Street – it was her world. And Tommy was her world as well.

Three

'Oh, no, I knew it, God help me!' Rachel leaned against the scullery door as her body clenched in a powerful contraction. 'Oh, why couldn't it come when there was school?'

Her face contorted and the muscles in her arms knotted tight. Her words were followed by a helpless moan of pain.

A queasy feeling grew inside Melly. Her mother was bent forward, her head bowed, dark hair twisted up and pinned roughly behind her head. A moment later she straightened up with a desperate gasp.

'Oh, no!' It was a sob.

To her horror, Melly saw a creeping pool of liquid move across the floor from her mother's feet. Rachel grabbed a rag and frantically wiped her legs. Melly's sick feeling grew. Had Mom wet herself? Not Mom, surely? She had never seen her mother like this before. She knew it was the baby but she didn't know what to do. When Kev was born she had been safely asleep in bed with Auntie here and Dad and a midwife.

'It's coming,' Rachel panted. 'Melly, go and get Dolly quick – tell her I'm having it!'

Gladys was out at church and Dad nowhere around either. Melly ducked her head against the rain pelting down into the yard.

'Eh, bab, where's the fire?' Dolly Morrison joked as

Melly hurtled in through the door of number one. Dolly was at the table, with Donna. Three of her lads were crouched round the fire, cuffing each other for something to do on a soaking-wet Sunday morning.

'It's Mom, she says can you come she's having it!' Melly babbled, still only half understanding that 'it' was the new babby Mom had said was on its way.

'Oh, my word –' Dolly leapt up. 'Come on, princess – you come with me.' Little Donna, seated at the table, was five now. Dolly scooped her up and dashed for the door. Melly followed.

'Rach?' Dolly took one look inside the door of number three. 'Melly, go back and tell one of the lads to run for the midwife – get Reggie to go, he's more chance of finding the way.'

Melly stalled for a moment. Her, order Reggie, who was six years older than her and had already left school, out into the rain! She wouldn't have minded asking Jonny or Freddie, the younger boys who were fourteen and twelve. But since Reggie had come to her rescue with Tommy the other day, she had started to feel a sort of awe for him, although he never took any notice of her. She was just a little squirt and a girl so far as Reggie was concerned, wasn't she? How could she tell *Reggie* what to do! But she ran back to number one, heart pumping even harder now.

Standing at the door, she found her courage to announce, 'Reggie – your mom says you're to go for the midwife.'

The three blonde boys all stared at her. They were good sorts really. But still lads. And older. Reggie raised his chin a little.

'Wha'?'

'You've gotta go,' she insisted. 'To get the midwife.'

To Melly's surprise, Reggie got up. She was taken aback that she had managed to make this happen.

'You gotta hurry an' all,' she added, gaining confidence, even though he was several heads taller than her. 'The babby's coming. Go on – quick!' Reggie pushed past her and she heard his boots clomping along the entry.

Back home, she found Dolly taking charge, putting on pans of water to boil, comforting Rachel and being motherly and reassuring. She had put little Donna, who was five, down at the table next to Tommy. Donna, plump-cheeked, with a head of wavy black hair like her mother's, was looking about her, seeming awed by what was going on. Kev was rattling about on the floor with his cars. Kev never kept still for long.

Melly stood by the table, at a loss. Everything felt frightening and strange. Although Mom had told her and Tommy that they were going to have another brother or sister, Melly had only dimly realized that the baby was inside Mom. She could hardly believe it. And she had no idea what was going to happen. She wanted comfort, though she hardly knew that was what she required.

'Come on, Tommy, Donna,' she said importantly. 'We're going to do some letters.' She liked being Tommy's teacher. Tommy had never been to school. Mom said there was nowhere for him to go, unless they put him in a home and she was never going to do that. Melly liked teaching him things she learned at school. 'Look – I'll write them out for you.'

As she leaned over to write big, careful letters in pencil, she could shut out the sight of her mother's agonized face. But she could not shut out the sounds. Rachel bent over, muffling her moans of pain with the end of her apron. As the spasm passed, she sank down on her chair close to the range.

'Oh, Dolly,' she burst out, her voice high and out of control. She seemed to forget they could hear every word. 'What am I going to do? What if this one's not all right? If I have another one like Tommy, that'll be the end of it. Danny'll go, I know he will. He'll just go off and leave us and then what'll I do?'

Melly felt the words like the blows of a stick. What was Mom on about? Dad, leave them? He had left them once before for a time, she didn't know how long and she didn't know why. But he had come back. It felt long ago, like a dream that she had forgotten until now.

She looked at Tommy. He was sitting in his special chair, his head slightly to one side, his body wavering slightly as it always did, eyes wide, looking across at Mom. Had he heard? Of course he had heard. Tommy heard everything, understood everything, no matter what anyone else might think.

'Oh, love,' Dolly was saying, leaning over Rachel with her arm round her shoulders. 'Shh.' She glanced back at Tommy for a second, then lowered her voice. 'Don't be daft. Why should it happen again? You had Kev all right, dain't you?'

'Well, why did it happen with Tommy?' Melly heard her mother say in a forced whisper. 'I still don't know. Was it something I did? Oh, God –' She broke off and pushed herself up to bend over the chair. 'Here it comes again.'

'Come on, bab – don't get all upset or you'll make it worse for yourself,' Dolly said, once the pains had receded again. Melly could hear a strain in her voice. She could tell that Dolly did not really know what to say either.

'See, Tommy,' Melly said to him desperately, trying to distract him from Mom's terrible words. 'Soon we'll have a new babby and you can play with him and we can show Cissy when she comes over . . .'

Cissy, Rachel's baby sister, was only two years older than Melly. They always called themselves cousins even though Cissy was really Melly's aunt.

'Why don't we get you upstairs?' Dolly was saying to Rachel. 'Let's get you sorted out. The midwife'll be here soon. Reggie went for her a while ago now.' She glanced round at the children. 'We can't send them to play out, Rach – they'll flaming drown out there today! All right, bab –' She gave Melly a reassuring smile. 'That's a girl – you look after your brothers. And you be a good girl, Donna.'

Rachel leaned on Dolly's arm as they went to the stairs and Melly heard Dolly encouraging her as they went up. Melly kept trying to make a little lesson out of everything as if she was at school, but Donna wasn't interested and sat with a faraway expression on her face, kicking her legs against the chair. Tommy, who was usually her willing pupil, was distracted and wouldn't pay attention. She felt tears rising inside her.

Noises came from upstairs, feet on the floorboards, groans, Dolly talking soothingly. Everything felt frightening and chaotic. Melly still felt sick. It was like the nasty feeling she sometimes had inside if she glimpsed into the Suttons' house across the yard – mess and dirt and everything being upside down and never knowing what might happen next.

'Oh, pay attention, Tommy,' she snapped, feeling tears forcing at the back of her throat. The kettle was gushing steam and she went to turn it off.

'Hello?' There was a light tap on the door. A smiling

face topped by a dark blue felt hat appeared, looking in at them. 'I'm the midwife – have I come to the right place?'

Melly got down from her chair, nodding solemnly at the woman who came in, carrying her bags.

'My goodness, what a day!' she announced, putting her things down on the floor. 'Raining cats and dogs!'

She looked about her, as if to check what the place was like and for the things she would need. Once she had put her bag down she removed the hat from a head of brown, collar-length hair clipped back from her face, then removed the navy mackintosh to reveal a pale green uniform beneath. Her face was calm and kindly. She looked up as a low groan came from upstairs.

'Is that your mother?'

Melly nodded again.

'And your brothers and sister?' She smiled at Tommy and little Donna who sat staring, awed.

'Donna's not my sister,' Melly said. Her voice sounded very small. 'Her mom's upstairs.'

'Ah, good – someone's with her then? And you've got some water on the go?'

The midwife came close to Melly and bent down to talk to her.

'What's your name, dear?' Melly thought her voice sounded lovely and smooth; she looked clean and bright and reassuring.

'Melanie Booker,' she whispered.

'Well, Melanie, I'm Nurse Waller. I'm a midwife and I'm going up to help your mother give you another brother or sister. You're a good girl, I can see – you'll be here to look after the other children, won't you? And soon it'll all be over, don't you worry.'

Melly nodded again. She would have agreed to anything suggested by this wonderful being in her crisp-looking uniform, with her pink skin and a light of kindly joy in her eyes. She seemed to have a power and wonder about her like no one Melly had ever seen before. Immediately the threat of chaos and fear died. This person would make everything all right.

As Nurse Waller's footsteps receded upstairs, she went back to the table feeling much better. 'All right, Donna – you can get down and play with Kev if you want. And Tommy – we'll play a game.'

Four

'What's going on?'

Melly's father, Danny Booker, burst into the house, his coat dark with rain, his face tense. 'Where's yer mother?'

'The babby's coming!' Melly jumped up. 'The midwife's up with her.'

Her father hung his cap on the door and drifted about the room, appearing restless and at a loss. Sometimes it seemed to Melly that these cramped little houses were not big enough for men to live in. Her father looked like an animal in a box that was too small for it. He looked round as if for something to do and at last said, 'Is there a brew on, wench?'

'In the pot.' Melly poured out a cup. She had already taken one to Nurse Waller. She had crept upstairs to the attic, straining not to spill a drop. She hurried in and put the tea down without even looking at her mother, in bed under the low ceiling, and scooted out again.

'Thank you very much, dear!' Nurse Waller called.

Dolly had gone home now, taking Donna with her.

It did not go on for long. By the time Melly had played a few games with Tommy, and Dad did some of his cartoon drawings with Kev, and Kev asked for the umpteenth time if they could get another dog because their little Jack Russell, Patch, a wanderer and philanderer if ever there was one, had gone and got himself run over and Dad said no, they didn't need any more mouths to feed or anything else to flaming well trip over – and they had all tried to close their ears to the footsteps and muffled cries from upstairs – Nurse Waller came down smiling, to tell them that they had another son and that Mom was in good spirits.

'Congratulations, Mr, er . . . Booker,' she said.

'Is . . . Is he . . . ?' Danny was sitting forward leaning on his knees, smoke curling up from the cigarette in his hand. He cleared his throat and started again. 'Is he all right?' Melly cringed inwardly at the question. She could see Tommy's steady gaze on his father.

'Yes, he's right as rain,' Miss Waller said cheerfully. 'Now – I see you've boiled me some more water. What a good girl you are, dear. You could make a marvellous little nurse one day!'

Melly's heart seemed to turn somersaults. Could she really be a nurse?

Picking up the steaming basin, a towel over one arm, Nurse Waller went to the foot of the stairs.

'I'm sure your mother could do with another cup of tea and I really wouldn't say no to one myself. We'll just get everyone tidied up and then you can all come up and see the little fellow.'

As the kettle boiled for tea, the heavy clouds cleared. Slanting spring sunshine managed to hook its way into the house in a sudden blaze of light. The midwife came down and had a quick cup of tea, saying that mother and baby were both having a nap. Melly stood watching her adoringly. She thought everything about Nurse Waller was wonderful and wished her father would be less brusque with her. He sat in his shirtsleeves, smoking and looking at the paper, not speaking to her. The young woman went upstairs for a last check before taking her leave. Putting her coat on, she said:

'Thank you for being my little assistant, Melanie. You've kept everyone in order and calm for your mother which is very important. Well done.' She looked round at them. 'Leave them be for a while. Perhaps you could go up a bit later?'

Melly watched her leave, feeling as if an angel was departing from the house.

Soon after they'd finished their tea they heard voices in the yard: Dolly greeting Gladys. Then both of them appeared at the door.

'Yer too late,' Danny said, looking bashful suddenly in front of the two women. 'It's another lad.'

They both came in, asking excited questions. Gladys's broad-hipped body was wrapped in a brown coat over a long black skirt, her thick salt-and-pepper hair piled up in a bun, fastened back with combs. She was an imposing figure as she claimed her usual seat at the table from where she could see out over the yard. She was queen of her home and gaffer of the yard. And she had taken all the rest of them in, first Danny, then Rachel, then all the children one by one.

'He's all right?' Gladys kept her voice light, but Melly saw her eyes meet Danny's. She glanced at Tommy, think-ing, *Don't you dare say anything else, not in front of him.* She knew how Tommy felt, that Dad didn't want him; that he'd never be a man, not the way a man should be.

'Midwife says he's all right,' Danny said.

'Thank heaven for that.' Gladys wiped her hands over her face. 'Is there any tea in the pot, Melly? I could murder a cup. And then we can go up and see the little feller.'

Rachel lay in bed gazing at her new son. She had said to the midwife that she wanted a nap to delay the moment when the family would come crashing up. She could hear their voices, a murmur of tones from downstairs punctuated by drips from the leaking roof into several pails and bowls round the room. She was not sleepy. In fact she felt so wide awake at that moment that it was as if she would never sleep again.

Six and a half pounds, the midwife had said, weighing him. Not a bad weight and good colouring.

'A fine little fellow,' she'd said, handing him into Rachel's arms. 'That was a good, straightforward birth, wasn't it, dear? Nothing to worry about.'

But when Tommy was born, she hadn't thought there was anything to worry about. He hadn't fed well, it was true, and he felt different, floppier, but it was only months later when he didn't sit up, just hadn't thrived the way Melly did. Only then, gradually, did they know.

'You're an expert now, with your fourth,' the midwife said.

'Fourth and last,' Rachel said. 'I'm as expert as I need to be.'

She felt like asking Nurse Waller if there was any way she could be sure of putting a stop to babies forever. But how could she come out with such private things and say, my husband is so . . . Well, he's so energetic and it's hard to stop him – I don't know what to do . . . It was all too embarrassing to know where to begin.

She leaned over and unwrapped the little boy from the white, gossamer blanket Gladys had knitted for him.

'Hello, Ricky.' She looked down at him. The sight of him made her smile. 'Richard Booker. How about that?' He looked back at her with a dozy expression, his eyes misty and puzzled looking.

'Well, you're a sleepier thing than our Kev was.' Kev

had fizzed with life from the very start, arms and legs going like little pistons.

Anxious, she tried his arms and legs, gently bending and straightening them. She was a fraction reassured. He felt different from Tommy – that was all she could tell for now.

She wrapped him up and settled down beside him, feeling battered and utterly exhausted.

'Please be all right, littl'un,' she begged him, her eyes filling with tears. 'God knows, you're mine and you're lovely, but you'd better be the last. I just can't stand any more.'

She heard Danny's feet on the stairs. He came round the door, her tall, wiry husband, his blue eyes full of longing and uncertainty. He came and looked down at them both, like a big child himself, Rachel thought. However old he grew, the hurt child was always there in Danny. The child thrown into the orphanage by his father and left to rot. God, she loved him, that she did! Even though he drove her to desperation at times.

'Is he all right then?' he asked.

She ached that this was the first question. It hurt her. As if he expected something faulty. No matter how much he pretended to accept Tommy, to be a decent father to him, she knew it always felt wrong and shameful to him to have fathered such a son, a boy who talked, but in a strange contorted way all of his own, who could only stand to shuffle from chair to chair, who could only climb the stairs with the greatest effort and difficulty.

Rachel nodded. She must appear sure and strong.

'He's all right. He's lovely, Danny. I thought we'd call him Richard – he looks like a Richard.'

Danny's face relaxed. He sat down on the bed and took in the sight of his boy.

''Ullo, Rich.' He chucked his cheek gently. The baby twitched in surprise and Danny gave a low laugh. 'You're a bit of all right, you are, mate.'

Rachel's tears flowed down her cheeks. She had given Danny two more sons now – the kind of sons he really wanted.

'Eh – what's all this?' Danny got up to move closer to her and take her in his arms. 'There's my wench. You're all right, ent yer?'

She nodded into his chest, still crying. All through the pregnancy she had felt faint and limp. It was hard ever to get enough to eat. 'I just want things to be right,' she sobbed. 'I don't want you to leave me.'

Danny stroked her, holding her close. 'I ain't going to leave you, Rach,' he said. He seemed puzzled. 'Why d'you think I am?'

She couldn't answer. It was just always a feeling she had. He'd left once before – he could do it again. 'No more, Danny. No more babbies – please. I've had enough and I keep thinking, with every one, that something will go wrong – something even worse.'

'All right,' he said, rocking her. 'All right, wench.'

They sat clasped together and she felt comforted by him.

'Eh,' he said after a while. 'D'you think he'll like the *Beano*? He'd better!'

'Oh, *Danny*!' she laughed, wiping her eyes. Danny and his comics.

He grinned at her, his freckly face close to hers. 'We'd better let Auntie and the littl'uns up to see him.'

*

Tommy sat in his chair, listening to the sounds from the rest of the family upstairs.

'We'll bring him down to you so you can have a look, bab,' Auntie had told him as they all went up.

He knew they would, but it felt bad being left alone down here. He could haul himself upstairs, but it took him an age. At night, Dad still carried him up to bed. He felt left out – again. Closer than the sounds of their feet on the bare boards, the exclamations and chatter, he could hear the clock ticking on the mantel. The ticking made him feel lonelier. He looked down at his hands, his right palm pressed to the tabletop, spread out. His left arm was clenched to his side. He couldn't control it the way he could his right. The muscles in his arm and hand wouldn't do what he wanted them to. When he was writing, which he could do well enough with his right hand, Melly had to weigh down the paper with a cup or a couple of brass weights from Auntie's cooking scales, so that the paper didn't slip about.

'Tommy's clever, Mom!' Melly said to their mother sometimes. 'Look at him doing his letters.'

Mom would nod in a distracted sort of way. He knew she was pleased – that it turned out he could do more things than she had feared were possible. But still.

Another boy. When Kevin was born, just before Christmas in 1948, Tommy had seen that his father had at last got the son he really wanted. And now, here was another boy. The sort of boy they wanted – a boy not like him. His eyes filled with tears and he started to get choked up. He wiped his eyes with his right arm. He mustn't cry – it made it so hard to breathe. He must just do what he always did – try to swallow his frustration. If he got upset, Mom and Melly were upset too.

'You're my brave boy,' Mom said to him sometimes. 'My brave little soldier.'

It seemed that his job was to be braver than anyone else, however much he wanted to break down and cry at the feel of his twisted arm, the pain in his hips or his way of talking which didn't sound like anyone else's. Up until the other day, he had been brave. Mom had taken him out sometimes in the chair. He had put up with people staring, other children calling him or his chair rude names, and the nasty, hurtful things some of the grown-ups said about him or Mom. He tried to pretend he hadn't heard. But there had been nothing before like those boys the other day. The horror of it rose up in him again. It had been terrifying, thinking they might tip him out of his chair, run off with him and throw him away somewhere. But the worst thing was their faces. They had looked so nasty and cruel as if they hated him for being the way he was. He was someone no one could ever accept. He never, ever wanted to see anyone look at him like that again. He wanted to stay where he felt safe, in the house, the yard. The outside world now filled him with foreboding.

'Tommy!' Melly came running downstairs. 'Auntie's bringing the babby down to you!'

Tommy felt warmed again inside, just a fraction. He arranged his face into his lopsided smile as they came into the room with the little bundle wrapped in a blanket.

II

1953

Five

2 June 1953

The Morrisons' house was packed full to bursting.

Everyone's eyes were turned in one direction – towards the new rented television, in its brown Bakelite casing which Dolly had polished to a sheen.

The children were crowded into the space in front of it, on the floor, all the kids from the yard and some others who had heard about the television's arrival. Melly sat among them, the cold hardness of the floor seeping through her knickers. Cissy was on her left and on her other side, Tommy's chair which Mo had kindly positioned so that he had a good view, despite Evie's sisters, Rita and Shirley Sutton, moaning that he was in the way.

The younger ones were wearing bonnets decorated with paper flowers, or cardboard crowns in honour of the young Queen who they could see, mistily, making her vows on the twelve-inch screen. Melly, feeling a bit silly now she was nearly twelve, had agreed to wear one too, though Cissy, who was going on fourteen, seemed happy with a white bonnet balanced on her ginger waves of hair. Cissy would always dress up, given the chance. Tommy's crown kept slipping down over his eyes and Melly reached up to adjust it for him.

'Got your bag of rocks safe, Tommy?' she whispered. Tommy nodded happily. Now that sweet rationing was over, they were all making the most of it. Tommy had a bag of sweets and liquorice strips tucked in his pocket. Melly was licking her precious toffee apple, making it last.

'Throughout all my life and with all my heart I shall strive to be worthy of your trust,' the young Queen's voice came to them.

'She must be ever so nervous,' Melly heard her mother say to Dolly. 'Think of having to do all that with all those people watching. My heart'd be out through my chest. I mean, she's younger than I am.'

There were roars of 'God Save the Queen!' and soon Elizabeth Regina emerged from Westminster Abbey. Melly gasped at the sight of her in her crown and a beautiful dress with tassels hanging from the shoulders. She was met by the huge crowds, cheering and clapping. Melly heard Mom and the others murmuring to each other behind her.

'Doesn't she look lovely,' Dolly breathed. 'Ooh, that gown she's wearing – that crown must weigh a bit . . . And look at all those people. Wouldn't you've liked to go, Rach?'

'What? Sleep out all night in the rain?' Rachel laughed. 'Well, maybe – if you'd gone an' all, Dolly!'

'Wouldn't catch me sitting out in the road all night,' Gladys remarked. 'Even to see the Queen.'

'More comfy watching it here, eh?' Dolly lit another cigarette and sat back, smiling. 'It's marvellous, isn'it though, Glad? Ooh and everyone together – our Wally back. If only Reggie was here . . . Bloody war goes on forever even when it's over.'

Melly's ears pricked up hearing Reggie's name. Reggie her distant hero. He had been called up last autumn for his two years of National Service. Wally, his older brother, had just finished his and come home.

'Right, everyone!' Mo announced after they had watched the procession. He had a natural authority with his burly body, pink fleshy face and cropped grey hair. Everyone liked and trusted Mo. 'Time for a party!'

As all the other children got up, cheering, bouncing with excitement, Melly went to Tommy. Her stomach was rumbling and they were all looking forward to the celebration food outside.

'We're going out to the party now, Tommy.' She could see he looked worried. He had been scared for so long now, of going anywhere other than in the yard. Even though he was now nearly ten years old, he had never been to school and he scarcely ever went out, except to the doctor's now and then. They'd given him a proper wheelchair, free on the National Health Service. Melly was his devoted teacher, trying to show him how to spell and count. His other friend and teacher was the wireless. And he stayed in the house and the yard where it felt safe.

'You coming with me?' he said. Each word cost him an effort, his muscles willing them out one by one. Tommy could make himself understood, so long as you gave him time.

'Course I am,' she said. 'It's just us. And there's going to be jelly.'

Tommy beamed with pleasure. Jelly was one of his favourite things.

She saw her father coming over to them. 'Come on, my lad.' Melly could hear the forced jolliness in Danny's tone. He tried his best with Tommy, but he just never knew what to do with him. It was so different with Kevin, who was four and a half now, and Ricky, who was two. Kevin was the real favourite, she could see. He was

45

a real live wire and she saw her father play with him, and toss him around. When Dad got out one of his comics or did his little drawings, he tried to share it with all his sons – but Melly could see that he was always relieved if he could just play with Kev.

She linked arms with Cissy, glad to stretch her legs after sitting on the cold floor.

'Come on, Ciss – Mom's bringing out the cake. Let's get us a good seat.' Melly wished Cissy could come more often. It was nice to have another girl in the family.

Cissy liked coming over to Aston to stay with her big sister Rachel and with Melly. Even though everything here was more cramped and poorer, and Melly and Cissy had to share a bed, at least she got a warm welcome. Peggy had never been a motherly sort and now that Cissy was long past the sweet baby stage, her mother had little time for her. She'd been much the same with Rachel.

'I don't know why you want to go and stay in that slum!' Melly and Cissy would take off Nanna Peggy in the snooty, languid voice she used these days. Their eyes would meet as they giggled over it, imitating the way Nanna crossed one slim ankle over the other as if to show off her shiny leather shoes. Rachel would say, 'Now, now, you two.' But she wouldn't be able to stop laughing either. It was how they all dealt with the hurt Peggy inflicted. And it was so much more fun for Cissy over here.

'We'll sit each side of Tommy,' Melly said, as they followed Danny who was pushing Tommy's chair along the entry.

Like so many other neighbourhoods, Alma Street was celebrating on this special, holiday Tuesday. Even if the weather was showery and not the best, everyone was determined it was going to be a day to remember. In the street they found tables arranged end to end. Women from the surrounding yards were carrying out plates heaped with the best that rationing and scrimping and saving would allow. Their yard had joined with the one next door, every possible stick of furniture carried out into the street to sit on. A few lengths of bunting fluttered along the houses and shops close by. The kids were lined up round the table in a variety of hats and crowns, the adults standing about behind. Everyone seemed in high spirits, especially the children.

Rachel, carrying a cake out to the feast, watched with an inner tremor, following behind the girls and Danny as he pushed Tommy's chair along. *Thank God I had Kevin,* she found herself thinking for the umpteenth time. Kevin, her healthy, skinny, uproarious lad. Never had she seen Danny so happy as when Kevin rose to his feet at fourteen months and toddled energetically round the room pushing a stool. Ricky had of course done the same. But she could see that Danny felt like a proper man once he had fathered Kevin. It was as if Tommy didn't count.

Lost in her own thoughts, it took her a moment to realize that Lil Gittins was walking just behind her. Lil and Stanley lived at number five in their yard, in the end house, abutting the metal spinning works. Rachel turned to smile at her.

'All right, Lil? How is he today?'

The very look of Lil was heartbreaking. When Rachel first moved to the yard, Lil's husband Stanley, a strong man and lively as a cricket, who had worked as a carter for the railways, had just gone off to war. Lil always used to wear her honey-blonde hair piled majestically on her head, and be made up with bright lipstick, full of fun and kindness. These days she was so thin that the bones in her face seemed overly large and her eyes were sunken. Her hair, still piled on her head, was now almost white, even though she was only in her late forties.

'Oh, he said he'll stop in today,' Lil said, trying to sound cheerful. As if Stanley stopping in wasn't what he did every day of the year. As if she didn't mind doing everything alone, trying to manage, as if her husband wasn't a member of the living dead.

Rachel could hear the tears building in her voice, but Lil stemmed them and raised her chin.

'Just the way it is, I s'pose. Make the best of it.' She shrugged and tried to smile, but she could not shift the desolate look in her eyes. Rachel reached out and squeezed her arm.

Stanley, who had been a radio operator on RAF fighters, had been shot down over the Mediterranean at night and floated in the black water for twelve hours before he was rescued. Within months, the plane he was in was hit a second time and he bailed out, on fire, again landing in the sea. By some miracle he was picked up once more by a British naval vessel, but was badly scarred all down his left side. His mental scars, though, were as bad, if not worse. Sometimes at night you could hear his screams across the yard. Quietly, the neighbours would say it was a pity he survived, that Lil would have to have him put away. But Lil could not bear to do it.

'He's my Stanley,' she would say quietly. 'For better or worse, I'll look after him. Anyway, our Marie's made her life in Liverpool now – what else've I got?'

Rachel carried the sponge she had made out to the table and placed it alongside the fish-paste sandwiches and jellies and dry cakes. She slipped past Ethel Jackman, who was hardly ever known to say an agreeable word, least of all to her own husband, and followed Danny who steered Tommy over to the corner of a table, where

Gladys and Dolly were standing. Gladys was wearing her usual dark clothes, though she had added a touch of colour with a vivid red scarf at her neck. Set against her dark chestnut hair streaked now with threads of white, pinned up in a thick, coiled plait, and her blue eyes, she looked very striking. She had been organizing everyone in the yard for weeks before the celebration, collecting money, making sure things got done. Dolly, beside her, was wearing a dress of green-and-red flower patterns. The two friends made an exotic pair.

Dolly was standing behind Donna, seven now, in a little crimson dress and looking as ever, utterly beautiful. The youngest Morrison boy, Freddie, was beside her. The others were far too grown up to be sitting with the children. The eldest, Eric, was on the point of getting married. Reggie was away and Wally and Jonny were standing about with some of their mates, all with hands in pockets, a distance back from the table as if they were holding themselves aloof from all this carry-on.

'That's it, good lad, Tommy,' Dolly said kindly, as he arrived. She saw Melly hovering about, waiting to look after Tommy. 'You and Cissy squeeze along there next to Donna, bab, and Tommy can come up next to you.'

Cissy and Melly immediately got on either side of Tommy. Rachel gave her daughter a fond glance. You could always rely on Melly. She felt a swell of pride when she compared Melly to those Sutton girls, Rita and Shirley, who were sitting opposite her, skinny little things with their long ratty hair and mean-looking faces. Rita was a bit older than Melly and Shirley a bit younger so Melly was stuck with them as they were the only girls her age in the yard. But they were right two-faced little sods. Nice as pie one minute when they wanted something; the next, she knew, they'd turn on Melly or whoever they were playing with and yank their hair or dig their nails into another kid's arm 'til they drew blood. And if anyone had anything – like that doll of Melly's that Gladys got her one Christmas, Irene Sutton would go and get something bigger and better. God knows how she affords it, the state they live in, Rachel thought. She'd had to go and get a doll – a big, hard plastic thing with blonde hair and eyes which opened and shut. Once they had something new they'd be all snooty and wouldn't want to know the other children. And they never, ever shared it with Evie. Evie was left out of everything. Rachel swelled inside with fury every time she saw the way Irene treated Evie, poor little mite. Even now, she was stuck on the end and they were all ignoring her. Irene stood behind her daughters, resplendent in a scarlet frock, her hair newly bleached and curled at the ends. Rachel looked at her, thinking, yes, not a thought for anyone else, but you can dress yourself up like a film star as usual, you selfish cow.

'I see the cripple's out today,' Irene remarked to a woman from the neighbouring yard, and not quietly either. The woman turned her head away, not knowing what to say. Rachel saw Melly's face tighten in fury and she herself was already poised to strike.

'What did you say?' she demanded. She felt Gladys clamp a hand on her arm to stop her rushing round the table to black Irene's eyes. It wouldn't have been the first time and by God she didn't half ask for it.

'*Don't*,' Gladys hissed down her ear. 'Leave it. She's just a silly bint – trying to get a rise out of you. Like a flaming kid, that one.'

Rachel looked daggers at Irene. She lowered her head, breathing hard, trying to control the impulse to go and tear Irene's hair out.

'In front of him,' she whispered savagely to Gladys.

'She cowing well said it in front of him. Just when he's . . .' Her eyes filled with angry tears. Tommy had come out to the street – that was progress.

'Just leave it,' Gladys said. 'Don't do anything – not today.' She nodded at the table of children.

Dolly, however, was not one for holding back. 'You want to look after your own kids,' she retorted across the table. 'Instead of poking your nose in about other people's. And where's your old man? Down the boozer as usual, I s'pose?'

Irene stuck her nose in the air and ignored them. Ray Sutton, dark-haired, full of charm when sober but frequently drunk and obnoxious, was nowhere to be seen.

Melly kept sneaking looks round at Wally Morrison. He and Reggie were quite alike and as brothers they were close. Both of them worked on milling machines for GEC, in Electric Avenue in Witton. Dolly had worked there before she was married and Reggie followed Wally there. But now Reggie had gone off into this unknown world of the army and Wally had just come back from it. Melly kept wanting to look at him, as if seeing Wally could somehow put her in touch with Reggie. It wasn't as if Reggie ever took any notice of her – not before and not now. But she was fascinated with him. He seemed to be everything a grown-up man should be – handsome, with a strong-boned face and thick blonde hair. He was tough and mysterious, not as talkative as Wally. The sight of Reggie always made her heart beat faster, even though she knew he had no time for her. After all, he was *eighteen*! For now though, all she had to look at was his older brother.

'What're you staring at?' Rita Sutton leaned across the table, her eyes narrowed in her sly way.

Melly whipped her head back round from another peek at Wally. 'Nothing.'

'You was staring. I saw yer.'

Melly could see the spiteful gleam in the girl's eyes.

'I *wasn't*,' she insisted.

She turned away as if to help Tommy, fussing over him unnecessarily.

'He's like a babby,' Melly heard Shirley Sutton remark. She kept her eyes fixed on Tommy's. *Ignore them*, her eyes said. *They're just nasty like their mom*.

Her own mom and dad were just behind them so she felt safe. She heard Mom chatting to Dolly. Rachel broke away for a moment from the group to call out to a friend up the road.

'All right, Netta? I thought you were going to come and watch it at Mo and Dolly's?'

Netta made some flustered reply and Rachel called back, 'All right then – see you tomorrow!'

Tommy was looking happy now and he beamed when they were presented with a bowl of orange jelly.

'Here y'are,' Melly said, reaching for a spoon to give him. Tommy could eat perfectly well with his good arm.

'It's disgusting, the way he eats,' Rita said, her eyes gleaming nastily.

Melly wanted to say, *Well, at least he doesn't have a face like a rat like you*, but she didn't dare. Rita was nearly fourteen and Melly was scared of her.

Seeing that Tommy was eating happily she glanced quickly round at Wally Morrison again. His blonde hair was slicked back and he stood more upright since the army, a swagger to him. He was all right, Melly told herself. But he wasn't Reggie. Reggie was quieter, kinder.

Around her was all chat and laughter. She could hear Mo's voice from down the other end of the table. Someone had rolled out a keg of beer and Mo, legs braced to hold his barrel-like body, was handing round cups, glasses, jam jars of it. Her mom leaned over to cut the cake. There was a pink seam of jam through the middle.

'Hold your plates out,' Mom said. 'One at a time!'

Mo worked his way along. 'Here yer go – a toast to Her Majesty!'

They were in the midst of drinking and cheering on the new Queen when an all-too-familiar figure came zig-zagging along the road, staggering into walls and out again across the pavement.

'Oh, look who it isn't,' Dolly said loudly, as Ray Sutton tripped into the gutter and almost fell. 'The ruddy Lone Ranger.'

'He's getting worse.' Gladys stared along the street. Melly knew that Auntie did not approve of swearing or bad manners or drinking to excess. 'When's he ever sober?'

Melly only half-heard what they were saying. The other half of her was dreaming about Reggie, imagining that he was here, that he would come and sit next to her and gaze deep into her eyes . . . She only looked up when there was a horrified outcry from around her. Ray Sutton was lurching along the road close to them, bashing into people who were shouting and telling him to get out of there, the state he was in.

'Wench!' he yelled, seeming able to focus at least on the fact that the ample woman in red was his wife. His voice was so slurred they could only just gather what he was saying. 'Get in the *****g house!' He staggered and nearly fell.

'Using the soldier's word – when you've never been near a uniform,' someone sneered.

Ray wasn't listening to anyone else. 'What're yer doing

out 'ere . . . ? Showing yerself off . . . Yer filthy trollop.'
He weaved round the end of the table towards Irene.

'Ray!' Irene shrieked, as he started to manhandle her.
Other voices were shouting at him to get off her.

'Knock it off, Ray!' Melly heard her father shout.
'Look at yourself – what're you doing?'

'Oh my God, here we go,' Rachel said contemptuously. 'Wouldn't you know it?'

'It's a party!' Irene shrieked. 'For the new Queen.
Come on, Ray – come and have a—'

But Ray managed to grab Irene's hair, poking a finger
into her eye as he did so. She screamed with pain and
continued to scream as he dragged her along by her
blonde locks and up the entry towards the house.

'Bloody disgrace!' Melly heard, amid other shouts
after them.

Her own heart was thumping. Now she was older, she
had become aware of the fights between Irene and Ray,
the shouts and screams late at night. Behind closed doors
was one thing, but this was horrible to see. Rita and
Shirley were hanging their heads. Melly looked at Evie.
She was staring ahead of her, her pale hair hanging in
sheets each side of her sweet, blank face, her eyes seeming
fixed on nothing, as if she wasn't there at all.

Six

'God Almighty,' Dolly said, appearing at their door one Saturday morning a few weeks later. 'Did any of you lot get a wink of sleep last night? I had to stop Mo grabbing the poker and going round to knock the pair of 'em out.'

Melly had heard them last night, the yells and crashes. Ray Sutton and Irene had had one of their worst-ever fights, starting after the pubs closed and going on for what felt like most of the night.

'Those two deserve each other,' Rachel said. 'It's Evie that worries me.'

'Come on – no time for canting, you lot,' Gladys said.

The Booker family were preparing to go to market, sleep or no sleep. There were piles of clothes on chairs. Gladys was rolling them into bundles.

'You know why, don't you?' Dolly said, propped importantly against the door frame, blowing smoke from her Gold Flake into the morning air.

'Why what?' Gladys said. 'Spit it out if you've got summat to say. We're running late as it is.'

'Kynoch's let him go yesterday. Take your wages –' This had been a wage packet that you couldn't bend – it had his cards in it. 'On your way. He keeps turning up at work so kalied he's bouncing off the walls. They've had enough of 'im.' She took another satisfied drag on her cigarette. Dolly always liked to be first with the news.

'It's a pity that one survived the cowing war,' Rachel

55

muttered, cutting a piece for Tommy. She spread a film of Stork on it. 'Someone should've dropped a bomb on him and had done with it.'

'Rach!' Gladys said. 'That's no way to talk!' She glanced round at the children who were all listening avidly.

Tommy did a soaring motion with his good arm and made a droning sound through his lips like a passing bomber aeroplane. Melly and the others laughed.

'That's it, son!' Danny chuckled and Melly saw her mother's face lighten at his approval of Tommy. Kev and Ricky both cackled loudly, even though neither of them really got the joke.

'Heaven help them now,' Gladys said, putting her bags by the door. 'They've been dodging the rent man for weeks, even with a wage coming in.' She straightened up. 'Ready, Danny?'

'You coming with me today?' Danny leaned over the table to Melly. 'You and Kev?'

She looked up into her father's eyes. Hers were so like his, everyone said. Big and blue. She swallowed her mouthful of bread. Against her will, she nodded, knowing she was pleasing him. Dad liked nothing better than taking her and Kev to work beside him and Auntie on the Rag Market, now they each had their own stall.

'All right . . .'

'There's no need to say it like that,' Danny cajoled, mock hurt. 'What's happened to my girl – you've always been at me to take you to the market!'

Melly didn't want to tell Dad how much she wanted to stay at home today. There were coils of excitement in her belly as if she'd swallowed a snake. Reggie Morrison was home! She'd just caught a glimpse of him crossing the yard in his khaki, his hair cropped shorter than she'd ever seen it. It made his face look thinner. If she stayed home she might have a chance of seeing him.

Gladys was already waiting, a bag in each hand. Dad was hustling Kevin along. 'Come on, mate – and we'll get us a comic, after, eh? What d'yer fancy – the *Beano* – or *Eagle*?'

'*Beano*!' Kevin cried. He knew it was Dad's favourite as well. Danny drew copies of the characters as well as making up his own. And Kevin liked going to the market. He hurried after his dad on his skinny legs. Almost as an afterthought Danny turned and patted Tommy's head.

'Ricky – c'mere. You can't go!' Rachel said, grabbing him as he started to crawl towards his father. Ricky started wailing loudly. He was quite a placid boy normally but he adored Danny and wanted to be with him wherever he went. 'You can go when you're bigger,' Melly heard her say as they all trooped out.

'Ta-ra, son.' Danny threw the comment to Tommy as an afterthought. 'We'll bring you a comic an' all, won't we, Kev?'

Melly saw her brother try to smile and pretend he was happy always being the one to stay behind.

The house fell quiet, once Rachel had managed to pacify Ricky and sit him on the floor with some of Kev's cars. Tommy watched her as he sat by the table in his chair, still eating long after everyone else had finished.

He was acutely sensitive to his mother's moods. As she straightened up from settling Ricky, a pinner over her old cotton dress, he could see the tiredness in her face, her thin arms and pasty skin. If only he could take Mom somewhere warm and nice like in one or two of those plays he had heard on the wireless, where she could eat everything she wanted and not have to work all the time. And where she could be free to come and go.

Because Tommy felt, all too painfully, that he was the reason for the dull, defeated look in his mother's eyes. The reason she was always stuck here, could never go anywhere much, and that neither of them could see an end to it. She was his world, his mom was, with her kind eyes and dark brown hair which was pretty when she got the time to curl the ends and dress it up a bit. She was fiercely protective of him. Although he was only coming up to ten years old, he could read her sadness and sense of defeat, as if her life was just passing her by in a round of weary toil. It made him ache inside that he could do so little to help or to free her. Though he could not quite have put all this into words, it was a burden he carried along with all his physical difficulties, with feeling left out of life.

He dipped his crusts in his tea one by one, to soften them. There was a niggling ache in his left hip and shoulder but he said nothing because the pain was a part of his life. Managing to cheat his thrusting tongue he took a mouthful. As he had grown older his control over eating had improved, his muscles strengthening, but today the food clogged his mouth as a lump rose in his throat. He coughed and spat it out.

'You all right, babby?' Mom rushed over from where she was washing up. 'You choking?'

He looked down at the soggy ball of bread on his plate.

'Just – coughed,' he said, with difficulty. Each word was a challenge for him, a contortion. He looked up at her and tried to smile. He did not want Mom to see in his eyes the swelling frustration and helplessness inside him. He knew his mom would do anything in her power for him – but what more could she do?

Day after day, all his life, he had watched the other children running about, moving easily in a way never possible for him. That terrifying morning when the boys attacked him, jeering and trying to tip his chair over, had given him a shock that burned into his soul. He knew he was different, he had always known that. He had heard comments from the grown-ups when they went out, though then he had been too young to understand most of them. But in the yard people had been kind. The Morrison boys always played with him and made him one of them and he had always had Melly to look to – and Cissy when she was about.

But Dad . . . He had been five when Kevin arrived. Old enough to understand that Kevin was the son their father had always wanted, one who could run and jump, not a cripple stuck in a chair. And then came Ricky, who was now walking as well.

'Mom?' He kept his eyes down on his plate, searching for the right words. With all those hours Mom and Melly had spent encouraging him to talk, he knew he could get them out when he wanted, with someone patient enough to listen.

'Umm?' She had moved away again, preoccupied as ever.

Tommy forced the words out, his mouth twisting with each word. 'When Dad – left . . . Was it – cos of – me?'

There was a silence. He heard her moving close to him again, leaning across the table, the pale green cotton of her apron level with his eyes.

'*What?*' Her tone was sharp, appalled, but she instantly realized that she did not want to have to force him to say it again. 'Tommy – I don't know what you're asking me.'

He looked up then, into her face, and saw her sad,

guarded expression. She *did* know, he could see. Her face already gave him the answer.

'Cos I – couldn't – walk?'

His mother folded her arms and looked at him, head on one side. Then she pulled out the chair and sat opposite him.

'Tommy – that was a very long time ago. You were only a babby then. Who told you your dad went away? Was it Melly? Is that what she said?'

'No!' He hurried to correct her. 'She never – she just – said – he left . . .' It felt as if he was crying inside but he kept the tears and his silent sobs from the outside. He didn't want to make it worse for Mom.

'Your dad did leave – for a little while.' Her voice was gentler now. 'Only for a few weeks. He was . . . You know, it was only months after the war ended, when when he'd first come home . . . A lot of the men who came back were in a state . . . Didn't know what to do with themselves . . . And Danny, your dad – it was just that he had to go off for a while, that's all. Because of how he felt. It wasn't you, son. It was just, being away and the army and everything. And then he came back to be with us – because that's where he wanted to be.'

He tried to smile. He felt that she was lying. Or half lying, or something. He didn't know. But he knew Dad wished he was different, or that he wasn't there at all. It was an abiding feeling.

'Now –' His mother leaned forward and ran her hand over his hair. He lowered his head, sniffing. 'Never mind all that – it was a long time ago. You're my boy – eh? And it's Saturday. You can go to Dolly's and watch your programme later.'

Tommy brightened. His favourite: *The Quatermass Experiment*.

His mother stood up. 'What shall we do while they're all out?'

He looked up at her. 'Paint – the town – red?'

'Oh, Tommy!' Mom laughed. 'Tell you what – I'll just clear up a bit and then we'll look at some of those books Melly's been reading with you, eh? And we'll have the wireless on.'

Melly felt the usual swell of excitement as the tall gates of the Rag Market swung open, come one o'clock. Outside the road was full of carts and cars and the crowds surged in, some pushing old prams, others holding bags, jostling and eager for bargains. She had been brought to this market all her life. It felt like a part of her.

'Come on, wench – help me hang these up!'

She ran to help her father. He had his own stall now – a proper one, not like in the old days when they sold from pitches on the floor. There were wooden tables with metal frames round them that you could hang things on. He was dealing in second-hand gents' clothing: suits and shirts, hats, coats, shoes, ties. And he had got hold of some new sets of braces and some cufflinks and collar studs.

Kevin, who at four was only just about as tall as the table, passed him up shoes and small items. Melly handed him the suits and shirts and Danny arranged them along the metal racks. She felt proud, working next to her nice-looking, energetic dad and seeing people greet him and share chat and jokes.

'What's this?' Bent over, he frowned, opening a bag which had ladies' hats inside. 'This lot's Auntie's, not mine – take 'em over to her, Melly, will yer?'

Melly hauled the bag along to where Gladys had her

stall, in a prime spot at the back of the Rag Market. Between them, covering ladies' and gents' clothing, they were doing very nicely. Several of the other stallholders called a greeting to her as she passed. Melly knew all their faces. The market felt like a family.

'Thanks, bab,' Gladys said, as she arrived. She pulled a little bag from the pocket of her dark green skirt. 'Want one of these?'

Melly reached in for one of Gladys's favourites – mint humbugs.

'Take your dad one. And tell him to get over here – he's left me with the float. The Toby Man's on his way round.' The Toby Man was in charge of collecting the rents, from the regulars who always had stalls, and the casuals who signed up to get one when they could.

Melly did as she was told. Dad's stall was up and running now and he went to collect the money which he kept in his jacket pocket. Melly saw that Kevin was under the table for the moment playing with a handful of marbles.

Melly stood by the stall and the noise about her faded. Much as she loved the markets, all the chatter and noise of the stallholders round the edges pitching their wares, the excitement of all the different things for sale – crocks and bedding, clothes and ornaments and the mouth-watering smells of food from the stalls and cafes around the market – her mind took her off into another place. . .

She walks slowly along the yard in Alma Street in her best, dark pink frock . . . He appears out of the Morrisons' house. She slows her walking to a dawdle.

Reggie stands for a moment, hands in his pockets and in that second he catches sight of her with amazement.

Who is that pretty girl? She walks closer to him and they stand face to face and—

'Eh, bab – you deaf or summat?' Melly surfaced from her sweet imaginings, which were very like a drama she had seen on Dolly and Mo's television . . . Two women stood before her, clad in bulky coats despite the summer warmth. 'I said 'ow much is that pair of trousers?'

That evening, as she walked into the yard with her father and Gladys, every nerve in Melly's body was alive with expectation. Would she see Reggie now? But the first person she saw was Evie, walking up the yard as if coming from the lavatories. She walked with her eyes lowered as usual, but as they passed, she looked up into Melly's face and gave her a vague half-smile.

'All right, Evie?' Melly said.

Evie stopped. 'Mom says . . .' She was speaking as if in a rush. She looked fearfully at her own house and at that moment Irene appeared at the door.

'Evie – gerrin 'ere – now!'

Evie lowered her head and hurried over to the house.

That night, it was quiet, despite being Saturday.

'No wage coming in, I s'pose,' Rachel said.

'P'r'aps he's got his feet up by the fire, having a nice cup of cocoa?' Gladys suggested and they all laughed at this unlikely thought.

The next morning, when she left the house to go to church, the door of number four was wide open. The downstairs room was empty, the house silent. The Suttons had taken their few frowsty possessions and done a moonlight flit – though there had been no moon to speak of.

Seven

All that hot August weekend Melly was full of an aching longing for Reggie to notice her. She was aware of him, wherever she was or wherever he was, in a way which made the hairs stand up on her arms.

On the Sunday afternoon all the kids were outside in the yard. She could hear the television coming from Dolly and Mo's. It felt strange and quiet without anyone in the Suttons' house. Even though she never liked the Sutton girls much, Melly felt unsettled at the change. Cissy was staying over, though, so she had company to take her mind off it.

It was so warm that, for once, Mr Gittins was out in the yard too. He was on a chair, close to the factory wall, half turned away from everyone. Melly kept looking across at his limp figure. She was fascinated by Mr Gittins. He always wore a hat – a battered trilby today. He had no hair, people said. His scalp was burned, puckered as a wasps' nest. The running, screaming children grated on his nerves and if they went close he would sometimes shout and lash out.

'Come on, Melly, I'm gonna do your hair up,' Cissy commanded. 'You get a chair from indoors and this'll be our salon.'

When Cissy bossed her Melly usually obeyed, though none too fast. She liked to put up a bit of resistance.

Gladys was sitting inside at her usual vantage point, at

the end of the table, looking out across the yard, fanning herself with a folded newspaper. She shifted to let Melly take a chair out past her. Melly carried it to their corner of the yard and put it down beside Tommy. She kept casting longing glances at the intent figures of Reggie and Wally Morrison up the far end, hunched over their pride and joy. The two of them had clubbed together to buy an old Norton motorbike. Wally had waited for Reggie to come back on leave before they went to get it, yesterday.

She kept sneaking a look at them. Wally the wider, stockier of the two, his hair a few shades darker than Reggie's. He was very aloof and always the boss. Reggie was slimmer, a shade taller than Wally now. They were completely absorbed in the bike. She could hear the rumble of their voices as they exchanged comments, heads bent over, smoking, treading the butts into the yard. Gladys would be after them to clear up, Melly thought.

Turn round, she urged in her mind, towards Reggie's curved back. *Look at me.* But the brothers were lost in the wonders of the bike's engine. Reggie didn't even know she existed. As ever.

As she settled on the chair, near Tommy, Kevin came tearing across with a couple of his little pals and nearly charged into her.

'Oi,' Cissy said, comb poised at the ready. 'Go on – shove off.'

'Just stop getting in the way, Kev,' Melly said. She felt scratchy and angry. *Reggie, Reggie* . . . His name beat like a pulse in her mind.

'Right – I'll put your hair up like mine.' Cissy's wavy ginger hair was caught up in a swinging ponytail. Melly winced as Cissy scraped the comb through her own boring old brown hair. 'Ow – go easy. That hurts!'

'Sorry,' Cissy said breezily. Melly caught glimpses of

her pale, freckly hands moving around her head. 'But beauty has to bear a pinch,' Cissy instructed. Hair and clothes were the main things Cissy seemed to think about. She leaned down and Melly felt her hot breath in her ear. 'Hey – you fancy Reggie, don't you?'

'No!' she retorted, all blushes. 'What're you on about?' She didn't *fancy* Reggie. The way Cissy said it made her sound silly and crude. She barely knew what it meant to 'fancy' someone anyway. She felt a hero worship, a sense of looking at a higher being. She didn't want Cissy anywhere near these feelings.

'He's too old for you,' Cissy decreed. 'He's not gonna want a little kid like you. Wally's *much* better looking, anyhow.'

Melly clamped her lips shut and sat with her face burning. Who the hell did Cissy think she was, coming and trampling all over this sweet, secret thing she felt? How did she think she knew anything anyway? At that moment she hated Cissy. Cissy didn't care about anyone – she always did just what she wanted. She, Melly, was the one who always had to look after people.

As she sat, red-faced, her head down, she realized Tommy was shifting about in his chair.

'You all right, Tommy?' she said. 'D'you need to go?'

'Yes,' Tommy admitted.

'Get off me.' She pushed Cissy away. 'I've got things to do.'

'All right,' Cissy said. 'There's no need to be so mardy. Just cos I said—'

'Just shurrit – all right?' Melly pushed on Tommy's chair. She felt important now, in charge of things. All her little life she had taken charge. It was what she did – keeping Mom and Dad happy; looking after Tommy.

She wheeled Tommy along to the lavs at the end of the

yard. He could stand out of the chair on his turned-in feet and shuffle in to do his business, so long as he held on to something.

She waited outside, aware that Mr Gittins was only steps away from her. It was as if his uneasy presence tingled through her. She felt she ought to do something though she didn't know what. He looked normal from behind. He was sitting on an ordinary wooden chair, positioned so that his view was mainly of his own house, number five, and an oblique view along the yard. He was another one, like Tommy, who scarcely ever ventured out on to Alma Street, let alone any further. Everyone was used to this, but now, looking at him, Melly felt very sad. Very rarely, one of his old mates came round to the house but mostly he just stayed in with Lil.

Melly moved closer to him. Stanley Gittins sat very still and seemed to be staring ahead of him, his only movements that of his right hand raising his half-smoked cigarette to his lips, nipped between finger and thumb. A broken thread of blue smoke rose from the tip of the cigarette. She ventured further. The right side of his face didn't look too bad so far as she could see.

'Hello,' she said.

Stanley Gittins moved his head slightly, turning to her. He had no eyelashes. She caught a glimpse of the left side of his face and it was a strange, shiny pink. She waited, nerves on edge, for him to shout, to tell her to get lost.

But he said, 'Hello, missy. All right, are yer?' His voice was low and gravelly but sounded ordinary enough.

Melly was taken aback. 'Y-yes,' she said. 'Ta.'

He didn't say anything else. She stood for a moment, thinking, he's all right with me. She had a feeling that people *were* all right with her. She seemed to soothe them in some way. She looked across to check whether Reggie

67

could see her talking to Mr Gittins. She ached for him to look up. Reggie threw her the odd word now and then, but nothing more. She was just a child in his eyes, she knew. He still had his head stuck down over the bike.

There seemed nothing else to say and then she heard the door of the lav open, so she went back to fetch Tommy, feeling gratified by what had happened.

She couldn't be bothered to be cross with Cissy any more and let her haul her hair up into a high ponytail while Cissy rattled on about her favourite subject – John Christie and Rillington Place, where all the murders had happened. Christie had gone to the gallows last month at Pentonville prison and Cissy had been full of it ever since.

'They found his wife under the floorboards!' she said, scraping Melly so hard with the comb that it brought tears to her eyes. 'Ooh – and those other women hidden in the kitchen. Just think of it – getting invited inside for a cup of tea, not knowing that you're never going to come out again!'

Just as Melly was shuddering at the thought of this, there came a loud throttling roar and the motorbike erupted into life, accompanied by loud cheers. Mo Morrison shot out of number one and across the yard, waving his arms.

'You've never got it going! God Almighty – I never thought you two prats'd do it in a month of Sundays!'

'See, Dad –' Wally, just turned twenty, stood proud, hands on his hips, yelling over the roaring engine. 'You owe me that pint!'

Reggie was grinning. Melly was filled with a helpless, melting feeling at the sight of him. She got up and inched closer, pretending to be interested in the bike. A second later the thing backfired like a gun going off. Everyone jumped and a terrible yell came from Mr Gittins. He leapt to his feet, his arms crossed over his chest as if he was collapsing in on himself. He crumpled forwards from the waist, howling.

'Oh, Lor'.' Mo went towards him. 'Eh – Stanley . . . It's all right, pal . . . It's just the bike . . .'

But Stanley straightened up and fled into the house.

'Oh, dear,' Wally said. 'Poor old fella.'

This put the dampers on the boys' triumph. Melly went up to Reggie, wanting to make it better.

'It's lovely,' she said. 'It looks ever so fast – and you've made it go . . .'

Reggie gave her a fleeting smile, which she folded into her heart, precious as a jewel. He would be gone again soon but at least she had this to hold on to.

'Yeah,' he said. He moved away immediately. 'C'mon, Wal – let's try her out!'

III

1954

Eight

August 1954

Rachel lay beside Danny in their attic room. Threads of moonlight seeped in through the cracks between the slates. Things scuttled about. It was a stifling night and in this room with its ceiling so low that they had to be careful not to bash their heads on the beam and with its tiny window, it was impossible to get any sort of breeze passing through. From across the yard, she could hear the grating cry of the sickly Davies baby.

Soon after the Suttons vanished, the Davies family moved in – or what remained of it. Mary Davies's husband, a foreman in a foundry, had taken his own life, leaving her with no income and three children, one of them very young.

'It did for him, that foundry,' Mary told her new neighbours in her plaintive whine. 'It ground him right down, my Bert. Sensitive sort of man, he was.'

Mary Davies was not a young woman: this had been her second marriage. Somewhere there were grown-up children. Her belly sagged and her teeth were as black-and-white as a crossword puzzle. Rachel struggled to recall the names of her children. Frankie – was it? – the eldest, was eight. There was a solid, silent girl called Carol, of about five. The babby, another boy a year or so old, seemed to do nothing but blart and Mrs Davies did a lot of shrieking.

They all felt sorry for her, but it was just that Mary Davies herself seemed enough to grind anybody down.

'That babby again,' she murmured to Danny. 'What is it about that flaming house? Why can't we get someone decent in there?'

Or better still, she thought, get out ourselves and find somewhere better than this.

Danny shifted beside her and flopped over on to his back.

'That place is in a worse state than all the others,' he said. 'You gotta be desperate to move in there.'

'There's plenty desperate,' Rachel said. She nearly added, *I'm* desperate. She longed with a passion to get out of here now, away from this stinking yard and cramped little house. None of it had mattered when the war was on, when she was young and in love. When she and Danny first had this room in the attic they had rejoiced to have a place and bed of their own. They hadn't cared then about the leaking roof or the mildew which crept along the walls, however many times they added coats of distemper, or the bugs and silverfish scuttling along the floor. None of that was important. They were together – and after Danny went away to war, she was too busy struggling to get by with Melly as a baby.

But these days she was tired of living under Gladys's thumb all the time on this mouldering old yard – in an ever worse state now with all the neglect of years. At least when the war was on, the right thing to do was to keep hanging on, hoping – but now what were they waiting for? Even rationing had finally ended, after they'd endured fourteen years of it, but somehow Rachel felt as though she was still waiting. She was exhausted and worn down with it all – struggling with the family, the short-ages all these years. And she wanted her own house. But plenty of families were crammed in together the way they were – and worse. Two families to a back house like this sometimes, or with lodgers squeezed in. There was scarcely a place to be had anywhere, especially from the council. Bloody Hitler had seen to that.

'God, it's hot,' she said. She felt dragged down and out of sorts. She blamed it on the muggy heat.

'It's warm, all right.' But it didn't seem to bother Danny. He'd had far worse in India. He reached over and she felt his hand on her breast, like a warm coal. He began fondling her nipple under her light cotton shift.

'Danny!' She wriggled. 'It's too flaming hot for all that!'

His face loomed over her. 'Too hot? You always moan enough when it's cold. Come on, wench . . .'

'*Danny.*' She grabbed his wrist. 'When're we going to try and get out of here? I'm sick of it. We're like wasps in a bottle . . .'

'We're all right.' His eyes were half closed. He was beginning to get lost in his arousal. 'There's plenty worse. Tell you what though . . .' His eyes snapped open. 'You know what we ought to do? Go to Australia. I met a bloke today, says he's going – ten quid a ticket!'

'Australia?' Rachel laughed. 'What the hell're you on about? I bet you don't even know where Australia is!'

'I know where you are though, gorgeous . . .' He ran his hand up her body. Rachel gave a low giggle, relenting. These were the times that made life worth living, she and Danny, close, in bed. Especially now Ricky was sleeping down with the others and they had the room to themselves again. She often heard other women muttering about men and their demands and what a dreadful thing it was, but she liked being with Danny like this, always had. Except that it led to babies and more babies . . .

Danny lifted her nightdress and started to reach between her legs. He shifted himself up and kissed her lips, starting to move himself on top of her.

'Danny –' she said, moving her mouth away. 'You'd better pull out this time. Don't you dare do what you did last time . . .' She was worried, always. Not another one – please God.

'Yeah, all right,' he murmured, reluctant.

Despite the fact that she was the one who had to carry the babies, she felt guilty making Danny pull away at the last minute. He was young and vigorous. And she wanted it too. She felt so tense tonight, so in need of something – closeness, comfort – that she wanted to feel something lovely. To reach the peak of lovemaking, not just to walk beside him as a spectator.

He kissed her ear. 'Sorry,' he murmured, close to her. 'I just want yer, that's all.'

'I know, but . . .' She felt tears rising in her, trapped between the opposing needs of lovemaking and avoiding another baby. It was so easy to give Danny what he wanted. To satisfy his desires in bed. To make sure she took on all the really difficult things: looking after Tommy, always here, doing the worrying, feeling the sadness of it. Danny worked hard, of course he did, and he clowned about with Kev and Ricky, did his cartoons, played football, took Melly to the market and all that. But when it came to his eldest son, however much Danny pretended, she knew he still could not really accept him the way he was. When it came down to it, she was on her own with Tommy.

She tried not to think about where this would all end. She was the one tied to Tommy, trapped inside this jerry-built little house. Sometimes it felt as though the walls were reaching in and swallowing her up. All her young life was tied to Tommy, who despite everything she loved with a burning fierceness. But some days, when she thought about her eldest son's future, she saw him only ever here with her. What would happen if she wasn't here?

If she allowed herself to think about what else her own life might have held, she just wanted to break down and weep in the sheer despair and exhaustion of it all. She tried so hard not to feel sorry for herself. She knew there were people worse off. Look at Lil Gittins with Stanley. At least she, Rachel, had a healthy, able-bodied husband. But sometimes it all welled up and got on top of her. Danny never seemed troubled by any of it. He avoided the things he did not want to do or feel. But she wanted him to care about keeping her happy too, not just to keep taking from her like another child.

As Danny kissed her more slowly, taking his time at last, she began to feel the tingle of arousal. She stopped hearing the yowl of the baby across the yard and became lost in her own feelings.

Danny moved off her for a moment. 'Take it off.' He nodded at her shift and she sat up and lifted it over her head. In the dim light they could just see each other.

'That's my girl. You're a cracker, you are.' His voice was warm and fond.

She was touched at him trying to woo her.

'Come 'ere,' she said and took him in her arms. Both of them were slender, but not skeleton thin the way they had been at the end of the war. When Danny had come home, he had been gaunt and sick from India and she had been a skinny shadow of herself from a life lived on low rations and nerves. Sometimes they joked that they could hold each other now without cutting themselves.

Danny stroked her back, kissing her deeply on the mouth, and gradually laid her down again, no longer able to wait, pushing deep into her.

'Shhh,' she giggled, putting a hand over his mouth as he thrust into her. Gladys and the kids were just below them. But she wanted him, pressed her hands against his strong back, the powerful spine, his flesh slick with sweat, her own pleasure eventually breaking over her so that they were both clinging and gasping together. She wept a little, released by the force of it.

In the silence, Danny licked a tear from her cheek. 'Don't cry,' he said. 'Why're you crying?'

'I'm not,' she whispered. 'Not really crying. It just happened, that's all.'

'Love yer, girl.'

More tears ran from her eyes. 'Love you too, you daft bugger.' *Oh, God, I didn't make him pull out. What if . . . ? What're we going to do?* She did want to weep then. But so many times over the years she had wanted to wail this question and she knew there was no answer. She didn't want to spoil this moment now.

Danny slid off her, both of them slippery wet. The air cooled her skin. He settled himself beside her.

'God, it's warm,' he muttered, as if he had just noticed. And she could already hear the sleep in his voice. 'Australia – that's where we should go . . . Start again . . .'

Rachel rolled her eyes in the dark. Danny was asleep.

Nine

October 1954

Rachel stood sorting through a pile of clothes on the table, ready for washing. She had lit the copper in the brew house, the steam curling out into the chilly autumn air. It was an ordinary morning, Kev and Melly at school, Tommy at home, Ricky playing out in the yard, Gladys out at the shops. Music streamed from the wireless.

'*That's amore . . .*' she sang, reaching over to stroke Tommy's head. He looked up from his comic and smiled at her. They found ways to keep him occupied. After his dinner he would go to Dolly's. He was too old for *Watch with Mother* really but it passed the time.

Rachel liked it when Gladys went out. Gladys had been good to them, there was no denying it. But as she got older and complained of rheumatism and her bunion on her foot she had become sharper, bossier. Rachel was fed up with living under her thumb. Gladys reckoned to be in charge of everyone – the household, the yard. Rachel tried to remain cheerful in front of Tommy, but she sighed as she bundled up the washing and her eyes filled.

She faced a morning of toil, turning the skein of sheets and clothing in the hot water of the copper, lifting it into the dolly tub to be pounded with the wooden dolly, rinsing it, mangling it, hanging it out. Her shoulders already ached and she had a dull pain in her lower back. On and on it went, the daily round, every week the same . . .

'Eat up, Tommy,' she said, more sharply than she meant to. She wiped her eyes and nose on the end of the sheet she was taking to wash. 'I need to get on.'

She didn't like to leave him while he was eating in case he choked. She thought, with longing, if only Tommy had been like Kev. Kev had done his first year at school already. The teachers said he was a bright little boy, if he'd only sit still long enough. Kev found his adventures with other lads on the bomb pecks of the surrounding streets far preferable to the classroom: the houses wrecked by bombing, the jungles of brick and plaster and weeds, the games and hunts for shrapnel. Kevin, energetic and restless, spent most of his time rushing about out there with them, even though he was one of the youngest. For a moment she imagined Tommy, whole-bodied, running about and a tear escaped down her cheek which she turned away from him to hide.

There was a knock on the door, an insistent rap.

'Bugger it.' Rachel shoved the pile of dirty washing under the table. 'Who the hell's that?'

She wondered if it was the welfare about Mary Davies's baby again. He'd been poorly on and off for weeks and they were keeping an eye on him. But they must surely know by now that he lived at number four?

'Coming . . .' She went to the door. Outside was a lady whose age Rachel could not guess. Her tobacco-coloured hair was collar length with a frizzy curl to it, brushed severely away from a straight right parting and held with a kirby grip. Her weather-beaten face bore not a hint of make-up and she wore a brown utility suit and brown lace-up shoes. Under her left arm were tucked some papers. Pebbly blue eyes looked intently at Rachel through horn-rimmed spectacles.

'Yes?' Rachel held the door close to her. 'What d'you want?'

'Good morning, Mrs – er – Booker. I'm here to talk to you about your son.'

'My – which son?' Rachel felt a stab of fear. She could see Ricky on his little trike along the yard. Had something happened to Kevin? She pulled the door closer to her. 'What d'you mean?'

She saw a kindly light in the woman's eyes. 'It's all right. It's nothing to worry about, Mrs Booker. In fact, I hope I might be able to give you some good news. My name is Miss Walsh. May I come in for a moment?'

Only a fraction reassured, Rachel relinquished the door and led the stranger into the downstairs room. It didn't look too bad, she thought, flustered. At least she'd managed to hide the washing.

'Ah.' Miss Walsh immediately spotted Tommy, in his chair by the table. 'This is who I've come to see. Hello, young man.'

Tommy, head slightly to one side, gave a convulsive wobble, his left arm clenched close to his body. He looked up at the lady with wide, wondering eyes. 'He – llo –' He managed to begin a greeting, but could not seem to get any further.

Rachel started to tremble. Although Miss Walsh spoke softly, she was afraid of her, of what power she might have. Was she one of those welfare busybodies? Could they make her give Tommy up, force her to put him in a home?

'What is it you want?' she said in a faint voice. Her legs went weak and she had to pull up a chair before she had even offered the stranger one, and sit down. 'You're not going to take him away?'

'Oh, my dear, *no*, nothing like that. It's quite all right. Let me explain.' Miss Walsh laid her hand on the nearest chair. 'May I?'

'Yes. Sorry,' Rachel said. Despite her fear, she could still feel a sense of trust in this woman with her soothing voice.

Miss Walsh descended on to the chair with a slow grace, resting her papers on her lap.

'I am a social worker – that's the best way to describe it. I am working with the welfare officers of an organization which you may have heard of, called the Midland Spastic Association – no? Well, you wouldn't be the first, believe me. It's people like yourself and this young man –' She looked questioningly across the table. 'What's your name, dear – can you tell me?'

'Tomm – y,' he said.

'Very good! Children like Tommy, with cerebral palsy . . .'

Rachel stared at her. 'Ce-re-bral palsy,' she repeated slowly. Not once had anyone said this odd name to her before. Not even the doctor. Tommy had always been a 'spastic' and a 'cripple'. *Cerebral palsy*. She tried to make sense of it. 'Is that –? I mean – are there a lot of them, then?'

'A lot? Well, I wouldn't say a lot exactly, but a number, yes. And there is now a special school for children like Tommy. Have you ever been to school, Tommy?'

'No,' he replied, wide-eyed. His sweetness melted Rachel inside.

'I guessed not,' Miss Walsh said, with a gentle smile.

'He doesn't really go anywhere much,' Rachel admitted. She looked down, tearful again. So much feeling welled up in her – the fierce protectiveness she felt for Tommy, the fear for him, rage at people's cruelty and the overwhelming, grinding exhaustion of it all. She felt as if her tears might flood the floor. She took a deep breath and looked up.

'I used to take him out when he was little – I tried, I really did. But people were so unkind and in the end he didn't want to go. And some lads – I mean, he had a bad fright one day . . . So I kept him in and his sister has taught him things and everything. But I never wanted him to go into one of those . . .' She couldn't say those words in front of Tommy. Home for Cripples. The sort of place her own mother, among others, had suggested she put Tommy and *just get on with your own life*. 'You know, those places . . .'

Miss Walsh nodded, leaning forward slightly, fingers of one hand to her lips, her back very straight. She was listening carefully. Rachel felt that no one had ever listened to her quite like this before.

'I just couldn't,' she said. 'And I didn't know what else to do . . .' Her tears were coming now, all the years of pent-up sorrow and desperation leaking out. 'My husband doesn't find it easy . . . He doesn't like . . .' She glanced at Tommy. She mustn't say any more, much as she longed to pour her heart out. Miss Walsh nodded slightly, looking at Tommy, as if she understood the problem. Desperately Rachel added, 'I did my best. I never knew anyone else and I didn't know what to do.'

'It's all right, dear,' Miss Walsh said. She looked at some notes she was holding in her lap. 'We were notified by one of the health visitors from this area. Do you have a health visitor now? When did you last see her?'

Rachel wiped her eyes. 'Oh – sometime after I had Ricky, my youngest. She still comes now and then.' She gave a watery smile. Fishing in the waistband of her apron she found a hanky and wiped her nose.

'Ah –' Miss Walsh's eyes searched the notes. 'It was a Miss Russell.'

'No,' Rachel said. 'I don't know her.' Then the memory dawned on her. 'Oh – no, I do! Yes, she's been one or twice.' The woman had been especially kind to Tommy, she remembered.

Miss Walsh smiled. 'Well, she was the one who mentioned you. I'm glad we've found you. We've been looking for children like Tommy, you see. Now, let me tell you . . .'

She explained that a few years earlier, two men of the city, both with wealth and influence, had each, in their own families, had a child with cerebral palsy.

'Like your son,' she added. 'It usually means that when the baby was born there was some damage to the brain, sometimes through lack of oxygen.'

She took in Rachel's bewildered expression.

'We don't know the cause in every case, dear. Now – one of the men was Mr Paul Cadbury, a member of the Cadbury's chocolate family, of course. Obviously he and his friend wanted to do the best they could for their children, but they soon saw how hard it is – even if you have money. They realized that there was nowhere for their children to go. So they started to wonder about other children in the same position. And they set up a school especially for them. It's called Carlson House and it's in Harborne. I don't suppose you've heard of it?'

'No,' Rachel whispered, shaking her head.

'What I'd like to do is have a look at Tommy. It appears very likely that we could take him to Carlson House to be assessed and – if they think it's right for him

– well, he could go to school. How old are you now, Tommy?'

'E – lev – en,' he managed to say.

'Only just eleven,' Rachel added. She was reeling. A special school, for boys like Tommy! 'But – Harborne . . .' Despair dampened her hopes. 'That's right the other side of Birmingham. I mean – how could I? I'd have to get him on the bus, and then—'

Miss Walsh raised a hand to stop her. 'There is transport provided. The school is a charitable foundation, you see, Mrs Booker. It wants to provide for children like Tommy. We are trying to trace children across the city who would benefit from it. So many of them are not getting any education at all and with a little help, a lot of them are capable of more than you might think.'

'I . . .' Rachel was still groping for words. 'I don't know what to say. I mean, I know Tommy's, you know, all there. He can read a bit and he can talk. I do a bit with him but it's his sister Melly – she's done ever such a lot. She likes teaching him, you see.'

Miss Walsh gave a gentle smile. 'How old is Melly?'

'Melanie's her real name. She's thirteen.'

'Well, what a wonderful daughter you have,' Miss Walsh said. 'It's not often you find a girl with as much patience and perseverance as that.'

'Yes,' Rachel said, surprised. She blushed with pleasure. 'She's a good girl.'

'She certainly is. So, Tommy.' Miss Walsh turned and faced him. Rachel could see in his eyes all the hope and uncertainty of his feelings after what he had heard. He was wavering and wobbling more than usual and she knew this was because he was in an emotional state. 'What do you think, dear? Would you like to go to school like the other boys and girls?'

'Yes,' Tommy said. He looked at Rachel and then at Miss Walsh. 'I – want to – go. If they're – not – un-k-k . . .' He stumbled over the word, but at last brought out, 'Unkind.'

Miss Walsh seemed moved by this.

'No, my dear,' she said. 'They are not there to be unkind, I can assure you. They are there to help.' She got up. 'May I take a look at you, please, Tommy?'

She spent a few minutes with him, feeling his arms, bending and straightening them, feeling how they responded. She asked him to stand, as Rachel had told her that he could, that for years he had slept in leg splints. He looked like a bent little man in his baggy grey trousers.

'I know – my – letters,' Tommy told her eagerly, once he was back in his chair.

Miss Walsh smiled down at him. 'Shall we take you over to Carlson House and see what can be done?'

'You really mean it?' Rachel still could not stop her tears as her boy's face lit up. 'There's really somewhere for my Tommy?'

'Yes, my dear. I'm glad to say there is. You don't need to be on your own any longer.'

At this Rachel began to sob. She put her head in her hands and wept, shaking her head.

'All these years,' she said at last, when she could get the words out. 'I've never thought he would have anything. There was nobody who wanted to know about him so in the end I kept him away from everyone. I didn't want him to be with people who were nasty to him. I never thought there'd be something like this . . .'

'If he is admitted to Carlson House,' Miss Walsh said, 'we also ask the mothers to become involved for a part of the time, in helping the children – for a day every week or two if you can. And don't despair if they don't take him into the school straight away. We are also trying to make sure that welfare officers will come to your home and you can ask their advice about anything related to Tommy. You need never be so alone again, Mrs Booker. And I'd say –' she gave Rachel's hand a squeeze as she got up – 'that this young man would fit into the school very well and get a lot of benefit from it. He's a bright little fellow.' She gave Tommy another kindly look. 'We'll be in touch, very soon.'

'Oh – thank you. Thank you!' Rachel said as the woman left. She realized, as Miss Walsh's footsteps receded along the entry, that not only had she not offered her a cup of tea, but that this extraordinary woman had, in just a few minutes, blown open the windows of her life to let in light.

Ten

As soon as she walked in from school, Melly knew something had changed. She picked it up before anyone said a word, a feeling of unease spreading through her.

Mom was by the gas stove, stirring baked beans. Her dark hair curled round her collar at the back.

'School all right?' she said over her shoulder to Kevin.

Kevin grunted.

'Spit it out.' Rachel turned. 'Did you get the cane again?'

Kev was at the table, filling his face with bread and Stork and twitching about as usual. He was obviously reluctant to say anything. Rachel stared him out.

''Er gave me a wap with a ruler,' he admitted, indistinctly through a mouthful. His fine, dark brows were frowning slightly but he did not seem very bothered.

'Wap,' Ricky echoed, with a gurgle of laughter.

'What for?' Rachel said.

'Not sitting still.'

'Hah – well, that hardly makes a change,' she laughed. There was something different in her laughter and Melly, helping herself to a piece of bread, could feel it. Something new, but she couldn't catch what. Taking a bite, she turned to find Mom watching her. She had moved over and was half leaning on the back of a chair.

'All right, Melly?'

'Umm,' she said, chewing.

Rachel's eyes seemed to search her face.

'You're a good kid. You know that, don't you?'

Melly looked up at her. Mom said that from time to time, absent-mindedly, when she wanted her to do something for her. *Take Tommy to the lavvy, will you? There's a good kid.* This time she was looking intently at her.

'All you've done with Tommy. Teaching him and everything. You've been ever so patient. Not many kids your age would've done it.'

Melly smiled, pleased yet confused. Mom was usually on at her for something. Why was she being nice suddenly? She looked at Tommy. He seemed different too, excited, a little grin coming and going, but het up, as if he might explode.

Mom moved back to the stove. 'When your dad and auntie get back, Tommy and I've got something to tell you.'

Everyone was looking at Tommy. He squirmed and half smiled and didn't know where to look.

'So who was this woman?' Danny asked.

Melly thought he sounded hostile, as if to say, how dare she come round here when no one asked her to and change things? Dad didn't like things changing. In that moment Melly realized that she didn't like it either. Tommy going across town every *day*? How could this be?

'I told you,' Rachel said. 'She was from the welfare. From this place in Harborne where they want him to go to school.'

'I've never heard of any such place,' Gladys said. She was sitting up very straight, tight-lipped and suspicious.

'I'm to take him to be assessed,' Rachel said. She

sounded proud, saying the word *assessed,* and defiant, as if to say, don't you dare try and stop me. To Gladys she added, 'It's been going a few years, this school, the woman said – Miss Walsh her name was. Since soon after the war anyway.' She told them about the man from Cadbury's and his child.

Melly watched her father sit back and light up, blowing whorls of smoke towards the ceiling.

'That's all very well. But how do they think we're going to go carting over to Harborne? Stick him on the back of my pushbike or summat?' His uncertainty came out as sarcasm.

'No, I *told* you, she said they'd fetch him. In a car.'

'A car!' Danny took a drag on his Woodbine and his mocking laugh was an outbreath of smoke. 'You really think they're gonna send a *car* all the way over here –' he nodded at Tommy – 'for 'im!'

Melly cringed inside at the way he spoke. She couldn't look at Tommy.

'Yes,' Rachel said. Melly could hear her anger and determination. 'That's what she said, dain't she, Tommy?'

'Seems peculiar to me,' Gladys cut in.

Melly watched her mother try not to lose her temper.

'It may seem *peculiar*,' she said. 'But this is how it is – and he's going. They're trying to find children all over Birmingham with, with . . .' She tried to remember the term again. 'With *cerebral palsy*, that's what she called it. And help them get some schooling.'

Gladys looked uncertain and pursed her lips. Melly could see that behind her suspiciousness, Auntie looked a bit lost in all this. It was outside her ken – beyond the world of Alma Street and the markets. She seemed vulnerable suddenly.

'Well, I've never heard of anything like it,' she said.

'Nor me,' Danny added.

'Well, aren't you glad for him?' Rachel stood over them, blazing at them both. 'Just because something's new and different doesn't make it bad, does it? They've set up a school specially. And Tommy wants to go. It's a chance for him – so we're going.'

Normally Rachel deferred to Gladys, but not this time.

'Well . . .' Gladys clasped her teacup between both hands. 'I s'pose if that's what they think best . . . What about you, Tommy, eh?' She reached round and stroked his cheek. 'What d'you think about going to this place?'

'I – I . . .' He was agitated, gasping for words.

'Take it slow, Tommy,' Melly said, leaning towards him. 'One word at a time.' She felt she needed to remind him and everyone that *she* had been Tommy's teacher up until now. *She* was the one who had helped him learn all the things he knew. She had a horrible shrinking feeling as if she was about to lose something very important and no one else was going to notice.

Struggling for each word, Tommy brought out, 'The lady – was – nice. I want – to – go – and – see.'

'What's it cost?' Danny asked, still hostile. 'There's got to be a catch somewhere.'

'You don't pay. It's some kind of charity thing,' Rachel said hurriedly. 'He's not in yet, not for sure – they have to look at him and then decide.'

'Oh, ar – I see,' Danny said, sitting back as if to say, well, that's the end of all that then. What's all the fuss about? Tommy wouldn't be going anyway.

'But she said she thought he has a very good chance,' Rachel insisted. 'And if they take him, they want me to go and help a bit – every so often, like. You know, with the kiddies.'

'Well.' Gladys sat back. It was all taking a while to sink in, but she knew, as Danny's aunt and the oldest there, that she had the authority in this house and she asserted herself. She looked round the table. 'It sounds to me like a good thing for the lad to try. If it's what they're making it out to be, any road.' She gave her nephew a sharp look. 'No need to stand in the lad's way if there's summat for him. If you're happy, Rach, we'd better let him.'

Rachel folded her arms. 'Oh, he's going.'

Danny didn't reply. He nudged Kevin. 'Come on, soldier – want to kick that ball around for a bit? And you, Ricky?'

Kevin leapt down from the table, full of energy as ever. The two boys went out, with Kevin's ball. Melly saw her mother frown, her eyes following Danny, and the expression in them was full of hurt and disappointment.

People who were out on Alma Street that morning stopped and turned uneasily to watch. A large Austin hearse rumbled along the cobbles at an unhurried pace, the driver craning his neck as if in search of the right address. He braked the heavy black vehicle at the kerb, wound down the window and called to a woman in a headscarf for directions. She straightened up, pointing, her face sober at the thought of a death nearby.

The driver, a rotund man with a remaining ring of black hair round a bald patch, switched off the engine and made his way along the entry, buttoning his jacket as he went. He searched out number three on the yard and the Mrs Booker he was looking for. He found her ready and waiting, her son with her in his chair.

Rachel pushed Tommy out along the entry, stopped and stared with incredulity at the car.

'Are you having me on?'

'No, I'm not,' the driver said, huffily. 'Sometimes they use our cars when the taxis are busy. They use cars from the Electric Garage and they've only got so many to spare.' As they got in he added, 'Any road, you're best off with me. Theirs're forever breaking down.'

A curious crowd gathered. The absence of any sign of a coffin or black funeral garb made the situation even more interesting for the Alma Street bystanders. Rachel felt hysterical giggles rising up in her. This would make Danny laugh when she told him later on.

'Off somewhere nice, are yer, bab?' some joker called from behind her.

'Come on,' the driver said, with an air of someone weary of merry comments about his vehicle. 'Let's get you inside.'

Rachel settled beside Tommy on the seat, his chair stowed safely in the boot. Tommy looked suddenly very small in the grand car, like a rag doll slumped on the seat. His face was solemn, his left arm seeming stiffer and more clenched than usual. He told her he had hardly slept. He was awed and nervous about the whole experience. Rachel worried suddenly that something might happen, that he'd wet the seat or something.

'You don't need to go, do you, Tommy?' she whispered as the car pulled away from the kerb. He'd been just before they left, but how awful it would be if . . .

He shook his head and managed a tiny smile. Rachel was filled with tenderness looking at him. Her poor little boy – he had hardly been anywhere in his life and now this. What a thing! She took his hand and squeezed it.

'I feel like a film star,' she said, letting some of her giggles out. 'Look, people're waving!'

And then they set off at a dignified, almost regal pace,

along Alma Street, past the Salutation pub and the Crocodile works and into Summer Lane, before gliding into Birmingham. She looked out at the centre of town which still felt like one big building site. As they crawled through, she stared out at the blitzed city trying to recover, at the jagged gaps between the buildings, the cranes, the scaffolding and dust and mess of it all and then they were out the other side and heading south towards the greener suburb of Harborne village.

As soon as Danny came home that night, she flung herself at him.

'They say he can go – he can go to the school! Oh, it's such a nice place – and I'm going to go and help!' She was so excited she hadn't been able to sit still since the car brought them back – a normal taxi this time, which had still caused a bit of a stir when they arrived home. 'They said it's the only school like it in the whole country. Oh, and everyone was so nice and they know just how to look after him!'

When they'd got to the school in Victoria Road and saw the buildings, the classrooms and garden and all the kind people working with the children she couldn't help it – again, she broke down and wept. That all this existed, that there could be such a place, all arranged specially for children like Tommy – it was a miracle! And as she looked round, seeing the children in their classes, the way everything was done to try and help each of them learn, even with all their varying difficulties, she was filled with astonishment.

'All right, all right, calm down, wench!' Danny said, trying to put down the bags he was carrying as she hung round his neck. But he was laughing at her enthusiasm.

'I just never knew there were people like that, Danny.' She was tearful again now. 'It feels as if . . .' How to say it, that everything felt different, that the whole world seemed to have changed when you could find all this help and kindness in it?

Danny looked round. 'Where is the lad then?'

'Upstairs having a kip,' Rachel said. 'He was worn out after all the excitement, poor little lamb. Oh, Danny –' She went to him again. 'I'm so pleased for him. I can hardly believe it.'

Eleven

Tommy sat in the back of the taxi as he did every afternoon now. They turned up Alma Street and parked in the usual place. It was Friday, the end of his first week at school and he was so tired he had almost fallen asleep on the comfortable car seat on the drive home.

'I'll just go and get your mother,' the driver said.

Tommy waited. He was always waiting for something. He could feel people peering into the car and he shrank down in the seat. If only he could jump out and run along the entry out of sight! He knew that later he'd go to Mo and Dolly's house to watch their television. He loved telly with a passion. It could take you anywhere. At school he had made a friend called Simon who loved telly as well and they talked about *The Quatermass Experiment.* Even though it ended months ago it still gave him churning, excited, terrified feelings when he thought about it. There was a new series on now called *Fabian of the Yard,* which was all about policemen and crimes. Tommy had seen one episode and was itching to see more of it . . .

Knuckles rapped the window. 'Tommy! Wakey-wakey!'

His mother opened the door. Her face looked white and tired. Tommy wriggled and slithered out of the car and into his chair.

'Thanks very much,' Rachel said to the driver.

'All right. Ta-ra,' he muttered, through his cigarette.

'How was it today?' She leaned down and he felt her breath on his neck and heard the anxiety in her voice. 'Taxi all right?' The driver of the hearse had been right – the old taxis which ferried the children around often coughed bronchially into silence on the way.

'Yeah. All right.'

It *was* all right. It was more than all right, sitting in the classroom with other boys and girls the same as him but each different in their own way. Some had far worse difficulties than his. They were trying him out doing all sorts of things. He showed them that he could write his letters as long as the paper was fixed down. People seemed to be pleased. Tommy felt happy but limp with exhaustion. So many things happening all day – it wore him out.

As soon as they got into the yard, Melly appeared. She came and helped Mom push the chair, although Mom didn't need help.

'Did you like your school today?' she asked, babying him.

He didn't say anything. Melly had always given him lessons when she got home from school. When he had been sitting not doing much all day, he had waited for her, wanting her to come home. But now when he got back he had been on the go all day and he was tired out.

In the house, Mom had cut him a piece with jam on it.

'When you've had that, shall I play a game with you?' Melly said.

Tommy was deep in one of Dad's comics. He shook his head. 'No – don't wan'oo.'

He didn't look at Melly. He knew she was good with games and lessons but he had proper teachers now. She took over everything. He wished she would leave him alone.

'Don't you want to do some letters?' Melly persisted. Tommy could hear the hurt in her voice but he carried on staring at the comic.

'Leave him, Melly,' Mom snapped. 'He's had enough. And that telly programme he likes is on soon anyhow. Why don't you go and see Cissy while she's here? It's not as if she gets herself over here often these days.'

Peering out into the yard in Cissy's direction, she added, to Gladys, 'We're gonna have to watch that one. She's up there by the works with Dolly's Fred again.'

Tommy could feel Melly standing by his chair, looking down at him. He didn't look up and after a minute she went to the door and slipped outside. No one called her back.

Melly stood at the side of the yard, in the dying light. She leaned against the wall, arms clenched across her chest. Cissy had come over after work to stay with them, but Cissy's idea of fun these days was hanging around with Freddie Morrison.

Cissy had left school now and was fulfilling Nanna Peggy's dream of having a daughter working in a big store. Well, almost. Peggy really wanted a daughter selling clothes or perfume at Lewis's or Rackham's. Cissy was working at Woolworth's, but at least it was Woolworth's in the Bull Ring and Peggy was sure it would lead to higher things.

Now she had left school, with a sigh and a flounce of relief, Cissy considered herself a Woman and Melly still to be a Child. Melly was fed up with her. Cissy used to come over to play with *her*, but she knew that these days, Alma Street was the main place where Cissy could meet boys. Cissy was full of new words these days. Everything was 'cool' or 'hip'. She wore full, swinging skirts and hoiked her ginger hair into a high ponytail.

Freddie, the youngest of the five Morrison lads, was fifteen, only a few months older than Cissy. Cissy had previously had a crush on Jonny, his older brother, but that hadn't lasted long.

'Jonny's boring,' she'd announced last year. Jonny, of all the Morrison boys, was the studious one. The others had left school and worked for various firms in the area, but Jonny wanted to be a teacher. Now that there were enough wages coming into the house from all the others, Mo and Dolly had said he could stay on at school. Jonny, at seventeen, had his nose constantly in a book and this was not good-time-girl Cissy's cup of tea at all.

So she had set her sights on Freddie instead. He was a jolly, uncomplicated lad who worked for a firm turning out brass pressings and stampings. As soon as he was finished at work, he was looking for fun and Cissy was eager to provide it. The two of them had lengthy, secretive chats in which Cissy did a lot of giggling. One of these chats was going on right now, by the wall of the wire works. Freddie, blonde and muscular, though not much taller than Cissy, was leaning one elbow against the wall, one leg nonchalantly bent. Cissy was laughing at everything he said even if it *wasn't funny*.

'I don't know why you bother coming any more if you don't want to do anything,' Melly had said to Cissy earlier. Cissy seemed to have no time for her these days. She just rolled her eyes, looked superior and didn't say anything back.

Melly was so fed up that she felt like hurting Cissy – slapping or scratching her. But it was the rejection she felt from Tommy that was the worst. He didn't seem to want anything from her now he was at school. Tommy had also told her that at school they had a proper frame to hold his paper, to stop it slipping. He was quite good with his right hand and his writing was coming on. What he could not do was to hold the paper still with his left hand. But he was now on to something better than having the paper weighed down with a tin of marrowfat peas and a packet of salt or whatever came to hand. Everything at Carlson House was marvellous and it seemed that none of the things she had done for him were good enough now.

Her throat ached with the need to cry. Earlier, she had wanted Tommy to see how near her tears were, to take pity on her. But he just kept staring at his comic.

Another outbreak of giggles came from along the yard and Melly turned her back on Cissy and Fred. The worst of it was, what Cissy felt for him wasn't even a tiny *fraction* of what she felt for Reggie, she thought furiously. Reggie was older and much more exciting than stupid old Fred. But Melly couldn't tell anyone about that because she felt embarrassed and no one would believe her. Reggie wasn't even here – he'd been away in the army for so long. Dolly kept saying he might be home for Christmas and every time she thought of it, Melly felt an electric thrill of excitement.

As she stood there Melly could hear the rise and fall of Dolly's voice inside number one over the murmur of the television. Frankie Davies, the boy from number four, kept trotting up and down hitting his own thigh and saying, 'G'won, Trigger!' Melly didn't want to know about Frankie. He was pale and odd, with adenoids. Beyond him, tucked against the far wall, was the Norton, Wally and Reggie's pride and joy, under an old tarpaulin. Wally tinkered with it at the weekends and took it out, with threats directed at any of the children in the yard as to what would happen to them if he caught them meddling with it.

Melly picked at the moss on the wall with her finger. The memory of her brother's bowed head kept forcing itself into her mind. Tommy wouldn't look up at her. Tommy, who before had turned to her for almost everything. She had been his companion, his teacher. Now he didn't want her. She was glad the light was bad because she didn't want to cry in front of Frankie Davies. She swallowed hard, feeling more lost and lonely standing there in the shadows than she had ever felt before.

No one seemed to want her. Mom only took any notice when she had a job for her to do and all she talked about now was Tommy's new school. She went in once a week to help and it seemed to have taken over all of her mind. Dad played with Kev and Ricky, never with her. She wanted someone to want her – need her.

A warm feeling spread through her as she thought about the nurse who had come when Ricky was born. *You could make a marvellous little nurse one day.* The idea caught hold in her mind. That was what she'd do – she'd become a nurse! Then she could look after people and they would need her and think she was special, the way she'd thought Nurse Waller was special. She'd work in a hospital and she'd be called Nurse Booker and she'd be the best nurse that ever was!

She was full of a burning passion, all in that moment, wanting it now, wanting it to begin. She thought about Lil Gittins. Lil always said what a good girl she was and how Stanley seemed to talk to her when he didn't to most people. That's what she would do. She'd go and see Stanley. She could help him; nurse him or whatever he needed.

Straightening up, she brushed down her grey school

dress. Pulling her shoulders back, she said to herself, 'Nurse Booker went to call at number five.' She walked in a dignified manner across the yard, past Cissy and Freddie. She waited for Cissy to call to her, 'Where're you off to, Melly?' But Cissy, propped in a provocative stance against the wall of the wire factory, didn't even look round. Melly reached number five and, after taking a breath, rapped on the door.

'Yes? Who is it?' She heard Lil's tense voice from inside. Poor Lil. That was what everyone called her. Poor Lil with her wrecked husband, her lost youth. But Melly could not remember Lil before the war. In her memory she had always been grey-haired and thin and nervy.

'It's . . .' She wanted to say, 'Nurse Booker.' Nurse Booker who strode across battlefields bringing balm and healing to injured men, like Florence Nightingale, who they had heard a story about at school. The men reached out to her, desperate, with trembling hands as she went past. They never forgot her. 'It's me. Melly.'

The door opened. Lil had a pinner on over her dress, hair half hanging down. She looked tense, her hands concealed behind her back. A nasty smell drifted out through the door.

'What is it you want, bab? I'm just doing . . .' She trailed off as if not wanting to finish the sentence. 'I'm just helping Stanley.'

'I thought . . .' Melly sounded silly now to herself. 'I just thought, I'd come and see Mr Gittins. Sort of help you look after him, like.'

Lil stared at her. 'You?' she said, bewildered. She recovered her natural kindness. 'Well, that's nice of you, bab, but I don't think . . . I mean, not now. You can't come now – I'm just sorting him out. It's not a good time for Stanley – and I'm doing our dinner. You could come back tomorrow, but . . .' She looked vague. 'I never know, you see, how he'll be. But . . .' She was already closing the door. 'Come back tomorrow, bab, if yer want.'

Twelve

'Where're you going, Melly?' Rachel said the next after-noon. 'Tommy'll be home any minute. I want you to help me get the tea.'

'I said I'd go and see Mr and Mrs Gittins,' Melly said. She made it sound official. 'They're expecting me.'

Rachel looked up from the table where she was rub-bing fat and flour for pastry. Irritably she pushed a lock of hair out of the way with her arm. 'What d'you mean? What d'you want to do that for?'

'Because I want to be a nurse,' Melly said. There – she'd said it – first time ever!

Rachel looked at her in amazement before bursting out laughing. 'A nurse – you! What the hell gave you that idea?'

Melly folded her arms. She felt cold and deflated. 'I just do. I want to help people.'

'Well, come and flaming well help *me* then,' Rachel said impatiently.

Before Melly could think of an answer there was a knock at the door. 'Carlson House – got your son out-side,' the taxi driver called and Rachel quickly wiped her hands and hurried after him.

The door of number five was ajar and she gave it a timid tap. Mrs Gittins appeared after a few moments and looked at her, dull-eyed. Mom always talked about how Lil Gittins had been before the war – a happy soul, always singing, dressed up. You'd hardly know her now. The woman who stood there now in a washed-out frock several sizes too big for her looked wizened and heart-broken.

'What d'yer want, bab?' She was speaking in a very quiet voice but Melly could still hear that she sounded irritated. 'Stanley's just having forty winks in his chair.'

'Sorry, Mrs Gittins.' Melly held her hands politely together in front of her. 'Only, yesterday you said to come back today. You said I could help look after Mr Gittins.'

Lil Gittins leaned against the door frame. She tilted her head so that it rested on the wood with its chipped remains of dark green paint. 'What d'you think you're going to do for him, bab? He's past helping, my Stan. He's asleep at the moment.' She turned her head and listened for a second. A faint sound came from behind her. 'Not that he ever sleeps for long. All right, come in then. I s'pose I should be glad anyone wants to see my old man. There's precious few of his pals take the trouble now. You can sit with us, keep us company a bit if yer like.'

Melly stepped into the downstairs room. She imagined herself in uniform, neat and knowledgeable, bringing information and comfort. She had never been in the Gittins' house before. It was gloomy inside, on this winter afternoon.

'I won't put the light on yet,' Lil whispered. 'He says it blinds him. Here –' Her essentially good temper was improving now that she had company. She reached for a rickety wooden chair from by the table. 'Come and sit by me, bab. It's nice of you to call. I'll make us a cuppa a bit later once Stanley's come to. Oh, dear . . .'

She went to shift a bucket that was near Stanley's chair. A grey cloth was draped over it. 'It's not that he can't walk,' she said in a whisper. 'But he don't like going outside – not even to the lav. He wants to be near me – all the time.' This was said with a brave desperation.

Seeing the bucket, Melly suddenly noticed the strong stink of wee in the room. Their own house stank of it often enough, since no one wanted to go all the way down the yard at night and they slopped out buckets in the mornings. But in here it smelt especially rank. She told herself nurses had to get used to that sort of thing. Lil hurried the bucket into the scullery, out of sight.

There was very little room to move. Two armchairs took up a lot of space near the old range. A mirror hung over the mantelpiece, along which were strewn a few dusty trinkets and a pair of brass candlesticks with stubs of candles in them. There was a table near the gas stove, and a chipped, white cupboard, curtained off at the front with a piece of brown-and-white flowery material. Another curtain, more like an old grey blanket, hung behind the door and the walls were covered in a drab, pale brown patterned paper which looked as if it had been there forever. In one corner, near the front of the house, the ceiling bulged downward as if afflicted with a cancerous growth.

Melly remembered the inside of the Suttons' house when Evie and the others were still there, the horrible squalor of it. These two houses, built against the wall, seemed to be worse than the other three. This one was not as bad as number four, but there was still that creeping, mouldy smell and everything felt old and damp and worn out. Gladys always made sure that her house was painted every once in a while and she liked to make new, colourful curtains and spread a cheerful cloth over the table. And the Morrisons' house was done up as well as you could do up these 'jerry-built rat traps' as Mo called them, because they now had several wages coming in. Not like Lil and Stanley.

Melly sank on to the chair which she placed quite close to that of her patient. In her head she was still play-acting. The nurse had come to call, to see how the patient was faring. Her eyes were drawn to his face. She couldn't help staring.

Stanley was asleep in his chair, his tilted head back. In the gloom she could see the dark hole of his open mouth and that with no hat on, he was almost bald. One side of the scalp was papery and distorted right up to his left eye, though the eye itself was intact. He was very thin, his nose pointed, cheeks gaunt, a thin layer of salt-and-pepper stubble covering the lower part of his face. For a second, in between breaths, Melly thought he looked as if he was dead. It was an unsettling feeling, like watching a statue breathe.

'My poor old boy –' Lil whispered, leaning closer to her. A powerful smell of body odour filled Melly's nostrils from Lil's dress. Lil nodded towards her husband. 'You'd never know he's the age he is – looks like an old man, don't 'e?' She spoke in a flat way, as if all feeling had long been drained out of her. 'Sounds cruel to say, but I lost him the way a lot of other wives did – in the war. The war took my man from me, chewed him up, spat him out. Only – my husband came back, like a ghost. They don't say anything about the ones like Stanley when they talk about heroes, do they?'

Melly was not sure what to say, so she shook her head.

'When I first met Stan, he was cock of the walk,' Lil said, a fond smile playing round her lips. 'Full of it, he was – handsome, lively, strong. Carted all sorts of stuff for the railways, up and down across Birmingham.' The light which had come into her eyes died abruptly. 'Our Marie can't bear to see him. Hardly ever comes near.' She touched Melly's hand for a moment. 'But you've come, haven't you? Tell you what, I'll put the kettle on now and then there'll be some water for tea when we want some. You'll have some tea, won't you, bab?'

'Yes, please, Mrs Gittins,' Melly replied. That made her feel more welcome.

Lil Gittins got to her feet and picked her way round the furniture. Melly watched her thin shoulders as she filled the kettle from a pail by the stove. As Lil lifted the kettle on to the gas the lid fell off and hit the floor with a tinny clatter.

'Oops-a-daisy!' Lil said softly, turning to look at Stanley. The noise made him jump and stir with a low, startled groan. Both of them watched him. He did not open his eyes, but moved restlessly in the chair.

'It's all right,' Lil whispered. 'The slightest thing makes him jump, see.'

Melly sat watching him, stern and floppy as a rag doll in the chair. He twitched and muttered. He didn't look happy, she thought. She wondered what she could do, what a nurse would do.

Glancing at Lil, who was laying out cups, she stood up and leaned over Mr Gittins. With the words, 'There, there, it's all right,' she laid her hand on his clammy forehead, the way a nurse would—

She was almost flung backwards. Stanley Gittins shot up in the chair with a yell. He did not get to his feet but threw her off and sat panting, staring wildly about him.

'Who? Wha' the . . . ? What was . . . ?' He caught sight of Melly. 'Who the hell're you? Oh – Lil – where are yer,

108

Lil?' he shouted, flailing back and forth in the chair, arms folded across him, groaning and beginning to weep.

Lil wove through the room at urgent speed. 'It's all right, love – Stanley . . . Stanley . . .' She knelt at his feet and took the distressed man in her arms, rocking him as he cried and murmuring to him. 'It's all right, babby – there's nothing wrong, your Lilly's here . . .'

Melly backed away towards the door. 'I'm sorry,' she said. 'I'm sorry, I never meant to . . .' But neither of them could hear her. She didn't like to leave. She stood by the door, crying tears of sorrow at what she had caused.

Eventually Stanley quietened. Lil got wearily to her feet and noticed Melly's tearful face.

'It's all right,' she said, her voice flat and tired. 'I just never thought you'd touch him.'

Stanley was staring at them both.

'Who's that wench?'

'It's little Melly from number three. 'Er just came in to keep us company. Come on, bab – sit down again. Just never touch him – he can't be surprised, ever. I'm gonna put the light on now, Stanley, all right?'

The bulb spread its weak light round the room. Melly found Stanley looking at her, his eyes now watery.

'Sorry, bab,' he said and with a shaking hand he indicated the chair that she had been on before. 'Come and sit down. I never meant to frighten yer.'

'I'll make us that tea,' Lil said. 'I might find the odd biscuit . . .'

Melly wanted to open the door and run home across the yard, but she went back to the chair, wiping her eyes, and perched on the edge of it. 'Sorry, Mr Gittins,' she said. 'I never meant to make you jump.'

Stanley sank back, clenching his quivering hands to try

and still them. 'I know, wench. It's just the way I am. You're all right. Sit and have yer tea.'

'Lil said you went in to see them,' Mom said on Sunday morning. She and Lil had been chatting in the brew house. She looked at Melly, seeming puzzled.

'I told you I was going,' Melly said, shrugging. Mom hadn't been listening.

Rachel put her hands on her hips. 'Well, it's an odd choice of company, I must say.'

Melly didn't know how to answer. She had a sense of pride that in the end they had sat and drunk their tea. Not much was said, but it seemed to be all right that she had visited and when she left Mr Gittins looked up and said, 'Ta-ra, bab,' as if it was normal that she should be sitting there.

'Come another time, if you want,' Lil said, sounding as if she didn't think this likely.

But Melly turned at the door and said, 'All right – ta, Mrs Gittins.' There was something she liked about being there. Everyone at home was so busy all the time and the one thing the Gittins had was time. She felt a bit useful.

'How is he, anyway?'

Melly saw her father look up. He was sitting forwards, leaning on his thighs in the way he often did, smoking.

'He's . . .' Melly hesitated. How would you describe Mr Gittins? 'He's jumpy.'

'You can say that again,' Danny said. He threw the stub on the floor and ground it out before picking it up again. 'Poor sod.'

Gladys was putting her coat on. 'You coming to church, Melly?' Gladys had her routines – church on Sunday, a matinee at the pictures one day in the week.

110

Melly nodded. Church meant her best frock and time with Auntie. She liked the atmosphere in the church and the singing. 'Can Tommy come?' She thought that now Tommy was at school and going out every day he might be all right with being out on the street. But Tommy was already shaking his head.

'No – don't want – to.'

'All right, bab,' Gladys said. 'No need. Come on, Melly, get a move on.' As they walked across the yard, Gladys said, 'Dolly said Reggie's coming home this week. She'll be glad to have him back . . .'

The words passed into Melly, a thumping excitement in her blood which rushed to her cheeks. Reggie!

'Oh,' she said, not looking round. 'That's nice.'

Thirteen

December 1954

'He's here!' Freddie Morrison came charging along the entry into the lamplit yard. 'He's just got off the bus!' He disappeared back out to the road again.

The Morrisons, who were eating their tea, came pouring out of the house.

'Hark at that,' Gladys said.

Melly rushed to the door. The others followed. Dolly and her boys had hurried out to the street and in a few moments the entry was full of shouts and laughter. Ethel Jackman poked her head out of number two to see what was happening, then went in again.

'Mardy old thing,' Melly heard her mother mutter.

Reggie came into the yard, cuffing Freddie round the head in a playful manner, and was immediately jumped on by Wally and Jonny as well. Once he had emerged from the tangle of lads, with Wally's arm round his neck, Melly saw a tall, muscular man with cropped hair, wearing a suit with wide lapels. She could see the glint of his teeth as he grinned and joked with everyone. She stood at the edge of the crowd, feeling as if a bird was beating its wings inside her. Wally might be as handsome as a film star but it was Reggie she knew was the one. Everything felt right now he was home for good again, like the biggest piece of a puzzle that had been missing.

There was a lot of ribbing and joking as everyone greeted him. Mrs Davies came out, wanting to be part of things, and Lil emerged, smiling, to see him. Melly watched, her excitement dulled a little by how grown up Reggie looked. He would be twenty in a few months. He had been out into the world, the army – why would he take any notice of her? She ached, remembering when they were both children: his cheerful, grinning face, the black-and-white rabbit he had adored for a few days as a pet before it escaped and was never found again; his rolling the rusty rim of a bike wheel across the yard to her, gently, calling out, 'Catch it, Melly – go on! Cop hold of it!' He was always older, of course, but back then they had all counted as the little ones. Now she felt the distance between them even more than before.

'Ooh, Dolly – hasn't he grown up,' Lil said, hugging herself in the chill evening. 'Even since last time he was here,' she said. 'He's a proper man now.'

Melly fixed Reggie with her eyes, willing him to look at her as he stood in the middle of the crowd chatting and greeting him. Dolly started rounding the family up.

'Come on in – tea's getting cold.'

As they turned towards the house, at last Reggie caught Melly's eye.

'All right, Melly?' he called to her.

'All right,' she said, quiet and shy.

And he was gone but inside her world was lit up.

Melly stood in the yard, shivering as the winter cold gnawed at her bare legs. It was a Friday evening, school had just broken up for Christmas and there was nothing useful she could pretend to be doing out there at this time of night. Tommy didn't want her. Cissy was here to see

Freddie. Again. Cissy had pleaded to be allowed to go out with him – to town, to the Odeon – but Rachel had refused.

'Ciss, don't ask me that. What would Mom say if she found out?'

'She won't,' Cissy pleaded. 'How would she, if you don't tell her? Anyway, when you and Danny—'

'That's enough,' Rachel snapped. 'You'll stay here and that's that.'

Cissy sulked for a while but was soon out there again, up by the factory, tittering away with Freddie. She had no time for Melly when he was about.

The light had already died and the yard lamp was giving out its feeble glow. But under it was the Norton and bent over it, with tools and a torch, were Wally and Reggie. Round them was a shoal of admiring little boys – Kev and Ricky and some other tag-alongs and Frankie Davies, their breath clouding the already smoky air as they shouted questions about the bike. Wally kept trying to start it. The machine made efforts but then coughed into silence.

'Out the way, you lot!' Wally kept shooing them back. 'I can't get round it with you in the way – go on, hoppit!' But they crept back, shoving each other, giggling. This was the most interesting entertainment on offer. Melly could see that Kev was fascinated with Reggie now he was back. She wished she could just hang around them the way the little boys did, but she wanted to hold herself apart.

Melly pulled her coat round her, willing Reggie to turn and notice her. She wasn't just a kid any more, she told herself. Reggie had grown up, into a man of nineteen. But she had grown too. Thirteen sounded so much older than twelve.

More often these days, she longed to be able to be on her own. What with sleeping in the same room as her brothers, with only a bit of curtain between them, and the house so full all the time, there was barely a moment to be alone. Mom tried to shoo the boys out when they brought the tin bath in by the fire. She would go first and they would follow after and Mom would make them wait in the yard. But of course Tommy was always there, being told to look away. She was never truly alone unless, on rare and special occasions, they went to the baths in Victoria Road and she could wallow in the big bath all on her own for twenty minutes or so.

Sometimes she would go into the scullery, climb on to an upturned pail to look in the dingy mirror nailed to the wall in which her dad shaved himself every morning. Looking back at her she saw a girl with a thin, pale face, shoulder-length mousey hair and big eyes which held a wistful expression. If she stretched her lips to smile at her reflection, big, slightly uneven teeth appeared. She hoped her smile gave her a friendly look. At least they didn't stick out like Lisa 'Bunny' Riley's at school.

If she wanted to see any more of herself she had to lean right against the wall and try to look down. That wasn't much good. But in shop windows she could see her long, thin legs. She was growing, becoming a bit gangly. She was thin and had barely begun to develop, but she could feel her body changing. Cissy was quite big at the front now. She had whispered to Melly importantly all about her Monthly. This was something Melly was still waiting to happen. She wished she was curvy and rounded like Cissy.

Trying to keep warm she shifted from one foot to the other. She kept thinking about going in by the fire, instead of standing around in this bone-aching cold. But she couldn't tear herself away. Five more minutes, she kept telling herself.

The bike roared suddenly into life. The little lads leapt back, yelling, and everyone cheered.

'Come on, Wal!' Reggie said. 'Quick, while she's in the mood – let's take her out.'

Wally was walking the Norton across the yard. The miracle happened then: a moment she would never forget. Reggie, beside him, caught sight of her standing there all alone.

'Hey, Melly – fancy a ride?'

For a second she couldn't believe he'd actually said it. Was he joking?

'What – me?'

All the boys swarmed round. '*I'll* go – I wanna ride!'

'Yeah, you!'

'Reg,' Wally protested. 'There's not room . . .'

'Ah, come on – she's only a tiddler. We can fit her in. Come on, Melly – come and try her out.'

'I want to go!' Kevin squeaked, furious at this betrayal, at them asking a *girl* out for a ride.

'Nah – you're too small,' Reggie said. 'Yer mom'd kill me.' To Melly he added, 'Come on then, if you're coming.'

She didn't give it a thought that Mom was about to call them all in for tea or about telling anyone where she was going or that it was freezing cold.

'All right,' she said.

'Come on.' Reggie beckoned her down the entry.

In the road, Wally got on at the front, settling himself with a bounce on the seat.

'Shift up a bit, Wal,' Reggie said. 'Right – you get behind him.'

Melly tried to do as she was bidden but it was hard trying to climb on, yanking her skirt up.

'Here.' Reggie's arms were round her waist, lifting her, and she found herself straddling the hard saddle and Reggie trying to climb on behind her. She had never felt more important in her life.

But there was scarcely room for two, let alone three.

'Look, it ain't meant for this,' Wally said, irritated, climbing off again. 'You take her for a quick spin and come back for me. But don't be long.'

'Shift back,' Reggie said. The next thing Melly knew, Reggie was leaping on to the bike in front of her.

'Right,' he said. 'Hold on to me.'

Hold on to me! She was shy of touching him but as soon as he pressed the bike into movement, she clasped her arms round him for dear life, her face sideways against the cloth of his jacket. The ice-cold air bit into her legs as the bike tore off along the road. They were going terrifyingly fast. She couldn't see anything behind Reggie and in any case she was so frightened of the force of the ride that she screwed her eyes shut.

The main thing in her mind, in the rush of it, the cold, alarming, gathering speed, was, I've got my arms round Reggie . . . Her hands were pressed against his ribcage, her face against his long, lean back as they turned one corner, then another. Opening her eyes a crack she saw the houses, adverts, lights rush giddyingly past. The engine was so loud that Reggie would not hear if she shouted anything. It was utterly terrifying and absolute heaven all at once.

It was over in five minutes but it felt to her as if she had been on the Norton for ages. She got off, her legs shaking and every part of her tingling with cold.

'Oops,' Reggie teased as she stood, unsteadily. He grinned at her. 'All right? Did you like that?'

She beamed at him. Did she *like* it? It had felt as if she

was flying, even if she couldn't feel her feet and her hands were blocks of ice! Reggie had taken her for a ride!

'Yes,' she said. 'Ta, Reggie.'

'Come on!' Wally was impatient to be off.

Melly watched, still trembling, as Wally got on at the front, him steering this time and Reggie riding pillion. Her face was still smiling of its own accord. She felt part of things, as if she had been invited to join a special club. Someone had taken notice of her and wanted her. And it was Reggie. Lovely, lovely Reggie.

'Have a nice ride!' she waved.

They didn't wave back but her smile was undimmed.

Wally set the bike away with a great roar of sound and she watched the two of them disappear round the corner.

When she walked in, everyone was sitting round the table, including Cissy who tried to look completely uninterested in her arrival, even though she was obviously dying to know all about it.

'Where've *you* been?' Danny asked, as she tried to suppress the grin that would not stop spreading itself all over her face.

'I *told* you, she went on Wally's motorbike,' Kev said, frowning furiously. 'He dain't let *me* go.' Even though Kev was only six, he had already decided that an experience like that would be wasted on a mere girl.

Danny looked at Melly with apparent surprise. 'Did yer – really? You wanna be careful. Dangerous, them bikes.' He seemed to see her with new eyes suddenly. 'You're not knocking about with them lads? They're too old for yer.'

'No,' Melly said huffily. She turned away. 'They just gave me a ride, that's all.'

All through the meal she could sense that Cissy was bursting to ask her about it but instead she acted as if she didn't care. Cissy burbled about Fred and about working in Woollie's.

Melly couldn't get away from Cissy because they had to share a bed. The boys all shared the biggest bed. Dad would help Tommy up the stairs, and Ricky was tucked at the bottom by Tommy's and Kev's feet. And tonight Melly would have Cissy's fulsome, creamy body tucked in with her. At least they kept each other warm.

Melly got in, turned on her side to face the wall and pretended to fall asleep straight away, despite Kev and Ricky talking and giggling. But Cissy was not having that.

'Come on!' Her fingers poked at Melly's ribs, making her squirm. 'You gotta tell me about it. Which one d'you fancy most, Reggie or Wal? Did either of them kiss you?'

'*No.*' Melly turned towards her and spoke in a cross whisper. 'Don't be *stupid*. They're years older than me. And I don't fancy either of them.'

'Come off it,' Cissy said. 'That Reggie looks right handsome now he's been in the army. You must fancy him a bit. He's more like Freddie now – only not as good looking as that, nothing like. Freddie's dreamy, isn't he?'

'He's all right,' Melly said, biting back a retort that of course Reggie was better looking than Freddie. Freddie was a mere child in comparison. None of them were as nice as Reggie even if everyone did say Wally was like a film star.

After a pause, Cissy persisted, 'So nothing happened?'

'*No.* We just went for a ride, that's all. Now shurrup and let me go to sleep.' She lifted her head and addressed her brothers. 'And you lot can shut it an' all.'

She was still awake even after the restless noises had stopped in the boys' bed and Cissy was breathing quietly beside her. She lay hugging herself, thinking back on all the memories she had of Reggie, which at the time she had not taken much notice of. Little freckle-faced Reggie when he got his first bike, handed down from Wally, and fell off it in the yard. Going with Reggie to feed the hens which Mo, for a very short time, kept in the brew house, and tittering over them together. His face when they lost the rabbit . . . Reggie and the others giving Tommy rides round the yard in his chair and Tommy squealing with laughter. That morning when he'd come to Tommy's rescue . . . And tonight – *'Fancy a ride?'* Reggie . . . Reggie . . .

She drifted into sleep with a big smile on her face.

Fourteen

Standing in the crush of passengers on the navy-and-cream bus, Melly could just about see out between Kev, Dad and a burly man. It didn't feel very nice standing pressed close up to strangers who stank of stale fags and sweat and oily chip pans. She shifted closer to her father.

Fog veiled the drab streets. Through the murk she caught sight of a few bare-legged kids running about on the open spaces of bomb pecks before another bus got in the way. It still felt peculiar not seeing trams, even though the last one had been taken off the roads over a year ago.

Kev was on to Dad about football as usual. Mom, looking smart in her black coat, had a seat, in front of them next to Auntie Gladys, who was holding a bundle on her knee. It was strange seeing Mom and Dad out and about together. She saw that they were younger than a lot of people on the bus and both good looking. It made her feel happy.

It was a rare treat, going to town, not just to work on the market. Any time Mom and Dad thought about an outing – to town, to the seaside (where they'd still never been) or to the September Onion Fair up the road, on the Serpentine ground – it never usually happened because they couldn't take Tommy. Recently Dad had been talking about buying a car, but as yet there was no sign of it.

'You go,' Tommy would say, his little face earnest, trying to make things better.

Melly always said she wouldn't go if he wasn't going and so they'd all end up not going anywhere. Occasionally, Dad would take Kev and Ricky to the fair and they'd come back with some chipped plaster-of-Paris ornament they'd won or a coconut. Dad said it was only right as he couldn't take Kev to the football at the Villa, with him being always on the market on a Saturday. Until now, Melly hadn't been able to bear to go out and see Tommy trying to look brave if they all left without him.

Now though, since Tommy obviously didn't need her any more, she'd decided she'd damn well do what she liked. Why should she stay in with him when he wouldn't miss her anyway? So Tommy and Ricky were going to stay with Dolly and little Donna while the rest of them went to see the Christmas lights and look round the shops before Dad and Gladys had to start work on the Rag Market.

She felt in the pocket of her navy wool coat for her secret, precious savings. There were halfpennies, farthings and the odd penny. She felt they must glow in there so bright that surely everyone could see them.

Ever since Reggie came home she had been saving, doing some extra jobs for a halfpenny or a farthing from Mom and Dad and not spending her coppers on sweets, despite the gorgeous array of chocolate, sherbet and gobstoppers you could buy now and eat as much as you wanted! To a child who had only known rationing, it seemed like a miracle. But she had resisted – though it was so *hard*! After all this scrimping she had one and eightpence and with that she was going to buy a Christmas present for Reggie. The very thought made her heart thump with nervous excitement. If he saw that she had saved all her money for him, surely then he'd know how much she felt for him? She kept imagining finding something nice, wrapping it up . . . She lay in bed at night, dreaming of Reggie's look of pleasure, of what he might say.

'Oh, Melly – that's just what I've always wanted. Oh, and I've bought you something too . . .'

Well, maybe not that last bit. That was pushing it too far. But perhaps it would dawn on him how nice she was.

She couldn't help herself these days. Where Reggie was, she wanted to be. When the lads were out tinkering with the bike, which seemed to need as much attention as a sick relative, she would be out there too, hoping they would offer her another ride. So far they hadn't. She asked questions sometimes – What's that? What does that bit do? – trying to care about the answer.

Wal and Jonny had started to tease Reggie. 'I see yer girlfriend's here again, Reg!'

The first time Jonny came out with that, Reggie was bent over the back tyre of the Norton. He gave a grunt in reply while her cheeks burned so much she had to go inside, agonized with embarrassment.

But he hadn't denied it, she told herself. Hadn't told Jonny to shut up. One day, oh, one day maybe it would be true! They might be engaged, the way Wally was now – to a girl called Susan who he had met at GEC.

As they drove into the centre of Birmingham she caught a glimpse of bright-coloured lights strung across the streets. It was so colourful and exciting! Surely, some-where, she could find something really nice for Reggie?

They climbed down from the bus in Colmore Row, among all the Christmas bustle. Rachel felt a swell of

123

excitement in the midst of her weariness. For a moment she had a pang of guilt that they had left Tommy behind. But he was doing well now at the school and she was there with him for a day, most weeks. She owed it to her other kids to do something for them.

'I'll go off,' Gladys said, handing Danny the bundle to carry. 'I'll get on quicker on my own. Ta-ra-a-bit – see yer later.' Her strong, matronly figure disappeared into the crowd, limping on her bunions.

'Keep together, all of you!' Rachel said. For a moment she went to reach for Melly's hand, before realizing that at thirteen she was too old for all that. And she was turning into a mardy little bit these days. She'd always been a good kid, there was no doubt, but these days she seemed lost in a dream world most of the time. Instead of being helpful she would shrug and look fed up if asked to do something. It got on Rachel's nerves when she had so much to do. Melly was a girl – she ought to help in the house.

Although Kev was only six he was a proper little lad, on his dignity and very much his father's son. He reminded her a lot of Danny at the same age with his bright energy. He wouldn't be holding her hand either, she thought, with a pang of loss.

They set off along the road in the press of shoppers.

''Ere – look.' Danny elbowed her. They were standing beside one of the furriers' shops in the city. 'That's the stuff you want to be selling. People'll pay the earth for one of them coats. D'you know, them rich people, they keep 'em in cold storage all the summer!'

'Do they?' Rachel smiled faintly. She wanted to think about Christmas, not about trading. Danny was doing well on the market but he was always restless, looking round for the next thing. He'd brought up this ridiculous idea of going to Australia again. Why on earth would they want to go right to the other side of the world, away from everyone they knew? And how the hell did he think they'd manage with Tommy? What a flaming ridiculous idea – it made her so cross. Still, she told herself, it was just Danny having one of his daydreams.

'What if we had a shop?' he said, half to himself.

'All that rent though, Danny,' she said. 'Come on –' She pressed his arm, felt it strong and thin inside his sleeve. 'Give it a rest – let's treat the kids.'

Danny turned to them, pretend serious. 'You two don't want to see Santa then, do yer?'

'Yes!' Kev yelled, so loudly that his face went red.

'Hey, shut it,' Rachel laughed. 'What about you, Melly? You're too old for all that, aren't you?'

Melly nodded. She would quite like to have gone to the Christmas grotto in Lewis's department store, but she knew she was too old really and, besides, she had much more important shopping to do.

'You take him, Danny, will you?' Rachel said. 'There's bound to be a hell of a queue.'

'All right then,' Danny said, reaching down for Kev's hand. 'C'mon, son.'

'I'm not holding hands,' Kev said, his arched brows pulling into a frown. 'I'm not a babby.'

'Meet you in the Bull Ring,' Rachel called after them. 'Eleven o'clock – outside Woollie's.' She looked down at Melly. 'We can pop in and see Ciss, when we get over there. Oooh – hark at that. The Sally Army!'

For the next hour, they wandered amid the chattering crowds, smelling the whiffs of cigarette smoke, of orange peel, of cooking meat, making their mouths water. From amid the vendors shouting to advertise their holly and mistletoe and Christmas wreaths and the flower lady and her daughter selling bouquets, floated the mellow sound of carols from the Salvation Army brass band.

Rachel bought a sprig of mistletoe from a man with one arm missing, the empty sleeve of his coat hanging limp. 'God bless yer, lady,' he said. She tucked the mistletoe carefully into her bag. They moved through the market, down into New Street, and she bought a pair of stockings for Gladys and some drawing paper for Danny. They stopped, by the Big Top site at the end of High Street, where New Street began. The buildings that once stood on that corner were lost in the bombing. The space had been cleared and there were rows of cars parked on it.

'What d'you want to do then?' Rachel said.

Melly shrugged. Rachel started to feel annoyed. Her grown-up little daughter was a mystery to her sometimes. Ever since she had had Tommy, when Melly was two, nearly all of her energy had gone on him. She wanted to give her daughter time now, but Melly, instead of blossoming under the attention, seemed preoccupied and distant. This was their chance of an outing and she might as well not be there!

'Look, what's up with you?' Rachel started to lose her temper. 'This was s'posed to be a nice morning out. What's the long face about? If you wanted to go to Lewis's with yer dad you should have opened your mouth and said so when you had the chance.'

Melly's eyes filled with tears. 'No – I dain't want to go . . .'

Rachel led her closer to the railings edging the site. A light drizzle was beginning to fall. She wanted them to have a nice morning but found her voice turning harsh. 'Come on, out with it – what's up with you?'

'I just . . .' Tears started to run down Melly's cheeks. Her voice went high and childish. 'I wanted to buy a present and I've . . . I've . . . You can't buy anything nice for one and eight.'

'One and eight?' Rachel quizzed her. 'Where did you get one and eight from?'

'I saved it – I dain't buy any rocks,' Melly sniffed, wiping her eyes. 'Not for ages.'

Rachel looked at her, astonished. Not buying sweets when every child in the neighbourhood was filling their face at every possible opportunity!

'But – why? What d'you mean a present – who for?'

Melly hung her head. Her coat was too short, making her legs look long and gawky. How had she suddenly grown so tall? Rachel wondered. Melly would be starting her monthly soon, she realized, her heart softening at the thought.

'F-for Reggie,' Melly admitted.

'Reggie. Reggie who?' Rachel said, bewildered. 'What – you mean Mo and Dolly's Reggie?' Her mind struggled to put these things together. 'You mean . . . ?'

But Melly could not say what she meant. She was too covered in blushes.

'What're you on about, Melly?' Rachel said. Without thinking, she burst out laughing. 'Reggie Morrison?' Reggie was nice enough, but he was a grown-up man now. He'd even been in the army. 'You haven't got a flame lit for Reggie? Oh, bab – he's almost old enough to be your father. I don't s'pose he's got eyes for you – in fact, I saw him with a girl the other day. You're going to have to get over that one, kid.'

As soon as she'd said it, Rachel regretted it. Reggie wasn't that old, only a few years older, in fact. But that wasn't the point. She saw Melly's mortified expression, her painful girlish embarrassment. And she remembered

Peggy, her own mother, the caustic burn of Peggy's views about Danny when the two of them were first together.

Melly turned her head away, fighting back tears. Rachel could have bitten her tongue out. She was filled with weariness. Why did she say that? Now she was going to have to deal with tears and tantrums and there was so much to get done this morning.

'Oh, come on, Melly,' she said, trying to jolly her along. They started walking again, slowly. 'Don't get upset. You're only young and there's plenty of fish in the sea. Let's get on with it, shall we?'

Melly kept her head down. Rachel found impatience rising in her. All this fuss – the girl was barely more than a child; not old enough for this. She took a deep breath.

'So,' she said carefully. 'You want to buy Reggie a present? Any special reason?'

There was no reply. Again she looked at Melly in her short coat and ankle socks, with her thin, little-girl legs.

'Melanie.' She stopped and made herself speak more gently. 'I didn't mean to laugh. I just thought . . . Look, just say what you've got to say.'

Melly raised her head, the drizzle moistening her already damp face. Tears were welling in her eyes, which held all her sweet, girlish longing. 'I just like him,' she said before looking down again, the tears spilling. 'But everything for one and eight is all just tat and rubbish.'

'I tell you what,' Rachel said. 'We've got to go to the Bull Ring. Let's see if we can find anything there, shall we?'

Melly looked up at her. Rachel saw the trust and hope return to her daughter's eyes and her heart was warmed.

'All right,' Melly said. She pushed her hands down into her pockets. As they walked down towards St Martin's and the Bull Ring, she said quietly, 'Mom – you won't say anything, will you? Not to Reggie, and not Cissy or Dolly or anyone?'

Rachel reached for her arm and gave it a squeeze. 'I won't, kid. I promise.' She found she had a lump in her own throat.

Fifteen

'Wakey-wakey, Melly – set the table for me, will you?'

Melly felt her mouth fill with saliva as she came into the steam-filled little room, so warm and cosy, and decked with paper streamers that she had made with Kev and Ricky.

Mom had been cooking the Christmas dinner while Melly went to church with Gladys. The smell of beef and potatoes in hot oil was mouth-watering even out in the yard and the delicious aromas filled the little room.

She had sat down next to Ricky, who was better at sitting still than Kev, to read *James the Red Engine* with him. But in between the little train's adventures her mind was wandering as it had done all through the hour in church with the crib and the carols and the walk back through the dull, wet midday, so much so that Gladys said to her, huffily, 'I've walked out with livelier dogs.'

'Sorry, Auntie, I was just thinking.'

'Oh, you don't want to be doing that,' Gladys said. Then winked at her.

But all the time her tummy was full of wobbly feelings. Her heart was pounding. Had he got his present yet? Had he opened it? And if he had – would he come round and say thank you? She kept imagining a knock on the door and Reggie appearing, smiling. And then she realized that if he did appear it would be terrifying and she wouldn't know what to say and everyone in the family would know she was *in love* and not just Mom and that would be awful. But had he got it? Did he like it?

She and Mom had wandered round the Bull Ring looking for something for Reggie. Melly's spirits fell lower and lower because she didn't have any idea what to get and, as she had feared, nothing any good could be bought for one and eight.

'What about some sweets?' Rachel asked.

'*No.*' Melly was grumpy with disappointment. 'He can buy them any time.' I want it to be *special,* she raged inside. From *me.* So that he'll think about me when he sees it . . .

They found a toy stall and Melly was just about to snap, not *toys,* that's silly, Reggie's grown up, when Mom said, 'Look – what about this? He'd like that – he would, you know. He's so mad about bikes.'

On the stall was a little cast-iron model of a motorbike and sidecar, the bike bright red and the sidecar pale blue with a little silver man sitting in it. It even had white rubber wheels.

'I don't think it's new,' Rachel said. 'But it's in good nick. Shall I ask?'

Melly looked at it. Was that the thing? She saw that it was nice – it would have to do.

'Three shillings,' the man on the stall said from under his moustache.

Despair coursed through her. She might have known she wouldn't have enough.

'We'll have it,' she heard Mom say. 'I'll give you the difference,' she whispered. 'Give us your pennies.'

Never in her life had Melly felt such a surge of love and gratitude for her mother. Soon the little figures were in a brown paper bag, nestling in her pocket.

'Thanks, Mom,' she said, all blushes. After a moment she slipped her hand into her mother's. Rachel looked down at her and smiled in surprise.

'Come on,' she said. 'We'd best go and meet your dad.'

Melly had wrapped the heavy little figure in red tissue paper. Yesterday evening, Christmas Eve, she had given it to Donna who was only eight but she knew she would not make fun of her. She told her to give it to Reggie from her.

Mom grinned knowingly as she passed her a handful of knives and forks. 'Come on – the table won't lay itself.' She was in charge today, dispensing orders before Gladys had a chance to start bossing them all about.

Melly set the places while cabbage and carrots boiled vigorously on the stove. Mom was tutting because she'd put her hair in curlers the night before to get the 'bouffant' effect.

'It'll be flat as a pancake again after this,' she muttered.

Gladys was singing 'Hark the Herald Angels Sing!' along with the wireless and soon Mom joined in and Tommy sang along as well in his chair. Then Dad and Kev came in and the room seemed fit to burst with people.

'I'm starved,' Kevin cried. 'What's for dinner?'

'What's for dinner?' Danny tugged on his ear. 'It's Christmas Day, yer prat – what the hell d'yer thinks for dinner?'

All day she waited, agonizing. What had Reggie thought of her present? Had Donna even remembered to give it to him? Did he like it? Or did he think it was babyish and silly? As she ate her lunch and helped wash up afterwards with Gladys, who said it was Rachel's turn to have a sit-down; as the adults snoozed, pink cheeked and red nosed from glasses of sherry and port wine; and Kev rushed outside to ride his new little bike; and she and Tommy did a puzzle that Gladys had bought for them, it was all she could think of.

On another day she might have been glad that Tommy wanted to play with her. But all the time her thoughts were in the Morrisons' house, wondering what they were doing. In her worst moments, she worried that they were all laughing at her. Nothing that day, not even the excitement of waking, knowing there were crackly little parcels at the foot of the bed from Santa – opening them to find a new jumper and some talc, a sugar lump and an orange – compared with the suspense of wondering how her gift to Reggie had been received.

'Are you going to see Dolly today?' she asked Mom later, as they all drank a cup of tea. She tried to sound casual.

'No,' Rachel yawned. 'They've got a houseful – her sister's over, with her lot. I don't know how they all fit in. Why?'

'Oh – no reason . . . Come on, Tommy – we've nearly got all the edge bits.'

On Boxing Day they had to go to Nanna's. Peggy said she thought she could manage them for tea.

'Mighty big of her,' Gladys remarked. She, of course, was not invited. Despite the fact that Peggy had worked on the Rag Market for a time, she had left all that behind when she married widower Fred Horton before the war. She always liked to think she was several cuts above Gladys.

'I'm surprised I'm even invited,' Danny said. He rolled his eyes at his aunt.

'It'll give you some peace,' Rachel said. 'That sounds a bit of all right to me!'

'Tommy and me'll have our own party, won't we?' Gladys said.

It was a long time since Peggy had seen Tommy. Rachel had made it clear to her that if she wanted to see her oldest grandson she would have to come to him. Even if Tommy had really wanted to go, it was impossible to get him there without spending the earth on a taxi. Peggy could have come quite easily. Rachel imagined her mother picking her way across the yard in Aston like Lady Muck – even though she had once lived in a worse place in Deritend herself. Not once had Peggy come over to see him.

Peggy and Fred lived on the Coventry Road, above the business, Horton's Drapers & Haberdashers. Fred was in his early sixties and Peggy, who was only fifty-four, had a major hand in running the business, a situation she complained about almost unceasingly, even though it was her own choice and she was in fact very good at it.

Cissy was delighted when they turned up, having been bored rigid all day. She had brushed her ginger hair into a high topknot with a flick of a fringe, and had on a dark green satin dress, flattering to both her colouring and her increasingly curvaceous figure.

'Ooh, you look nice, Ciss,' Rachel said, kissing her.

'So do you, Rach – that red suits you.'

Melly found herself hugged by Cissy. She felt Cissy's breasts push against her and blushed. Cissy was really growing up. Since Freddie Morrison was not about, Cissy was evidently going to bother with her company today.

Peggy was draped back in her chair as if in a state of profound recuperation. Fred was snoozing by the fire and didn't even hear them come in.

'Ah – you're *here*,' Peggy said, like a siege victim relieved at last. 'Help Cissy make the tea, Rachel – I'm absolutely all in. I couldn't move if the house was on fire.'

'Happy Christmas to you too, Mother,' Rachel said between clenched teeth, heading to the kitchen. Melly and Cissy went with her, Cissy giggling at Rachel's words.

'You should've heard her cooking the dinner,' she hissed. She glanced round the kitchen door to see if anyone was following, then closed it firmly and started doing imitations of their mother, an arm languidly across her forehead. 'Oh, if only I had some proper help. Someone who'd *understand*. Here am I – shackled to an old man ... Every year it's the same – slaving away up here! No one ever invites me round or cooks for me ...'

'I'm not bloody surprised,' Rachel interjected, slamming the lid on the kettle, but she was laughing. 'So did she think Fred was just going to keep getting younger then or what?'

Melly was beginning to giggle, watching the two sisters let off steam. When Cissy was a baby, Peggy had doted on her for a little while, but she soon lost patience and was just as rejecting and self-absorbed in her behaviour as she had been when Rachel was young.

'I'm a martyr to this family!' Cissy went on, with dramatic exaggeration. 'No one knows what a struggle my life is!'

'Shhhh, for God's sake!' Rachel was really laughing now. 'She never said that?'

'She did,' Cissy spluttered. Soon the three of them

135

were helpless with laughter. Melly was no more fond of her grandmother than the two sisters. She had heard Peggy say things about Tommy that made her blood boil. 'That cripple child of yours,' she called him.

'Come on,' Rachel said once they'd made the tea. 'We'd better go and rescue your dad.' She had left Danny making desperately stilted conversation with Peggy and trying to keep Kevin still. 'I hate going to Nanna's,' he'd grumbled all the way over. Peggy had never approved of Danny – he wasn't good enough – and she thought Kevin was wild and out of control, none of which was helped by the fact that as soon as he set eyes on her, he seemed to *feel* wild and out of control. He had brought some of his cars to play with and was down on the rug.

They managed to compose themselves enough to carry in a tray of tea. Fred sat up with a start, suddenly realizing they had arrived.

'Ooh – hello, girls,' he said, rubbing his head.

'Hello, Fred,' Danny said. Fred wasn't too bad really. And he was right under Peggy's thumb these days. His own son, Sidney, who had lived with them when Rachel was young, never showed his face there any more.

Rachel put the tray on the low table in the middle of the room.

'There's a fruitcake I made,' Peggy said. 'Fetch it, will you, Cissy – oh, and plates and . . . Oh, dear, I'm so tired I can barely even think.'

'Don't worry, Mom, I expect we'll manage,' Rachel said. Melly knew she was always sick of her mother within minutes of arriving at her house. She came over here less and less.

They sat round, asking the usual questions – how was the business here? How was the Rag Market? This was always asked by Peggy in a tone which implied she was picking up something dirty as she said it.

'It's good,' Danny said. He leaned forward, the one person in the room not totally drained of energy. 'I'm thinking I'll buy a car soon.'

'Oh – really?' Peggy said, sounding put out. She and Fred did not have a car. 'Seems a terrible expense.'

'It'd make things a lot easier,' Danny said. 'We could branch out . . .'

'Tommy's doing well at school,' Rachel said.

Peggy rolled her eyes. 'School!' It was said with such contempt that Melly wanted to shout at her. 'I suppose they have to call it that – though most of them are cabbages.'

Melly saw her mother struggle to control herself.

'Luckily,' Rachel said, 'thanks to Melly, Tommy could read and write when he got there. They were really taken with him. He's doing ever so well. And he was in the nativity play – he was Joseph. We've got a picture.' This photograph was in a prime spot on the mantelpiece at home, Tommy standing, solemn, in a brown robe with a cloth on his head.

Peggy rolled her eyes again and changed the subject.

'Come on,' Cissy whispered, beckoning to Melly.

The girls went into the bedroom and Cissy twirled round in front of her in the green dress.

'Mom made it for me for Christmas. D'you think Freddie'd like me in it?'

Oh, Melly thought. Here we go.

It took two buses to get home. By the time they got back it was dark and foggy and everyone was frozen and all in favour of buying a car. They were also at screaming pitch after a few hours with Peggy.

'I don't know why I bother,' Rachel ranted as they waited for the bus in town. 'She's so wrapped up in herself. She can never see what anyone else might have going on, or—'

'She's not gonna change, Rach,' Danny said, putting his arm round her shoulders. Melly was warmed by the sight. How must it feel to have a man love you? she wondered, with dread and excitement bubbling in her again now they were on the way home. Suppose when she got there, there was a note waiting for her – from him? Maybe Reggie would be too shy to come himself?

'It's all right for you,' Rachel was saying. 'You just let it all wash over you.'

'She's still your mother,' Danny said. His own mother had died when he was nine.

'Huh,' Rachel said. She looked cold and deflated. 'I'm not doing this next year. She can bloody well come and see us.'

There was no note waiting at the house. Nothing. Melly looked to see if Gladys had anything to tell her – had Reggie been round while they were out? But no. They were all tired out after the day of high emotions and more indulgent eating than usual. Melly went up to bed soon after her brothers, shivering in the freezing room. Ricky was grizzly but Kevin went out like a light, his wiry body tucked in beside Tommy.

'Night, Tommy,' Melly whispered and heard him mutter a reply in the darkness.

She lay there, her feet icy, allowing herself to feel miserable and hurt. But she told herself that Reggie might not have wanted to come round with everyone there. Maybe he would speak to her himself, when they were on their own . . . And very soon she was asleep too.

The next thing she heard was screaming and she leapt up in bed, thinking it was one of the boys having a nightmare. The noise was so loud she had thought it was in the room. Then she realized it was coming from outside the window.

'Oh, my God!' It was a woman, hysterical, beside herself. 'What're we gonna do? How can we get there?'

Other voices joined in.

'Melly?' She heard Tommy in the dark. 'What's that?' Kevin and Ricky still seemed to be asleep.

'I don't know.' She got out of bed and sat on the boys' bed. There were more noises – Gladys's door opening; hurried footsteps on the attic stairs. There was a further mix of voices outside, male and female, more hysterical shouting, more crying. Melly went to the window. In the lamplight she could see a knot of people.

'It's Dolly,' Melly said, horrified. Happy, kindly Dolly Morrison, sounding utterly distraught.

At last the noises died away. She heard the grown-ups come back into the house and shut the door but they didn't come upstairs.

'I'm going to see,' she told Tommy. 'I'll be back in a tick.' She had a terrible thought growing in her. If it was Dolly, did that mean something had happened . . . ? Could something have happened to Reggie?

She found Mom and Dad and Gladys all standing downstairs. To her surprise, the clock on the mantelpiece said that it was only half past eleven. She felt as if she had been asleep for hours on end. All of them turned to look at her.

'I heard everyone shouting,' she said. 'What's going on?'

Gladys sank into a chair. She was shaking and seemed unable to speak.

'Oh, Melly –' Mom came over to her. 'Poor, poor Dolly and Mo. There's been an accident. The two of them were coming home on the bike – Wally and Reggie.' Mom knelt down, putting her hands on Melly's shoulders. 'They hit a lorry. We don't know anything much yet – they've gone to the hospital – but . . .' She shook her head and looked down for a second. 'It's bad by the sound of things. We don't know if either of them are alive.'

Sixteen

'My boy! Oh, my lovely boy – he was always the sweet-
est of the lot of them! And all his life before him. Why
did this have to happen? Why?'

Dolly raged and sobbed, sitting bent over their table in
number three, looking as none of them had ever seen her
before. Her pretty looks were mangled by grief and she
seemed aged by years.

Wally was dead: twenty-one years of age and engaged
to be married to Susan. He was steering the bike when
the truck pulled across in front of them out of the fog and
darkness on Constitution Hill. Reggie, riding pillion, had
taken the impact on his right side as the bike slewed
round. He was badly injured, his right hip smashed up.
They didn't know if he would ever walk again.

Melly sat quietly in the corner by the fire. She had
barely been able to eat anything since the news came, two
nights ago. She felt sick constantly. The grief around her
seemed to invade her so that she didn't know who she
was upset for most – for Dolly and Mo, for Reggie, for
herself. It was as if the pain belonged to all of them and
enveloped all of them.

She had never seen Gladys as emotional as she was
during those days. She comforted Dolly, her old friend,
but she was stunned and unable to do anything. Her face
was gaunt, her eyes rimmed with red.

'I feel as if . . .' She struggled to find words for Rachel and Danny. 'I just feel as if I've been knocked for six.'

In a quiet moment the day after they heard, Rachel had sat Melly down, upstairs in the bedroom.

'You know – Gladys had a little boy once.' Melly looked at her mother's pale face. 'This was something she knew, but had almost forgotten. 'I think – what's happened to Dolly and Mo – it's brought it all back for her. She's upset for them, of course – but it's more than that. I've never seen her in such a state.'

Melly nodded, her legs dangling over the edge of her bed. She didn't know what it meant to lose your son. She just knew that all of it was wretched and terrible. Everything had changed overnight, like a cloud blacking out the sun forever. She felt ashamed of her nerves on Christmas Day, wanting Reggie to thank her for her silly little present. Reggie could be dead now, like Wally . . . Her eyes filled with tears.

'Mom – is Reggie going to be all right?'

Rachel moved closer and squeezed her hand. Mom had been unusually tender with them all since the news. 'I think so, bab. It'll take time. I don't know much about what's up with him, but he's alive – that's the main thing.' She tilted her head and Melly felt her looking into her face. Mom's eyes were red from crying, like all of them.

'Maybe, when he's a bit better, you could go in and see him?' Rachel said.

Melly looked at her in horror. Go and visit Reggie? No, she couldn't possibly! This had taken Reggie right out of her reach. He was so much older and now, his body badly hurt, his brother dead. How could a child like her face him – he wouldn't want to know!

'No.' She shook her head and looked at her hands, holding a hanky in her lap.

'All right,' Rachel said gently, getting up. As if to herself, she said, 'I wonder if he'll be all right to get to Wally's funeral.'

Everyone in the yard did everything they could think of to look after the Morrisons. Mo, only just sixty, turned into an old man overnight. His strong, solid body moved slowly, with more effort, his good-natured features sagged, borne down by his suffering. His hair, already well on the way to white, took the last stage at a run.

The family stuck together. Eric, the oldest, who was married, called every day. Jonny and Freddie helped every way they could and little Donna seemed to grow up almost overnight. She became thinner and quieter and helped Dolly about the house.

One night, just before the New Year, Rachel and Danny were lying in bed together, still awake, though it was late.

'You don't know what to do for them, do you?' she said, lying in Danny's arms. The calamity had brought them closer again. 'If it was one of ours – I mean, I don't think I could stand it.'

Danny didn't say anything, though she felt the muscles in his arms tighten around her. Sometimes it frustrated her when Danny wouldn't talk about things, but she knew that it was his way of keeping terrible memories at bay.

'Sorry, Danny – does it bring it all back? Losing your mom and everything?'

When Danny and his sisters were in the orphanages – he in one, they another – his middle sister in age, Rose, died. She was only ten. The other two, Jess and Amy, eventually came back to them, but by then they were all strangers to each other. They both had lives now, outside Birmingham, and Jess was married, but the bond between them had been broken forever. They no longer knew where Amy was living.

'A bit,' he said, at last. He kissed the side of her head in the dark. 'I s'pose all you can do is try not to think about it – when you can't do anything, I mean.'

'I can't stop thinking about it,' Rachel said. 'I hope to God Reggie's going to be OK. Dolly and Mo went to see him – they said he's in a terrible mess. He knew them though, thank goodness.'

'He'll be all right,' Danny said. 'He's a good strong lad.'

'Shh – what was that?' A sound, muffled but definite, had come from somewhere outside.

They heard it again: a cry, a howl of anguish from the inside of one of the houses. It came three times, then no more. The sound was so primal, so desolate, that it brought Rachel to tears again.

'That was Mo, wasn't it?' she whispered.

'Must be,' Danny said. His voice was husky as well.

'Oh, God, Danny, the poor man,' she wept. 'Poor, dear old Mo.'

'But they're not Catholics, are they?' Rachel said, when Gladys told her where the funeral was to be. 'I've never known them go to church.'

'That's what I said,' Gladys reported. 'But Dolly said her mom was Italian and they used to go to church as kids. Made her First Communion, white dress and all that. After that I don't think they bothered with it.'

'So – we are going to go?' Rachel asked cautiously. Her friend Netta was Catholic and Gladys who was staunch C of E had always been a bit sniffy about it, Italian mission to the Irish and all that.

Gladys looked at her in astonishment. 'Of course. What're you on about? We'll be there with our boots blacked. I wouldn't miss going for anything, whether it's smells and bells or whatever it is. That's not what matters.'

On a bitterly cold day in the fledgling new year, they filed into the church of the Sacred Heart and St Margaret Mary. Melly looked about her fearfully. Even though she went to the parish church with Gladys most Sundays, this felt strange and different, the walls at the front of the church glowing with gold, the candles burning, the statues up near to the altar and the smell of wax and incense. It was beautiful, not dark and frightening as she had expected.

Everyone went, Tommy as well. They took it in turns to push him the mile or so across Aston to the church in Witton Lane.

Melly was at the end of one of the wooden pews to the left, with Tommy close beside her in the aisle. Gladys was seated to her right. They could see Dolly up in front of them with her two sisters, with little Donna and with Susan, Wally's intended, who they could hear trying to stifle her sobs. Everyone was in black and Dolly and her sisters, like most women in the church, were wearing black lace mantillas over their hair. Dolly had given one to Mom and Gladys to wear as well, so that they did not look out of place.

The boys were waiting at the back of the church, all in sharp black suits. The church was almost full including a group of people who, Melly realized, had worked with

Wally and Reggie at GEC. And Dolly and Mo were much loved: between them, the family knew a lot of people. But there was one person missing. Melly had seen no sign of Reggie. She wondered if he was too badly hurt to be moved, though Dolly had said she thought he was going to come. Eric, her eldest, was to bring him in a taxi. Melly couldn't see Eric either. She sat waiting in the hard pew, awed and nervous.

Just when it felt as if the service must surely begin, heads turned along the middle aisle and she caught sight of Eric, pushing a wheelchair. Her heart pounded hard and she had to remind herself to take a breath. There he was – there was Reggie! She felt ashamed of the effect seeing him had on her. He was sitting back, stiffly, and she only caught sight of the left side of his head as Eric pushed him past and round the front pew to the side aisle, arranging the chair to Dolly's left. Dolly leaned across for a moment to kiss him, her arm encircling the back of the chair.

Eric walked back speedily up the aisle, head down, and Melly exchanged glances with Tommy. She felt grateful to Tommy for the sympathetic way he looked at her. Almost as if he knew what she was feeling. For a moment she thought about holding his hand, until she remembered that he did not want her mothering him any more.

Within a moment, the organ began to play and Mo, Eric, Jonny and Freddie Morrison, with Mo's two brothers, carried Wally's coffin along the church and rested it on the bier in the middle, covering it with a black velvet pall.

All the way through, the priest sprinkling the coffin with holy water, the stream of words in Latin, the incense and the sound of suppressed weeping and mutters of 'Amen', Melly could not stop her gaze from returning to

Reggie. She had liked Wally well enough, and he had always been around since they were all children. The sadness of it weighed upon her, for all of them, the terrible loss and grief of the family. Reggie felt so far away now. His injuries and the death of his brother had closed about him, shutting her out. In her mind Melly tried to fold away her feelings for him, seeing them as childish. Why had she ever thought Reggie would be interested in her? By the time the Mass was finished and they all trooped out into the grey morning, she felt numb and cold – and older.

Gladys was going to the cemetery with the family.

'We'll go home, Auntie,' Danny said. 'Take the kids. You gonna be all right?'

Gladys squared her shoulders in her black coat. Her face, too, seemed to have sunk in on itself in the last terrible days. 'Course. See you later.' She turned and walked towards Dolly and her sisters, who stood in a close huddle, their arms about each other. Mo, pushing Reggie's chair, was with his brother and sons, a cluster of dark suits.

From a distance, Melly saw Reggie's fair hair, his head lolling just above the seat of the wheelchair. His right leg was outstretched and braced straight. There were dressings on his face. She thought he looked very uncomfortable but knew this must be nothing compared to his pain inside. People were going up to him, bending to say something to him. She saw her father talking to Reggie, gentle-faced, laying a hand on his shoulder for a moment. She couldn't go to him, just couldn't. She looked away, unable to bear it.

She saw Gladys go up to Mo, and hold out her hand to him. But Mo threw wide his arms, drawing Gladys into them and clutching her close, his face contorted in agony.

IV

1955

Seventeen

February 1955

Rachel slipped out of the overall which protected her clothes, shouldered her coat on and stepped out through the front door of Carlson House, Tommy's school. Inside, the children were having a sing-song to end the day and she knew she was not needed for the last twenty minutes or so.

It was an iron-hard winter day, the sky low and ash coloured. But it was dry and Rachel was glad of a break. Hugging her coat round her, she lit a cigarette. These days she found cigarettes more and more of a comfort. She leaned against the front wall, luxuriating in the few moments of quiet, smoke unfurling in front of her. She had had her hair cut into a sleek bob, parted on the right, the hair on the left pinned back, the way some of the teachers at the school wore theirs. The brown skirt and cream blouse she was wearing felt smart and she knew fitted well on her slim figure. For the first time in years she felt more like a young, slender and attractive woman with a thread of life going on.

Getting out to the school one day a week had changed her life. It was so good to escape from the same four walls of the house, the grimy old yard, always in some grubby and tattered frock, with Gladys bossing her to do the same round of chores. Coming over to Harborne had changed her view of things. It was an escape.

Everything in Alma Street now was tainted with grief. These days, Mo and Dolly were not the people they had been before. Sometimes it felt as if grief was sucking them down into a deep, dark place that they could not get out of. Both of them looked older, more faded. Everyone missed Mo's sunniness and jokes. He tried to keep cheerful but even if he was trying to smile and be his usual old self, sadness weighed down every line of him.

Rachel ached with pity for them, and for their other boys. Jonny had taken refuge in his lessons and hardly raised his head out of a book. But he was also waiting to see when they would call him up for National Service. While he had been dreading it before, Rachel realized he might now be glad to get away. Freddie had become solemn and quiet. Cissy couldn't get anywhere with him any more and their friendship had cooled.

Gladys was also more tired, bitter and short-tempered. And Rachel, with the children getting older, the constant worry that she might have another one, the endless work and demands, increasingly felt bone tired. The yard in Alma Street which had once been a refuge from her mother, a place where she and Danny could make a home, now filled her with desperation. It was true that Danny had finally bought a car – a rather battered old black Standard – which eased things a bit. But it made no difference to where they lived. Her friend Netta and family had recently managed to move a bit further out of town, into a house that was still very scruffy, but was at least bigger. Seeing it when she went to visit had brought home how everything in Alma Street was old and filthy and rotten. All she could see was the bug-ridden griminess of those leaking little houses, the slimy floor and mould in the brew house. If only they could get out, to somewhere new. She dreamt constantly of a place of their own, a nicer, cleaner house with more space. If Netta and Francis had managed it, why could they not find somewhere else as well?

From inside the school she could just hear music, some of the children banging cymbals and drums. This place was a constant source of amazement to her. From having thought her son would have to fester at home all his life, with no help or chance of doing anything, now Tommy was doing well. The teachers were saying that one day he might even be able to get a job!

As soon as she had started at the school with Tommy, had walked into his classroom where rows of children, each with their individual difficulties, sat at little desks, each being helped and encouraged, she had thanked God for it every day. Tommy was writing well now. So long as his paper was held still with big spring clips, into a frame to stop it slipping about, he could write as well as anyone. He read and did sums and now they were talking about teaching him to type. They helped him with his eating and speaking and also encouraged him to walk more, using sticks. The doctors had taken great pains with him and he was about to go into Woodlands, the orthopaedic hospital on the Bristol Road, for an operation on his left leg. She hardly knew where to begin telling them how she felt – her gratitude for all this. But people seemed to understand.

And every Thursday she travelled across town with him and spent her time helping in the classroom and at mealtimes. She had got to know the other children, the teachers and other mothers. Some of them said she was really good with the children. Had she ever thought about becoming a teacher?

Rachel had laughed at that. Her, a teacher! Stay on at school! Little did they know how things had been in her childhood, her father's disgrace and death, Peggy's struggles, falling pregnant with Melly when she was only fifteen – these were things she would keep to herself. But she was flattered all the same. It was nice to have someone to tell her she was good at something.

Life for her had definitely got better – at least, until last night and the conversation she had had with Danny. She had not spoken to him this morning, she was so angry with him.

It had begun with something she'd said. Her idea. She had thought it a week or two ago, when she was walking along Victoria Road in Harborne, where Tommy's school was, past the neat brick terraced houses lit by the morning sun.

It looks so nice, she thought. It's even nicer than where Netta's gone. I wish we lived in a house like that with its own garden, not on a yard. I bet they have their own bathrooms as well. And then the thought came to her, what seemed at first an unthinkable thing: why don't we move and rent a house over here nearer to the school? It's not as if they couldn't afford it. The market made them a good living. And they had the car now to get to the market. Everyone said it was impossible to find anywhere to live these days but surely some people must be able to find a new house?

Of course she hardly dared mention it at first. Leave Alma Street? It still seemed almost unthinkable. And what about Auntie? She found herself longing to get away from Gladys – just to be in their own place. Would Gladys come with them? Surely not. Gladys had lived in the yard in Alma Street for more than two decades, with Mo and Dolly there, through good times and bad. They were almost family. Gladys was stubborn and it was hard to imagine she would ever leave Alma Street. But even moving with Gladys would be better than staying stuck where they were.

She pushed the reality of the acute housing shortage out of her mind. She just thought about her dream. And the more she thought about it, the more she had a tingle of excitement inside her. She argued it back and forth in her head all week.

Last night she had been about to broach the subject herself, when they went to bed. It was the only time they had any privacy. Though the council had finally installed electric light in the houses a few years back, there was still no light in the attic. She lay waiting for Danny, a candle burning on a saucer on the chair by the bed.

Danny's shadow moved huge, on the wall. He pulled off his shirt and trousers in his fast, restless way, every line of him slender and strong, Rachel's stomach knotted with nerves. She wanted Danny to agree with her, to long for what she longed for.

He thumped his way into bed so that the springs screeched.

'For God's sake,' she hissed. 'You're like a flaming herd of elephants!'

Danny grinned and grabbed her, pulling her into his arms. 'I'm the great big bull elephant, kid!'

'Gerroff!' She wriggled free, giggling. Normally she liked it when they were joking and teasing together but tonight she had too much on her mind. 'Stop it, Danny – there's something I want to say to you.'

He looked down at her, leaning on one elbow. He looked excited. 'There's summat I want to say to you, missis, an' all.'

'What?' she said through a yawn. She hadn't expected it to be anything much.

'Let's go to Australia.'

Rachel groaned, infuriated. Just as she had been about to say what she needed to say he had to put this stupid thing of his in the way.

'*What?*' Her anger came through clearly. 'You're not still on about that, Danny?'

'Ten pound each – that's all. On this ship, the SS *Asturias*.' He made a movement with his hand, from side to side, a ship's ocean glide. 'The kids go free.'

She had seen the posters too, advertising this offer of a passage to the other side of the world. But that didn't seem real either. She stared at him. He was joking, he must be? No . . . He wasn't.

'Are you mad?' She sat up, annoyance rising in her at all this, at being thwarted in what she wanted to suggest. 'What're you saying? We can't go to Australia. It's . . . It's the other side of the world. It's . . .' She could barely find the words. It was all so beyond her. 'What about Gladys? And what about Tommy, for that matter? His operations and all the other things?'

'Kids go free. Tommy could have what he has here . . . And the rest of us – think of it, Rach. There's loads of jobs, open space, warm weather. I could trade there – there's always that . . . I mean –' He made an impatient gesture with his hand. 'What've we got here? They kept saying everything'd be better after the war and look at it – still the same old bloody thing. Stuck in these jerry-built ratholes. I want more for us, Rach – I dain't go all through the war to come back here and rot away.'

She saw, appalled, that he had been thinking, dreaming of it. But he hadn't thought – not really.

'Danny – no. *No!* Don't be stupid – you're not rotting

away. You always say business is going well. And you've got the car. We don't know if Tommy could go to school there, even if we got him over there. This is the only school in *this* country, never mind Australia.'

Danny shrugged. 'Well, he could stop at home again. He'd be all right. He's had a bit of schooling.'

She stared at him. She could have killed him for that shrug, those words. For the way he dismissed everything that was so precious to her, dismissed his son and his chance of a life, dismissed the prospect of anything but her being locked at home with Tommy again. It was a betrayal that felt like a physical blow. Was he hankering after Australia because he had once clung to the dream that his father had gone there? Longed for him to have made good and summoned his children to join him? That empty old dream?

'But we can't leave Gladys,' she managed at last. If Danny didn't care about Tommy, surely he'd mind about his aunt? 'She's lost everyone, Jess and Amy – then you . . .'

'She could come too,' Danny said breezily. 'Why not? Fresh start in the sun.'

'Oh, you've thought it all through, haven't you?' She pushed the bedclothes away as if wanting to escape from him. 'Even if you don't count Tommy as a person – because you never have, have you, Danny?' Tears came suddenly, running down her cheeks. 'What about Melly and the boys? What about asking the rest of us? Me, for a start? D'you think I want to go and live all the way over there, away from everyone I know?'

Danny stared at her. 'Well, don't you? It's nice over there. You can make money – and have a much bigger house.'

Rachel seized his hand, speaking urgently. 'Danny –

157

I've been thinking. Don't keep on about Australia – for God's sake, just stop it. I'm not going to Australia and nor are our kids and that's that. I've got a much better idea. Why don't we move to Harborne? I know it's difficult to get a house. We might have to wait. But if we look out – there might be a private landlord, and we could put our name on the list as well . . .'

'Harborne?' This idea seemed beyond Danny's comprehension. 'We can't go to Harborne!'

Rachel sat back, laughing. 'Why not? It's not the other end of the earth, Danny – it's just across town. I go there every week.'

'Oh, we can't do that,' he said. 'I mean, what about Auntie? She'd never leave here.'

'Danny,' she said, exasperated. 'You're on about going to the other side of the world but you won't even think about moving just a few miles away. We can hardly swing a cat in this place. And anyway, the way things're going, we'll all have to move in the end. All these neighbourhoods – they're taking it all down, bit by bit. Look what they've done in Ladywood. And those blocks they've put up over at Nechells Green – they're knocking it flat and putting new roads and such in. We'll be next. It's in the plan – get rid of all the slum housing. We live in a *slum*, Danny – it says so in the paper.'

'Yeah – well, like I say, let's get out of here and go to Australia. If we're all gonna be like rats from a sinking ship, we might as well get out early before it starts.'

Rachel thumped her fists down on the mattress. 'You're the end, Danny Booker! You go on about going to the ends of the earth – and then you think it's too much to move a few miles across town! I've told you – I'm *not going* to cowing Australia.'

They never resolved it. Both of them fell asleep angry

and Rachel woke still furious with him. She got up to get Tommy to school, ignoring Danny. Australia, indeed – what did he think he was playing at? He'd better get that idea out of his head right quick.

'You go then, if you're that keen,' she murmured, carrying on the conversation to herself as she leaned against the front wall of Carlson House. 'But I'm not bloody going.'

'Excuse me.'

She had been so lost in her thoughts that she had not seen a man walking up the road towards her.

'Sorry,' he said. 'I didn't mean to make you jump.'

'That's all right,' Rachel said, putting out her cigarette against the wall. 'I ought to be moving anyway.'

'Is this –' he eyed the building, and read, *Midland Spastics Association* – 'another special school?'

Rachel could not have placed his age, but he had a mild, kindly face and short brown hair. His hands were pushed down into his coat pockets and he looked hunched and cold.

'I don't know about *another*,' she said. 'It's for spastics – children with cerebral palsy. It's the only one there is.'

'Oh, I see. That's good.' Hesitantly, he asked, 'Are you – I mean, do you have a child . . . ?'

'My son.' To her annoyance, Rachel felt herself blush. The fact of Tommy's state, his difficulties, burned in her as guilt, no matter how many people said she should not think of it as her fault. There *must* have been something she did wrong. Looking over at the building, she said, 'They've been ever so good with him. I don't know how we got on without it now.'

'I know. My little girl, Ellen, goes to the blind school. That's why I was asking. I didn't know about this place, even though I don't live far off.'

159

They had a brief chat, agreed it was wonderful that there was help for children, and the man passed on. Rachel put him out of her mind then. She was far too busy feeling annoyed with Danny.

Eighteen

March 1955

'I could go on ahead,' Danny said.

They were having another heated conversation in the bedroom, even though it all had to be conducted in whispers.

'What d'you mean, "ahead"? Without us?'

Rachel was sitting on the edge of the bed, throwing words over her shoulder at him. She felt so hurt and bereft that he was still even thinking about this. Danny, her Danny, came home from the war saying all he wanted was to be at home, with her. Never to have to go anywhere again. And now here he was, talking about taking off to the other side of the world. Was he trying to leave her? Is that what he really wanted? To go away like he did before – but this time not come back?

But even these fears could not change her mind. Even if Tommy had been like the others with no problems, she still would not have wanted to go. And now there was another reason why she couldn't go, one that she hadn't yet told Danny. For two days she had woken feeling unmistakeably queasy. Both times she had drunk a cup of tea to try and settle her stomach and had to hurry out to the lavvy to be sick. This morning, hanging over the stained, smelly lavatory pan, she vomited until she was empty, and tears began to trickle down her cheeks.

'No,' she whispered. 'Not again. I can't do it all again. You sod, Danny Booker – you bloody sod.'

'Just for a while.' Danny kicked off his shoes and came and sat beside her. He spoke in a gentle, persuasive tone. He really wants this, she thought, sinking inside. 'To get settled. 'Til I get a job. We could have so much more over there – a whole new life. Then you could come over with the kids.'

'On my own. On a ship. With Tommy – and the others?' She spoke harshly, her voice sarcastic in her hurt. 'Oh, that'll be bloody marvellous, Danny. And then when we get there, we don't know a soul . . .'

'You'd get to know people – you're friendly, you are. People like you.'

'And there won't be a school for Tommy. For God's *sake*, Danny – Carlson House is the only school in England. It might be the only school in the world for all I know. There's not going to be one in Australia, is there?'

'Well – you know all about it now. You could start one!'

He seemed full of confidence, of enthusiasm. She felt shut out. What had come over him?

'I met this bloke in the Barton Arms – told me all about it.'

'Oh – he'd done it, had he? So what was he doing in the Barton Arms if Australia's so cowing perfect?'

'No – but his pal has. Happy as anything over there, got a job in the motor trade, spraying cars.' Danny was talking facing the window now, the dream of it all in his voice. 'Made a good bit of money in no time. And he said it's ever so nice over there. Warm and sunny. You can go to the beach – beaches like you wouldn't believe. Christmas is one of the hottest days over there. Imagine it – Christmas on the beach!'

For a moment it sounded attractive: a whole new life. That was what she wanted, wasn't it? But no. She couldn't. Not like that. She felt sorry for not being able to climb on board and ride on his dream but she just couldn't. And she felt so sick and exhausted; she couldn't cope with much more anyway. She would tell him about the baby, but she wanted to be sure he knew this was not the main reason for her refusal to go.

'Danny.' She spoke softly, but with iron certainty. 'I'm not going to Australia. I know you wish your dad had gone – that he was going to send for you and there'd be this perfect new life over there. But he never did, did he? That was your dream, not his. He never went anywhere and he's most likely dead by now – a drunk in that hostel or workhouse or whatever it is.'

Swallowing down the tears that were rising in her, she went on, 'You go, if that's what you want. I love you, Danny, but I can't do that, not even for you. Things've got so much better – for me and for Tommy, after all this time. I thought I'd spend my whole life stuck here with him and there'd be nothing for him, ever. There've been times when I've sat here, between these four walls, and it's felt like a prison.' She wiped her eyes, feeling her chest tighten around a well of tears. 'I've tried not to show it, tried not to let it get me down – but that's how I've felt. And you haven't had to do that – none of it. There's a chance now – a little chance of something different. And there's Auntie and friends – everything that matters to me is here.'

She looked into his eyes with intent seriousness. 'If you go, we won't be coming with you. We won't be coming over after to join you. If you go, you're leaving me and our marriage. You need to know that.'

She watched Danny take this in. He got up slowly,

walked round to the other side of the bed and sat, leaning on his thighs, head down. He didn't say anything.

'Danny?' There was no reply, so she went on. 'We're . . . There's another one on the way. Another babby. I've been being sick.'

He turned then. He liked her having babies. Danny craved family.

'Oh, Rach!' His face lit up. 'But that's all the more reason to go! Over there we can have a nice big house and—'

'Danny!' She got to her feet and came round to speak right into his face. '*Listen* to me. Just hear what I'm saying, cloth ears. *I'm not going!*'

A couple of days later, Rachel was at home trying to get the washing finished with Kevin running about under her feet. Finally he shot out the door to play outside.

'Don't you go anywhere near the cut!' Rachel shouted after him.

It was a habitual warning, now the weather was warm. It was dangerous enough, kids swimming in the canal, at the best of times. Now, any body of water was a potential killer, harbouring polio. A boy up the street died of it. Everyone knew a child in leg irons as a result. And Kevin was just the sort to go and jump in anywhere the fancy took him, even if he couldn't swim!

'Yeah, awright –' Kevin tossed her a backward shout. He had heard this so many times before.

Rachel shook her head as he vanished into the yard. 'What'm I going to do with him?'

Kev was only six and she already felt rather awed by him – he was so bright and energetic. Sometimes she looked at Kev and wondered what Danny would have been like if his life had not been so hard, his dad dumping him in the home, the poor life they had had before. Her Danny was a restless soul. A sense of anguish filled her. Was she now what was stopping him from fulfilling himself, using all that energy?

'Right –' Gladys said, folding her arms once they were alone. 'What's going on?'

Rachel had had the feeling Gladys was working up to a confrontation. She and Danny could hardly say a civil word to each other.

There was no getting out of it. Gladys was in her usual vantage point at the table, a pinner over a pale green, spotted frock, her arms folded. Usually she sat watching the goings-on in the yard – but today her attention was fixed on events indoors.

Gladys was sixty now, still an impressive-looking woman with vital, big-boned features. Even at nearly thirty herself, Rachel still felt like a child in relation to Gladys, who had been like a mother to her. You didn't argue with her, however much you might want to, and now there was a look on her face that gave no room for evasion.

'How d'you mean, "going on"?' Rachel said, though she knew exactly. Neither she nor Danny would back down. And she wasn't sure if Gladys had noticed her hurrying out to be sick. Gladys never missed much. She would have to confess that her house was soon going to have to take in yet another person.

'What's the vow of silence all about? It's like living in a flaming monastery in this house, with you two.'

There was silence for a moment. Rachel folded her arms and leaned against the stove where the kettle was heating, emotion swelling in her.

'It's Danny.' Tears escaped and she wiped her cheeks.

Gladys was not greatly in favour of blarting, unless something truly terrible had happened, as in Dolly's case. 'I'm having another babby. And he wants to go to Australia.'

It was not often in her life that Rachel had seen Gladys startled, but this was one of the few times. Her expression changed from tetchiness to astonishment. She felt very grateful to Gladys in that moment.

'What? You're having me on!'

'I'm not. He's been on about it for weeks now.' She couldn't help crying, after keeping it all to herself. 'He wants us to go and start a new life. Now he's keeping on about him going on ahead . . .' She poured out all her worries about it and about Tommy especially.

'We'll be back where we started – me at home and nothing for Tommy,' she wept. 'That's the worst of it. It's not just that I don't want to go and leave you, and everyone – although he said you could come too—'

'Big of him,' Gladys remarked.

The kettle was gushing steam. Rachel prepared the pot.

'He just doesn't seem to see what it'd be like for me,' she said. 'And now Tommy's at school – he just talks as if it doesn't matter.' Rachel carried the tea over and sat down, weeping quietly. 'And now I'm expecting . . .'

'Does he mean it?' Gladys seemed bewildered. 'I know there's been a lot going over there. But what would he do?'

Rachel looked up, a bit riled that Gladys was taking this seriously at all.

'Why – would you go?' she asked.

'Me? Oh, no. I'm not going nowhere.'

'Well, I'm not going either. He says he could get a job. I daresay he could. The thing is, Auntie . . .' She decided to risk talking about her own ideas. 'I sometimes wish we *could* move – to somewhere with more room. What if we went over nearer the school – to Harborne, say? It's nice – much nicer than here.' The words came tumbling out. 'We could live in a proper house – we could afford one, couldn't we?'

Gladys looked doubtful. 'I don't know, bab. I've been in this house a long time. I know it's not the best. They're a verminous load of rubbish really, these houses. But I've had mine patched up and got it the best I can. And I know everyone – Mo and Dolly – I can't imagine it, not living by them. It's just how it is. Anyway, they say there's no houses to be had.'

Gladys seemed vulnerable suddenly, humble, saying this. She drew her black shawl round her shoulders as if protecting herself from any more change. Wally's death had hit her hard. She'd known the lad all his life and she was deeply upset for Mo and Dolly. Rachel realized that his cruelly premature death had also brought back the loss of her husband and her own little boy. She hadn't the heart to remind Gladys that the houses on the yard like this, miles of them, cramped, airless and damp, were on the list, in 'development areas' to be knocked down.

She took a deep breath, trying to quell her frustration. Why could neither of them see what a good plan it would be to move across town? But she could hardly say, 'All right then, we'll just go without you,' because she couldn't get any sense out of Danny either.

'I know that, Auntie,' she said carefully. 'I know what Mo and Dolly mean to you. So you're not going to want to go to Australia either, are you?'

'Oh, no,' Gladys said. She slipped a barley sugar into her mouth and offered the little white bag to Rachel, who shook her head.

'No, ta.'

'Do you good.' She nodded at Rachel's belly.

She took one after all and put it in her mouth. The sweetness made her feel a bit better.

With a bulging cheek, Gladys said, 'I'm not going to flaming Australia. What would I want to go there for?'

'And you don't think I should go?'

Gladys shook her head. 'I can't see why you would. You'll just have to tell the lad not to be so silly.'

As if it was that easy, Rachel thought.

'Can you tell him, Auntie?' she asked.

For the first time in a long while she felt in unity with Gladys.

Rachel was at the school with Tommy all the next day. Once the sickness in the morning eased off she did not feel too bad and was glad to get out. After that she kept forgetting she was expecting and the memory of it would come back with a jolt.

When the day ended, she and Tommy went out to wait for the taxi to take them home. It was another cold but dry afternoon. Tommy struggled along, using the chair as a support. The school liked to encourage him to walk as much as he could, not just sit all day. He had been to the Woodlands hospital for his first operation to straighten his left leg and he was due to go in again. Tommy knew it was good to move as much as he could, but when they reached the gate he sat down again with relief.

Rachel saw him wince.

'Hurts you, doesn't it, babby?' she said.

Tommy gave a faint nod. He didn't like fuss, especially in front of the other children who were coming out. Some of them were much worse off and could not even stand.

Again, fury filled Rachel. This was another reason why

Danny was being so stupid and thoughtless. Think of all the attention Tommy was getting here in Birmingham! She had hoped Gladys might say something last night, but Danny went out to the Salutation with Mo – and she could hardly begrudge Mo. By the time he got back it was too late.

As they were waving off some of the others, Rachel heard a voice say, 'Hello again.'

She saw the man who she had spoken to a few days ago, walking past, hand in hand with a girl with straight, white-blonde hair and a pale, sweet face.

'Oh – hello,' Rachel said. There was a moment's awkwardness, so she said, 'This is Tommy – my son. Say hello, Tommy.'

Tommy squinted up at the man. 'Hel – lo,' he said.

'Hello, Tommy.' The man smiled and Rachel noticed that his lips were full, his top teeth square and widely spaced. His expression was very appealing, lighting up his face. He looked neat and trim, in fawn-coloured trousers and brown tweed coat, well worn, like an old friend. He nodded at the girl, affection in his eyes. 'This is Ellen, my daughter.'

Ellen smiled in their general direction and said, 'Hello,' shyly. She looked about fifteen, Rachel thought. She wondered about the man's age. Older than her, certainly. She guessed that he was in his late thirties.

'We're just having a little walk now school's over, as it's dry today,' the man said. 'Ellen goes to the blind school. You're all just finished as well?'

'Yes,' Rachel said. 'I'm waiting for our taxi – we live the other side of town.'

'Oh,' he paused, seeming shy, hesitant. 'That's a way to come.'

She explained briefly, about the school, how Tommy

had come to attend there, how it was the only school like it, about the taxis from the Electric Light Garage.

'That sounds very good,' the man said.

'Yes – we're very lucky,' Rachel said. She looked into his eyes, grey, crinkled at the corners, sympathetic. She looked away again, down at Tommy.

'Us too.' He looked at his daughter. 'They've helped us so much.'

They didn't know what to say then.

'I'm Michael, by the way,' he said, holding his hand out. 'Michael Livingstone.' He was well spoken, not posh exactly, but a gentleman. Rachel sensed something in him which drew her. It was as if beneath his diffident manner lay a strong need to talk to someone. And he treated her with respect. She told him her name.

'I don't know if . . .' He hesitated. 'Sorry, this must seem rather forward. But Ellen and I are on our own. We don't see much company. I wondered if . . .'

Just then the taxi pulled up at the kerb, the driver waving to them.

'Not today, obviously,' he said. 'But perhaps you and Tommy could come to our house for a cup of tea? We only live round the corner.'

'Oh, all right then – thanks!' Rachel said. Flustered, she hardly knew what she was saying. She needed to get Tommy into the car. 'That'd be nice – but I don't know. The taxi always comes at the same time, you see.'

'Well –' Afterwards she wondered if he would have said this had they not been so hurried by the taxi arriving. 'Just you, if you like. A morning?'

'We'll have to see.' She wasn't here any other morning, only when she came with Tommy. She helped him into the car. 'Bye for now.'

It was only as they drove home and she let it sink in,

that it struck her this was all a bit startling. She thought about telling Danny when she got home, the way before she would always have told him things that happened in the day. He was her friend as well as her husband.

But the memory thudded back to her. Australia. He was still going on about it. It seemed to be all he could think about. Whatever she said she couldn't get through to him. No – damn Danny and his plans which seemed to leave all of the rest of them out. Danny didn't feel like her friend at the moment. This was something she wouldn't tell him. It wasn't as if she had time to go and have tea with Michael Livingstone anyway.

Nineteen

'I want a word with you, Danny.'

Gladys waited until all the children were in bed. Rachel had just come back downstairs, feeling queasy, her head swimming with tiredness. When she heard Gladys start on this conversation, she woke up again immediately, for once happy that Gladys was taking charge.

Danny was hunched over the table with a pencil and paper, his cigarette burning on an ashy saucer beside him. He looked up from his drawing, irritated at being interrupted.

Gladys's tone left no doubt she was serious. She was still standing, one hand on her hip, forbidding.

'What's all this nonsense about going to Australia?'

Danny gave Rachel an accusing look. Her eyes shot back the reply – you never said don't talk to Auntie about it. Why shouldn't I?

'Stop looking daggers and say summat,' Gladys ordered. 'Did you think you were just going to take off without saying a word, lad?' She lowered her voice, more hurt than angry. 'Just like that? After all these years – after . . .' She gestured with her free hand. 'Everything?'

Danny stared down at the tabletop under the assault of these shaming words. It was Gladys who had taken him in when he came out of the orphanage, who had brought him up in Alma Street, who had given him work on the Rag Market, who had taken Rachel in when they were expecting their first child, when still hardly more than children themselves. Gladys helped them get married and helped Rachel to look after Melly and Tommy when Danny was still in the army. And she had been staunch to Rachel over keeping Tommy at home. Gladys Poulter was tough as a pair of old leather boots, but she had always been there for them. They owed her everything.

'I . . .' Danny shrugged and looked up at her. 'I was thinking about it, that's all.' He looked at Rachel again. She knew her eyes were full of hostility.

'Well, when did you think you were going to mention it to me – eh?' Gladys said. 'From what Rach says, you're thinking of taking off, leaving your wife and all your family – in my house, don't forget. And what did you think Rach was going to live on while you was gallivanting about round the world? Did you think of that, Danny?'

'I'd send money home!' Danny erupted, full of indignation. He got up from the table, furious now at being ganged up against. 'I wasn't going over there to lie on the beach, you know. I was going to work and make a place for us to live – a house, a new start. You as well, Auntie, if you wanted – all of us.'

'Not for "us",' Rachel reminded him acidly. 'Cos as I said, I'm not coming, Danny, and nor are the kids.'

'She won't even think of it, Auntie!' Danny burst out in frustration. 'Why won't she even think of it when we're all stuck here in this filthy bloody warren? You wouldn't have to work. And it wouldn't matter how many kids we had! Think of it, Auntie – it's hot over there, not rain and fog day after day. We'd all be together over there instead, that's all. There's a whole new life to be had.'

'A new life?' Gladys's voice dropped. 'Why d'you

173

think I need a new life, Danny? Don't you think I have a life? I earn all my own money, I've got a roof over my head, I've got family and friends just a stone's throw away who I wouldn't change for gold. I couldn't leave Dolly, especially now. Not after Wally . . . What other life d'you think I need at my age?'

'Well, all right – not you then,' he said. 'But us – we're young. We've got things we want to do—'

'Stop talking about me as if I want what you want!' Rachel burst out, seething with frustration. 'I've told you, Danny, I'm not—'

'*Some* wives,' he interrupted, leaning towards her so aggressively that she thought he might hit her, 'do as they're flaming well told. Dain't you promise to obey me when we were standing there in that church? If I say we're going to Australia, then you should be saying, yes, Danny, all right. If you think, as my husband, that we should go and live in another country, then my job is to come with you and make the best of it. That's what a proper wife should do.'

He stood back, glaring at her. Rachel met his eyes, stunned by this. She had never heard Danny talk this way before. All these years they had muddled on through life like the two young pals they were when they first married. Then the war came and he was away for four years, leaving her first with Melly, then Tommy and all that went with his difficult little life.

And when he came back, they were no longer children. They had both fought their battles separately and survived – she as well as he. To obey, in the way Danny meant her to obey, would be like being a child, a little helpless thing with no mind of her own. And she was not that child any more.

'Who've you been talking to?' Gladys said. She pulled

out a chair and sat down. 'Who's put these ideas in your head?'

There was no answer. Danny and Rachel carried on staring each other out, their gazes locked ferociously together. Neither wanted to be the first to look away. Rachel could see the burning feeling in Danny's blue eyes, the desire and restless frustration. But she too was full of a strong, immovable feeling.

'Obey?' Her voice was icy. She felt steely and calm. 'Danny – why the hell d'you think I should obey you? I'm not a child. I'm not a soldier, marching to your orders. You're not thinking of any of us and you're wrong to ask me to go to Australia with you, however much you want to go. *You* go, if you want it that badly. But no one'll be coming after you. We live here. If you want to lose your family, you buy that ticket and off you go.'

She stood up and leaned across the table, her fist clenched.

'And don't *ever* talk to me about obeying you again. I don't care what it says in those vows – I've known you since we were knee high and, if I know one thing, it's that I'm equal to you. I brought up your kids for years when you weren't even here. I'm not having you pushing me around. And, *for the last time*, I'm not going to sodding Australia neither.'

Danny got to his feet. At last he broke the look which had sizzled between them and lowered his head. With an abrupt movement he picked up his cigarettes and flung out of the house, slamming the door so that the walls shook.

Rachel and Gladys sat in silence for a moment. Rachel stared down at the tablecloth, the crumbs on the blue-and-white checks.

'Am I wrong, Auntie?'

Gladys sighed. 'Danny's father, Wilf – he was a restless so-and-so as well. All stuck in these little yards, no space to move – you can't see further than across the street. Even going to war to get shot at's an adventure, I s'pose.'

'If it wasn't for Tommy, I might go,' Rachel said. She looked up at Gladys. 'I can't do it to him.'

'No,' Gladys said. She started to stack the cups that were on the table. 'I know.' She stood up. 'Danny'll get over it. He'll have to, won't he?'

Twenty

April 1955

'Tommy?' Melly said. 'I'm just popping over to see Lil and Stanley. I won't be long, all right?'

It was a Saturday and the others were all out. Dad and Gladys had taken Kev with them to the Rag Market and Mom had said after dinner, 'I just need to go out for a while – pick up a few things. You'll stay with the boys, won't you?'

Melly nodded. Not that Mom was even waiting for her reply. They're always telling me *I'm* the dreamy one, she thought grumpily. Mom seemed to have her head in the clouds these days. She and Dad were in a mood with each other. Nothing had been said but they just ignored each other most of the time. Yesterday while they were having tea Auntie had suddenly come out with:

'I'm sick of this, you two – for heaven's sake!'

Melly saw Mom and Dad glare at each other. They each carried on, cross and stubborn, eating their tea. Melly and Tommy exchanged looks and Tommy rolled his eyes. But they didn't know what was going on. They're silly, Melly thought crossly. If we did that they'd tell us to make it up and have done with it.

And Mom was getting more involved with Tommy's school – another morning a week now. She always seemed miles away these days.

It wasn't that Melly minded staying with Tommy. He was used to his school now so it didn't make him quite so tired. He had established his independence from her and they were getting used to things so that now Melly felt more as if he was her brother again. He didn't want her to teach him, but they would play things together. They had already played noughts and crosses and hangman and Ludo. But she had had enough now. The afternoon was hanging heavily.

The games had helped keep her emotional thoughts at bay, but now she was finding it hard to sit still. Dolly Morrison had come over last night. Usually Dolly came over and cried because she said Mo couldn't stand seeing her cry at home. Through her tears she'd say things like, 'I haven't got five children – that's wrong. I've got *six*. My family feels like a table someone's sawn one of the legs off.'

But last night her face was lit up the way they hadn't seen it since before the accident.

'He's coming home!' she announced. She was just back from her long journey across town. Reggie was in Woodlands, the orthopaedic hospital in Selly Oak, where Tommy had had his operation. 'They've said he's ready – at last!'

Reggie's injuries had led him to have two operations on his right leg and hip, having to convalesce from one before they began on the other. His recovery had taken several months. Dolly said he was beginning to walk now, with crutches.

'Oh, my boy's coming home!' she said. 'You should've seen Freddie's face when he heard!'

Gladys went and embraced Dolly, which was an occasion in itself as Gladys usually held back from emotion. But she knew how empty the Morrison household – and the yard – had been during these months. With Eric married and gone, Wally so brutally taken from them, Reggie in hospital and now Jonny – to his enormous annoyance – waiting to be called up for National Service, suddenly it was just Freddie and Donna left. Dolly was bereft. 'I'd have another if I wasn't over the hill,' she said to Gladys sometimes.

Melly felt this news of Reggie's return go through her like a shock. She didn't show it and made her face look pleased for Dolly. She *was* pleased for Dolly and Mo, but she felt terrified of facing Reggie. She had tried to shut away any feelings she had for him, telling herself it was a schoolgirl crush and that he had found it ridiculous. Now it was all the more difficult. How could you face someone who had been through such a terrible thing and lost his closest brother in the process? Dolly said he was due to be brought home sometime during the following week.

There was no one she could talk to. If things were different, if Cissy had been around more – if she was not, well, *Cissy* – maybe she could have confided in her like a sister. But Cissy was having a fine old time, earning her money and defying Nanna, getting up to all sorts that Peggy would have a pink fit if she heard about. She was going about with some man called Teddy. Cissy talked endlessly about him on the few occasions she had come over and bunked up for the night (only when Teddy was busy, it seemed). Teddy worked in a big firm in Coventry, doing exactly what, Cissy never seemed to know. But he had a car – a sports car!

'It's an Austin Healey 100!' Cissy recited. 'Bright red – a real hot rod and it can go ever so fast!'

'How fast?' Tommy asked. Cissy often conducted her secret conversations up in their bedroom in front of Tommy as she knew he wouldn't tell on her. Kevin and

Ricky weren't at all interested in any of Cissy's doings and would play with cars along their racetrack – the offcut of green carpet between the beds.

'Oh – I don't know,' Cissy said impatiently. '*Fast*. He can goose it straight up to sixty! It makes a proper mess of my hair – Teddy says you have to cover your head.' Cissy patted her hair to illustrate the point. 'I feel like Grace Kelly, sitting there in a silk scarf!'

Melly was already rather tired of hearing about the wondrous Teddy. Cissy would blather on endlessly about him but if you asked her any questions, she'd put her head on one side and say scornfully, 'Are you writing a book?'

She wouldn't say how old Teddy was but she wasn't even sixteen yet and it seemed funny that she knew more about his car than what he did for a living. Heaven knew what she told Nanna and how she managed to get away with it. Melly felt very annoyed with Cissy, partly because she seemed to be having such a very good time! Cissy always seemed to fall on her feet, whatever.

With her thoughts churning round, she wanted some distraction and someone who was pleased to see her. At least Lil and Stanley seemed to like her coming round. As their daughter's so far away, Melly thought, I can go and see them instead. Lil sometimes made a plain cake or bought a bun or two for them to share, as if it was a special occasion. It made Melly feel wanted, like someone who was doing good. At least Lil talked to her.

'Hello, bab,' Lil said. 'You come for your tea, have yer? Stanley – here's our little visitor!'

The downstairs room was in its usual cramped, smelly condition, but as it was warm and Lil was keeping the door open, the room felt a bit fresher than usual and there was a sour whiff of Ajax.

'Hello, Stanley,' Melly said, going over to him slowly, careful never to make him jump. As ever he was in his chair.

'All right?' he muttered. He had grown used to her. Melly even thought he liked her coming in for tea. She was often a bit bored sitting there, truth to tell, but she liked to feel as if she was doing something useful.

'How're you today, Stanley?'

He gave a nod, as if to say, what do you expect? But it was friendly, not hostile.

Lil made tea and Melly sat on the wooden chair beside Stanley. Sounds came through the door, Ricky chattering to himself across the yard and Mrs Davies's whining voice, 'Frankie – get in 'ere, *now*!'

She didn't know what to say to Stanley – what, in the life of a thirteen-year-old girl, could be interesting to a man like him? The news that was burning inside her – Reggie was coming home! – was not something she wanted to talk about.

But Lil, after announcing across the room, 'I've bought a couple of Chelsea buns,' said, 'I hear Dolly's lad's coming home at last.'

'Oh –' Melly's heart set off like a piston. Her cheeks flamed. What was the matter with her? She had got over Reggie – hadn't she? 'Is he?'

'The poor lad,' Lil said. 'I hear it's touch and go if he'll be able to walk.'

'I think he can,' Melly said, lowering her face to hide her blushes. 'With crutches, Dolly said.'

'Well, let's hope so, for all their sakes,' Lil said. 'He'll need a job. A young man needs a job, doesn't he?'

They drank their tea and shared the sugary coils of

bun. Lil kept up a bright conversation, asking about the markets and how Tommy was doing. Soon after he had finished his tea, Stanley seemed to have fallen into a doze, his hands slack in his lap.

'Poor old thing,' Lil said softly. 'Look at him. He's bad at night, that's why he's so sleepy in the day.'

'Doesn't he *ever* go out?' Melly asked. She had not seen Stanley outside the house for a long time now. She could hardly imagine being forever inside this room, with barely space to move. 'Couldn't he go and see somebody – go to the pub?'

'The pub – hah!' Stanley erupted, so furiously that both of them jumped. They had thought he was asleep. 'You won't catch me setting foot in a pub. Drink myself to death like my old man!' He subsided, shutting his eyes again.

'Stanley's father . . .' Lil hesitated, unsure how to say it to a young girl. 'Well, when he came home from the first war, he wasn't himself, was he, Stanley?'

Stanley made an angry sound, a hissing through his teeth, eyes still closed.

'The thing is –' Lil leaned forwards, taking a drag on her Woodbine which hollowed her cheeks for a moment. She puffed the smoke towards the sagging ceiling. 'You're too young to remember, bab, but after the first war – oh, the men who came back! The state of them. They couldn't say what they'd seen, most of 'em. They were either wild as horses or limp as rags. Stanley's father was hardly sober from the day he got back. It did for him, before long.' As she finished, her eyes settled on her husband and Melly saw a well of sadness in them. 'Oh, well . . .' She petered out. 'Anyway, Stanley likes to stay in the house. I get out a little bit – shopping and that.'

She smiled, the weary lines of her face lifting. 'You don't want to hear about us old things.'

Melly felt so sad for Lil and Stanley, especially when Mom told her what they used to be like. But she didn't know what to say. She nodded at the teapot. 'D'you want me to top you up, Mrs Gittins?'

Lil nodded. 'Thanks, bab. It's good of yer to come and sit with us. We don't have much young life around us now. Stan – you'll have another drop, won't you?'

A bit later she got up to turn on the wireless.

'He likes his match results,' Lil said. 'It's getting on for the end of the season now – it's not the same in the summer without the football. He don't care much what the Australians do with theirs.'

She switched on the wireless. A voice droned out the scores. The light began to fade outside and Melly, bored with the football, washed and dried the cups and put them away.

'I'd best be off,' she was saying to Lil, when they all heard the voice bellowing out in the yard.

'I've done it! I've bloomin' well gone and done it! *Ye-e-e-es!*'

They looked at each other; even Stanley opened his eyes again.

'That's Mo,' Lil said, and she and Melly rushed to the door.

Outside, Mo was lumbering up and down like a dancing bear in shirtsleeves, boots slapping on the bricks and waving a piece of paper in one hand. Years seemed to have lifted off him. Everyone came to their doors, Ethel Jackman with her stringy arms folded as if resenting anyone else having good news.

'What's bitten you, Mo?' Lil called to him, laughter in her voice.

Dolly appeared outside then and Donna, both looking excited and bewildered at the same time.

'Mo reckons he's had a win,' Dolly said, hurrying over to Lil. 'He was sat there watching the teleprinter thing on the television and he says – well, it looks as if . . . It's the group of them, at the Salutation . . . God, Lil, I feel all shook up – look at my hands – I'm shaking like a leaf!'

Everyone crowded round, close to Lil and Stanley's door. Melly stood aside so that Stanley could see out.

'Eight score draws!' Mo cried. His face was pink and beaded with perspiration. 'I can't believe it – I was sat there in front of the television and the first two come in . . . Then it went on and there was nothing, a long gap and I thought that's it then – then there was another and another and then another. I said to Doll, look, I've got five and she said – well, she weren't even listening really, were you?'

'I was doing the ironing,' Dolly giggled.

'And it went on and I thought, well, that's good – but that's it. And they got to Scotland and there was three more – all in a row! And we got 'em all!'

Just then, Gladys, Mom and Dad appeared along the entry. The three of them stopped on seeing the little crowd at the end of the yard.

'What's going on?' Gladys called out, putting her bags down.

'It's Mo –' Dolly dashed over to her. 'Mo and the others! Look – come and see. They've picked eight score draws and they've all come out!'

'Blimey, Mo,' Danny said. 'That must mean . . .'

'What did it say?' Rachel asked. 'Afterwards, I mean?'

'It said, "Telegram applications only",' Dolly said.

They all looked at each other, trying to make sense of things.

'Well,' Gladys said. 'I s'pose that means . . . God, Mo – you lot must've won a packet!'

Twenty-One

Rachel had gone to the Rag Market on her way back across town, late that afternoon. First, she called in to the Bull Ring for some knock-down fruit and veg. When she turned up in the Rag Market to help Gladys and Danny pack up their stalls, she wanted it to look as if she had come into town to go shopping. She found herself enjoying the deception, angry and excited, like a child playing with fire.

She had come from Harborne. Michael Livingstone had asked her to visit for a cup of tea with him and Ellen. She had found him waiting outside the school a few days ago. 'You and Tommy,' he had said. But she couldn't take Tommy across town without the taxi. And there was always Melly to look after him. For once she could go on her own.

Michael and Ellen lived in War Lane. She had the journey across town, first one bus, then another, to ask herself what the hell she was doing, sneaking off to see this man, without Tommy, without an excuse. She and Danny had had another row that morning in furious whispers. It was the same old thing.

'You go then – just bugger off and leave us all if that's what you want. Go to the other side of the world if you think it's so flaming marvellous. But don't ask me to come – I don't want to and that's that.'

'Oh, come on, Rach!' Danny calmed down and tried to plead with her. 'Give something a chance for once!'

'Give something a chance!' she raged back at him. 'How about carrying your child when I wasn't even sixteen, how about leaving my family and moving across town? I've done enough giving it a chance. I want a nice life and a better life than in this hovel – but not in cowing Australia!'

They hadn't made it up. Early in the afternoon, Rachel had slipped out, telling Melly she was going shopping. She took two cloth carriers with her. Buying from the Bull Ring on the way back was also a way of settling her conscience.

Once she got off the bus in War Lane, walking in the thin spring sunshine, there was no more time to think about Danny or to tell herself that all she was doing was going to drink a cup of tea with someone. Someone who happened to be a man, who made no mention of a wife. She was being drawn along, despite herself.

When she saw him, Michael Livingstone seemed both taller and more hesitant than she had remembered. For a second she almost turned and fled. What was she doing, walking into a strange man's home? How had this happened?

'Hello,' he said, opening the door of his terraced house. 'It's nice of you to come. Especially all this way. Come in.'

'It's all right, it didn't take long,' Rachel said, stepping past him. The hall was narrow and she was conscious of having to walk close to him, to his slender body in a green-and-white checked shirt, the fawn trousers.

'Ellen's in the front,' he said. 'Would you like a cup of tea?' He spoke hurriedly, obviously nervous, but Rachel liked his quiet, gentle manner and agreed that she would.

In fact she had begun to feel a bit sick again and was not sure if it was the baby or her nerves. She hoped a cup of tea would settle it.

'Ellen –' He stood at the door of the back room. 'Here's our friend Rachel to see us – Tommy's mother.' Rachel liked the way he said 'our friend'. It sounded both warm and innocent at once. And it *is* innocent, she thought defiantly.

Rachel entered a cosy little room with a table and chairs in the back corner and two armchairs at the front, near the window. Ellen was sitting in one, holding a skein of white knitting, her hair falling forward until she raised her head and smiled in the direction of the door.

'All right, Ellen?' Rachel said, relieved that the girl was there. It made her visit seem safe and legitimate.

'Have a seat,' Michael said. 'I've boiled the kettle – I'll just get the tea ready.'

Rachel obeyed, and chatted to Ellen.

'That's nice – your knitting, I mean. Can I have a look?'

Ellen held it out. Rachel was impressed to see that the girl was making almost no mistakes.

'They taught us at school,' she said. 'Once you've got the hang of it, it's something you can do by feel. I can't use a pattern yet, though – I'm only knitting easy things.'

'No socks for sailors yet,' Michael joked, carrying in a tray of cups and a plate of biscuits.

Rachel smiled up at him. 'Socks are difficult. You need more needles – for the heels.'

He shrugged. 'I don't know. I've never knitted anything in my life!'

Michael went out again and Rachel looked approvingly round the room. How lovely to have a front room and back room – this was just the sort of house she longed to live in!

The chairs they were sitting in were of well-worn brown leather. The floor was covered by two sections of green patterned carpet. On the table were a blue-and-white striped jug containing dried flowers, a pile of books and a camera. For a moment she thought of Coronation Cameras where Danny had worked for a short time. But her attention was drawn to the lead fireplace and the shelf above it, on which were two framed photographs.

She heard Michael's footsteps returning from the kitchen again as she gazed hungrily at the wedding photograph – a young, slim man who must have been Michael, arm in arm with a woman whose features Rachel could hardly make out under a gauzy veil. Where was this woman? It already felt as if she was not here – otherwise why would he have invited her?

The other picture was of Ellen, a smiling infant propped on a white blanket, though there was already an unseeing blankness to her eyes. And then she had to stop looking because Michael appeared with the teapot.

As he poured, she examined him. It seemed so strange to be close to another man when she was used to Danny's broad, freckly face, his bright blue eyes like Gladys's which had reproduced themselves in Melly and Kev, his wiry, muscular body. Michael seemed a calmer person altogether, brown hair falling across his forehead, thinning a little on top, she noticed as he bent to pour the tea, and eyes of a colour she could not quite pin down – greenish, hazel – she was not sure. There was a gentle grace to him, as well as the upstanding bearing of someone who, she guessed, had been in the forces.

'How's Tommy getting along?' he asked, bringing a chair over from the table and arranging it between the armchairs for himself.

'He's doing all right,' Rachel said. 'They're ever so

good. We never thought he'd walk at all when he was little but he can manage a bit with a stick when he needs to. He finds it ever so tiring but it means he's not always in the chair. He's doing well at the school too. They say he's clever.'

'I'm sure he is,' Michael agreed, stirring his tea. 'And Ellen . . .'

'Oh, she's clever, all right,' Rachel said. 'Her knitting's better than mine for a start!'

They all laughed.

'I made so many mistakes when I started,' Ellen said. Rachel wondered if her mother had the same pale hair. There was still no mention of her.

'It's marvellous what they can do in those schools,' Michael said. 'I can hardly bear to think where we'd be without them.'

'I know,' Rachel said. 'In fact, that's where we were before we found out about this place. A lady came and told us about the school. We were . . . Well, I couldn't believe it at first. Tommy had never been to school before.'

'Good gracious!' Michael said.

They talked for a long time about their children. She realized that it was a relief for him to have someone to talk to who knew what it was like to have a child who was different, whose life was such a struggle.

He was fascinated when she said they worked the Rag Market and wanted to know all about it and she asked him about his work.

He smiled, topping up her teacup and offering the biscuits again. She took a Bourbon, nodding her thanks. She definitely felt better for something in her stomach.

'I was always mad about taking pictures,' he said. 'My uncle had a camera, just a little box Brownie, that he let me loose on when I was only about seven. And that was that. It was all I ever wanted to do, really. As soon as I got out of school I went and got a job with a photographer here and – well, I've been at it ever since. In the war the navy let me carry on – Fleet Air arm, reconnaissance photographs.'

'You mean out of aeroplanes?' She was impressed.

'Mostly, yes.'

'Did you take that one?' she asked, nodding at the portrait of Ellen.

'Oh, yes – and I've got a much more recent one, just done it in fact.' He jumped up with nimble energy and went to the table where from a paper folder he produced a close-up of Ellen, obviously very recent. She was facing the camera diagonally as if looking dreamily at the corner of the room, her hair arranged softly back over her shoulders. Her face wore a sweet but wistful expression.

'It's lovely.' The girl looked beautiful in it, a little older than in real life. It had captured the essence of her. 'You're so pretty, Ellen,' Rachel said, and then a wave of discomfort passed through her – she's probably never seen her own face . . .

But Ellen just smiled.

'You'd be rather photogenic, I think,' Michael said. He stood back and appraised her, a professional at work suddenly. 'You have very good cheekbones.'

'Do I?' Rachel blushed. No one had ever said that before! 'That's news to me I can tell you!'

'You only have to look in the mirror,' he said. 'Here –' For a second he ran a finger down her cheek, so softly that it was barely a touch, a butterfly's footsteps. 'They create interesting shadows. Perhaps you'd let me photograph you one day?'

'Oh – well!' Rachel laughed, startled. 'That might be nice, yes!'

Michael sat again. He told her that he had been born in Kings Heath, not far away, and lived all his life in the area. His parents were dead but he had a brother who lived in Shirley.

Rachel wondered how old he was. Ellen was about Cissy's age, but the couple in the photograph must have been . . . Well, obviously older than she and Danny were when they set out. She thought Michael must be well on in his thirties.

In turn she relayed a little about herself – that she lived in Aston, that she had a daughter about Ellen's age, two more sons of six and four. Somehow she never quite mentioned Danny or that she was carrying another child.

By the time she got up to go, they had had an amiable couple of hours of talk and laughter. It had been such a relief to talk easily, to feel a kind friendliness coming from him. There was nothing to be ashamed of. Yet, going to the door to leave, she felt self-conscious about being seen leaving his house.

'Rachel,' Michael said as she stepped outside. She turned. He was speaking in a low voice and sounded suddenly tense. He joined her out on the step and drew the front door almost closed.

'I didn't want to explain in front of Ellen. It's not that she doesn't know, obviously, but she doesn't like to hear me say it . . .' Rachel waited.

Michael spoke, looking down at the blue bricks of the front path. 'Ellen's mother left me. We were married in 1940 and the year after that I went into the navy – the Air Arm. Ellen came along the next year. She was born blind. They don't know why, of course . . .' He shrugged. 'Just one of those things, I suppose. By the time I came home, she – Nancy – had had another child, by someone else. She . . . Well, she didn't want Ellen in her new life. Never

191

really could accept the fact that Ellen was never going to be able to see. It's not so bad in a baby, but of course as they get older and start to move about . . .'

Rachel listened, horrified. Fancy leaving your child, leaving a nice man like Michael. Then she ticked herself off, inwardly. Who was she to be judging other people, when she had just spent the afternoon visiting a man who was not her husband?

'She left Ellen with me when Ellen was nearly six. Of course, it all took a lot of getting used to, for both of us.' He stared grimly along the path. 'There've been times, I can tell you . . .'

Rachel felt tenderness awake in her. This poor man – what a homecoming!

He shrugged again and gave a strained smile. 'It's just all rather lonely. People don't really want to know, do they? So it's been nice to have some company – especially someone who has some idea . . .'

'Yes,' Rachel said. 'I've barely met anyone – not 'til Tommy started at the school.'

They stood for a moment, not speaking.

'Well –' Michael became brisk and cheerful. 'I must let you go. But if you've ever got time – I'm usually here.'

'Don't you go out to work?' she said.

'I rent a place where I have a darkroom and I can do studio portraits. I'm there some of the time. I have to be flexible – because of her.'

'I suppose . . .' Her heart beat faster. She looked up at him. 'I could . . . Maybe, I mean, manage a morning in the week?'

Michael smiled. The flesh round his eyes crinkled and the clown-like curve of his lips made her smile back.

'That'd be nice.'

A turmoil of feelings swirled in her on the bus back

into town. There's nothing going on, she told herself. Danny could have sat in that room with them all afternoon. But the feelings of ease with this man, of understanding, tenderness – Danny could not have seen that, still could not see it.

In town, with her bags of fruit and veg, she walked into the bustle of the Rag Market. The stallholders were all shutting up now, folding away the clothes, packing up bags and prams and basket carriages. Rachel smiled as she looked around. The place brought back so many memories, both good and bad, but above all of her early days with Danny, of the Danny she had adored . . .

As she moved towards their two stalls, both along the back wall of the market, Danny was busy piling up pairs of men's trousers and jackets and talking to the man on the stall next door. She drew closer and then he looked up and caught sight of her. He stopped what he was doing. For a second he looked startled, then faintly hostile, and then she saw a hunger in his eyes which seemed to say, *My wife – here she is . . .* As if all their quarrels were behind them.

He thinks I've come to make up, she thought, with a longing in her. But nothing's going to be made up unless he gives up this stupid idea of going to Australia . . .

She breezed up to his stall. 'Thought I'd come and help,' she said. She held up her bags to Gladys. 'Got some fruit and veg.'

'Stick it under here,' Gladys said, indicating her stall. 'You can help me fold up this lot.'

By the time they got home, their argument had gone off the boil for the moment and when they reached Alma Street and found Mo dancing about the yard – for the time being, all else was forgotten.

Twenty-Two

'*How* much?'

Gladys seemed hardly able to take in the news when Dolly told her a few days later. She had come straight round to see them as soon as they'd heard.

'You'd best sit down as well, Dolly,' Rachel said. Dolly's face was very pale and she looked as if her legs were about to give way. 'I'll make some tea.'

'Got anything stronger?' Dolly said, lighting a cigarette with trembling fingers.

Gladys nodded at the half-empty bottle of port wine next to the wireless on the sideboard. It might have been only ten o'clock on a Monday morning but this was medicinal.

'It's . . .' She gulped, accepting the glass of port. 'God, I can hardly say it, Glad. It's . . .' She lowered her voice to a whisper, '*Thirty-two grand.*'

Rachel heard herself gasp at the same time as Gladys. *Thirty-two thousand pounds!* It was an unimaginable amount of money. It was beyond thinking of, beyond envying. If Dolly had said five hundred, she might well have burned with desire for it to be hers.

'So that means . . .' Gladys struggled to get her mind round it. She took a fortifying mouthful of port. 'There's four of them, did you say?'

'There's Mo and Alf and Fatty Jenkins and – oh, I can't remember but yes, four. It's going to be in the papers,

Glad. Only we've asked them not to print our names.'

'That's eight thousand each,' Rachel said. Even that was beyond seeming real.

Dolly looked from one to the other of them, wide-eyed like a little girl. 'I feel all knocked for six. I mean, you think you might win a tenner – or even a hundred quid if you get a really good day. But this . . . I don't know if I'm coming or going at the moment.'

'The lucky bastards,' was Danny's comment. 'Lucky, lucky bastards.'

He said it with such feeling that Rachel felt even further from him than she had before. Of course Mo and Dolly *were* lucky and she tried to be glad for them, especially after losing Wally and all the sadness they had endured. It was time they had some good fortune. But there was a feeling that this changed things, and no one knew quite how yet.

She couldn't help thinking about all that money, though. Imagine what we could do with some of that, she thought. A nice house, away from here; a decent car. She didn't ask what Danny would do. It would probably have involved taking off across the world and she didn't want to hear it. The two of them had come to an uneasy truce for the moment, but there was still a quarrel between them and neither of them would back down.

The money brought its complications. The yard was full of talk about it, jokes about buying a mansion, a yacht. Everyone bought copies of the *Evening Mail* to relish the news. But even though the names of the four families were not published, somehow people found out.

'We're getting these letters,' Dolly told Gladys, with a

195

bewildered look on her face. 'From people we've never even heard of. They've all got a sob story.'

Everyone was full of it and Mo and Dolly were in shock. Eight thousand pounds was a fortune. What, in reality, did you do with a fortune? After the initial euphoria – and on top of the other shocks they had suffered – it sent them into a tailspin of uncertainty.

And in the middle of all this turmoil, of celebration and heart searching, Reggie came home from hospital.

The day Reggie Morrison came back, Melly walked home from school sick with nerves. Kev and Ricky were whirring round the yard with Frankie 'Trigger' Davies and Tommy wasn't back yet. She dashed into the house and went straight upstairs.

'Cat got your tongue, has it?' Rachel called up after her. 'You get back down here, Melly – I need you to peel some spuds.'

Melly didn't answer. Mom was even more scratchy with her these days, forever ordering her about. In the bedroom she stood to the side of the window and looked across the yard. It was full of children, a go-kart, a little red tricycle and several lines of washing slanting in the breeze. But of Reggie there was no sign. Her nerves unrelieved, she clomped back downstairs again.

'Why don't you ever make Kev help?'

Rachel turned to her, looking irritated. 'Kev? What use would he be? Anyway, he's a lad. Here –' She pushed a large pan across the table, full of potatoes and water. 'Get started on these. I'm running late.'

'Why are you running late?' Melly asked, as if to say, is that *my* fault?

Rachel kept her eyes on the pastry she was thumping

away at on a floured patch of the table. 'I just am, that's all.'

Melanie wondered if she imagined the blush that crept up her mother's cheeks. Mom was being strange these days.

The question that was gnawing at her had to come out. Lifting a potato from the muddy water, she asked as casually as she could, 'Dain't Dolly say Reggie was coming out today?'

Melly did not see Reggie until the next evening.

She was coming back across the yard from the lavs and he stepped out of the house, leaning on a crutch under his right shoulder. He set out in her direction, limping painfully, favouring his left leg.

Melly's blood raced and she was filled with panic. There was no one she wanted to see more, no one who she longed to avoid more as well. But there he was. With a jolt of shock she took in his gaunt, drawn face, hardly like the Reggie she remembered. He was looking at the ground, concentrating on walking, and he seemed sad and far away.

An agony of feelings filled her. She pitied him, wanted to say something nice and comforting, but she had no idea what to say across the gulf of age and of all that had happened. In the seconds during which they moved closer she almost put her head down and walked past without saying anything. But as they met she forced herself to look up.

'All right, Reggie?' Her voice sounded thin and young to her.

'All right,' he murmured, raising his head a little.

She couldn't bear for that to be all, even though the conversation felt excruciating already.

'Is . . . I mean, are you better?' She could have cut her tongue off at the stupidity of the question. All she wanted to say, that she was sorry, so sorry about Wally and about his leg and everything, was locked inside her and seemed unable to get out.

And to her horror, Reggie, in a voice so bitter that it was unbearable to hear, replied, 'Better than what? Dead?'

'No!' She said, 'No, I mean . . .'

But he was already moving away. Despair filled her. Why had she said that? Tears burned her eyes. She got everything wrong when all she wanted was to say something nice. And then, while she was already punishing herself for these things that were not really her fault, she thought with a terrible pang of the little Christmas present she had bought for him, what seemed now like years ago. A motorcycle! Did he still have it? And if so, did it just remind him of nothing but the accident and the death of his brother? If she had tried she could not have bought a worse present!

Hurrying back to the lavatory she bolted the door and stood in the half-dark, crying quiet, despairing tears. She had said and done everything wrong. She had her little weep and went back inside to peel the potatoes in silence. More tears fell in the bowl of water but her mother didn't notice.

As she lay in bed that night her thoughts went round and round. None of it meant anything – she could see that really, with her more grown-up self. Reggie gave her no thought in the first place and he had much bigger things on his mind. Bigger things than her, certainly. Dolly had said that GEC were going to take him back and make sure he had a job where he could sit down. Thank goodness, she thought, at least he'd be at work like any other lad. But now he was around again. She'd keep bumping into him, if she did not do her best to avoid him.

A few days later, Rachel came along the entry into the yard in time to see Gladys walking back into the house with her stiff, rocking walk. Rachel had noticed that Gladys was moving more slowly recently, what with her bunion and her sore hips. But today there was an extra heaviness about her, as if life was weighing her down. Rachel often felt intense irritation towards Gladys, having to live in her house and do things her way. And her desperate feelings now that she had another baby on the way, as well as secret meetings with Michael Livingstone, were making her both more restless and more guilty and tense because she could not seem to help herself.

But seeing Gladys's face this afternoon, the feelings drained away. Gladys was sixty now. In that moment Rachel saw, almost as if for the first time, how much Gladys had changed. There was a fragile, papery look to her skin. From being the most active, fearsome person Rachel knew, she looked suddenly tired and faded. As Rachel walked into the house she saw Gladys sink down at the table with a heavy sigh.

'You all right, Auntie?' she asked, finding a gentleness in herself. However much she resented Gladys sometimes, she knew how much she owed her.

Gladys slumped down, leaning her head on one hand. 'Oh – I dunno.' For a moment she eyed the bottle of port wine again. 'No . . . Pour us a cuppa will yer, bab? I've just filled the pot. I need summat to pull me round.'

Rachel poured them both one and sat down with her. 'It's Mo and Dolly, isn't it?' she said.

Gladys straightened up again, sugared her tea and sipped it.

'Dolly says she wishes it had never happened. The pools. In a way. And what with Reggie . . .'

They had all seen the state Reggie was in, pale and thin, only able to get about, agonizingly, with the crutch and very low in himself.

'I know Doll would give anything in the world to have Wally and Reggie both back as they were, rather than the money,' Gladys said. Her eyes filled. 'Cruel. Terrible cruel.'

They sat for a moment in silence before Gladys heaved another sigh.

'And now they're talking about buying a house. Course they are – with all that money they could buy a dozen houses.' She rolled her eyes. 'If there were any houses to buy, any road.'

'You mean leave here?' Rachel said.

'Well, of course leave here,' Gladys said brusquely. 'Why would anyone live in a dump like this when they'd come into a fortune?'

Rachel saw then why Gladys was upset. She had banked on her old friends always being here. If Mo and Dolly left Alma Street and this yard, nothing would ever be the same again. They would be leaving everyone behind in more ways than one. But in her own heart Rachel felt a guilty jolt of hope. If Mo and Dolly were to move out of number one, then what was to stop them getting out of number three as well?

'We don't know what to do for the best.' Dolly came round the next afternoon, after Melly was home from school. She sat at the table smoking one cigarette off the end of another, offering them round. Rachel took one and lit up. 'All these letters we keep getting.' She mashed her cigarette butt into the pale blue saucer on the table.

'That'll soon die down,' Gladys said.

'I know, but I just feel as if I want to run away and hide somewhere, I really do. If we give something to one person we'll have to give to everyone and where will it end? But all these people who say they're at their wits' end and that . . .' She shook her head, blowing smoke from her lips. 'Having all this money makes me feel all sort of peculiar. And Mo keeps saying, we've got to be sensible, Dolly, or it'll all be gone and then where will we be? What would you do, Glad?'

'I really don't know,' Gladys said. There was more than a hint of sarcasm in her voice. 'Can't say I've ever been well enough off to find out.'

'Mo's had to go to the bank and open an account,' Dolly went on. She sounded awed. They had never thought of such a thing before. 'The bank manager was ever so pleased to see him.'

'I bet he was,' Gladys laughed, but again there was a dryness in her tone.

'Said if he wanted him to recommend an estate agent, he could help,' Mo said.

Gladys said nothing. Melly felt a tense silence come over the room.

'D'you think you'll go?' It was Rachel who asked.

'Well,' Dolly said. 'It'd be daft not to, wouldn't it? All that money – we could get out of here at last. No more bugs and rain coming through the roof! And it might help Reggie. And Jonny can stay on at school . . .'

'We could go as well, Auntie,' Rachel said. Melly saw her look back and forth between Gladys and Dolly. 'It won't be the same here without Mo and Dolly – you keep saying that.'

'We could help you!' Dolly said. 'We've got enough to—'

'No need for that,' Gladys said, sitting up proudly. Melly saw her mother frown. Gladys was such a stubborn old soul. 'We make enough to rent for ourselves, ta.'

Dolly looked rather hurt, Melly thought.

Once Dolly had gone, Rachel turned eagerly to Gladys. 'Can we, Auntie? I know you never would've moved if they were staying. But it's all going to be different now. The yard won't be the same with them gone, will it?'

Gladys put her teacup to her lips. She didn't answer.

Over the next few weeks, Dolly and Mo were blown about in all directions.

'Every time I see them they're going somewhere different,' Gladys complained. Rachel could tell she was hurt to the core. Even though you could hardly blame them – who wouldn't want a nicer house if you could get one? – none of their plans seemed to take into consideration anyone else around them. How could they?

They mainly saw Dolly who would come round and give them the latest bulletin about places the estate agent suggested they might live. One day it was, 'He says there's this nice house for sale in Four Oaks and we could afford it!' The next it might be, 'We could go to Sutton Coldfield. Or right out into one of the villages somewhere. But then there's a house for sale in Bromsgrove that he says would suit us down to the ground . . .'

'I'm sure the commission'll suit him down to the ground an' all,' Gladys said.

'Oh, Glad,' Dolly begged. 'Don't be like that. We don't know what to do.'

'Well, don't look at me,' Gladys retorted. 'I'm not the one to tell you, am I? Why don't you just let me know when you've decided?' On that occasion she ended the conversation by picking up a pail and walking out of the house.

'Oh, dear,' Dolly said to Rachel, tears filling her eyes. 'I don't know what to do for the best, I really don't.'

Twenty-Three

May 1955

Rachel felt she was living two separate lives that hardly connected. As the spring months passed, she went through the motions of everything at home, the housework, care of Tommy and the others, while most of her mind was completely elsewhere.

After his confrontation with Gladys, Danny had not said another word about Australia and Rachel had not raised it. He was quiet, his mood flat. She had no idea what he was thinking and she realized they were avoiding each other. This was at least half her fault.

She saw Michael Livingstone every week. She told the family she was working each Thursday morning as a volunteer in the office at school. Tommy was in class and could not know whether she was in there or not. Instead, she would travel over with him in his taxi, kiss him goodbye just inside Carlson House and watch as one of the assistants wheeled him away to his classroom, before slipping out and round the corner to Michael's house.

On Thursday mornings, Ellen was at school as well. The last time Rachel had visited, the two of them had sat talking as usual, in the front room, side by side on the chairs. As time went by, though, Rachel became aware of a change of mood between them. Usually they chatted easily, but now there were silences and the atmosphere became intense. Michael leaned forward and put his cup down. As he sat back, he turned to her, his eyes seeking hers, and reached for her hand which was resting in her lap. His own hand felt large and warm and she did not pull away as she knew she should have done. They sat in a loaded, awkward silence for a couple of moments. She could feel a slight tremor coming from him and she felt shaken herself. She did not meet his eye, not then. She looked down at the clasped hands, her heart going like mad, and she could still feel his hungry gaze on her. Full of panic she had said she had to go home and they stood up, released their hands and tried to talk normally as if nothing had happened.

This time, as she sat beside Tommy in the car, she tried sternly to bring the two sides of her life together. She was expecting Danny's child! She had not mentioned this to Michael. Nothing was showing yet. Michael knew now that she was married, but it was as if their time together was separate from all other life and reality. It was a kind of dream that did not feel as if it could have any consequences in her real life. In this dream they could kid themselves for a little while. She kept telling herself that nothing was going on, nothing had happened except Michael grasping her hand, once, for those few moments. Was that so bad?

But she knew really. Now every time she saw him, the air would be charged between them. Even before he took her hand, she had sometimes seen it in his eyes, the way suddenly, while they were talking like friends, about their children or their daily lives, he would go quiet and give her a brief, intense look of longing. It would make her blush and look away. But sometimes she looked back into his eyes and felt a prickling in her skin. It could not go on. She knew where it was leading, this feeling. It was wrong. She was nearly four months gone with the baby and soon it would begin to show. That was her life. That was what was real . . .

But in the meantime there was this interval of excitement, of this secret bliss, of being listened to, looked at like that, wanted . . . As the car carried them along, she was on the point of lapsing into another daydream.

'Mom,' Tommy said. Then louder, 'MOM!'

'Shh, Tommy – what?' She knew she sounded irritable. Her nerves were at screaming pitch. She ticked herself off. Her boy was beside her, Tommy who needed her – and all she could think of was her . . . Her what? What should she call Michael? Words failed her.

'Miss – said I'm – very – good at – typing.'

She took a deep breath, praying for patience as Tommy reached for the words.

'I know,' she said. 'That's ever so good, Tommy. You know, Miss said to me the other day that you're one of the boys she thinks might be able to get a job somewhere one day. That's good, isn't it?'

Tommy's eyes watched her face. 'A – job?'

'Yes – in a firm or something. You're good with figures, and if you can type . . .'

'Did she – say – that?' He looked worried and pleased at once. Such a thought had never crossed his mind before, she realized, feeling tender towards him. He had written himself off.

She squeezed his hand. 'She did, love.'

And all the time she was talking to him her heart was beating hard and she was thinking, soon, in half an hour, I'll be with him . . . But she had to tell Michael today, had to. It had to stop – her being there, the way they looked at each other and where it might lead. She had to prick the bubble of this dream. She was sorry, but . . . Or if not today, very soon, perhaps one more week or two . . . She felt as if her life was whirling away from her, out of control.

Last night, in the privacy of the attic, Danny had finally said to her, 'I feel as if you're just not here most of the time, Rach.' He looked really hurt. 'What's going on?'

'I've told you,' she said. She could hear the hardness in her voice. When had she ever spoken to Danny like this before? Just once – when he came home, after disappearing after the war, when she was the one who was hurt and bereft. She thought he had settled since then, that everything about their life was solid. But now it felt as if he wanted to leave her all over again and the thought of it sat between them like a mountain.

'I don't want to go to Australia. I don't want you to go.' Tears came into her voice. 'You're wrong to try and make me, Danny. It's cruel of you to try and force me.'

A long silence followed.

'I don't want to force you,' he said. 'I just want you to come with me.'

She turned over and refused to say any more.

Walking to Michael's house, she watched her feet, in her well-polished navy shoes with neat heels, taking one step after another, as if they were someone else's. She always felt as if she was in another world over here.

The whole city was still in recovery after the bombardment of the war and years of neglect. Harborne was grimy and shabby like everywhere else. But even so, it was a much neater, nicer place than where they lived. There were more trees and houses and far fewer factories. She ached to be somewhere like this, instead of the cramped, industrial streets of Aston, their scrubby bomb pecks and squalid yards of houses. In her mind there played a fantasy: what if she was to stay here, with Michael? Just disappear and never go back?

Her mind filled with memories of him holding her hand, of his eyes on hers and the shock of desire his looking at her sent through her body. As she walked towards his door, her limbs felt weak. She knew she could barely trust herself, as if she had no will to stop events and was being swept along.

The door was dusty black with its dull brass knocker. There was no woman in the house to polish such things and Michael did not make time for it or even notice.

I am outside, she thought. In a minute I'll be inside and what will happen will happen . . .

She raised her hand and knocked. The door opened seconds later. She knew he would be waiting.

'Rachel,' he said, trying to sound ordinary and calm. But in his voice she could hear a catch of something that was anything but calm. 'Come in.'

In the hall they were too close for a moment so she stepped away. Things had come to a pitch between them over these weeks of talking, of sitting together in a small room, of eyes meeting. Neither of them could seem to help themselves. And now, more than ever, there was an atmosphere of things unspoken, of feelings tangible in the air.

'Nice to see you,' Michael said, in his polite way. 'Cup of coffee? Tea?'

'I'll have tea – thanks.'

Michael took her coat and they went into the back room. Following him, she was aware of every line of him, the slender body moving within his clothing, the way his hair sat above his collar at the back.

'Ellen all right?' she asked.

'Yes, she's doing well. Getting over that cold. She's a very patient girl, really. Always has been.'

Patient like her father, Rachel thought, standing in the kitchen. She had a feeling still that she was in the dream again, watching Michael fill the kettle. A tap indoors, water there whenever you wanted it! She burned with longing for a new life, for everything to be different. He put the kettle on the stove and turned, before lighting the gas.

Their eyes met. Rachel felt a plunge of acknowledgement inside her. The way he was drinking her in: surely there was no mistaking it, the look in his eyes? He opened his mouth, as if about to say something, and then closed it again. A moment later, he managed to speak.

'I –' he looked down in confusion – 'I try not to think about how things really are . . . D'you know –' he looked up at her again, a desperate expression on his face – 'what I mean?'

Slowly, she nodded, not looking away. She knew it was wrong, she was wrong. She ought to walk out of this kitchen, away from this man with his sad, longing eyes, and never come back here again. But she could feel the force of the need in him that matched the need within her.

The second he stepped towards her, she knew there was no stopping it. They had both waited. They were both already so primed that as soon as they stepped into each other's arms they were lost. She felt his arms around her, smelt him, a mixture of soap and tobacco, felt the force of him against her and they kissed with hungry urgency.

Her mind was caught up in him, the taste of him, the feel of his back under the white shirt, of the heat and press of their bodies and the way desire built on itself, each needing more because of the need in the other. But at the same time, there was the strangeness of it mixed with desire, the realistic little thought creeping into her mind – I have never kissed any other man except Danny – until now. And now, what does this make me?

Michael drew back and his tawny eyes looked into hers. 'Please,' he murmured. 'Come upstairs with me, will you? I know I shouldn't even ask. But I just ache for you – all the time. I can't seem to think about anything else.'

She took his hand, walking slightly behind him as they climbed the narrow stairs. The dream continued. Who was this woman, following a man upstairs who was not her husband, not Danny? With every step she thought, I shouldn't be here, I should stop, say no, turn round . . . But she was caught up in Michael, filled with desire to see him naked, for him to see her, for them to discover each other . . . The sense of daze continued as they reached the top of the stairs and she was looking through the door of a bedroom: a chair under the window with a black jersey folded and hung over the back, a cupboard, at a wide, marital bed with a pale green coverlet . . .

'No!' She stalled at the door. 'Oh, God, Michael, no! I can't. I'm sorry . . .' She gabbled at him. 'I can't go on like this! Look – I've got to go home.' She pulled away and turned to go down the stairs again. 'Just – I don't know – forget all about me. I don't want to lead you on. I just can't . . .' She was close to tears.

'Rachel – wait.' He took hold of her forearm while she was on the top step, before she could retreat down the stairs. 'Look – it's all right. I'm sorry.' He sounded miserable, but not angry.

He looked down into her eyes. Already she knew her gaze was clouded with shame and she could see the same in his face as well. She had pricked the bubble of the dream. He kissed her cheek gently.

'I'm sorry,' he said again. 'Oh, God . . .' He sounded utterly wretched. 'What a way to behave.'

'No,' she said gently. 'It's not your fault – it's just both of us. It's how things are.'

Now that they had pulled back from the moments of acute desire, he felt strange to her again, as if she had been through something and had now passed out the other side. Michael's body was alien to her. They did not belong. He was a nice man but he was not her man, however much she liked him. Danny was her man, had always been.

He had let go of her. They were not touching now. She stepped up to stand beside him, on the tiny landing at the top of the stairs. 'Look,' she said. 'I must go. We mustn't—'

'No!' he agreed. 'We absolutely mustn't. God, you're a married woman . . .' This was the first time they had ever acknowledged this openly.

'I'm so sorry,' he said. He looked down, embarrassed. 'I just miss it – I miss being married.'

'It wasn't just your fault,' Rachel said. 'It was mine as well. And we mustn't do it again. I can't keep coming round here – not when Ellen's not here, or it'll just keep happening, won't it? And I should be at home really, looking after Ricky. But Michael –' she leaned to him and kissed his cheek – 'you're a nice man. Please let's be friends.'

'The problem is –' he looked down at the floor in a troubled way – 'I'm not sure if I can now. It's ridiculous, I know. But every time I see you I'll just want . . . This – and more. Maybe it's because I'm a man. We're just a bit, I don't know, primitive like that.' He looked back at her again and his dark eyes were sad. 'It's not that I don't want to see you, it really isn't. It might just be better . . . Well, not for a good while, anyway.'

Rachel nodded. However much she understood, this felt hurtful, as if she was being rejected. Her eyes filled with tears and she wiped them impatiently away. The dissolving of the dream had left an emptiness behind.

'All right,' she said. Her tone was flat, she couldn't help it.

'I'm sorry,' he said again.

'You're right.' She began to go down the stairs and he followed. 'I know you are.' She looked over her shoulder. 'I know we've been wrong, but I'll miss talking to you, Michael.'

She felt him touch her shoulder briefly, in acknowledgment.

They did not kiss goodbye. Walking back along the street to the bus stop, Rachel looked down at her feet again. Everything felt different now, the street quiet and in some way sad. Things were back to normal, with no dream, and she had to face it exactly as it was. Danny was her husband and she his wife. She had to go home to him and bring him home to her.

'Danny.'

She lay in bed and he stood and looked down at her. Even in the poor light of the candle she thought he seemed wary of her, as if wondering whether she was going to have a go at him.

'Let's . . . You know.'

'Oh?' His voice was bitter. 'Want me now, do yer?'

She had lain turned away from him so many nights,

refusing even to speak to him, angry with him. She had dreamt of Michael, of lying in his arms.

She held her hand out. 'I want us to be . . . To be *us*. The way we should be.'

There was a long silence. In a husky voice, he said, 'So – you won't come with me?'

She felt anger flare in her again but she swallowed it down. She felt sorry for not wanting something he wanted so badly.

'I just can't. I'm sorry.'

He sank down on the bed with a sharp sigh. 'I want . . .' He trailed off. 'Something . . .' He made a frustrated sound and slapped his thighs. 'I can't say it. I just want more, that's all. More life – outside of here.'

She laid a hand on his back, on his familiar body and it felt right, felt like home.

'I want more too. Just not the other side of the world. Why do we have to go so far? You might hate it and then what? We're not that poor, Danny, not like some people. Auntie could have moved out of here to a better house ages ago, but she stayed because of Mo and Dolly. But now . . .'

Danny turned his head. 'Everything's changing.' She wasn't sure if he sounded pleased about this.

'Don't be angry, Danny.'

After another silence, he said, 'You're my missis.'

'Yes,' she said.

He turned and knelt on the bed, still in all his clothes, looking down at her and she looked back.

'Don't leave me,' he said softly.

'I won't, Danny.' She was astonished. What had he sensed in these weeks to make him say something so deeply vulnerable, to acknowledge this fear that he would never normally admit to? 'Why would I leave you?' She

213

tried to keep things light. 'Where d'you think I'm going to go, eh? I thought you were the one who was going to leave me.'

'No.' He lowered his head for a moment, then looked up at her again. 'No. We'll have to think of summat else, won't we?'

Twenty-Four

Late July 1955

A postcard arrived one morning for Rachel.

> Come over and see me as soon as you can. I need to talk to you about Cissy,
>   Mother

Rachel showed it to Gladys.

'Got your marching orders then,' Gladys said, after reading it.

'Well, she could get herself over here if she wants to see me that badly,' Rachel grumbled. Guiltily, though, she realized she hadn't seen her mother for weeks. She'd been too busy, too caught up with Michael and everything else. Peggy didn't even know she had another baby on the way.

Gladys frowned. 'What's up with Cissy?'

'How should I know? She hardly ever darkens our doors these days.'

But they were all very fond of Cissy, even if she was exasperating. Rachel wondered what was wrong. Wouldn't Cissy have come to her, her big sister, if she had a problem? When I get a minute, she thought, I s'pose I'll have to traipse all the way over there and see what's going on.

Feeling annoyed with her mother once again, she went

215

out into the yard to fill a bowl of water for washing clothes. It was overcast but warm. The children who were too young for school were outside, Ricky and a couple of other little lads poking about with a ramshackle go-kart at the other end of the yard.

As she went to the tap, Rachel found Dolly, leaning against the wall in a patch of sunlight, smoking a cigarette. Seeing Rachel, she pushed herself off from the wall, blowing smoke back over one shoulder.

'All right, Rach?'

'Yeah – ta. I hope the cowing water's on today.' She put the bowl on the ground. A miserable trickle emerged from the tap. 'Huh. Better than nothing.'

'Getting on for six months now, is it?' Dolly eyed her front which was now taking on an unmistakeable shape. 'Keeping all right?'

'Yeah,' Rachel said grumpily. From the day she left Michael, she had not been back to his house and he must have steered clear of the school because she had not set eyes on him. She was happy, knowing things were better with Danny, that she had done the right thing in the end. But she missed Michael. She missed the excitement of going over there under false pretences, however bad that was, missed the desire she saw in his eyes. And she missed his friendship.

In all the other kerfuffle going on in the yard, and because she was expecting now, no one had even commented on her not going out on Thursdays any more. And no one would ever have guessed why she was in a disgruntled mood. Her chest ached with sadness and she felt she was in mourning, no matter how much she told herself to buck up and stop being so silly.

'Oh, it's not all bad, bab,' Dolly said, thinking she was just down about the baby. 'I feel empty-handed now my

Donna's gone to school. You want to make the most of it.'

'Yes. I s'pose.' Rachel made an effort not to be so bad-tempered and looked at Dolly properly. 'Ooh, you look nice! Isn't that a bit posh for around the house, though?'

Dolly had her hair up in a scarf and a pinner on, but under it, Rachel could see the skirt of one of her new dresses. Dolly, with money to spend, had been splashing out. All the family had new clothes.

Dolly smiled, pulling up the apron to show a full skirt of scarlet material covered in big white polka dots. She had on a smart pair of white high-heeled shoes.

'It's only cotton,' she said. 'But yes – I s'pose I should've left it off 'til later.' She sighed. 'It's nice, buying a few things you haven't made yourself – I can't pretend it ain't. But none of it'll bring my Wally back. If I could choose . . .'

The gaggle of little boys came tearing past just then, two of them dragging the go-kart.

'Eh – d'yer wanna knuckle san'wich?' the oldest of them bawled at one of the others.

'Oi!' Dolly berated him. 'Watch it, you – none of that! What's that Smith lad doing here anyway?' she added to Rachel. 'He ought to be at school.' The lad was from the neighbouring yard.

'Probably "off sick" again,' Rachel said. 'She can't be bothered to make 'em go. Ricky!' she shrieked after her youngest. 'You stay in the yard where I can see you!'

'Oh, *Mom*!' Ricky yelled. He was immediately full of a four-year-old's boiling frustration. 'I wanna go out there. We ain't doing nothing. We was next door but Mrs Smith told us to gerrout – 'er said 'er'd tan our arses if we—'

'*Ricky –*' Rachel advanced on him, hands on her hips – 'I don't give a monkey's what Mrs Smith said. You *stay in here*. The other's'll be back in a minute anyway – look, they've left the kart behind.'

Ricky slumped to the ground with an air of misunderstood tragedy and sat with his shoulders hunched, legs crossed. Rachel walked back to Dolly who was turning the tap off for her.

'Glad all right?' Dolly asked, trying to sound casual.

'Think so.' Rachel looked at Dolly. Dolly had been Gladys's friend for years on end and Rachel had known Dolly and her direct kindness too long herself to hide anything from her. 'I s'pose she doesn't want you to go. Or anything to change.'

Dolly sighed, looking down at her feet, the cigarette held up close to her face.

'D'you know – I don't know if I'm glad any of this has happened, even if I have got a new frock or two out of it. My Mo's in a right state. He keeps saying to me, "Dolly – should we just give it all away and have done with it? Go back to how we were?" He's not sleeping, Rach. It'd be all right if we could just decide. We want to get out of here – live somewhere better. Look at this place – who wouldn't? The writing's on the wall anyway – they'll come and knock the lot down soon. And there's the boys to consider.' She took a drag on her cigarette.

Rachel realized Dolly badly needed a listening ear, had been waiting out there to unload her worries on someone.

'Reggie – maybe he could find some different work, or do summat else. And our Jonny – he wants an education when he gets back from the army. We can let him have it now.' She shook her head and her eyes filled. 'I don't want to leave Glad behind – we've always been neighbours. We'll still be friends. But it's so difficult to make up our minds what we want. We've never *had* to make up our minds before, not like this.'

'You've not decided then?'

'I have these dreams,' Dolly said, with a wistful smile, 'of somewhere out in the country with fields round us and chickens and everything lovely, all trees and flowers. Clean, with space to move. The air not stinking of chemicals and swarf and smoke. And you could all come out and see us. But –' she flicked ash on to the ground – 'I can't believe in it, not really. I've been round here my whole life.' She looked about her. 'These old walls.'

Rachel smiled. 'But that sounds lovely, Dolly. Just cos you've always been here doesn't mean you can't change. I want to get out of here, Dolly, I really do. Somewhere better, with a bathroom, even a garden for the kids – think how that'd be.' She thought of her mother again. Perhaps she was more like Peggy than she realized.

'Well – you tell 'em!' Dolly squeezed her arm. 'Gladys and Danny make enough money – you don't have to stay here.' Her face fell for a moment. 'Only it'll be hard to leave. It's what we're used to.'

Within a few days, Mo and Dolly had made up their minds. They came round to show everyone a picture of the house they had decided to buy. Rachel watched Gladys's face as they made the announcement and saw her clenching her jaw as if to steel herself.

Mo did the talking. He looked bashful, flustered, unused to all this.

'They offered us all sorts – all over the place so we hardly knew if we was coming or going. I started to feel as if my head was gonna spin off!' He looked around with his boyish blue eyes. 'I've never had much choice over anything before, 'cept for marrying Doll here and that was – well, that was easy.'

Dolly blushed and raised her cup at him. 'Oh, Mo!'

'You'd think it'd be nice to be able to have anything you want,' Mo said, still sounding bewildered, 'but when it comes down to it . . . Any road, we've tried not to act hasty, like, but when we saw this place –' he tapped the sheet of paper he was holding to his chest – 'I said to Doll, how about this, wench? It's a palace of a place but it's still in Brum. When it comes down to it, we're Brummies – I don't know how we'd get on out there in the sticks miles from anywhere.'

'Well, come on then – let's see it,' Danny said, standing ready to look over Mo's shoulder.

'Where is it?' Rachel asked.

'Moseley,' Dolly said, unable to keep it to herself any longer. 'And it's ever so grand!'

'It's only a stone's throw from the main road as well, Glad,' Dolly put in.

'Moseley?' Rachel said. 'That's on the number fifty, isn't it?'

Mo solemnly laid on the table a sheet of paper with a grainy photograph on it of what looked to all of them an absolutely enormous house. Everyone gasped and admired.

'There's a little park at the bottom of the garden, with a lake!' Dolly said, her face lit up with excitement. 'It's . . . Oh, it's . . . Well, it's all pretty scruffy at the moment because an old couple have had it, but . . .'

'You having it – for definite?' Gladys asked. She was trying to sound pleased but not doing very well at it. Mo and Dolly were like a big liner, steaming on past her, leaving her in a little rowing boat.

'We agreed today,' Mo said. He looked at Dolly. 'We still can't really believe it – can we, Doll?'

'It's got seven bedrooms!' Dolly said. 'Can you imagine? We could have our grandchildren live with us!'

Gladys was very quiet.

'It sounds lovely, Dolly,' Rachel said, trying to make up for Gladys. 'We'll all come and see you.'

Twenty-Five

August 1955

A van drew up to the kerb in Alma Street and braked at the end of their entry. Mo had arranged for it to come as soon as he finished work on Friday afternoon.

It was a muggy day with the close, blanketing heat which bodes a storm. Melly's temples were throbbing and Gladys was sitting with Tommy at the table indoors, a wet cloth pressed to her forehead, her eyes closed. It was disturbing to see Auntie looking so lost and sad.

Danny was helping Mo and some of his pals carry things from the house and out along the entry: the television and the few worthwhile pieces of furniture the Morrisons possessed and wanted to take with them. Kev and Ricky kept running up and down getting in everyone's way and being yelled at.

Melly watched from the doorway, close to tears at seeing the house they had all known so well for so long being emptied. She had to keep swallowing the lump in her throat. The Morrisons were going – all of them. Including Reggie.

It was a torment to her whenever she saw him. She had no idea what to say to him and was haunted by painful, guilty feelings. None of what had happened was her fault in any way, she knew, yet the feelings persisted.

Reggie's walking was improving, supported by a stick

now, not the crutch. It seemed he would always have a limp. He had gone back to work at GEC and as far as anyone could see he was getting on with his life. But Dolly would confide that he was very low in himself. Electric Avenue was a painful reminder of Wally, because the pair of them had worked there together before.

Melly ached for him, but he showed no sign of wanting to talk, either to her or to anyone else. All his pain was locked inside him and Dolly was desperately worried. Melly was upset that the Morrisons were leaving. It felt like the end of things being normal and as she had always known them. They would see them again, of course, but not often. It wasn't going to be the same at all. But not seeing Reggie was going to be an enormous relief. It would spare her the helpless torment of wanting to talk to him and not being able to, of feeling that things were ragged and unfinished.

'Oh, Glad –' Dolly came fluttering into their house, a rag in her hand with which she was wiping her nose and eyes – 'I don't know if I'm coming or going today.'

'Going?' Gladys suggested caustically. She hauled herself to her feet and without looking at Dolly, started sorting through a pile of clothes.

Her bitterness was lost on Dolly. 'I've just said goodbye to Lil and she was so nice and kind – oh, I do feel for her, stuck there all the time with Stanley, the way he is. If only they could get out of here too. You'll go and see them, won't you, bab?' She looked at Melly. Melly nodded, tears in her own eyes. 'You're such a good girl, going in to visit the way you do. Course, *that* one –' she jerked her head towards number two and Ethel Jackman – 'was as tart as ever.'

'Oh, ar?' Gladys said, peering at a rent in the lace

collar of a blouse. 'Well, that one'd be miserable if she was invited in at the Pearly Gates.'

Melly watched Auntie as she took up a long navy coat to fold. She felt like ticking her off but didn't dare. Auntie was hurt, Melly knew. But she shouldn't be angry with Dolly, who was her best friend and was still suffering even though life had delivered a slice of luck.

There had been tearful scenes only last week when Jonny had finally been called up for National Service. Dolly sobbed as she hugged him goodbye. They all knew that the army was the last thing quiet, scholarly Jonny wanted to be doing now. He wanted his books and to see if he could win a place at the university. But that would all have to wait now that another of those brown envelopes had arrived and he had to set off for Catterick for training.

'Make us a cuppa tea, Melly, will you?' Dolly asked. She knew better than to ask Gladys at this moment. 'There's a good'un,' she said as Melly went to the stove. 'I want to sit here 'til we have to go.'

Rachel came in then, from the yard, draped in washing, a few clothes pegs in her hand.

'All right, Dolly? You nearly packed up?' she said. Melly saw her mother take in that she was making tea, so she sat down as well, next to Tommy.

Melly stood listening, leaning against the stove and drinking in these moments. Last moments. Tears prickled in her eyes. Gladys and Mom and Dolly sitting here, canting as they called it, had gone on all her life. Now, something that had gone on every day seemed so precious.

It's ending, she thought, a hand on the kettle's handle, feeling its vibrations. This is how it feels when things end . . .

'You'll come and see us, won't you?' Dolly said, her

nerves making her chatter and perhaps not wanting to leave any space for Gladys to have a go at her. 'It's going to be awful without all of you – and you must come too, Tommy, eh?' She smiled at him. 'Mo's going to learn to drive as soon as he gets a minute. He wants to carry on at Norton's, see. Drive across town. And he was worried about leaving the Salutation – he'll be back every other day, I should think!!'

They all smiled. The Salutation along the street was Mo's favourite watering hole for all eternity.

'He sat up in bed the other night – like that Frankenstein's monster – and he said, "Dolly – I'm not gonna be able to go to the Salutation!"'

They all laughed at the thought of pink-faced Mo doing a Boris Karloff.

'So I said to him, "Don't be daft – course you will. You can go over. Your pals'll still be there." That cheered him up. He thought the world had ended for a moment there! But –' her voice became anxious – 'I'll be able to pop over to you, won't I? And you've got to come and see us. It won't feel like home without all your mugs about.'

'What about Reggie?' Melly dared to ask as she poured them their tea. 'What's he going to do? I mean –' she gabbled – 'it'll be hard for him on the bus, with his leg and everything.'

Dolly turned to her and gave a tender smile. Melly blushed. She imagined they didn't know she had been soft on Reggie. They hadn't guessed, surely?

'He's going to find summat else – once we're over there. And Fred can get a job . . .' Fred had just finished school. She shook her head. 'It feels ever so odd not having to worry about every penny. But I'm frightened of

225

it all running out. Mo's being ever so careful – saving for when we need it and that.'

There was a silence as the three older women sat together, as they had so many times before, Dolly smoking. She had offered Rachel a cigarette, but she shook her head. Melly, watching them, felt her throat ache with coming tears.

'Oh, I'm gonna miss you all!' Dolly burst out again, with a sob.

Soon all the women were crying and trying to laugh at themselves at the same time. Seeing them all, Melly couldn't help letting her own tears flow as well.

'It's not going to be the same without you at all, Dolly!' Rachel sobbed. Melly was surprised by how much Mom cried. Once she'd started she couldn't seem to stop.

Gladys wiped her eyes, seeming not to trust herself to speak. A second later they noticed that the doorway had gone dark. Mo stood, leaning against the door frame, Danny just behind him.

'Oh, good God,' Mo said, 'what's this – the Wailing Wall?' His eyes seeking out his wife, he added more gently, trying to hide his own emotion, 'We're all loaded up, Doll – time to go.'

Everyone trooped moistly out to the street. Melly pushed Tommy's chair along the entry, so that they could all stand outside amid a gathering crowd of neighbours and general nosey parkers, to wave off a family who were much loved in the area.

Dolly hugged everyone, her dark eyes especially seeking out Gladys, to look intently at her.

226

'You're my best pal,' she said. 'Always have been. Get yourself over to ours soon, won't you?'

Gladys nodded, her eyes swimming. She seemed unable to speak. Donna, who was nine now, clung to her mother, sobbing.

Melly stood behind Tommy's chair as Mo, Dolly and Donna climbed into the front of the van. Reggie came limping out, with Freddie. They looked round at the crowd, shy and awkward. Melly's heart bucked at the sight of Reggie, his fair hair, his thin, strained-looking face.

He ran his eyes over the crowd and gave an awkward wave to everyone. She knew he was not looking for her, that he never had been. She stood quietly, saying goodbye to him without words. She must close the door for good on those little-girl dreams, she thought, though the tears started in her eyes again. The boys climbed into the back, closed the doors and Reggie was gone from sight.

The van started up loudly and as the driver pulled away, everyone waved and shouted and whistled.

'Bye, mate – bye for now!'

'Get yerself back to the Salutation, Mo – we'll keep yer seat warm!'

'Good luck – don't do anything we wouldn't do!'

'Ta-ra-a-bit!'

Tommy raised his good arm and Melly waved with the rest of them. 'Bye, Reggie,' she mouthed, silently. There was a strange unreal feeling to the afternoon, to them all standing there on the pavement and watching Mo and Dolly and their few things in the old green van disappear along the street, Dolly waving her little rag out of the window until they had disappeared into Summer Lane.

*

227

They were slow to disperse. The little knot of people stood in the mellow afternoon, men with sleeves rolled up, women in summer frocks. They were all still part of the occasion and they lingered there, not wanting to break it up.

Melly was at the edge of it, staring dreamily along the street, half thinking of Reggie, with a lightness now that he had gone, half hearing the conversations going on behind her. A breeze played on the hairs of her arms. She saw people come and go into the huckster's shop along the street. A bus pulled up, let people out, roared up to them and passed, coughing fumes.

Someone among the little group who had been on the bus was striding fast along the street. It was a woman in a dark dress, a white bit of lacy stuff about the neck, an urgent but disdainful air about her. It took Melly a few seconds to see that the woman was familiar as she got closer and her features came into focus.

'Mom.' She turned, looking for Rachel. 'Mom!'

Rachel half turned, not wanting to interrupt her talk with Lil who was out there with them.

'*Mom!* It's Nanna!'

That got her mom's attention all right. She came over quickly. By now Peggy had almost reached them.

'Mother?' Rachel hurried towards her and Melly followed. 'What on earth are you doing here?'

Peggy stopped. She was breathing heavily and Melly could see a sheen of perspiration on her forehead, under the thatch of frizzy hair. She looked very agitated.

'I asked you to come and see me and did you bother?' she demanded in a low, furious voice. 'I knew there was something brewing with that girl. You might've been able to knock some sense into her – and now it's too late.'

'Well, I only got your card a few days ago,' Rachel said. 'I haven't had time. What's the—?'

'The *matter*,' Peggy snapped, 'is your sister. Cissy. Is she here with you?'

Bewildered, Rachel shook her head. 'I haven't seen her.'

'Oh!' Peggy cried, not caring now if anyone else noticed. 'I knew it! I've looked everywhere for her – there are things missing from her room. I knew she was planning something. Cissy's gone missing – she's run away!'

Twenty-Six

They had no alternative but to ask Peggy in. Things must be bad, Rachel thought, for our mom to grace the doors of a yard house in Aston. On any other such occasion she would have had a smell under her nose but this time she was preoccupied. She looked round her in spite of herself, out of curiosity. Peggy had never set foot in Gladys's house before, though not because she had not been invited.

Rachel could see that Gladys was still in a state after watching Dolly depart so she took charge.

'Sit down, Mom,' she invited. It felt very odd seeing her mother in this house in her stiff navy frock.

'What the hell's going on?' Danny whispered as she went to the stove. 'What's she doing here?'

'It's Cissy,' Rachel told him, not bothering to lower her voice. 'She's run off – or Mom thinks so anyway. She's most likely with that Teddy bloke she never stops going on about.'

Peggy's head shot round. 'Who's Teddy? She's never breathed a word about him at home.'

'She talked enough about him round here.' Rachel couldn't be bothered with sparing her mother's feelings. Peggy had never spared hers. 'Some bloke with a fast car. She's been knocking about with him for a few months.'

Peggy's mouth opened and closed. At last she managed

to say, 'And you let this go on? You didn't think to say anything to me?'

Thinking about it now, Rachel realized she probably should have asked Cissy more, tried to find out about Teddy, asked his age. She had never thought it was anything serious and she had no idea how old Teddy was. But he seemed to think it worth coming all the way from Coventry for. They just seemed to go gadding out to the pictures. She had also rather enjoyed the idea of Cissy pulling the wool over their mother's eyes, the way she had done herself at Cissy's age.

She turned to fiddle with the lid of the kettle. 'I didn't think it was anything.' Rachel looked back at Peggy. Everyone else, Danny and Gladys, Tommy and the others gathered round the room, was listening. Ricky looked astonished by the appearance of this grandmother of his who he hardly ever saw. 'Didn't she come home from work then? She can't have got far in that time, can she?'

'She never came home *yesterday*,' Peggy said.

Her words fell on the room. Rachel felt a curl of real dismay inside her then.

'Yesterday?' Gladys said. 'All night, you mean?'

'I thought she'd come over here.' Peggy sounded furious, as if it was all their fault that Cissy was gone. But she needed their support. 'And then I had a look in her room and . . . There were things missing – clothes.' Her face creased then, the real worry showing through. 'Where can she be? I don't know what to do.'

'I suppose it depends,' Danny said, 'how long you want to leave it before you go to the police.'

'*Police?*' Peggy stared at him in horror.

'Well, if no one knows where she is,' Danny pointed out.

231

'Come on, Peggy.' Gladys got to her feet. 'We'll go to the nick in Victoria Road – I'll show you the way.'

There was nothing they could do except wait and worry. After going, like a lamb, to Victoria Road with Gladys, Peggy went home to Hay Mills. For all she knew Cissy might turn up there at any time. The police had agreed to start making inquiries.

'The little minx,' Rachel said to Danny when they finally got to bed. She was reeling with exhaustion but knew it was going to be very hard to sleep. In spite of her worries for Cissy, a giggle escaped her. 'Mom's face when Auntie said she'd march her down to the police station. I'll never forget it!'

Danny laughed as well, climbing into bed beside her. 'Bit of a comedown for old Peg, I must say. I thought she was going to blow a gasket!'

They both laughed, but after a few moments, Rachel's face became solemn. 'All the same, though – where the hell is she? Stupid girl.'

'If she doesn't turn up tonight, you'd better go over there,' Danny said.

'What – to Mom's?'

'Yeah. She's worried to death.'

Rachel turned to look at him, surprised by this consideration for his mother-in-law who had never had a moment's time for him.

'After all,' he said. 'That's her second daughter gone to the bad.'

'Danny!' She thumped him, playfully. It felt so much better that they were friends again. 'But you're right. Melly can stay with the boys. I'd better go and see the old girl.'

*

Cissy did not arrive back that night, nor the next. Rachel went across town to Hay Mills and spent Saturday with Peggy and Fred as they tried, distractedly, to keep up the running of the shop. Rachel was glad to help, cutting lengths of cloth and selling needles and zips. It was something to do.

Fred Horton, Cissy's father, his once gingery hair almost white, bumbled in and out of the shop, seeming stunned. Rachel felt sorry for him. She'd never warmed to Fred but he hadn't really ever done her any harm and he loved Cissy. It was Peggy who had the sharp tongue on her.

At dinner time, when Rachel was standing in the back kitchen, Peggy came in. Staring hard at Rachel, she said in a disgusted tone, 'You're not expecting again, are you?'

Rachel was getting on for seven months pregnant. It shows how often Mom bothers to look at me, she thought. Her mother's distaste made her feel defensive, almost proud.

'Yes,' she said, trying to sound glad. 'Due in October.'

'But that'll be *five* children!' Peggy said, as if this was a fact Rachel might have omitted to notice.

'Yes,' Rachel said, cutting a slice off the loaf without asking. She was starving and had to eat. 'That's right.'

Peggy went to switch the gas on under a saucepan. 'I should've thought you might ask if you want something to eat in my house.'

Rachel didn't reply. She had spread the bread with as much butter as she thought she could get away with and munched away on it.

Peggy was tutting. 'Breeding like rabbits . . . Never a thought for the morrow . . .'

Rachel watched her stiff unloving back with a sense of

233

detachment. If she had ever expected anything from her mother she had stopped doing so a long time ago.

Sunday was much more difficult. There was no shop to distract them. Rachel almost resorted to going to church to get out of the house, but she was too tired to make the effort in the end.

'Where can she be? My poor, silly girl? What are the police *doing*?' Peggy kept wailing. She hadn't been able to wail in the shop, though the evening before had seen a fair bit of it. On Sunday morning she sat in the upstairs sitting room and gave herself up to fretting.

While Rachel was very worried about Cissy herself, Peggy acted as if she was the only person ever to care. For the umpteenth time she demanded, 'Who is this man she's gone off with?'

No one could answer this, other than to repeat that his name was Teddy and he drove a red car.

'Teddy – oh, I can just imagine what he's like,' Peggy moaned. 'He'll be one of those *dreadful men* . . . We may never see her again! She's been sold into the white slave trade – ruined!'

'Don't, Peggy,' Fred said, sitting across from her, quietly anguished. He sagged in his chair, his hands never still on the arms. 'Don't say that. The police are looking for her. They'll find her – she'll be back.'

Rachel sat thinking longingly of home. She complained enough about the yard in Alma Street but now she was dying to get back there. I'll have to go back tonight, she thought. There were so many things to do and she didn't think she could deal with another day in the same house as her mother.

In the afternoon, unable to stand any more, she took

herself off for a walk round Yardley cemetery, enjoying the peace of it, the quiet companionship of the graves. Stopping to look across the tightly packed space, she breathed, 'Oh, Cissy, you silly girl – where are you?'

Her mind raced from thought to thought. One moment, she found that while she was worried about Cissy and wanted her to come home, she did not believe that anything terrible had happened to her, the way Peggy seemed to. She found a faith in her little sister's luck and good sense. Thinking of herself at the same age, running off with Danny, she understood Cissy and the desperate desire she must feel to get away from Peggy, to look for someone to love, who would show that they loved her.

The next moment, doubt and terrible imaginings filled her mind. Supposing Cissy had gone off with some brute who was doing awful things to her even now? What if she never came back? Now and again there were stories in the paper. Her stomach churned with nerves. If only she'd come over when she'd received Mom's card. Maybe she *could* have found out from Cissy if there was something going on.

When she walked back into the house, Peggy and Fred leapt to their feet at the sound of her feet on the stairs. When she saw them, both at the sitting-room door, frenzied with hope, her heart really went out to them. They were desperately worried and all they could do was wait.

'Oh!' Peggy burst into tears. 'We thought . . .'

'I'm sorry,' Rachel said, and she really felt it. I'm sorry for not being Cissy.

Somehow they got through the rest of the afternoon, each tick of the clock a loud marker of the seconds slipping away.

Twenty-Seven

Cissy sat on her bed, sobbing extravagantly. 'I'm not a silly girl and you're all wrong – about everything!'

Fred, relieved that his little girl was home in one piece, left the women to perform the interrogation and went to telephone the police and say that Cissy had returned safe.

Cissy, already in a storm of tears, had rushed up to her room. Rachel and Peggy followed.

'What's been going on? Where've you been, you dreadful girl? Who is this man? What's he done to you?'

Peggy's questions rained down on Cissy who had flung herself on the bed and hidden her face in the eiderdown, quivering with sobs. Rachel sat on the side of the bed. Peggy was having none of this. She seized Cissy's shoulder and shook her.

'You sit up, my girl, and tell me what's been going on. We've had the police out looking for you – the shame of it! All weekend we've been here, beside ourselves with worry. You *damn* well sit up and speak to me before I put you over my knee!'

The idea of manhandling Cissy's voluptuous frame was absurd, but Peggy was beyond reason.

'You've got to promise me never to go anywhere near this *dreadful* man again,' Peggy decreed.

Cissy shot up on the bed to defend herself.

'No! Teddy loves me and I love him and we want to get married.'

'Oh – *married*!' Peggy sneered. 'What – to a man who steals you away from your family without a word or a by-your-leave and takes heaven knows what liberties . . . We've never even met this person you've been sneaking off to see . . .'

'I only sneaked off because I knew you'd try and stop me,' Cissy retorted, her freckly face blotchy from crying. 'You don't want me to be happy – you only want me to do what you want.'

Though Rachel could see that Cissy was overwrought and she herself was still highly suspicious of this Teddy person, she could not disagree with Cissy here. She remembered when she had felt just the same. Being with her mother this weekend had brought it all back, Peggy's self-absorption, her unreasonableness.

Hands on hips, Peggy continued the interrogation. 'You're not even sixteen yet. *Marriage*.' She made a contemptuous gesture with her head. 'What nonsense!'

'I'm nearly sixteen!' Cissy argued, shifting to sit on the edge of the bed. 'And Rach was sixteen when she got married.'

'Yes, but that was only because . . .' A cloud of suspicion crept over Peggy's face. 'You're not . . .? Right, madam – you'd better tell me the truth, right now. What's been going on? Because if you're in the family way, I'll—'

'You'll what?' Cissy sneered. 'And no, I'm not, so there. But I love Teddy and he loves me and he's going to ask you, as soon as I'm sixteen. It's not long to wait when you love someone,' she added. Cissy, born the day war broke out, was fast approaching her sixteenth birthday.

'And we'll say no, your father and I,' Peggy declared. 'How old is this person, anyway?'

Cissy looked down, knowing what reaction she was

going to get. 'Teddy's thirty-four – but he's ever so young.'

'*Thirty-four!*' Peggy erupted. 'He's old enough to be your father.'

Rachel was shocked at this too. This Teddy person was four years older than she was!

'No, he's not,' Cissy argued. 'My father's old as the hills.'

'Well, he's old enough to know better. He's playing with you, girl – you're too young to see it but it's plain as the nose on your face. I bet now he's had his way with you you'll never see him again.'

'You're wrong, Mom,' Cissy said, sitting up straight, tear-stained but with a dignity that Rachel could only admire. 'Teddy says he wants to come and meet you both – and you too, Rach, if you can. He wants to do things properly.'

'Well, if that's what he wants he's got off to a very bad start,' Peggy said. 'Taking you off without a word, scheming and—'

'It was my idea,' Cissy said. 'Teddy thought . . . Well, I told him . . .' She blushed. 'He thought it was all right, that's all.'

Rachel managed to get a word in then. 'How old does Teddy think you are, Ciss?'

Cissy's blush grew deeper. She picked at a thread on the eiderdown. 'I might've told him I was seventeen . . . Sort of by accident. But only to begin with – he knows how old I really am now.'

'Oh, *Ciss*,' Rachel said.

'It's just, he came in – when I was at work—'

'He picked you off the counter at Woolworth's!' Peggy scoffed. 'Well, that doesn't say much for his taste, does it!'

'He said he spotted me and I was the most terrific girl he's ever seen. And the thing was, I liked him. He's sweet. I thought if I said I was fifteen straight away, he'd just give me up.'

Rachel put her head in her hands for a moment, and then looked at her sister. 'Ciss –'

Cissy looked up into her eyes, her own pleading for Rachel to be on her side.

'You're so young. I know I married Danny young. But it's not always for the best.' She glanced up at Peggy who looked as if she was getting worked up for another outburst. 'Look – if this Teddy really wants you, he'll wait a bit, won't he? Let him come round and meet Mom and Fred . . .'

'I want him to come round and meet them,' Cissy flamed with emotion again. Rachel was surprised by her determination. Cissy had always seemed flighty before. 'And you'll see he's not what you think. I will tell him and it won't make any difference. Teddy loves me. And when I'm sixteen –' she glowered at Peggy – 'I want *you* to say we can get married.'

'What's he like, then?'

Rachel found an eager audience when she returned home a week later from another visit to Hay Mills. Cissy's goings-on had been a distraction from the sad emptiness of the yard now that the Morrisons had left.

She had gone over for Sunday afternoon tea, to which, Cissy had announced, Teddy would be coming.

'Well . . .' She sat down at the table, enjoying the attention, all eyes fixed on her.

'Cissy's not getting married, is she?' Melly asked. Her

reaction had been one of complete bewilderment. Cissy was only a couple of years older than she was.

'We'll have to see,' Rachel said.

'Come on – spit it out,' Gladys urged her. 'What's the bloke like?'

Rachel had started out feeling highly suspicious of what this Teddy bloke was after. She had expected him to be sinister, to have cast a spell in some way on her little sister. She was looking for a villain from the pictures, with a thin moustache and an odd, cold manner. Why would a grown man choose someone who was barely more than a schoolgirl? The whole situation seemed suspicious. But she couldn't honestly say that he had seemed all that terrible when she met him.

'I don't know what I was expecting,' she said. 'He's all right, I suppose. He's called Teddy Meeks. He's got money – or his father has. Meeks's is in Coventry – car components – and he's done all right for himself. Teddy works in the business.'

He had said he worked in the offices. Something to do with the accounts. He had a reasonably intelligent look about him, Rachel thought.

'I saw the car – very swish. And he's all-right looking. Brown hair, nice enough face. Quite ordinary really. Good manners. Seems quite a gentle sort, nothing, you know, nasty. His teeth stick out a bit. He looks a bit like a squirrel – big cardigan. Looked as if his mom had knitted it. Only he hasn't got a mom – I remember he said she died when he was quite young.'

'A squirrel in a cardigan,' Danny said with a grin. 'Doesn't sound too much of a bounder.'

The kids all laughed, especially Kev. 'Has he got a tail?' he chortled.

'Sounds like love's young dream.' Gladys couldn't

help her lips turning up as well. 'Good job his name's not Cyril.'

'No,' Rachel laughed. It was good to let off steam. 'He's really all right, I think. I could see Mom and Fred trying to ask him leading questions and find out something they could get rid of him for. But he was quite relaxed and nice with them. They didn't even take him to task too much about the previous weekend – which they spent in Buxton, by the way – because he came along so serious about marrying Cissy. And he's mad about her, you can see.'

'Well, she is a looker,' Gladys said. 'But she's only fifteen.'

'I know.' Rachel shook her head. 'And he knows. He kept saying, "I know there's a bit of an age gap, but we don't seem to find that it matters." That was the thing – the only reason you could say that any of it was wrong was that he's twenty years older, nearly.'

'Doesn't seem natural,' Danny said.

They all agreed that it didn't seem natural, but even Peggy and Fred had not been able to find reasons just to turn Teddy Meeks away there and then.

'So've they asked him to wait?' Gladys said.

'Well, Cissy's mad to get married and he seems pretty keen as well. Mom and Fred didn't exactly say they could, but . . .'

They all looked at each other. No one wanted to say it in front of the children but Rachel was thinking, if Cissy was in fact expecting a baby . . .

'Time'll tell,' Gladys said. 'She might've changed her mind by Christmas.'

V

1956

Twenty-Eight

July 1956

Rachel walked along Harborne Park Road with Sandra asleep for once, in the pram. At the baby's feet, tucked into the pram, were Rachel's bits of shopping: a loaf, potatoes, bacon and salad.

She pushed the pram along slowly, gripping the handle hard to still the tremor in her hands.

I can't go home, she thought. Not yet.

Usually she still felt a tingle of excitement each time she went back to their new home in Harborne. The novelty of it all – seeing that miraculous 'For Rent' sign, Danny giving in at last, the move across town – would take a long time to wear off. At last she had got what she wanted! It all took getting used to. She felt on her best behaviour in Harborne. But still – it was a new start and she was excited by all of it, the extra space, the television in the front room, the kitchen with taps and a bathroom with a lavatory indoors!

But today was different.

She steered the pram into the park on Grove Lane, found a place away from anyone else and sank on to the grass, trying to still her breathing. Her heart was banging like mad, an ache spreading across her chest. She stared, unseeing, across the green swathe in front of her.

For the first time – amazing that it was the first time

now that she thought about it – since they had moved to Harborne, she had just seen Michael Livingstone. She came out of the bakery and there he was, across the street. He did not see her, she was certain. The reason he did not notice her was because he was not alone: he was walking arm in arm with a woman. The sight sent a jolt through her: the woman was dark-haired, pretty. Rachel had turned away immediately and hurried in the other direction.

Each school day now, either she or Danny pushed Tommy along the road in his wheelchair. The taxis were no longer needed. Rachel was not working at the school for the moment because of just having had Sandra. She missed it and now she was stuck in the house all the more. They took the same route to Carlson House each day, straight down to Victoria Road. She knew that other than that first time she met Michael, when he had taken a detour for a change, he had no reason to walk down there.

From the day she left his house, she had never seen Michael again. She had known she must cut off from him completely, otherwise she would go back and back, drawn in by his need and her own, and by the excitement of knowing that someone wanted her so badly.

For a time afterwards she grieved, feeling as if she had a heavy stone in her chest. Many times she thought of running back there to him, into his arms, his life, even though she knew that Danny was really her man and always would be. Lovely, gentle Michael had given her something warm and new and satisfying. During the rare times she could be alone, she would sit and weep and dream of him. But then she and Danny made it up and he put away the idea of taking off to Australia. And everything seemed to go back to normal again.

She put Michael and what had happened behind her,

especially once Sandra was born last October – a good birth, a quick one and another girl at last! – and she was again overwhelmed with a new baby. Any thought of him receded. By the spring, all those familiar queasy feelings were back – she was expecting again. She even wondered if something guilty in her body was still making it up to Danny for her thinking about another man. Silly as it seemed, she wondered if that was why she had fallen pregnant again so quickly after Sandra.

Gazing across the park, she watched a blue-black crow stalk its way across the green. The grass was short and she caught the fruity smell of half-decayed grass cuttings. When she realized, just a few weeks ago, that she was carrying yet another child she had felt as if it was some kind of punishment.

Lowering her head she allowed the pain to seep through her. It was a pain of longing, loss, jealousy. Michael had longed for her. Now, presumably, he longed for someone else. She had no right to him, to feel any of these things. But feel them she did. She ached with unreasonable jealousy, with the loss of that specialness that she had felt with him.

She took a few deep breaths and raised her head. Thank God I saw him, she thought, calming gradually. Now, if it happened again, she would be prepared. She could say hello and move on. She got to her feet. In the distance she heard the excited shrieks of children. The end of school. A feeling of great weariness came over her. Summer holidays. Kids at home, all the time. She had to try and pull herself together.

'Go up and get her for me, Melly, will you? She's awake again.'

It was the first thing Mom said as Melly came in through the door.

Melly went upstairs, dragging her feet. 'What did your last slave die of?' she muttered to herself. She went into the front bedroom where Mom and Dad slept, where her new sister, Sandra, now ten months old, was lying in a cot next to their bed. A cot – that was a new thing – none of the rest of them had slept in a cot!

Sandra's face was screwed up ready to let out another yell, but at the sight of a face above her, she stopped, looking mildly surprised. Standing over her baby sister, who everyone said looked very much as she had done at that age, Melly let out a sharp sigh.

'All right, all right – don't start that.' She picked up the little bundle, warm, moist and wide-eyed from sleep. Sandra let out a squeak. 'You're a noisy so-and-so, you are. Why can't you stay asleep a bit longer? You've put Mom in a right bad mood again.'

Melly was not in the best of moods herself. They had moved to Harborne in February when she only had a few more months left at school. She had travelled across to Aston each day, having to get up early and catch two buses, and half felt as if she had not really left. She popped in most days to see Gladys. Gladys had dug her heels in and refused to move.

'They can carry me out of here in my box,' she said. 'I'm not being pushed out of my home.'

Sometimes she went to see Lil and Stanley. They were also hanging on in the old yard.

'Where else've we got to go?' Lil would say. 'It'd be out of the frying pan into the fire.'

Mrs Davies was still shrieking. The Morrisons' house was occupied by two bony-cheeked women who looked like sisters but Lil told her were a mother and daughter, and there was a young boy with them. Lil, trying to look on the bright side, said they were nice enough, but Melly could see she was missing the old familiar faces. She seemed really glad to see Melly when she came in now. And Melly liked to see them. Harborne was very different: quieter, greener, more genteel. But it was nice to go back and visit Auntie and the familiar old end. She was drawn back to Aston in the same way Mo kept going back to drink in the Salutation where he knew everyone.

But today the term had ended – her last ever day at school! She knew she would miss some of her friends from that side of town, but leaving school with her references for a job had been exciting. She was fifteen – a grown-up ready to go out in the world.

When she got home, released with all the other school-children, she walked into the house almost expecting a fanfare. Melly's left school!

Fat chance. She wished she'd gone to see Auntie today instead. At least she would have remembered.

No one was taking any notice of her at home because Tommy was away in hospital having further attention to his leg and Mom was about to set off and visit him. As usual, Tommy was all she could think about. Kev and Ricky, who had moved to a local school, were out, most likely tearing about in the park with a bunch of other lads. When Melly walked in, Mom didn't even look up.

'Hurry up,' Melly heard her mother call after her as she dragged her way upstairs. 'I can't stand that blarting.'

'All you ever do, eat and cry,' Melly said to Sandra.

She loved her little sister really, but Mom was expecting yet again now and Sandra didn't sleep well. They all heard her yowling in the night. Mom was forever tired and bad-tempered and she, Melly, bore the brunt not just of that, but of a lot of the work.

If they don't want more babies, she thought crossly, why keep having them? Her knowledge of these matters had increased since Cissy married Teddy Meeks in May. In the way of a queen dispensing favours to her commoners, Cissy informed Melly of the intimate facts of life, sometimes in rather more detail than Melly really required. But Cissy had no intention of having babies yet.

'I want to have some fun before I get into all that,' Cissy declared. 'I don't want to spoil myself. I'm not like Rachel.'

Despite everyone's misgivings, Cissy had kept on and on until Peggy and Fred relented and let her marry Teddy. Despite the difference in their ages, they both seemed like a pair of children together. And Teddy was treating her like a queen. Cissy didn't even have to go out to work!

Carrying Sandra downstairs, Melly handed her to Mom who held out her arms absent-mindedly, saying, 'I'll go straight over to the hospital after this.' She latched Sandra on for a feed, her cardigan draped carelessly over her for modesty's sake.

'Oh,' Melly said. So she'd be cooking tea and looking after the others then. 'Good.'

'What's up with you?' Mom asked, sounding irritated.

'Nothing.'

She stomped to the back of the house, into the little rectangle of garden, and stood against the back wall, tilting her chin to catch the sun on her face.

'What would you care anyway?' she whispered.

Staring morosely up at the cloud-dotted sky, Melly thought, all Mom ever does is have babies and clean the house and cook. Every time she thought about her own future and what it might hold, she was filled with dread.

Was that all there was? Leave school, have babies, stink of bleach all your life, then get old?

Cissy had the right idea, even though she didn't see a lot of point in Cissy's life either. All she seemed to do was prettify the enormous house Teddy's father had bought for them. She had met a couple of other young wives – older than her, but all looking for company – and they went out to milk bars together in Coventry. On Saturdays they went to the golf club where Teddy played. Cissy claimed that it was all marvellous.

Staring across at the backs of the houses in the next street, Melly muttered, 'When I'm older, I'm never going to be like any of you. I want some *life*, not just babies.' A sense of mission filled her. 'I want to *do* something.'

Twenty-Nine

They'd already had words about what exactly she was going to do when she left school; one wintry evening, soon after they moved across town. They were all sitting round the tea table. The fire was lit in the back room and it felt very cosy as they had their tea, but it didn't stop Melly leaving the table ready to explode with anger and frustration.

'You'll come on the market,' Dad had said. 'You're a market trader through and through. If you start off with me, we could put you on a list for your own stall. P'r'aps we'll move into a shop.' He was forever on the lookout for something else, for expansion, branching out. 'You could take over Auntie's pitch.'

'Who says she's ready to give up?' Rachel said. 'It'd be the death of her.'

They were all haunted by the sight of Gladys, that morning they had moved out of the yard, standing in the road, looking suddenly very small, watching them drive away in Dad's new car. She didn't wave.

The car was parked outside now. Dad had wanted something flash and American but he'd come home with the old grey Standard vanguard in the back of which he could pile a lot of sale stuff for the market.

'She could take over mine,' Danny said, getting excited. 'I'll start something new.'

Melly was sick of everyone talking over her head.

What if I don't want any of these things? she thought. Just as she was about to argue, to her surprise, her mother said:

'P'r'aps Melly ought to get another job, to start. Get some other experience – in an office or a shop.'

Danny looked impatient. 'What's the point of that?'

'The point of that,' Rachel argued, 'is to give her a chance to do something different – something a bit more, I dunno . . .'

'You sound just like your flaming mother now,' Danny said, slamming his teacup on to the saucer. 'You mean summat more *respectable* – selling ladies' make-up or perfume.' His tone was mocking. 'Like Peggy wanted you to do instead of marrying someone common like me.'

Melly watched Mom and Dad square up for a ding-dong. She saw the word 'Yes' forming on her mother's lips and before she could come out with it, Melly interrupted.

'I don't want to work in a shop and I don't want the market. I want to be a nurse.'

There was a shocked silence. Only seven-year-old Kev muttered, 'Nursie-nursie,' with a grin on his face, to break the awkwardness of it.

'Shut up, Kev,' Melly said. 'You don't even know what a nurse is.'

'I *do*!' he shouted.

'A *nurse?*' Rachel said, her brow wrinkling. 'You're not still on about that?'

As she said it, Melly realized that being a nurse was what she had always wanted – not that anyone had ever asked. Kev was so clever that his new school were already talking about him taking the eleven plus for the grammar school. No one ever mentioned her. Bitterly, she felt like the house dogsbody.

She looked down into her lap, blushing. It was a tender admission, in front of all these incredulous faces. She wanted someone to be on her side and say, 'Oh, Melly, you'd make a wonderful nurse!'

'A nurse?' her father said, in a scoffing tone. 'What the hell'd you want to do that for? It ain't for people like us. And any road, it's all wiping arses and being ordered around by old harridans.'

'Danny,' Rachel said crossly.

Melly looked up, amazed to hear that Mom seemed to be taking her side.

'Melly – would be – a good . . .' Tommy started saying but no one let him finish.

Mom said, 'You don't want to be a nurse, Melly. You don't know anything about it.'

'I *do* . . .' This was not very true. She had barely any notion of what was needed or how to apply or anything, but the more they went on at her the more certain she became that this was exactly what she wanted.

'But I don't want you just going on the market as if that's the only thing.' Rachel looked round the table. 'You go and get another job for a bit and see if you want the market after that.'

'Well, you'd better want it.' Danny sounded resentful. 'It's our livelihood – it's what keeps you in shoe leather, wench.'

Melly wanted to open her mouth and shout, *Why don't you listen to me? Why don't you ask me what I want instead of bossing me around all the time?* But she knew it wouldn't get her anywhere and Kev and Ricky would just laugh and tease her about it. She didn't say another word and in bed that night she wept, quietly, not wanting anyone to hear her. Why didn't they *listen*? All

Dad could ever see was the market and Mom wasn't really on her side.

The worst of it was, although she did like the idea of being a nurse, she had no idea what to do about it or who she could ask. Even as she lay there she was half resigned to giving up the idea. Maybe Dad was right. People like them didn't do things like that. She'd have to go and work in Woollie's like Cissy used to.

With no encouragement from anyone at home she began to lose heart in the idea that she might be a nurse, putting it down as a silly childhood dream. She thought about talking to Auntie about it, or to Lil, but she was afraid that they might be just as bad as Mom and Dad.

It was only a few days after the end of term when she finally left school, that she met someone, as if sent from heaven, who changed everything.

She was strolling back from the shops, along Harborne Park Road. It was a warm, hazy day and her mind had wandered off into a dream world. She found herself thinking about Reggie Morrison, even though she tried not to. Since the Morrisons had moved to Moseley they had been over numerous times to see their huge house with a long garden, four floors, an enormous, cosy kitchen and windows that seemed to hold half the sky. Dolly was very excited to see them every time they came. Gladys said Dolly was lonely over there. It was not easy to make friends.

'It feels like old times with all of you here,' she said, every time they went. And she laid out an enormous feast of scones and cakes and pints of tea.

Only once was Reggie there. Since moving across town he had had a bit of luck. Instead of working in a factory he had been taken on to train as a gardener in Kings Heath Park. He seemed calmer, happier; he had filled out again and looked solid and strong. Even though he still walked with a pronounced limp, he appeared to be well able to do the job. Melly only exchanged a few words with him. He seemed removed from them all, as if he had grown into another life.

Wistfully now, she thought of Cissy and Teddy. The age gap between herself and Reggie was nothing compared with theirs, but she didn't have whatever it was that Cissy had, that made men mad for her. For a moment she imagined living the sort of life Cissy had, only with Reggie. It didn't feel real at all.

As she walked along, a bicycle passed her on the road. When it drew ahead, she saw that it was ridden by a nurse in a navy coat and hat, pedalling steadily along, looking around her as if in search of something.

Melly's heart started to beat faster. Even seeing one of them in a uniform filled her with longing. Could she ask her about how she too could become a nurse?

But the district nurse was cycling on ahead and Melly realized she was not going to be able to catch up, let alone stop her. She would just have to look out for another nurse in the area. But then, before reaching the corner, the nurse braked, steered her bicycle into the kerb, climbed off and looked around again. As Melly approached she was reading the road sign on the opposite corner.

'Excuse me,' she said to Melly as she came close. 'Am I right in thinking I'm near Albert Road?'

She was a young woman, wearing steel-rimmed glasses. She looked kind, Melly thought, though hot and flustered.

'Yes,' Melly said eagerly. 'It's just round the corner there. I'll show you.'

'Thank goodness – I'm nearer than I thought,' she said, panting. 'I might as well walk the rest. I'm new on this patch and it's a nuisance having to keep getting a map out. There's an old gentleman I've got to visit and then I've got to go all the way back into town. You get strong legs in this job!'

Melly thought that the woman, pushing her heavy bicycle along, was going to natter non-stop all the way and leave her no chance. When she paused to draw breath Melly had to dive in.

'Miss?'

'Yes?' The nurse looked at her with amused eyes.

'How d'you get to be a nurse? I mean, where d'you start?'

'Why?' Her face grew more serious. 'Do you want to be a nurse, dear?'

'I . . .' She blushed. It was so odd for someone to listen and take her seriously that she hardly knew what to say. 'I think so.'

'How old are you, now?'

'Fifteen – nearly.'

'I see. Well, you're a bit young as yet. You can't start training properly until you're over eighteen, you see. And you have to apply to a hospital. So as you live round here you might go to, let's see – the Dudley Road, perhaps? Or Selly Oak?' She considered for a moment.

'I think sometimes they take on junior nurses at sixteen, to be dogsbodies really. You could do that. But if I were you I'd get another job and see how you like that. It's good to know about other things. I used to work with horses – much easier than people, I can tell you!' She chuckled again. 'If you still want to be a nurse when you're a bit older, you could, couldn't you?'

Melly stared at her with adoration. She made it all sound so easy. Above all, she made it sound possible.

'So why do you think you want to be a nurse?'

'Because . . .' She was blushing again. Because . . . She thought nurses were wonderful. They did things for other people. They were kind and made people better. 'I like looking after people,' she said, thinking guiltily of Sandra, probably screaming her head off at home. It wasn't *always* true! But she knew it was what she wanted.

They reached Albert Road and the nurse looked at the house numbers.

'I need to go further down. You needn't come out of your way. But best of luck, dear. Just remember – you can find out from one of the hospitals how to apply. Write to them. My mother was a nurse so I didn't have to find out. Or the library perhaps . . .' She was walking away. 'I'm sure you'll make a splendid nurse!'

Melly held this glowing coal of encouragement inside her. Even if Mom didn't want her to leave home, even if she did have to do some other job until she was old enough, it felt like the thing she was meant to do – whatever they said.

VI

1959–60

Thirty

October 1959

Melly stood in front of her mother in the back room, the letter held between her trembling fingers.

She was to go for an interview at the General hospital, somewhere in the middle of Birmingham.

'You're not on about that again?' Rachel snapped at her, bending to pick up her youngest child, who would be three in a couple of months, who was yelling at the top of his lungs. 'Pack it in, Alan – stop that blarting!'

She hauled the little lad up into her arms, his plumpness contrasting with her own skinniness. 'Just give it up, Melly – you don't want to go getting into all that, not at your age.'

Melly felt rage flame in her. 'At my age?' She gave a bitter laugh. 'What d'you mean? I'm eighteen, not sixty-five! What you mean is, *you* don't want me to do it. You don't care what I want!'

She had become harder over the years, she could feel it. It wasn't something she liked about herself, but why the hell should she stick around to look after Mom's kids – no one asked her to have them, did they?

Rachel stared at her with unmistakeable hostility over Alan's tear-stained face. He was quietening now, sensing that something else was going on around him. He reached an arm out for Melly but she did not move towards him.

'You've got that nice job at Chad Valley,' Rachel said. 'What's wrong with that? I thought you liked it?'

'It's all right – I don't mind it.' Her voice rose with impatience. 'But I had to do something, didn't I? They won't take you for nursing until you're eighteen.'

'But you don't know anything about it.' Mom seemed to be reaching for every argument she could find. Because she wanted a skivvy at home, Melly thought. 'And what about that nice lad, Paul? You'd never see him.'

'Mom.' Melly stared down at the crumb-strewn quarry tiles, straining not to lose her temper. After all, if she was going to be a nurse, her temper was something she was going to have to rein in. 'Paul's more of a mate.' Paul was nice enough for a night out at the flicks, but there was no more to it, not for her. She raised her head in defiance. 'They say I have to go to the General – for an interview.'

'Well, what about Tommy?'

'What about him? Tommy's all right. He'll have a job of his own soon.' Her temper nearly got the better of her then. 'Since when does Tommy need me for anything? It's Sandra and Alan you really want help with. But you're their mom, not me.' She bit back the words, *I never asked you to have them . . .*

Her mother stared at her. 'You're getting above yourself these days, my girl. And I don't know what your father will say.'

'Yes, you do. And so do I.' Melly turned away. 'But whatever he says, it's my life, not his – or yours. I'm going – so don't try and stop me.'

Over the past three years her determination to be a nurse had grown. Not that these years hadn't been fun in some ways. Her first jobs after leaving school were in a grocer's shop and then a laundry. And most Saturdays she worked the Rag Market as well.

After a year she decided to go for something new. She applied to work in the toy factory at Chad Valley. When she first arrived she had been assembling colourful tin spinning tops. She found everybody friendly. A middle-aged lady called Elsie had taken her under her wing to begin with. Elsie had been at Chad Valley all her working life and she told Melly all about when the firm had made little dolls of the royal princesses in 1936 and the princesses even came for a sitting. She also told her how she had spent most of the war making tent poles and it was lovely when they went back to making all the new toys.

That Christmas, Melly had spent some of her wages on the game Escalado for the family. It still gave her a warm feeling remembering that Christmas, all of them playing the horse-racing game, taking it in turns to whizz the handle round to move the horses along, which Tommy could manage as well as the others. Kevin and Ricky had loved it and Dad as well. Sandra had sat cackling at the sight of them all laughing and yelling on their horses to win.

Buying the game still felt like one of the best things she had ever done. And she did like Chad Valley. But she did not want to be like Elsie, still there in her fifties. She wanted more. And she had an ambition of her own.

Things had moved on for the family. Unlike the years in Aston when they hardly went further than the middle of town, things had branched out. For a start they were back and forth visiting Gladys in Aston and the Morrisons in Moseley.

Tommy, now sixteen, was one of the small chosen number at Carlson House who had been encouraged to sit some O-levels and he was working hard for those.

Kevin had taken the eleven plus and got into the grammar school. Mom and Dad had not been too sure about that but she was the one who had stood up for Kevin. They weren't a family who could not afford the uniform, were they? Why not let him go?

Sometimes it felt as if Mom and Dad – and Gladys when they consulted her – were against anything anyone tried to do to better themselves. All they knew about was selling things and they were not very open-minded about anything else.

Kevin, who was the liveliest and sparkiest boy in the family, was thriving at the grammar school. He was clever, quick, and good at sport. Melly secretly found courage in Kevin. He didn't fret about whether he was good enough or clever enough. He just got on with it.

Well, Melly thought, if Kev's that clever, maybe I'm a bit clever too.

And she was meant to be a nurse – wasn't she?

Thirty-One

February 1960

Melly carried her suitcase downstairs that cold, bleak morning.

The case was a cheap thing she had bought from the market and it now contained her few clothes and belongings. It felt momentous, exciting and, all of a sudden, sad. She felt herself well up as she watched her feet, in the new black lace-up shoes she had bought in preparation, take each step downwards towards her fate.

She paused for a moment, near the bottom. Was she doing the wrong thing, leaving like this? In those seconds her familiar home seemed so precious, all the everyday things that made a family life. She knew that as soon as she left, things would never be the same again. What if she stayed, gave it all up and went back to Chad Valley, having an on-and-off sort of friendship with steady old Paul, carrying on with things as they were?

But the very thought made her feel shut in and depressed. No – she had to do something else with her life while she had the chance!

Earlier she had said goodbye to Tommy. He had done very well at Carlson House. The operation on his left leg had straightened it a fraction, though he was still in pain some of the time, but he could walk, slowly, painfully, with a stick when necessary. The school were currently looking for a firm who might take him on as a book-keeper, once he had done his exams.

It was a long time since Melly felt that Tommy actually needed her in the special way he had since she was little. But now he looked her in the eye and hugged her clumsily with his good arm.

'You know, sis,' he said in his quiet, slow way. 'You'll make – a really – good nurse.'

Looking into his earnest face, as he worked to finish the sentence, Melly felt a great rush of love for her little brother and her eyes filled with tears.

'Bye, sis. Good – luck. Don't – be a – stranger – will you?'

'Course I won't.' She gave him a watery smile and squeezed his arm. 'Good luck to you as well.'

Her other brothers said hurried goodbyes on their way out to school, Ricky, who was eight, not really taking in that she would not be home again. Kev understood but was in a gruff, eleven-year-old rush to get out of the house.

Dad had gone out early this morning. Only Mom was left with Sandra and Alan. Mom was sitting at the table, the midday dinner cleared away.

'Well,' Melly said. She was due to arrive at two. 'Time I was off.'

Her mother stood up. Melly saw that while she had been upstairs packing, Mom had changed into one of her best dresses, in royal blue wool. She had swept her hair and pinned it into a sleek pleat. Melly was struck by how nice she looked, how much younger suddenly.

'I'm coming with you,' she said.

'But – there's no need,' Melly said, astonished. 'It's only a bus ride.'

'I want to,' Rachel said. Melly saw her eyes fill with

tears and her own throat ached. Mom did care that she was leaving! 'See you off, proper like, as you're going. Anyway, I want to see where you are, you know – make sure it's all right.'

It felt as if she was going to another country, not just a short ride round the outer circle bus route.

Mom didn't say much to her on the bus. Sandra and Alan sat unusually quiet, as if in awe. Soon they were walking along Raddlebarn Road to the red-brick hospital. When she went for the interview, Melly had taken to Selly Oak hospital immediately, with its flower-edged gardens and airy corridors.

It was Selly Oak that had given her a chance. She had been sent there from the General for an interview – Selly Oak were prepared to take students who had no formal qualifications, so long as they were prepared to work hard and learn.

The porter's lodge directed them to Willow Road. They soon reached the gabled building which was Woodlands Nurses' Home and was to be Melly's abode for the next three years.

'Oh, my goodness,' Rachel said, looking at it with a doubtful expression. It did look a bit forbidding.

Even Melly felt a tremor of misgiving, but she made herself ring the bell. The wide front door opened a few seconds later and a woman in uniform, with a friendly face, greeted her and said that she was the Home Sister.

'Time to say your goodbyes,' she kindly instructed Sandra and Alan who were wide-eyed on the step. 'Nurses only in here, I'm afraid.'

Melly turned to her mother, conscious of the Sister standing there. She could see that Rachel felt constrained by this as well, but in a way it made it easier to say good-bye quickly.

'Ta-ra, Mom.' She hugged her mother briskly, as if already taking on a professional nurse's attitude. 'I'll come and see you all soon, I promise.'

'Bye, babby,' she heard her mother whisper. She drew back, her eyes wide and sad, but forced a smile to her lips. 'Good luck, kid.'

After swift goodbyes to her little brother and sister, Melly was inside, behind the closed door.

'I'm starting to be a nurse,' she thought, sinking on to the bed in the room to which the Sister had led her, after a walk along so many corridors that Melly wondered if she would ever find the way out again.

The new intake were housed, for the first three months, in 'the huts', a wooden structure at the back of the home where lots of doors opened into little rooms off the corridor.

Her room was small and simple, containing a bed, wardrobe, chest of drawers and chair. It smelt of a mixture of disinfectant and polish. Melly could hear sounds, people moving in to the other rooms, and every so often, voices in the corridor as another new recruit was shown her quarters. Her stomach was fluttery with nerves. Who were they all? What would they be like? Would she be able to fit in?

Beside her on the bed were laid a collection of garments – mauve uniforms and a collection of starched-looking white items – aprons and cuffs, she saw, sorting through them, and collars and caps. Her uniform!

The Sister had said she needed to put a uniform on in readiness to meet the others for tea at four o'clock. Melly looked doubtfully at some of the white bits and pieces, wondering whether she would be able to sort out what went where. There was also a lovely, warm-looking navy cape. She stroked its red silky lining in wonder.

Unsure what else to do, she opened her suitcase and was in the process of stowing away her things in the chest of drawers, when she heard a voice with a strong Irish accent from the corridor outside.

'Does anyone in this place have an idea what you're supposed to do with this?'

Melly crept to the door and opened it a crack. As she stuck her head out she saw a number of other heads appear from nearby doorways. A couple of the faces were those of black girls. Most were white and mouse-haired like herself, one blonde.

In the corridor stood a skinny young woman, herself with short, almost boyish brown hair, very pale skin and a mischievous expression on her face. She was holding up one of the aprons with its long, trailing straps.

Everyone emerged and started admitting, amid laughter, that they had no idea what to do with most of it and how exactly *were* they supposed to put it on – did anyone know?

The Irish girl was called Berni O'Reilly. Soon, though Melly did not then realize it, while chatting and laughing over the uniform in that corridor and later having tea together in the nurses' home's common room with the others, she had met the group of girls who would be her friends – Berni, from Dun Laoghaire; Jen, the blonde girl who came from Alcester and Margaret, a soft-spoken, twinkly-eyed girl, one of the two who had come from the West Indies to begin their training.

*

A bell was ringing somewhere. Melly opened her eyes and looked round at the bare room in utter bewilderment. The nurses' home! For a few moments a sick, bereft feeling filled her. It was the first time in her life she had not woken up at home, with her brothers and sister and Mom and Dad, with all the old familiar things and voices around her.

She lay fighting back tears and the sudden urge to run along the road and catch the bus back home – as if this new life was all a dream, full of strange rules and regulations.

A host of details had been reeled off to them the night before: about wearing black regulation shoes, *polished*, and darning their black stockings if any hole or ladder appeared. There was to be no jewellery worn and very little make-up; nails must be kept short and no nail varnish, ever. They had learned how to fold their frill-edged 'Sister Dora' caps and pin them on with kirby grips. Melly, whose hair was straight and long enough to fasten into a bun, found that her cap stayed on quite easily. With all the rules about where they could study, what time everything was expected to happen, and trying to take in everyone's names, her head felt as if it was bursting by the time she went to bed.

But then she remembered the tea last night and the warming feeling that most of the girls were friendly and not snooty and that they were all just as nervous about everything as she was. They sat round, tucking into the stodgy spread that was provided and drinking cup after cup of tea.

'My sister's a nurse,' Berni had told her last night. She, like everyone else, looked fresh and suddenly professional in her mauve uniform. 'The things she tells me.

Jaysus –' she rolled her eyes comically – 'it's enough to frighten the life out of you!'

Melly had liked Berni immediately and she also took to Margaret with her neat, wiry hair and dark eyes which danced about, always looking ready for a joke.

'My mother said to me, you gotta do something with yourself – you work as a teacher or a nurse, some profession. And I thought, I am *never* going to make a teacher – huh!' She shook her head. 'Children *vex* me.' Warily she eyed the cake in her hand as if it might explode. 'What's *this*?'

'Rock cake,' Melly laughed. 'It's nice – promise. Haven't you ever had one before?'

Margaret took a cautious nibble. With crumbs on her lips, she went on, 'So – nursing for me, I thought. The lesser of two evils!' Seeing their shocked faces she finished with a wink. 'I'm joking. It's a serious vocation.'

'I've always wanted to be a nurse,' Jen said, piling sandwiches on her plate. They would learn that Jen, blonde, blue-eyed, skinny as a stick insect, could eat like a horse and was almost as strong as one. 'I read all those stories about heroines – you know, Florence Nightingale and Edith Cavell – and bandaged up my teddy bears. Only thing is, teddy bears are nice and clean and fluffy. Goodness knows how I'll be with blood and . . . whatever else.'

Berni told them she had been working as a 'skivvy', as she put it, in a hospital back home since she was sixteen.

'My mother kept on about me going into an order – I've eight older sisters and she'd've had me into the Sisters of Mercy like my sister Cath and oh, good God, I wasn't having that. I thought I might as well escape across the water and get trained up properly so I can earn my own living and please myself.'

271

'You know there's a convent just round the corner, don't you?' Melly teased her.

Berni actually looked worried for a second, and then burst into laughter. 'Well, I'll be keeping well away from there, I can tell you! And you – Miss Melly – are you a born nurse then?'

'Me? Oh – no. But I s'pose . . . It was the midwife who came when my mom had my brother, one of the ones after me—'

'Well, it would have to be after you really, wouldn't it?' Jen put in and they all laughed. Melly smiled at the silliness of what she had said. But there was no malice in Jen, she could see.

'She first gave me the idea and I just always thought it was the best thing to be.'

'Well,' Jen said, holding up her teacup as if in a toast. 'We're soon going to find out, aren't we? At least they don't let us loose on a ward straight away. Here's to Preliminary Training!'

The thought of seeing these girls, who she already liked, who she hoped she could fit in with, drove Melly out of bed, to join the throng of them as they went over to the hospital canteen for their first breakfast as nurses.

Thirty-Two

'Huh,' Danny said as Melly walked through the door for her first visit home. 'Packed it in then, have yer?'

They were all there that Sunday afternoon – even Gladys. Though Melly had only been away for two weeks, it felt so strange that home should still be here, going on just the same. As soon as she walked in, four-year-old Sandra was clinging to her legs, wanting to be picked up. She hauled the little girl up into her arms, too happy to be annoyed by her father's comment. She felt as if she had grown up years in the last fortnight. It didn't matter what anyone said.

'No, Dad.' She beamed round at everyone. 'I *love* it. Every minute of it!'

Though this was not quite literally true – getting out of bed in the morning was always a struggle and in parts of some of the lectures, especially in the afternoon, she felt like dozing off to sleep.

So far she had done two weeks in the Preliminary Training School and was starting to become familiar with all the routines and the layout of the hospital and classrooms. She had settled in happily and rubbed along with everyone – especially with Berni, Margaret and Jen.

Together, when they had time off, they had explored Bournville Green, just near the nurses' home, where they had sat out one fine afternoon on the wooden benches, nattering and sucking sweets from one of the little shops.

Though it was cold, the sun was shining and a carpet of snowdrops and yellow, mauve-and-white crocuses blazed their colours across the green. They caught mouth-watering whiffs of chocolate from the Cadbury works close by and heard, from across the road, the sweet-toned bells of the carillon ringing out. It was such a pretty place.

Last Sunday, as she was used to going to church with Gladys, she went to St Francis in Bournville with Jen. Berni was a Catholic and went off to St Edward's along the road. Margaret, who was from Nevis, said her family were Moravians. She and Denise, the other girl from Nevis, found out that Moravians were just starting to meet at Sparkhill Methodist church so they went all the way over there. The rest of the time they were all together and got along well, unified by the training, by the laughter, successes and mistakes, the sharing of new experiences and all the things they were learning.

Selly Oak hospital had already begun to feel like home.

It was tough at times and she knew it would get tougher when they started on the wards.

'Just remember,' one of the senior nurses told them. 'If you work hard and study hard and are prepared to do the things required of you, you can all be good nurses. There will be difficult times. I don't know a nurse who has not been in tears in the sluice during her working life and more than once for many of us. But you can do it. Just remember that.'

Melly was prepared for all of it. She wanted to do her very best, to *be* the best, most hard-working and caring nurse ever. She had found the thing that was right for her and which seemed the most noble work anyone could do. She was in love with the whole thing!

Mom and Dad looked at her, uncomprehending, as she sat at the table with them and told them all about the school.

'We have a dummy to practise on called Mrs Bedworthy,' she said, laughing. 'She's very patient. And we do anatomy on Jimmy the Skeleton!'

'I – bet – he's a – bit – bony!' Tommy said. They all laughed.

Gladys seemed slightly awed and she could see Mom and Dad were listening, though they didn't know what to ask about any of it. Sandra and Alan were too young to understand any of it. They got down from the table to muck about on the floor and Kev and Ricky started muttering to each other about football and yesterday's Villa match.

'We're learning about nursing practice and hygiene,' Melly bubbled on. 'They're going to take us to a sewage works – and a dairy.'

'What the hell for?' Danny said, reaching to flick ash on to a saucer. 'You're not looking after cows, are yer?'

The boys tittered at this. Melly felt annoyed.

'It's all about learning how to prevent infection,' she said importantly.

'Are you getting enough to eat?' Mom said, gathering up the crumb-strewn plates.

'Yes, Mom.'

'And the rooms – are they—?'

'Yes,' she said impatiently. 'The rooms are clean. Of course they are!'

'You – been – in the – wards yet?' Tommy asked. Tommy knew a thing or two about hospitals, having spent weeks at the Woodlands.

'Not yet,' Melly answered, grateful that someone was

actually taking what she did seriously. 'We're in the classroom for a bit to begin with.' She smiled at her brother. 'How's it going, Tommy?'

His eyes twinkled at her. 'They're – working – me – to the bone.' He finished with a grin.

Mom and Gladys were clearing the tea things and had started talking about one of the neighbours, someone who was poorly, who Melly didn't know. She could see that her family only had limited interest in anything going on outside their own world. It felt as if she had been away a lot longer than two weeks. For a moment she felt sad that they didn't share in any of her interests. She turned to her father.

'How's it going on the market?'

'Good,' Danny said, sitting up, suddenly full of energy. 'I've been down London this week, down Petticoat Lane – with some of them Jewish lads. Thought I'd have a go and I bought some leather coats, three-quarter length . . .' He sawed the side of his hand against his leg just above the knee.

'Leather?' Melly said. 'What – new ones? I bet they cost a bit, didn't they?'

'Seven quid each, I paid.'

Gladys laughed. She had just refilled the teapot and she limped over to pour them out more tea. 'You dain't have much luck with 'em yesterday, did you, Danny?'

Danny looked pained. 'Nah. They're great heavy things. Hard as hell – all creases in the arms. You have to work 'em in like a pair of shoes. *Warm*, though. As toast. Any road, I'm thinking what to do – summat with a bigger return instead of grubbing about round all these jumbles sales and such.' He was happy now that she was talking the trade he knew. 'Seconds – that's the way forward.' He tapped his nose, his face boyish now. 'I'm working on it, kid.'

Melly grinned. 'I bet you are, Dad.'

Thirty-Three

One Saturday that summer, Melly arranged, on her day off from her first ward placement, to go and visit Cissy.

When she got through to her, from a telephone box, Cissy sounded ecstatic to hear from her.

'Course you can come. I wish you'd come more!' she said. 'And anyway, I've got something to tell you.'

Melly pictured Cissy in the enormous living room of her and Teddy's house – mansion, to be more accurate. She could hear a faint echo over her voice because the room was so big. Cissy truly lived in another world.

In the almost four years since Cissy's marriage, Melly had only been over there a handful of times. Cissy, who was a lady of leisure, preferred to come back into Birmingham to see her friends and family and have a good look round the shops. Rather to Melly's surprise she never gave the least hint of being unhappy out in her Warwickshire lap of luxury.

'I'll come on the train,' Melly said. 'Would Teddy be able to . . . ?' On previous visits, Teddy had either come to Coventry station in his sleek car, smelling inside of leather and Teddy's expensive cigarettes, or they had urged her to summon a taxi for which they would pay.

'Teddy'll be at the golf club,' Cissy said. 'But don't you worry – you stay at Coventry station and I'll come and pick you up. Teddy's bought me a little runabout.'

'You've learned to drive?' Melly said, finding this hard to imagine.

'Yes.' She heard Cissy's infectious giggle down the phone. 'I took the test four times – but now I'm safe to be let out on the road!'

Coventry railway station was a building site. Amid all the racket of banging and rumbling machinery, she waited for Cissy. When she saw a very shiny cream, open-topped sports car come shooting towards her, driven by a woman with blonde-white hair tucked under a red-and-white floral scarf and scarlet lipstick, she was still looking for someone else. But the car braked alongside her and the woman leaned over the passenger seat and flung open the passenger door.

'Here we are – hop in!'

Only then did she recognize Cissy's face.

'God, Ciss!' She hurried into the car, Cissy revving off as she shut the door. 'I'd never've recognized you!'

Cissy grinned at her. She was wearing a crisp cotton frock in bright red and white candy-stripes, and on the foot pedals Melly could just make out white, very high-heeled shoes. Cissy seemed plumper, her bare arms fleshy, creamier looking. There was a little wad of flesh under her chin. All in all she was looking mighty pleased with herself. Melly smiled back, with a rush of fondness.

'D'you like the look?' Cissy said.

'Oh, yes – you look like a film star!' Melly said. And she did.

'Well, I'd never get away with this lipstick with my real colour,' Cissy said. She patted the silk scarf covering her hair. 'And Teddy loves it.'

'Gentlemen prefer blondes,' Melly said and Cissy giggled. 'And this car's yours?'

'Teddy bought it for me – early present for my twenty-first!' Cissy shouted back. 'It's the new Daimler. Course, Teddy likes a go in it as well. But he's got his Jags.'

Melly nodded. Teddy seemed to her an old man of tweed and leather and smoke, while at the same time childish, a boy no older than Cissy.

'So how're you, littl'un?' Cissy yelled as they roared out of Coventry.

'All right,' Melly said. She didn't want to go into any detail while she was having to shout over the buffeting air as Cissy tore along. They were out of the city and in green lanes between hedges and fields; cows swishing their tails back and forth.

Soon, Cissy turned into the drive of Rawson House, the white, four-square building with four acres of land stretching around it which, to everyone's continuing astonishment, was her marital home.

'Teddy said he's sorry not to see you,' Cissy said as she braked at the front of the house. A twisting wisteria, all mauve bells of bloom, stretched itself across it.

'Not to worry,' Melly said. She didn't mind not seeing Teddy, though he was affable enough. She had spent a long time at the beginning looking for something suspicious about him, some dark motive in him for marrying a girl like Cissy, so many years his junior, who he had plucked out of the city. But she could not find one. Teddy just plain adored Cissy. In fact, he seemed to be happy with his monied life, his bits of work in the firm here and there, his golf, his passion for model aeroplanes and good cigars – and a pretty wife on his arm. There was really no more to him than that.

Melly had waited for Cissy to get bored with titivating the house and herself. Everyone had almost given up speculating about when they were going to have a baby. But Cissy did not seem bored. She was just like Teddy, Melly realized. They were made for each other. It also made her see how much more she wanted herself – a life with more challenge and things to do.

Cissy climbed slowly out of the car. Melly, who had nipped out in her lithe way, thought, my, she's turning into a middle-aged woman.

Cissy led her through the front door, into the capacious hallway, its parquet floor covered by modern rugs in bold blocks of reds and green, its mock-antique furniture. The panelled walls were hung with paintings of ships and aeroplanes, all modern and in bright colours. Melly looked at them and thought, as she had thought every time she visited, well, I wouldn't want them on *my* walls.

'He's got a new one, I see.' She pointed at a picture high up, above another painting.

'Oh, yes,' Cissy said fondly. She pulled the scarf off, turned to a little ornate framed mirror on the wall and patted her blonde hair which curled up at the ends. 'His Spitfire. He loves it. Anyway – come and see the kitchen. Mrs Rogers isn't here today, so I'll make you some dinner. Soup all right?'

'Yes,' Melly smiled, knowing how hopeless Cissy was in the kitchen. She had never much liked cooking, or any work. Now that she had a housekeeper and several gardeners to tend to all the land that Teddy owned, she could sink back happily and not bother.

Melly followed Cissy, with her white high heels clicking along the floor. She felt rather drab in her blue-and-white floral dress, compared with Cissy's bright, striped one. But she had always felt drab in comparison with Cissy. She minded a lot less now. She liked her own life.

'Oh!' she exclaimed as they went into the large kitchen. 'Blimey, Ciss – this is different!'

The old-fashioned kitchen and range had been swept away. She had never seen a kitchen like this one! At home they had old handmade wooden cupboards and the white sideboard with the flap that came down. Mom did have a refrigerator, though, which was quite something. The Morrisons had a lovely big kitchen in Moseley, but it was cosy and old-fashioned with a big scrubbed table and all Dolly's pans hanging from hooks. The only other kitchens she knew were the old house in Aston and the kitchen in the nurses' home, with its tiled floor and big black range.

What she saw now was an array of cupboards fitted all around the walls, some high up and all with sugar-pink doors. The window curtains and even the cooker were pink. There was a small table in the middle with a pink-and-white checked cloth and at one side, beneath a row of overhead cupboards, a strip of bright white surface, with two white plastic chairs on moulded stems, almost like wine glasses, pushed underneath.

'D'you like our breakfast bar?' Cissy giggled, pointing. 'It's the new thing. We love it!'

'It's . . .' Melly could hardly take it in. 'It's ever so modern, Ciss!'

'But d'you *like* it?' Cissy pressed her, her hands clasped together. 'I said to Teddy that if it was going to be a colour it had to be pink.'

'Yes – it's lovely!' Melly said, almost truthfully, though privately thinking it was a good thing Cissy had dyed her hair blonde instead of ginger. Her scarlet clothes were an eye-aching enough clash.

Cissy rummaged in one of the cupboards and pulled out two tins of Campbell's soup concentrate.

'Here we are – chicken or mushroom?'

Melly was almost too hungry to care either way. She seemed to have an enormous appetite ever since she started nursing. 'Mushroom, please,' she said.

'We can eat in the dining room,' Cissy said, laughing in her good-natured way. 'Sorry I haven't got anything better. Mrs Rogers does so much I still haven't learned to cook.'

'Never mind, Ciss,' Melly said. 'I s'pose we can't all be beautiful *and* practical.'

The dining room, at the back of the large Edwardian house, had deep red flock-patterned wallpaper and glass doors opening out to the garden, its beds at present blooming with flowers.

'I'll open the door,' Cissy said, laying two places at the end of the long, mahogany dining table which would seat at least twenty guests. There was a silver candelabra in the middle of the table and glass-fronted cabinets arranged at the edge of the room full of porcelain and china ornaments.

Goodness, Melly thought. I'd be afraid to move in here.

A quiet lay over the place, except for a banging every now and then, as if someone was knocking in a post somewhere in the distance. The faint buzz of bees and scent of flowers came in on the breeze. Cissy left the room and Melly looked out at the carefully arranged beds of roses and other beautiful flowers which she could not name in white and pale mauve, pink and blue. What a lovely place it was!

Cissy returned with half a loaf of bread, a pat of butter and a lump of what looked rather mousetrap sort of cheese.

'I thought there was some better stuff but I can't find anything,' Cissy said. She sank down at the table as if exhausted. 'Hop in and pour the soup for us, will you? It's bubbling.'

Melly brought the greyish soup in and set the bowls in their places on the white cloth Cissy had laid at their end of the table.

'You all right, Ciss?' she asked as she sat down. Cissy was looking rather pale suddenly.

'I will be, when I've had a bit to eat,' Cissy said. She looked up coyly at Melly. 'I haven't told you my news – and you haven't even noticed. Look!'

Pushing her chair back she stood up and smoothed the soft material of her dress close down over her belly. Only then, Melly noticed the round bulge of it. She looked at Cissy, who was beaming at her.

'I'm getting on for five months!'

'Oh, Ciss – that's lovely!' To Melly's surprise she found tears in her eyes. 'Have you told Nanna Peggy?'

'Not yet. I wanted to be really sure, you know . . .'

'Well, I'm happy for you,' Melly said. 'You know, we all began to wonder, with Teddy being so much older and . . .' She stopped, realizing how tactless she was being.

'These things can take time,' Cissy said. She blushed, looking down into her soup.

'Sorry, Ciss.' Melly reached to touch her arm. 'I didn't mean to be nosey. The main thing is, the baby's on the way! I'm so glad for you.'

'I can't wait!' Cissy beamed, before taking a ravenous bite of bread, thickly buttered.

They both ate hungrily and talked about the baby and how Cissy and Teddy were having a room decorated and Cissy was buying clothes and a cot and everything new.

'Gladys'll be knitting for you as soon as she knows,' Melly said. 'Or finding all sorts of stuff for you off the market.'

'Ah, yes,' Cissy said, looking a bit pained. 'I suppose she will. I'm not sure that . . .'

'Don't offend her,' Melly said. 'She loves babies and she's known you since you were knee high. Just take what she gives you and say thanks – she won't know if you use it much, will she?'

'Yes – course.' Cissy smiled. 'Dear old Auntie. How is she? How's everyone?'

'She's all right, I think,' Melly said, sawing off another slice of the soft white bread. 'Says she's stiff these days. She's hanging on in Alma Street still – they haven't knocked the old place down yet, but it's sure to happen. She's putting a brave face on it all. She said Stanley Gittins's got bad, though. Lil's barely managing. But I don't see much of anyone at the moment.'

'Of course!' Cissy gasped. 'You're doing your . . . Being a nurse! Oh, what's it like? Ooh, I could never do what they do.'

Melly, glad to be asked, was just launching into a description of her life in Selly Oak when, from the garden, a voice, moving closer, called out low and teasing:

'Hello-o-o? Hello there – Miss Cissy. Where's my little pumpkin got to then?'

It was a deep male voice, with a strong country accent.

Cissy dropped her spoon, splashing soup on the cloth, and dashed to the door.

Melly saw a tall, robust-looking man, dressed in working clothes and a rather crushed brown trilby hat, appear close to the doors. His face, so far as she could see, had a ruddy, healthy look to it. Cissy, hurrying down the step to the garden, went over on one of the high heels and had to recover herself. The man caught her as she staggered forward.

'Eh – careful with yourself, my lovely!' he said. 'Don't want our little Petey coming a cropper, do we?'

'For God's *sake*,' Melly heard Cissy hiss at him. Her lips moved closer to the man's ear and she added something else that Melly could not hear. A second later the two of them parted and Cissy came back in. She was making obvious attempts to look nonchalant, but her hair was rumpled by her tripping and she looked flushed and tense.

'*Really*,' she said crossly, sitting back down. With both hands she tried to settle her hair again. 'Sometimes having staff is more trouble than not!'

'Oh, dear,' Melly said, not sure what else to say. She was not yet thinking very clearly, except that what she had just seen happen seemed mighty odd. She just looked at Cissy.

Instead of carrying on eating, Cissy put her hands in her lap and hung her head.

'I know what you're thinking,' she said.

'Do you?' Melly said. She wasn't sure what she was thinking herself.

'He's . . .' She looked up with a kind of desperate defiance. 'He's the same colouring as Teddy, almost exactly. Teddy'll never know. He can't, you see. Can't seem to give me a baby, and . . .' She put her hand over her face for a moment, and then drew it away again. 'But now he thinks he can. That it can just take that long. He's so *pleased*. It's made him younger again just thinking of it.'

Melly stared at her, the pieces of this puzzle only just beginning to join up in her head.

Cissy leaned towards her in deep earnestness. 'You won't say anything, will you? *Please*, Melly.'

Melly was reeling with astonishment. She had still had so little to do with men that all this felt beyond her. This lie of Cissy's – such a big, awful lie. And then she thought, what would happen if Teddy knew, if everyone knew? Would it help, or make anything better? She looked at Cissy's pleading face. What on earth other answer could she give? It wasn't her business to interfere.

'Course I won't, Ciss,' she said. She took Cissy's hand and squeezed it.

Thirty-Four

October 1960

Tommy bent over the lavatory, retching up a tan gush of tea.

He had got up at six, having hardly slept. He was so charged up with nerves that he knew he would need time to steady himself for the day to come. Creeping down to the kitchen he had put the kettle on and sat sipping scalding tea, hoping it would take away the queasiness, but he had had to hurry out to the lav, downstairs at the back, and only just made it.

He flushed the lavatory and washed his mouth out over the basin. For a moment he leaned against the wall, breathing hard. A chill spread through him, but at the same time he could feel that his new shirt was already clammy with sweat.

I can't do it, he thought, staring at the tooth-coloured enamel of the basin. All these years he had led a protected life, surrounded by family or Carlson House. Today he was expected to venture out into the world, to travel right across town and start work. A proper job. What if he couldn't manage any of it? But his next thought was, I've got to. What else am I going to do? I can't stop at home all my life.

Some of the welfare workers at Carlson House had

visited firms in the city to find out who would be prepared to take on disabled employees. When it turned out that Tommy had passed five O-levels and that they were told his disabilities were not nearly as severe as those of some children, he had been one of the first to be offered a job.

He was to go to the offices of Joseph Lucas's in Hockley. What he would do when he got there he was not sure. Whatever it was, he found the prospect terrifying.

By the time Mom came down to get the others off to school and make breakfast, he was already dressed and ready to go.

'You're up early,' she said.

'Umm.' He was sitting at the table in the work clothes they had bought: black trousers, white shirt, jacket, all strange and crisply new on him.

Mom sounded nervous and it made him want to seem as if he wasn't. Carlson House and the Midland Spastic Association clubs and socials had become her little world as well. It had protected both of them.

Dad came down and ate standing up, a wedge of bread, slurping tea. Tommy felt the atmosphere of awkwardness coming from him that was always there when he had to do anything with his eldest son – uncomfortable, trying too hard.

'You had your breakfast?' Danny asked in a gruff voice.

'Yes,' Tommy lied. 'Ready – when – you are.'

Dad was to drive him for the moment. For a start he needed to know the way. But someone from the Midland Spastic Association had told him that there was now an organization from where you could get motorized tricycles for invalids. He was excited and nervous about the thought of being able, at last, to get about by himself.

'One thing at a time, love,' Mom had said. 'Let's get you settled in the job first. See if it works out.'

He heard in her voice the thought that it might not.

Rachel stood outside, waving them off in the old Standard. Tommy gave her a brief wave, then faced the front, dignified, not even looking at her. She had tucked him into the car, overdone it, she knew that. Even now that her eldest son was setting out to begin his first job, she found it hard not to baby him. A job – Tommy! – it was the miracle they never thought would happen.

She stood with a white cardigan draped over her shoulders, watching the car slide away down the street, and gave thanks for Carlson House, for the years of kindness and attention, of speech therapy and lessons and all the care that went into trying to help children like Tommy have the best they could manage in life. Tommy, as it turned out, had become a star pupil there, actually passing national exams. The cleverness of her children amazed her. She had never thought herself anything special.

Yet as the car disappeared, she shivered. The road was quiet, a breeze blowing little clouds across the sky, and a cold, empty feeling came over her. She was not needed any more – not by Tommy, to whom she thought she would be tied for life. And while there was a lightness, a relief, she found she felt bereaved.

Melly was gone – she came home once a month or so and seemed happy as anything with her new nursing life – and now her little Tommy too. The two children who had been her whole life throughout the war years, when she was barely older than Tommy was now.

She stood for a moment, close to tears. Then she

reminded herself that her job was not over yet. There were plenty more children still to look after and that Alan was inside the house getting up to who knew what! She hurried indoors.

Tommy and Danny did not talk much in the car.

'You'd best watch the route, son,' Danny said as they set off. 'You need to know where you're going.'

Tommy nodded and watched queasily out of the window as they made their way across town, to Hockley. He had been once before, for a brief interview, but as Dad braked near the imposing factory buildings in Great King Street, he felt once more overawed and scared. Lucas's was one of the great, famous Birmingham firms, started by 'Old Joe' Lucas as he was fondly known, who had started out in the nineteenth century selling paraffin from a barrow. Once he started manufacturing oil lamps, the company grew and grew.

Tommy stared up at the buildings, wishing he could see through the walls to the lathes and presses, the engineers and workers, and all the machine parts pouring out of the factory. Now, he was to be one of the tiny cogs in the Lucas machine.

'Well – here we go,' Danny said. 'I've got as close as I can. That's the door you need.' He sat for a moment, the engine cut off, hands braced on the wheel.

Tommy didn't want to get out of the car, not yet. Streams of people were making their way into the works, some glancing into the car. A small covered walkway across the road divided the offices from the manufacturing section of the works.

It felt as if Dad had something to say. The discomfort of it grew in the car.

'Look, son,' Danny came out with at last, staring through the windscreen. 'You're a good lad. You'll do well, I'm sure. But people can be unkind. They don't always know how to deal with you . . .'

As if I need telling, Tommy raged inside. As if his guts weren't in turmoil because of these very thoughts swirling in his head. He just wanted to get out of the car. To begin and get it over with.

'Yeah,' he said. 'I'd better go, Dad. Don't want to be late.' He saw Danny move to get out. 'S'all right,' he said quickly, grasping his stick. 'I can manage.'

On the pavement with his stick, he felt exposed and foolish, but he stood tall and waved his father away. Danny gave one of his brief gestures of parting with the flat of his hand against the window. And, amid the sea of hurrying workers, for the first time he could remember, Tommy was out in the world, alone.

'Here y'are, mate – you can sit here.'

The supervisor stood over him as Tommy sank, still panting from the effort and worry of getting up the stairs to the office. Already he felt exhausted. He was in a room with windows along one side, at a seat among a row of desks which, though not a production line exactly, was how he imagined a production line would look. Only this was a production line of papers.

The man treated him in a breezy, infantile way, not sure how to talk to him.

'Here you are – this is the invoice department.' He spoke slowly as if he was explaining things to a small child. 'Now – I'll show you what you have to do.'

The job, Tommy learned, consisted of tearing off the invoices – in this case for L-plates – sorting the copies and stapling them together. While easy as falling off a log for someone with two working arms and a working brain, Tommy was minus one of the working arms. He eyed up the work before him, the stapler. He could manage it, one movement at a time, and he set off. It was laborious and slow, lining up the sheets of paper. He soon worked out a way of tucking the front inch or so of an invoice over the edge of the desk and pressing his body against it while he used his right hand to staple the corners.

There was a young lad on one side of him and a girl on the other. The boy was ginger-headed, with very pale eyelashes and about his age. Tommy felt sure they were working far quicker than he ever could and he felt tense and foolish. It was not as if it was a difficult job.

The girl was pale, black-haired, plump-faced and sleepy looking. She had a very big chest which Tommy found his eyes drawn to in fascination. Neither his mother nor Melly was anything like that. Among all the females he knew, he had never seen one quite that shape before. It gave him an excited feeling. Once she caught him staring at her and made a rude face at him. He looked away, his cheeks burning. By asking a few questions throughout the morning he ascertained that neither of his work fellows had any O-levels.

As soon as the lunch break arrived, both his neighbours fled the office to the company restaurant or the shops without asking him if he needed anything. Mom had sent him with a pack of sandwiches and he ate them at his desk, wondering where the lavs were. He found out when the ginger-headed boy came back, tucking into a greasy and delicious-looking sausage roll.

'Wha's yer name?' he asked Tommy, swallowing so that his Adam's apple wobbled.

'Tommy.'

'Mine's Micky. Tha's Con.' He nodded at the busty girl's empty chair. 'Wha's the matter with you?'

'Nothing,' Tommy said, irritated by the way he said it. 'Nothing's the – matter – with – me.'

'But you talk funny – and you're a cripple, ain't yer?' He took another bite and added, muffled, 'Tha's what Con said. You're from the home – the cripples' home.'

How did they know where he was from? Tommy wondered, a blush spreading across his face. He looked down at his desk.

'I've – never –' Because he was tense his speech became more contorted. It always did. 'Been in – a – home,' he said as firmly as he could manage. 'I – live in – Harborne.'

Micky stared at him, swallowing the last of the sausage roll. 'Oh, ar,' he said finally. 'Well, you look like a cripple to me.'

It was going to be a very long afternoon.

When he made his way out of the building at clocking-off time, the grey Standard was waiting almost where Danny had dropped him off.

'All right, son?' Dad said, as he got in.

'Yeah.' He felt like crying.

Dad pulled away from the kerb. 'Well, you seem to be all in one piece. How d'yer get on?'

'All right,' Tommy said. He just wanted to curl up somewhere and be very quiet.

'Well,' Dad said, seeming cheerful. 'You've done your first day's work!'

Work, the work he was apparently so lucky to be doing – was one of the most dismal experiences of his life. Was this all, from now on?

He could see his father was more at ease with him because he could work like anyone else. And there were people he knew at Carlson House, like his friend Martin, whose twisted bodies would never let them enter that world the way Tommy had done. He ought to be feeling happier, he told himself. He *had* survived it. And he knew he must put on a brave front to go home and face Mom.

She was waiting, obviously hovering as he came through the door, in her apron, a spoon in her hand which she had carried from the kitchen on hearing the door.

'Hello, babby – Tommy, I mean – how did you get on?' Her breathless anxiety was all too apparent.

'All right,' he said. 'Yeah.' He forced a smile on to his face.

'Is that the lad?' He heard Gladys's voice from the back room. Auntie – had she come over specially? 'Come in here, Tommy, and tell yer auntie all about it.'

So much happiness that he had a job, that he could lift the burden of himself from their shoulders. He limped into the back room to tell Gladys that the day had been good and people were nice and it was all right.

Only later, in bed, in the little box room he had to himself, did he let himself cry, muffling any sound with the bedclothes. He thought of Kev, of all the football and cricket he played at the grammar school, things he could never ever do himself. He might have been like Kev – mightn't he? They said he was clever. Had a brain. But his body let his brain down.

And now he was faced with this, day in day out. A few of the older ladies were kind and motherly to him. But with the younger ones, like Con, they either ignored him or treated him like a curiosity or an idiot. Without a flaming O-level between them! he reflected bitterly. The near presence of Con's breasts would not leave him alone. At least that bit of me works all right, he thought, as he hardened with excitement. But his arousal cast him into further gloom. No girl was ever going to look at him, was she?

At Carlson House he had seldom been frustrated because the life there was tailored to his needs and so many of the others had had bodies that were even more uncooperative than his.

But now, he thought, this same body shaking with sobs, now it was always going to be like this. Like hell. Only he'd have to keep quiet about it – and be grateful for having anything at all.

Thirty-Five

December 1960

Rachel crumpled up the last of the paper streamers which had sagged in colourful lines across the room. The kids had had a lovely time making them and she smiled at the thought of Ricky, Sandra and Alan round the table before Christmas, for once not squabbling too much over the squeezy little bottle of glue and the cut-out strips of coloured paper and old magazines Danny had brought home for them to use.

She hurried out to the back to put them in the dustbin, her head bowed in the drizzle. It was a horrible grey day and she felt flat and sad.

Just before Christmas she had had a visit from Cissy with the baby boy she had given birth to six weeks earlier, Andrew as she had called him. Cissy was besotted with the little lad who, like his mother, looked plump, creamy and satisfied. She reported that Teddy was over the moon at the birth of his son. Rachel's own children had loved meeting Andrew. And then there was all the excitement of Christmas, the children up at crack of dawn to find their stockings and all the cooking and enjoying being together, all of them around her. Gladys had come over and it had been one of the happiest family times she could remember.

Rachel sighed as she shut the door behind her. Funny,

she thought, how you want your children to grow up, but then again, you feel lost when they do. A feeling of grief rose in her for a moment and her eyes filled.

Danny was at the table in the kitchen doing their accounts for the market. Kev had gone to see a pal of his and she could hear the other three upstairs, playing at something, not fighting for the moment. Rachel filled the kettle, wishing there was no one else in the house just for a while.

As she tidied the kitchen her mind wandered to Tommy and she felt immediately anxious. It was Melly who had forced her to see what was in front of her eyes.

Melly had come home for Christmas but she had only been able to stay one night. She was on an early shift on the ward on Christmas Day, so Danny had had to go and pick her up afterwards. Rachel felt a bit hurt that she did not appear to mind this. Her daughter had been sucked into the life of the hospital and did not seem to need them any more.

But Melly had taken her aside, upstairs, that evening.

'Mom –' She closed the door of the bedroom she was now sharing with Sandra. They stood between the beds, on the runner of blue carpet. 'I want to talk to you. What the hell's wrong with Tommy? He looks terrible!'

Rachel was on the defensive immediately.

'What d'you mean?' But she knew. She had been trying not to notice because she had no idea what to do about it.

'He looks . . .' Melly tried to find the words. 'Not like Tommy. He looks sad and not himself. I asked him about the job again – I mean, he'd said he didn't like it very much. Now he won't say anything.'

'Well, he's only been there a little while,' Rachel said, turning away to sit down on Sandra's bed. She tried to sound as if it was nothing to worry about. 'It's bound to be difficult, isn't it? He'll take longer than most people to settle in. And everyone has to do jobs they don't like sometimes.'

Melly folded her arms. Rachel felt as if her daughter could see right through her and was suddenly older than she was. This made her bristle with annoyance. After all, she was the one here with Tommy day after day – why did Melly always think she knew better?

'I'll talk to him,' was all Melly said.

She hadn't said anything else. Rachel wondered now whether she had managed to get anything more out of Tommy. He went off to work with Danny every day, uncomplaining. Perhaps if he got one of those trike things he would be able to go on his own. Maybe that would cheer him up, she thought. He never complained, but try as she might to tell herself that he was all right, she could see he was shrouded in misery.

But what could she do? Rachel made tea and placed a cup in front of Danny, who muttered, 'Ta'. She stood, looking at his bent head. He was barely aware she was there. She climbed the stairs to gather bits of hand-washing.

As she worked she felt a pang of envy for Melly, full of her new job, a life all before her. Melly didn't know she was born. Not that she would have wanted Melly's job. The thought of it made her shudder. At her age, Rachel thought, I had two kids already. No life of my own. And God, she'd been so young. All because of Danny. She would have followed Danny anywhere then, done anything for him.

Back downstairs with an armful of washing, as the tap ran into the pail, she turned and looked at Danny again. Skinny little thing he used to be. He had filled out and was now a strong-looking man getting on for thirty-seven, his face still handsome. His hair had darkened from fair to brown but there was still plenty of it. She looked at his hunched shoulders in his dark blue jersey, suddenly filled with tenderness. What else could she have done at fifteen? With a mother like Peggy and bloody Fred Horton in tow?

Once Cissy, Fred's own child, arrived she had felt like an outsider, a cuckoo in the nest. Cissy was the one who had given Fred and Peggy everything they wanted. And now Cissy had given them Andrew – a proper grandchild, of both of them. No doubt there would be more fuss made over Cissy's kid than there ever was over any of her six, Rachel thought sourly. Not that she blamed Cissy. She was delighted for her sister, had worried for her that she might never have a baby as it was taking so long. It was her mother's snobbery she couldn't stand. Even now she was only just about polite to Danny.

She turned the tap off and tilted the packet of Omo – *Adds brightness to cleanness and whiteness . . .*

'Danny?'

'Ummm – what?' He turned to her.

She wanted him to look, to notice she was there. She smiled. 'Nothing – doesn't matter.'

To her surprise, he grinned back, as if he had heard something in her voice. 'What?'

'Nothing.'

Their eyes met for a moment before they turned away again.

She did still love him, that was all. It was one of the moments when she stopped and knew it. She pushed the dirty clothes down into the white bubbles, smiling to herself.

Thirty-Six

March 1961

'Melly – you seen the list?' Margaret slouched against the door frame of Melly and Berni's room in the nurses' home. 'I'm on with you this time – A3, male medical.'

'Oh – is the list up?' Melly said. They always waited anxiously to see where they were going next. 'Good! We'll be on different shifts, though.'

'At least we can compare,' Margaret said. She came and sat on the edge of Berni's bed.

Now they were no longer the new intake and were seasoned second years who had survived their first-year exams, they were no longer in the 'huts' outside, but in the nurses' home. Some of the girls had rooms to themselves, but Melly had been allocated to share with Berni. Berni's cheerful, freckled face could always cheer her up and their room was often the meeting place for some of the others who came in with cups of cocoa and sat chatting and laughing on the beds. But today, Melly and Berni were sitting propped against the pillows, studying. This was their last week of the latest training block in the classroom and there was a lot to cram into their heads.

'Did you see where I am?' Berni asked.

Margaret frowned. 'C4, I think – women's medical and ENT.' Her face broke into a grin again. 'With Mavis.' Mavis was the least agreeable girl in their group.

'Jaysus, Mary and Joseph!' Berni groaned, stretching and yawning, hands above her head. 'I don't know how that one ever makes anyone better – she looks like the wrath of God.'

'So I'm with you?' Melly smiled at Margaret.

'Yes, brainbox, you are,' Margaret said, pouting. 'Don't go showing me up.'

'I'll try not to.' Melly gave a happy smile.

To her amazement she had achieved the second-highest mark overall in the exams in October. She had come first in anatomy! And she was only a couple of marks off the girl who had come first. The glow of finding out that she could do something well, of being praised by the nursing tutors and finding that anyone could look up to her for something had still not worn off.

'Being a nurse isn't about passing exams anyway, is it?' she added, not wanting to seem too pleased with herself.

'Ohh, C4!' Berni groaned. 'Ladies – they make so much fuss – and they can't pee into a bottle. Give me men to nurse any time!'

'Well,' Margaret said, 'I'd say it's about the only chance they get to make a fuss.' She eyed the open packet of custard creams beside her on Berni's bed. 'Can I have one? Or two?'

'Help yourself,' Berni laughed.

Melly had grown to like Margaret a lot and she admired her determination. Both she and Denise, the two West Indian nurses, had met with hostility on the wards. Melly wondered how they stood it. Denise, who was a quiet girl, never said much about it. Margaret got angry, but not in front of the patients themselves.

'It's something new for them,' she would shrug, trying not to show how hurt and insulted she was. 'Foreign. Maybe they'll get used to us.'

Sometimes being kind to unkind people was the hardest job of all.

The first year had passed with what seemed to Melly like amazing speed. She had never in her life been so happy. As well as flying through the exams – though not without slogging very hard for it – she had completed two ward placements, one on ENT and one men's surgical, and between those, a block of nights on women's surgical. It had been strange and nerve-racking at first. They had visited a couple of wards during the classroom period. And they had learned the basic work, of bed-making and how the ward was to be arranged and giving bed baths.

When she walked on to her first ward for a placement, though, the strangeness of it hit her all over again. There were the hospital smells of disinfectant and soap; and human smells of excrement, the acetone aroma of the very sick, ether and sweat; and sometimes, intermingled, a whiff of flowers. Appearing in uniform, she knew that most patients did not realize she was a new student nurse and would expect her to know what to do. And there was the challenge of dealing with real patients instead of the uncomplaining Mrs Bedworthy with her blank smile.

Melly had made her mistakes – misunderstood and brought the wrong things for senior nurses, got procedures awry, not arranged pillows the perfect way that Sister required and all sorts of human things.

She had, as predicted, found herself sobbing in the sluice, the room at the end of the ward where there were sinks and where they emptied and disinfected the bedpans and sterilized instruments. Sometimes she had cried not out of shame for her own stupidity but out of shock and sadness. A death, or the sadness of someone's life or someone in pain. She had shed a lot of tears already and learned that this was a part of nursing.

But she learned fast. And she loved it. Every time she started on a shift she felt excited. In the long Nightingale wards with the beds in rows along each side, you could see everyone, more or less. There was the caring for people, making them feel better even by just replacing a sheet, smoothing a pillow or giving a kind word.

Melly loved the feeling of restoring order, of tidying and rearranging, making everything fresh and right. It gave her a motherly, protective feeling. Every spare moment she had, she would move about the ward tucking in a sheet here, straightening the wheels of a bed there. Some of the other nurses teased her about it. 'Miss Perfect', Jen called her.

But she did feel she wanted things to be perfect. It was bad enough that people were sick and in pain. The least they could do was to keep the wards looking cheerful and neat and under control.

Each day was like watching a story unfold. She hardly thought about anything else, wondered about her patients even when she was off duty and they were safe in the care of another team of nurses. Sometimes she found herself thinking about Mr So-and-So or Mrs So-and-So and hoping they were not having a bad night.

'You never know a ward,' one sister told her, 'until you've seen it at night. That's when people are at their most fragile.' She learned that people who were most ebullient in the daytime were sometimes the most vulnerable at night.

Despite the hard work, tough on the back, the feet, the emotions, Melly loved almost every day of it and was looking forward to starting on a new ward. She was riding high. This was what she was made for and she wanted to be the best nurse ever.

She had no idea that things could tilt downhill so quickly.

'Welcome to the ward.' Sister Anderson, a stern-looking woman in her forties, dressed in her navy uniform, brown hair scraped back tightly under her frill-edged 'Sister Dora' cap, greeted Melly when she arrived for her first early-morning shift.

Once they had received the handover from the night staff, Sister Anderson drew Melly aside with a first-year nurse who was beginning her first placement, an Irish girl called Cath O'Shea with black curly hair. She was so frail she looked as if she would snap in half and was trying hard not to appear terrified.

'You'll be all right,' Melly told her, also trying not to look terrified and to seem like an old hand.

'Now –' Sister Anderson's tone had an edge of sarcasm – 'do pray tell me, what is a medical ward?' She looked from one to the other of them.

Melly could almost feel Cath seize up with nerves beside her, so she spoke quickly.

'It's for diagnosing and treating illnesses that do not require surgery, usually with drugs,' she recited.

'Good,' Sister Anderson said, without warmth. 'Now – Nurse Jenkins over there will be working with us and the SEN and auxiliary nurse.'

Nurse Jenkins, a third-year student, was a homely-looking girl in her twenties who Melly had often seen around the hospital. She looked nice, Melly thought.

'If you have any questions, never be afraid to ask. Always better to find out than do something wrong because you're afraid to question. Right – now the morning work needs to begin – ah, no, no, stop!'

They both turned, immediately feeling guilty of wrongdoing. But it was the newcomer who was at fault.

'Your apron straps are not crossed correctly at the back,' Sister told her. 'Sort them out immediately. Nurse Booker, it would be quickest if you could help her.'

Melly quickly refastened the girl's apron, unable to resist feeling proud of her own seniority. She could remember her first days on a ward and how ham-fisted she had felt.

'You'll soon be doing it standing on your head,' she whispered and the girl gave her a grateful glance.

Breakfast was over and the first job was the bedpan round for those patients not allowed up. After that, they made the beds, moving the top sheet to the bottom and supplying fresh pillowcases, before the beds were wheeled into the middle of the ward for the cleaner to come and mop the floors. The junior nurses' job was to wipe all the lockers with disinfectant before the beds were pushed back against the walls.

Melly worked as hard and quickly as she could, keen to prove to Sister Anderson that she was an excellent nurse. Over the past months she had become lithe and strong. She liked the feel of her muscles working as she pulled the beds and bent, tucking in a sheet, making it neat and tidy at the corners. She also loved the approval of the senior staff and had worked hard to get it, wanting to be looked upon as a good student, a hard worker and a promising young nurse. She zipped around the beds, proud that she knew what to do and loving comments from the patients, the older men especially who would say things like:

'You're a nippy little thing, aren't yer? They must've put some good batteries inside you, bab!'

And she smiled and smoothed a sheet here, tidied the top of a locker there and felt like a nurse, a radiant, efficient, caring nurse which was what she had always wanted to be.

All that first morning, as they passed round hot drinks, performed bed baths and readied the ward for the dinner trolleys, she gradually got to know the patients lying in the rows of beds: men with bad hearts or lungs, the heavy smokers gasping for breath, mostly older men but a few younger ones too. There was a man of twenty-four who had come in after trying to take his own life with pills and who no one seemed to want to talk to. He lay at the far end of the ward, on his back, staring at the ceiling. And amid all the white faces was that of a black man, thirty-five years old, called Clinton Palmer, who Melly learned was suffering from an inoperable tumour on his lung.

He was a slender man with cropped hair and a slow way of talking and even slower of moving, which made Melly realize how ill he must be feeling. He was lying propped on his pillows, breathing with difficulty.

'Hello, Miss Nurse,' he gasped to her whenever she came close to do anything for him. He peeled his lips back in a smile. Even that seemed to involve effort. His voice was husky. 'How are you this fine day?'

It was sunny outside now, all breeze and daffodils.

Melly smiled, holding his water jug to be refilled. 'All right, thank you. How are you?'

'Doing well, doing well.' He winked at her. 'Never better. I'll be well again – soon as I get to Jamaica.'

'Are you going to Jamaica, Mr Palmer?' she asked,

surprised. This was the first she had heard of it. Surely he was too poorly to travel anywhere?

'That's me.' He gave a chest chuckle. 'God willing. Off and away, home to the West Indies. Isn't that right, Jim?' he rasped across to the man in the next bed, a skeletal-looking fifty-year-old called Mr Stafford, who had been admitted with a suspected gastric ulcer. 'I been telling him.'

Mr Stafford, pale and sunken-cheeked with thin brown hair flat to his head, was lying back dozing. He opened his eyes and made a non-committal sound. A sour expression came over his face. Melly thought he did not look very nice.

By the time Melly had gone to fill up the jug and returned with it, Mr Palmer's head had lolled to one side and he seemed to be asleep. Mr Stafford, however, was wide awake and his expression seemed one of even more terrible revulsion.

'Nurse!' He sat up with sudden urgency. 'Quick – give me the bowl. I'm gonna be sick again!'

He started heaving and coughing. Thank heaven there was a bowl ready on the locker. Melly grabbed it and thrust it at Mr Stafford. She yanked the curtain across between him and Mr Palmer before closing the other side as well. She went to stand beside him.

Mr Stafford gagged, bending forwards, and let out a whimper of pain. He retched and Melly saw a thin jet of pink liquid hit the bottom of the bowl. He panted hugely, gathering himself to be sick again and then again. The torrents spewed into the bowl were blood red and arriving in horrifying quantities. Mr Stafford gave an anguished moan.

'Oh!' Melly gasped. 'Oh, my goodness. Hold on, Mr Stafford – I'll get help!'

In her panic, all the ward rules about never running and presenting a calm exterior went right out of Melly's head. She leapt out from behind the curtains and tore along the ward. 'Sister – Sister, help!'

Sister Anderson, who was bending over another patient, looked up with a thunderous frown on her face.

'Come quickly, please, Sister – it's Mr Stafford!' Melly gasped, skidding to a halt. She did at least manage to lower her voice to hiss close to the Sister's ear. 'He's vomiting blood – *masses* of it.'

Thirty-Seven

Melly lay on her bed, the horror of the morning playing in her mind. She could not stop seeing the gush and splash of red into the white bowl, the terrifying force of Mr Stafford's body expelling blood, splashing his pyjamas, the bedding, the floor . . .

Even though she told herself that the doctors had come and taken over, that he was being cared for, the experience had gone through her like an electric shock.

While the emergency was on, all Sister's attention had been on getting Mr Stafford seen to. It was only later, when he had been rushed away into surgery, that she had had the time to tear a strip off Melly. She ordered her into the sluice. Even though Miss Anderson was not a large woman she seemed to tower above Melly, her expression so grave that Melly felt her already wobbly legs turn to water.

'Nurse Booker – don't ever, *ever* let me see you behave like that on a ward again!'

'I'm s-sorry, Sister.' Melly struggled to speak, her chest was aching so much. She could not hold back and burst into tears, which made things even worse. 'I was so . . . It looked so awful – there was so much blood. I thought he'd flood the ward.'

'Don't be ridiculous,' Sister Anderson said, though she too seemed shaken. 'We are professionals. We do not go panicking and dashing about the ward alarming our other patients. You walk – quietly and swiftly – to where you need to be, without making an exhibition of yourself.'

'Yes, Sister.' Melly looked down at her already well-worn black lace-ups. 'I'm sorry. It won't happen again.'

'I should think it won't,' Sister Anderson retorted. 'Now – wipe your eyes and return to work.'

Somehow Melly had composed herself for the remaining hours she was on duty. She locked her distress away inside her and worked as well as she ever did. But once the end of the shift came and she was back in her room, she sank on to the bed to unlace her shoes and started shaking. Lying back on the bed she had a cry, overcome by shock and the humiliation of being so soundly told off.

Now, she said to herself after she had sobbed quietly for a while. This has to be over. That was what you had to do – have a cry, put it behind you and move on to the next thing.

Feeling slow and unusually exhausted, she pulled herself off the bed and went to wash her feet. She spent the afternoon and evening trying to get things done – stockings to darn, books to read, and Berni came in later after her shift on C4 with stories of the ladies there. Berni could always see the funny side of things. But at any quiet moment, the horrifying rush of blood forced itself into Melly's mind again.

Later in the evening, while Berni was having a bath, there was a tap on their door.

'Hello?' Margaret came in, after her late shift. She saw Melly lying on her bed. 'You all right? You're looking pale as the sheet.'

'I'm all right.' Melly sat up. 'How did it go?'

'Oh – all right.' Margaret sat down beside her. 'They say you had an emergency this morning.' Her cheeks dimpled. 'Sister Anderson gave us a lecture about running on the ward. Wasn't you, was it?'

Melly blushed. 'It was horrible. He started vomiting and it was like a dam bursting. And all blood! I thought he was going to bring up all his insides.' She shuddered and drew her knees in closer. 'I can't stop thinking about it. How is he – is there any news?'

'Torn stomach,' Margaret said with a detached air. 'A perforation. He's all right. On a surgical ward. Sister said he'll be coming back to ours soon – on a sippy.'

The 'sippy' diet was given to ulcer patients involving small but frequent meals, mainly of milk and small amounts of cereal and egg.

'Thank goodness he's all right,' Melly said. It was hard to believe anyone could be all right after all that.

That should have been the end of it, but it wasn't. That night she dreamt that she went into the bathroom in the nurses' home and the bath was filling with blood, the level rising so fast that she could see it would soon be over the side. She backed out of the bathroom, knowing that she must not run, must not shout for help, and walked, hurrying desperately, all round the rooms of the home, then all round the hospital and there was not one person there.

She went back on to the ward and continued to work.

'That poor man,' Mr Palmer whispered to her the next day. He must have heard everything through the curtain. Though he was speaking, he could barely keep his eyes open, his eyelids a deep plum colour. He made a sucking sound through his teeth. 'He going on all right? What happen?'

'I believe he is, yes,' Melly told him. She explained that Mr Stafford had been moved but would be coming back. 'And how are you today, Mr Palmer?'

'Oh . . .' he sighed. 'Strong as a horse, me. Dreaming of Kingston.' He opened one eye. 'You coming with me?'

'All right then.' Melly smiled, a pang in her heart. 'If you like. I'd like to see Jamaica.'

'You would,' he managed to say, though his eyes were closing again. 'Paradise on earth.'

The next day when she came on duty, Mr Palmer's bed was occupied by a new patient, a white face where there had been a black one before. Melly stared at it. Margaret had not said anything – she had been on the late shift.

'Where's Mr Palmer?' she asked Nurse Jenkins.

Hope rose up in her. Had he gone, the way he said he was going to? Was he now on his way to Jamaica, to the sun and sea and palm trees he had longed for?

Nurse Jenkins looked up sadly at her. 'He died in the night,' she said.

'No!' Melly protested. 'No – he can't have done!'

Nurse Jenkins gave her an odd look. 'His cancer was very advanced,' she said. 'You knew that. There was nothing anyone could do.'

'But . . .' Melly was about to say, *He was going to Jamaica* . . .

'No,' she said. 'I suppose not.'

Mr Stafford was back within a few days, looking much the same as he had before, though if anything even thinner. Despite her fear of approaching him, Melly went up to him, her hands clammy with nerves.

'Hello, Mr Stafford,' she said. 'I'm glad to see you're back and all right.'

He nodded. He was a man of few words. 'Ta, nurse. Nasty that was. Very nasty.'

'But you're on the mend now, I hope,' she said.

He nodded and looked back down at his newspaper.

I'm more upset about it than he is, Melly thought.

Later in the morning Sister ticked her off for writing up the results of a urine test wrongly. It was a small thing and Sister was not even very cross, but Melly broke out into a sweat and found herself shaking. Making mistakes was always uncomfortable, but this seemed to assume huge proportions in her mind.

She did not feel right in herself. Before, she had often felt as if she was flying through her shifts on the wards, even though sad things happened. They were nurses, after all, dealing with people who were sick and sometimes dying. But now she felt as if the ground under her feet, firm before, was uncertain and shaking about.

One morning when she came on duty, the Night Sister told them during the handover that there had been a new admission in the night.

'A Mr Alexander, aged thirty-six,' she said. 'He's been in here before, more than once. Chronic asthma – he had an attack in the night. He's stable but his breathing is still laboured. He has a Becotide inhaler now but he still suffers very severe attacks.' She glanced along the ward to a bed on the right-hand side. 'He's asleep at the moment.'

When Melly and the others went to begin their morning routines, she saw Mr Alexander in the fourth bed along, or rather she saw a head of black, wavy hair and only the tip of a cheekbone of his sleeping face.

All she thought then was what a pity it would be to disturb him with all the busyness of the ward after he had suffered such a difficult night.

Thirty-Eight

Melly did not have anything to do with Mr Alexander at all that morning; he was being cared for by Nurse Jenkins and one of the first-year students. But by the time they were getting ready to bring round the dinners he was awake, propped groggily on pillows, wearing green pyjamas and reading a book. He wore spectacles and looked serious, studious. She could see his chest working hard as he breathed.

Among the many grey heads of the ward he stood out. His dark, strong hair and the round, horn-rimmed spectacles drew her attention back to him each time she passed. Something about him fascinated her.

As she hurried back and forth, carrying out all her duties, she could sense his presence. There was an intensity to him, a quiet isolation, as though he had a blanket of silence wrapped about him.

He stayed awake for a time, then fell asleep again, apparently exhausted. He was still sleeping when she went off duty.

The first time she spoke to Mr Alexander was the next afternoon when she was on a late. During visiting hours, Melly saw a woman come in and sit beside him. She was small, with blonde hair cut in a bob, and she moved about the ward as if she was used to hospitals. She brought grapes and daffodils. Melly saw her looking for somewhere to put the flowers and as she was not engaged in a task just then, she went over to them.

'If you give them to me, I'll put them in water for you.'

When she brought them back, their yellow heads just starting to open in the warmth of the ward, they both thanked her quietly and the woman smiled. She had a neat, pretty face and darker eyebrows than her hair.

'I brought him in his books.' She nodded towards a small pile on top of the locker. 'He usually ends up here for a few days. That is all right, isn't it? Shall I put them in the locker?'

'Yes, that might be better,' Melly said.

The woman obeyed immediately. It still felt strange to Melly that her uniform made people who were older than her seem to think she had authority over them.

'He does like his poetry,' she said.

Mr Alexander smiled at her and Melly saw that he looked nice when he smiled.

She left them, wondering if they had children and if so, how old.

It was she who handed Mr Alexander his tea later, when the visitors had gone – a ham salad with coleslaw. As she stood next to him for a moment, Melly could hear his lungs wheezing.

'I'm not sure I'm up to eating much,' he said. The effort of talking made him cough. He had a quiet, well-spoken voice. 'These attacks knock the stuffing right out of me.'

'Never mind,' she said. 'Just eat what you can.'

He stopped coughing and looked up at her, very directly, his dark eyes meeting hers. It had an effect on her, this curious frankness, though she could not have said what the effect was. But an impact of some sort, instant and strong. Her pulse picked up speed.

'All right,' he said, reaching for his fork.

She didn't like to say any more to him when he was about to eat and she had other meals to hand out. She went to collect his plate later. 'I attempted a raid on it,' he joked, handing her the only half-empty plate. 'But the raiding party ran out of steam.' And she smiled and said, 'Well, it's good that you've eaten something.'

Unlike the busy morning shifts, the evening shift sometimes offered pools of calm when the nurses had more time to speak to patients. While they were doing the evening TPRs – taking the temperature, pulse and respirations of each patient – Melly's fingertips had felt the strong pump of blood at his wrist as she counted. She picked up Mr Alexander's chart to record his results.

Mr Raimundo Alexander, she read.

'Raimundo?' she said out loud, without meaning to. She blushed, fearing she had sounded rude.

'Yes,' he said. 'My mother was from Spain.'

'Oh,' she said, adding foolishly, 'that's nice.'

It explained his dark hair, she thought.

Of all the patients it was Mr Alexander she wanted to go back and speak to.

By eight o'clock there was a lull. Melly was walking back along the ward, looking from side to side to check whether anyone needed anything when a low voice from her left called, 'Nurse!'

She turned to see Mr Alexander.

'Sorry,' he said. 'But could you pass me the socks from in my locker, please? My feet are icy cold.'

'Oh, dear, are they?' Melly said. It was hard to imagine being cold on the ward when she was rushing around so much.

She found a pair of black socks in the locker, beside his pile of books.

'Don't move – I'll put them on for you,' she said. 'We don't want to bring on another attack, do we?'

'Oh, I don't think it'll do that, but I must admit, I do feel washed out,' he said.

She folded the covers back. Mr Alexander's slender legs stretched along the bed. He had delicate feet, the dark hairs of his legs giving out at the ankles, the skin very white. She eased a sock on to each foot and covered him up again.

'Shall I see if I can find you another cover?' she said.

'No – it's all right.' He took a wheezing breath, having to lift his diaphragm. 'It's only my feet. The socks will make all the difference.'

'Do you need any of your books out of there?' she asked.

'Oh – now you mention it, yes, please. What did she bring? Would you read the spines to me?'

Melly leaned down to look. 'W. B. Yeats,' she read.

'Yeats.' He chuckled. 'It's pronounced Yates.'

'Oh.' She felt foolish again.

'But then there's Keats,' he said, seeming to enjoy himself, 'spelled with an a but pronounced Keets.'

'Oh, dear,' Melly said. 'You can't win.'

'No, indeed. Who else?'

'Pablo Ner-u-da,' she read slowly.

'Ah, yes – pass me that one, please.'

She handed him the book and put the others back in the locker.

'Is he Spanish?' she said.

319

'Yes. Well, he writes in Spanish. He lives in Chile.' He saw her look vague. 'In South America.'

'Oh.'

She liked the way he talked to her, friendly and not talking down. She lingered by the bed.

'Are you a poet then?'

'Me? No!' He gave a wheezy laugh. 'I design prosthetic limbs. You know – your wooden leg!'

'Oh,' she said. 'That's . . . That's good.'

'Yes, I suppose it is. And you – you're . . . ?'

'Just a second-year student.'

'Marvellous. You look very young—' If he had been about to say something else, his talk was cut off by a long bout of coughing. Melly waited as he curled into himself, his lungs sounding drenched. She wondered if he would rather she went away but she thought she might need to help in some way. As the coughing died, he looked up, took a deep, effortful breath and said, 'They say you're getting old when the nurses start looking young!'

'Nearly twenty,' she said. 'Not that young.' But she realized he was almost twice her age.

'It's a noble thing to do,' he said. Looking up into her eyes, he added, 'Not without its struggles, I'm sure. I suppose everyone wants to believe you're all angels.'

Melly was startled. She had rather hoped that people *did* believe she was an angel.

She shrugged, blushing. She wanted to ask about his work but did not know how to begin.

'My brother can't walk very well,' she said. 'He doesn't have a wooden leg but he's had operations on his left leg.'

'Oh?' She had his attention. 'Why's that?'

She told him about Tommy, about the way he had walked and talked when no one thought he would. An ache filled her as she talked about him. She missed him. And she was worried about him.

'And he's working, you say? Unusual – he must be quite a lad, that one.'

'He is. He's at Lucas's, in Hockley. In the offices.' And he hates it, she thought. Even though he wouldn't say. She must go home and see him. It was so easy to get caught up in life here that she almost forgot about home.

She wondered about Mr Alexander's family, whether he had children.

'Mrs Alexander not in today?' she asked.

'Mrs? Oh, yes – Mrs Alexander. She is, in fact – she's my brother's wife. Very good sort. I lodge with them, you see. No family of my own, sadly.' He gave her a valiant smile.

'Nurse Booker!' The other Sister who was on duty this evening called softly from the middle of the ward.

'Ah,' Mr Alexander said. 'Duty calls. Thank you for your help.'

'Well, you look a bit happier,' Berni observed as Melly came into their room after the shift. She had just arrived back from her own shift on C4, had already removed her cap from her carroty hair and was sitting on the side of her bed untying her laces.

'Phoo!' She picked up her shoes, screwing up her face in disgust. Aching, smelly feet went with the job. She rotated her ankles, starting to do the exercises they had been taught to soothe their feet. 'I bet those men are easier than the women. I spend half the day in the lavatory, I tell you! Then Sister ticked me off because I started off to walk through a door before her.' She brought her right hand across as if shooing away a fly from her face and picked up her shoes. 'These can stay *outside* the door.'

Melly grinned. She found she was bubbling with happiness. 'Yes – we had a good shift.' She told Berni about Raimundo Alexander.

'Raimundo?' Berni chuckled. 'God, he sounds like a proper charmer.'

Melly felt a bit deflated. Berni was so lacking in romance. But once Berni had gone off muttering to the bathroom to wash her feet, Melly looked in the mirror in the bedroom. She *did* look happy. Her face had a peachy glow, her eyes were bright. She let her hair down. For the first time in her life she looked in the mirror and actually felt pretty.

'Hello.' She smiled at her reflection. 'It's nice to see you.'

Then she felt silly. Who the hell was she talking to? Herself? First sign of madness?

She was on an early the next day and she realized she could not wait to get back on the ward. Before, all her heightened emotions were negative ones. Now it seemed to be the opposite. The effect Mr Alexander had had upon her in such a short time felt like a sudden lightning bolt. She wanted to be back there, seeing this man with his romantic name, warm brown eyes and friendly manner. After that she had two days off and he might have gone by the time she was back on the ward. At least tomorrow he would still be there and she might have a chance to talk to him. She had never met anyone like him before.

Thirty-Nine

'Ah,' Mr Alexander said when Melly presented him with his breakfast the next morning. He was looking shinier about the eyes, less ill. 'I see my favourite nurse is back on duty. Do they ever let you have any time off in this place?'

Melly laughed. Berni was right – he *was* a charmer. But in a lovely way. It felt genuine. 'I'm off tomorrow, for two days.' She felt a pang of loss even as she said it. Normally she relished her days off but this time she wanted to keep working while this wonderful man was there, his presence like a glow along the ward.

'Oh, no!' He pulled a mock-disaster face as she laid a boiled egg and toast on his table.

'Sorry.' She pulled her mouth down for a second. 'Toast's burned again.'

'Ah, well –' He drew in an audible breath. 'These things are sent to try us. Actually, I rather like burned toast.'

He was well enough now to get up and wash himself so he did not need a bed bath. She would feel him throughout everything she did on the ward that morning, like a constant tingle of awareness. She told herself not to be so silly; why should he be interested in her? But almost every time she looked over in his direction, he *was* watching her and would give a slow smile if she held his gaze long enough.

Mr Stafford was recovering very slowly with the help of his 'sippy' diet. Melly was often the one who had to go and hand him his regular glass of milk. Though she was ashamed of the feeling, she was frightened of going anywhere near him. Every time he took a sip she was afraid some new horror would erupt out of him. But she gave him encouraging smiles and tried not to show him how she felt.

Everything seemed to be going her way that morning. She was the one to make Raimundo Alexander's bed, with Cath, the young Irish nurse, while he sat out on his chair. All the time she was doing it, her heart beat faster and she was full of excitement as if all her feelings were intensified again. And he talked to them, or rather to her, asking more questions about Tommy and about her family. They had been told not to talk about themselves to patients, to ask only after them, but with Mr Alexander it was difficult because he was so curious about other people. When she admitted that her father worked on the Rag Market he seemed very interested.

'What does he sell?' he asked.

'Clothes,' she said, glancing round to check that Sister was not within earshot. 'Lately he's trying to set up something new – leather coats and sheepskins, things like that.'

'How fascinating,' he said. 'He must meet all sorts of people.'

'Yes – I s'pose he does.' She was so used to it she had hardly thought.

Something about him touched her. For a grown man who was sturdy and good looking he also seemed frail. Patients were often childlike in hospital. Grown men put themselves in her hands as if she was the elder of the two of them and she was suddenly like their mother. It was

324

not quite like this with Raimundo Alexander. He had been in and out of hospital with his asthma and was more used to it than some. But there was a sweetness about him, a wistfulness. And he seemed genuinely to like her and to enjoy her company.

As for her, she had to admit to herself, over this short time she had become very preoccupied. She only had to look in his direction and see him looking at her, to feel weak at the knees. It was the first time, she realized, that she had felt this about a man since Reggie Morrison. The thought of Reggie filled her with sadness. She hadn't seen the Morrisons in ages. Gladys went over there every so often, but since they had stopped being neighbours nothing was ever the same. She had barely seen Reggie in years.

Perhaps I just like older men, she thought. She'd been out with a few boys, like Paul, who was nice enough to spend a bit of time with, but neither he nor any of the others had come close to stirring her feelings like this. She found herself thinking about Raimundo constantly, in a besotted sort of way. As often as she could, she went to see if there was something she could fetch for him – water, books, anything!

'A little chat?' he said once when she asked if there was anything he wanted.

'Sorry,' she said, eyeing Sister along the ward. 'No time at the moment.'

He gave a conspiratorial smile. 'No – I can see that. Later perhaps?' And this thrilled her.

But as it was the early shift with all the usual tasks to get through and with two new admissions to the ward, one with terrible bedsores from being nursed too long at home, the other with an intravenous infusion in his arm, they were kept very busy. Melly was dispirited that she only just managed to find time to have a word with Mr Alexander as she was going off duty in the afternoon.

'I'm going now, Mr Alexander. I've two days off, so I don't know if you'll still be here?' She spoke in a bright and cheerful voice, as if to any patient, while her heart was going like a drum.

'So you're deserting me, are you?' He looked up at her. In the second their eyes met, Melly felt quite wobbly about the knees again. 'Oh, dear. Is that really so? Well, I'm sorry to hear that. I shall miss my favourite nurse.'

She felt like rushing to see if she could exchange shifts with someone, rearrange her days off. But it was too late.

'You might have gone, I suppose,' she said, 'by the time I get back.'

'Oh, I don't know about that,' he said. 'They seem to keep me in interminably whenever I have one of these attacks. But just in case . . .' He held out a hand to shake hers. 'It's been a pleasure to meet you, Miss Booker.'

He had remembered her name! Her cheeks blazed red, she was sure of it.

'You too,' she said.

She turned to go, then looked back at him and said in a formal tone, 'I hope you feel much better soon.'

As she walked away along the corridor of the hospital she found, to her surprise, that she had tears in her eyes.

Before going home for a visit, Melly took two buses and went to see Gladys in Alma Street. She hoped Auntie would be in. She had not said she was coming. Being a weekday she might be out, getting stuff for the market.

Aston came as a shock to her now as she did not go there often. It was familiar, in one way, but whereas before she had taken it all for granted, now she was struck afresh by the cramped, mildewy houses and decaying yards, shops boarded up with half-rotted fly posters blowing in the breeze, the blank walls of factories, the smells of rotting rubbish mixing with factory smells.

When would Auntie stop being so stubborn and call it a day? She could move out any time, Melly thought. They could help her look for somewhere.

The door of number three was ajar and she heard, 'Come in, Melly, bab,' as soon as she knocked. Gladys was in her usual place, looking out over the yard, a half-drunk cup of tea in front of her.

'Fancy seeing you,' she said dryly.

'Hello, Auntie.' Melly smiled. The room looked just the same as ever. It was good to be back. 'You all right?'

'I'll do,' Gladys said. 'You'd better make a fresh pot, bab. My feet're killing me today.'

'Anything going on?' Melly nodded towards the yard as she filled the kettle from a pan of water Gladys had ready.

'Oh, you know . . .' Gladys said. She sat up straighter, looking out. An air of sadness hung over her. She seemed tired, defeated in some way. 'The usual. The Davieses have gone – I don't know where. More Irish moved in.' She rolled her eyes, speaking in a flat tone. Melly saw in the hard daylight that her hair was now more white than anything. The colours had been in competition and now white was winning.

'How're Lil and Stanley?' Melly came and sat down.

'Oh – you won't've heard . . . She had to have them take Stanley. He went for her – she had two black eyes. He hardly seemed to know who she was any more.'

'Take him?'

'To the asylum.' Gladys jerked her head in the general direction of Winson Green.

'They call it the mental hospital now, Auntie,' Melly pointed out.

Gladys shrugged. 'It's the same place.'

'Oh, Auntie.' Melly's heart ached for Lil. 'She never wanted to do that. How is she?'

'You know Lil. Bearing up. She goes over to see him, twice a week or so.'

Melly made tea and they talked about the family. Melly didn't tell Gladys she was worried about Tommy. She talked a bit about the wards and dug out one or two of Berni's stories to make Gladys laugh.

'I'd better be off soon,' she said when they'd had their tea.

'Oh – I forgot,' Gladys said. 'I tell you who I saw the other evening – Sat'd'y, after the market. That youngest wench of Irene Sutton's – Evie, wasn't it?'

'Did you? Goodness, she'd be seventeen by now, like Tommy!' Melly said. 'Did you speak to her?'

'No. I'm sure it was her, though. Coming out of the Drover's on some bloke's arm.' Gladys frowned. 'She saw me but I don't know if she'd've known me after all this time. I tell you summat though – she's still pretty as a picture.'

'Poor Evie,' Melly said. 'That awful mother of hers. I hope she's all right. Look, I'll see you soon, Auntie. Ta-ra for now.'

'Ta-ra.' Gladys got to her feet and to Melly's surprise, said, 'Thanks for coming to see me, bab.'

Melly waited for the bus back into town, feeling sad, for Auntie and for Lil Gittins and the changes that life had brought them.

On the bus, part of Melly's mind was still on the ward, thinking about what they would all be doing now and wondering how Mr Alexander was this morning. The image of his face swam in her mind.

Her mother came to the door in her apron, Alan, who was now four, trailing behind her.

'Oh – hello – I wondered if you'd be coming,' Rachel said distractedly. 'No, Alan, stop that – go on, find something to do.'

'Hello, Alan!' Melly greeted him. The little boy looked overjoyed to see her and came to her for a cuddle. 'You bring something for me to do with you,' she said to him. 'Your cars? I'll play with you while we have a natter.'

Rachel sank down by the table. 'Oh – I'll be glad when that one goes to school, that I will. He's hard work on his own.'

Melly laughed. 'I s'pose you haven't had one on its own since me,' she said.

'Not for long, no,' Rachel said.

They talked over the racket of Alan rolling his cars along the table.

'Tommy all right?' Rachel asked.

'He's all right,' Rachel said. She didn't look Melly in the eye. Melly saw she looked tired. 'He's a bit quiet, that's all.' She was holding her cup between her hands. She had to shield it from a crash with one of Alan's Dinky cars. 'All right – that's enough,' she snapped. 'You get down and do that on the floor. Or do something else. You're getting on my nerves.'

Alan slid to the floor with a dark look at his mother and scooted the cars up and down the tiles.

'Dad still taking him over there?'

'Some days. When he's not out early. He's going to Somerset every week now – buying sheepskins and that. Tommy gets the bus. It takes it out of him, though.' She looked across the room, still avoiding Melly's eye. 'It's like blood out of a stone with him and Tommy at the moment.'

Knowing Mom, Melly thought, she wouldn't have tried very hard either. But she could have a go herself. Suddenly she felt like the oldest child in the family again, someone who had a place and could be useful.

'Dad all right?'

'Oh, yeah,' Mom said. 'Your father's all right. Always is.'

She was not planning to stay overnight but she waited until the others were back from school and then Tommy from work.

Ricky and Sandra got home first and were glad to see her. Kev walked in, tie all adrift, shirt unbuttoned. 'All right, Melly?' he said with manly disdain. But she could see he was pleased to see her.

Tommy came in with Danny and disappeared upstairs.

'All right, wench!' her father said. 'They given you a day off, have they?'

She smiled. 'Yeah – couple of days.'

'I wouldn't've worked you as hard as all that, you know. Eh –' he came over to her, full of enthusiasm – 'you should come with me. I'm starting to get cabbage from the furriers, and second-hand – beautiful stuff, some of it. Them shops are summat else, you want to see 'em. There's one at Five Ways, got an elephant in the shop – huge thing it is!' He nudged her. 'You'll have to come.'

Melly laughed, enjoying hearing the old market names for things again – like 'cabbage' for seconds, or damaged goods. 'All right, Dad – you take me one day.' She told him she had been to see Gladys and all about Lil and Stanley.

'Shame,' Rachel said. 'It shouldn't have to come to that.'

'I don't want you putting me away,' Danny called from the sink where he was washing his hands.

'Don't tempt me,' Rachel retorted.

Tommy came back down, walking with his stick. As he came through the door, the noise of the telly from the front came in a burst before he closed the door again. He gave Melly a wan smile and sank into his chair, seeming relieved. He looked paler, thinner and more worn than Melly could ever remember. His work trousers hung on him as if made for a bigger man.

'All right, Melly?' She was helping Mom cook tea – egg and chips. The potatoes were seething in the hot oil.

'How's it going, Tommy?' She filled with pleasure at seeing his sweet, familiar face.

'OK. What about – the – hospital?'

'Oh, that's nice. I like it.'

'You're – lucky.' He looked away.

She was, she knew. Mom cracked eggs into the pan and they sizzled and spat. Melly lifted the chips from the fat and let them rest a moment. Mom had a metal basket now specially for cooking chips and it made delicious ones.

'They treating you all right?'

'Umm.' Tommy looked away. She lowered the chips back into the fat. The room smelt of it. Their clothes would too.

'I'll put some beans on,' Rachel said.

'Hey – look – what I – bought.'

Tommy got up again. In the corner, on the sideboard, he showed her a record player in a little red case.

'Oh, Tommy!' she said, excited. 'I didn't notice that. Did you get that with your wages?'

'It's second-hand,' Rachel said. 'Nearly new, though.'

Tommy was beaming now. 'I've – only – got one –

record.' He put it on, a 45 of Bill Haley. They listened, jigging to 'Rock Around the Clock'. Melly felt her spirits lighten.

'Get something nice and romantic next time,' Rachel commented. But she looked pleased.

Once they had all eaten tea and cleared up, Melly thought, soon I'll have to get the bus. The thought of Raimundo Alexander came to her for a moment, almost like a pain.

'Tommy . . .' The others had gone to the front room to watch the television. 'You all right?' she asked. 'You'd say if you weren't?'

'Yeah.' He looked away.

Something in his face filled her with sorrow for him. He seemed so defeated and disappointed. But he would not say any more.

Forty

When she got back to the nurses' home late that evening, she went straight to her room to find Berni, who had not long come off duty.

Berni already had her shoes off and was lying, collapsed, on her bed.

'You all right?' Melly said, fearing the worst. 'What's happened?'

'Nothing.' Berni sat up, yawning. Her hair hung in a loose coil behind her head, having just been released from being up all day. 'Why should anything be up?'

'I just wondered.' Melly sat down beside her. 'Anything new?' She both wanted and did not want to bring up Raimundo Alexander's name. She was very afraid that he might have been discharged.

Berni thought, lying propped on her elbow. Then she said, 'Not really. Mr Stafford's still sipping away. The feller with pneumonia's gone home now. Your Mr Gorgeous with the asthma's still wheezing and coughing his head off—'

'Coughing?' Melly said. 'What – worse than before?'

Berni twinkled up at her. Melly had so often seen those naughty blue eyes looking at her across the room of the training school and had been reduced to giggles. The pair of them had often been in trouble for it. But now Melly thought she saw something knowing in them, teasing her. 'Now – why would you be asking about him?' she said. 'Go on now – do I see pink cheeks?'

'No!' Melly laughed it off.

'His cough's got worse – or at least it's not better. They were talking about him going out at the beginning of the shift and they'd changed their minds by the end.'

She told Melly a few stories about the nursing staff which made her giggle and she went to bed happy. Even though it was her day off the next day, it sounded as if Mr Alexander would surely still be there when she went back to work.

She was restless the next day. There were the usual chores to catch up on, washing underwear and her stockings which needed holes darning in them as well and polishing her shoes.

In the afternoon she walked down the hill through Selly Oak. It was a damp, cold day and she had to put her umbrella up for half the walk. She bought apples and chocolate. On the way back, on impulse, she stopped at the library next to the railway bridge and went inside.

She had hardly ever been in a library before and she immediately felt apologetic, as if she was bound to do something wrong. There was a hushed, brown atmosphere inside and a smell of paper. An old man with yellow-white hair greased to his head was sitting at a table reading the paper with his face very close to the page. She could smell him across the room. He coughed and his chest rattled.

The pale librarian at the front desk looked at her over half-moon spectacles.

'Can I help you?' He looked at her suspiciously, as if she might be about to commit a crime.

'I . . .' Whispering, she went on. 'I wondered if you had any poetry?'

The man, who had chopped brown hair and a pudgy face, made a superior sort of gesture with his neck as if to say, *Well, what do you expect? This is a library!* He led her across the room, with its long windows, to a shelf in the corner.

'Poetry,' he said, snootily. And walked off.

Melly looked along the shelves of worn old spines, trying to find any of the names that she had seen on Mr Alexander's books. She had memorized them: Keats, Yeats, Robert Lowell, Pablo Neruda . . . At first she thought the library did not have any of them until she came to the last shelf and found an old blue book. *W. B. Yeats* she could just read on the spine.

The poems made her feel stupid. A lot of them were very long and she did not understand the language or what they were about. She felt sad and disappointed looking through the book. How could she have thought . . .? But what had she been thinking, really? That Raimundo Alexander was interested in her? That she could be his equal? But he read these books as if they were simple as ABC, or so it appeared to her. And she could barely understand this one at all.

There were some shorter poems in the book. One that caught her eye was called 'A Friend's Illness'. The poem was only a few lines, saying how the friend's illness had put a new thought in his mind:

Why should I be dismayed
Though flame had burned the whole
World, as it were a coal,
Now I have seen it weighed
Against a soul?

She read the poem over and over again, trying to make sense of it. Did he mean that one person, one soul, was more important than all the world if that person was someone you loved? Or did it mean something else completely? She put the book back and walked to the hospital. She still felt stupid because she did not really know what the poem meant.

But it was about a sick friend and a sick friend was the thing always at the front of her mind.

She was on duty again in the morning, glowing with happiness not only that Mr Alexander was still there, in the same place, but that he looked up in his quiet way when she came over to him and his eyes were full of warmth.

'Ah, I see my favourite nurse is back.'

Melly beamed at him. He *did* like her – even if only as his 'favourite nurse'. 'How are you, Mr Alexander?'

'Doing all right. The cough won't leave me be, though. They decided to keep me in a few more days.'

'Well, I'm sure you'll be on the mend soon,' she said, not wanting to add that she was glad he was still here. It would sound as if she wanted him to be ill.

The morning was very busy. She was not assigned to make his bed, but she enjoyed her work, knowing that he was there. She felt efficient and energetic, as if someone had lit a fire under her and she was burning with energy.

'Heavens,' Nurse Jenkins said, half in complaint, when they were making a bed together. 'Days off have certainly perked you up! It isn't actually a race, you know!'

'Sorry,' Melly laughed. She knew she was feeling a bit frantic and she tried to move in a more measured way.

She was waiting for an opportunity to speak to Mr Alexander again, wanted to tell him about the poem.

There was no chance during the morning, because there was so much to get done. But when the dinner trolleys appeared and Sister was supervising, she handed Melly a plate of meat in gravy with vegetables.

'Here – for Mr Alexander,' she said.

Melly's pulse speeded up. She carried the plate over.

'Dinner time. Looks like a nice stew,' she told him, though she didn't think it looked all that marvellous.

'Ah – thank you,' he said, and coughed.

Setting the plate on his table she said, 'I went to the library yesterday and had a look for . . .' To her annoyance she hesitated. She still wanted to say 'Yeets'. 'For Yeats. I read a bit. He's good, isn't he?'

'Oh – did you?' He looked surprised and pleased. 'Yes, he's wonderful – some of them, anyway. I don't necessarily read all the long ones.'

Melly was delighted to hear it. She had to go then.

'Tell me, when you have time,' he said in a friendly way. 'What you read, I mean.'

'I will.' She smiled and went back to Sister, hoping that later in the afternoon, before the shift ended, she might have a chance to go and sit with him.

While they were clearing the dinner plates away on to the trolley, she saw Mr Alexander get up and walk along the ward towards the bathrooms. He was quite able to move about now and did not need much assistance, which Melly was mainly relieved about though it would have been another chance to talk to him. He did not look in her direction as he went past and she thought it was because he was heading for the toilet.

She went round the ward gathering plates. It was buzzing with noise. People tended to perk up a bit when they had had a bit to eat, before wanting to sleep, and some of the patients were chatting. Someone was coughing along the ward and someone else laughed. The rubber wheels of the trolley squeaked on the polished linoleum.

'Right,' Sister said when they had all the plates back on the trolley. 'Take it out now, please, Nurse Booker.'

She was wheeling the trolley towards the main door of the ward. She could hear the coughing, louder now, and she thought that must be Mr Alexander. They were right to keep him in – it did sound bad.

There was a commotion then, by the door into the bathrooms. Cath, the first-year student, came flying along the ward in obvious panic. Melly saw, as if in a dream, that someone was lying on the floor in the doorway into the bathrooms, and Nurse Jenkins was there and Cath was saying, 'Sister – quick, he's collapsed!'

Sister Anderson was along the ward in seconds. She dropped to her knees beside the prone figure. Nurse Jenkins hurried across to the ward telephone. Melly moved towards them, feeling as if her destination was never coming any closer. Somewhere about her, patients were making comments, craning to see what was happening.

Mr Alexander was flat on his back. His eyes were closed and his body looked slack in a way which made Melly freeze. Sister Anderson was over him, breathing into his mouth, pressing on his chest. She looked more frantic than Melly had ever seen her.

A doctor appeared, crashing through the doors to the ward, white coat flying behind him. He saw immediately what the situation was and joined Sister Anderson on his knees. He felt for a pulse, asked questions. What happened? How long . . . ? They deliberated for a moment. Then the doctor laid a hand on Sister's arm. Her eyes met his and he gently shook his head.

'No!' The sound came out of Melly's mouth without

338

her knowing it. They glanced round. She put her hands over her mouth to stifle the scream that wanted to tear out through it.

'He was only thirty-six,' she heard Sister Anderson say to the doctor. There was shock in her voice. And sorrow and bewilderment.

She looked round at Melly, and almost in a confessional tone she said, 'I'm afraid he's gone.'

Forty-One

She lay in the dark, the blood thumping round her body. Every night now it was the same.

Berni was asleep across the room, making little popping sounds with her mouth like a fish. They sounded like gunshots to Melly. Sleep was completely impossible. Every cell in her body was in a jarred, surging state that would give her no rest.

The room was completely dark. She wondered what the time was, but if she switched on the light Berni would wake up and complain. If only she could read to try and quieten her mind. She considered creeping out to the common room, but she thought she might be in trouble if she got caught. And all she really wanted was to lie down and be able to sleep.

It was like this every night now. Since Mr Alexander died, four days ago, she felt she had not slept at all. Desperation filled her. So far she had kept going during her ward duties, full of a crazed energy. But the body and mind needed sleep. What if she started to make terrible mistakes on the ward? It had been a close-run thing already.

The first night, over and over again she had seen Raimundo Alexander's body on the floor along the ward, then herself moving towards him, unable to turn away and not see . . . Sister moving up and down over him, trying and trying to pump the life back into his body, his crumpled look, the closed eyes.

How could he be dead? He was only thirty-six.

Asthma, Sister said afterwards, can affect the heart. The lack of oxygen, the extra strain on the body. His asthma was severe.

Thank heavens Melly had not been one of the ones to lay him out. Instead, she could remember him alive and smiling at her.

She knew really that Mr Alexander had not been interested in her *like that*. He was a nice man and he had seemed to like having a chat to her and having her look after him. She barely understood her own tender attachment to him – not like being in love exactly, but involved so that her emotions fixed so strongly on him. But none of this really made sense of why, now, she was in such an overwrought state. Every night her mind was like a flickering light, sending fast, broken-up images until she thought she might go mad. Eyes open or closed she could not stop it. Her chest was tight and she had to keep reminding herself to breathe deeply.

Lying here, now, she turned on her back once more and stared up into the darkness. He was there. Then he was gone.

She had seen other patients die, or known of them dying. This one was different. The sudden, abrupt wrongness of it.

He was a beautiful man . . . The thought wrung her, but still she could not cry. If she could only shed some tears she might begin to get past it, but they would not come. She felt like a dry stone.

There was nothing she could say to anyone. They all had their shocks and things to face on their own wards. Margaret had said to her, 'Such a shame about that nice man, Mr Alexander. And you were there? Terrible thing. Must've been a shock.' She clicked her tongue, shook her head. That was all. It was a straight line for Margaret, it seemed, out the other end. For Melly it was a circle in which she was trapped, which just kept swirling her round and round.

'Nurse.'

Melly was walking along the ward. A hazy feeling filled her head, as if she was not really there. Everything felt like a dream.

'Nurse!'

'Melly – Mr Hopkins is calling you.'

Luckily it was Cath who saw her. She gave Melly an odd look but was not in a position to tell her off.

Melly went over to Mr Hopkins, a bluff, bald, pink-faced man with a heart problem. His legs were swollen with oedema and sometimes seeped astonishing amounts of liquid.

'You with us, bab?' he said wheezily. He was a kindly person, embarrassed by his condition. 'Only, er . . .' He whispered. 'I need to, er, I need to go, Nurse.'

'Sorry, Mr Hopkins,' she said wretchedly. God, she thought. I must pull myself together.

'I'll help you. You'd prefer to go along to the bath-room, rather than a bedpan?'

'Oh, yes, I would,' he said fervently. 'I'd rather be private, Nurse, if I can.'

She supported him slowly along the ward. He made a gallant joke about them walking arm in arm. Like getting married, he said, and she managed a laugh. She delivered him to the lavatories.

'I'll be outside,' she said.

She stood just by the door, almost in the spot where Mr Alexander had collapsed. Melly closed her eyes for a moment. Right there, by her feet, was where he had lain. For the first time, tears welled behind her eyelids. Oh, God, not now. I can't cry now. She swallowed them away and quickly wiped her eyes. Mr Hopkins took a while. She began to be afraid. Supposing his heart gave out while he was sitting on the lavatory and she didn't notice in time? Or what if he was in there haemorrhaging to death and was too faint to call out?

'You all right, Mr Hopkins?' she called to him.

'Yes, ta, bab. Not doing too badly,' she heard.

Eventually she was able to take him back to bed.

Nothing went wrong, she thought, with relief. She realized she did not trust herself. Even making beds, one of the easiest jobs on the ward, seemed fraught with danger. Taking patients' TPRs, sometimes she had to start again several times because she drifted off.

'Sure you can count?' one man said to her sarcastically, when she had taken his pulse for a ridiculously long time.

Odd things kept happening, or seemed to her to be happening. She saw calamity everywhere: gushes of blood, horrific torrents of diarrhoea, unstoppable vomiting, all plagued her mind. Every time a patient had anything wrong in that way, she froze with panic, terrified that something extreme was about to happen. She saw chaos breaking out everywhere.

Over and over again she tidied up; the beds, the ward. It was such a busy place that things got out of order very quickly. If only she could keep everything tidy, nothing would happen. Everything would be kept at bay.

'Nurse . . .' Sister Anderson came to her one afternoon in the laundry cupboard, where she was folding and

343

refolding pillowcases, pyjamas. Sister frowned. 'What are you doing?'

'Just tidying, Sister.' She felt hunted. Was she doing something wrong? She just wanted to be busy, to keep things under control.

Sister Anderson looked around the little room with its neatly stacked shelves. Then she looked at Melly.

'Are you all right, Nurse Booker?'

'Yes, Sister. Thank you.'

'The laundry room is quite tidy enough. We have a new admission coming this evening – Mr Davis is going to be discharged today. I shall need your help with that. In the meantime, go and make the patients' drinks, please.'

'Yes, Sister.'

She felt Sister Anderson's eyes on her as she walked towards the kitchen. She had a moment's relief. Making drinks was a soothing, easy job. Nothing terrible could happen.

Working wards was becoming more and more difficult but despite all the worry and uncertainty it caused her, it was the nights she dreaded most now, going to bed and lying there in a scattered agony of mind, unable to fall asleep. Sounds echoed loud in her head. Images flashed and dashed across her mind.

She felt as if everything was sliding from her grip, but she did not know how to say so, or who to say it to. Nurses were not supposed to have emotions, or not for long. They were meant to get over them. She was ashamed of the state she was in. It was unprofessional and weak.

'You've been restless at night,' Berni – who slept like a

log – observed one evening, a week after Mr Alexander's death.

'Sorry,' Melly said, amazed that Berni had only just noticed this. 'I'm not sleeping very well.'

It didn't get any better. A few days later, Berni tackled her about it again. Sitting on the side of her bed, she studied Melly's face.

'Are you still not getting your rest? I heard you moving about last night. You really don't look any too good, you know. You're all black under the eyes. And you're getting thin.'

Melly knew it. In the mirror a white, gaunt face looked back at her. Her uniform belt felt looser and she could easily circle her wrist with the finger and thumb of the other hand.

'What's ailing you?' Berni asked, head on one side. 'You look worse than some of the patients!' She gave her laugh and Melly forced a smile.

'Oh, I don't know. Time of the month.' She pretended to busy herself. 'Better get my shoes polished.'

They were lovely March days, sunshine brightening the chill and spring flowers like a bright carpet across Bourn-ville Green. But Melly was too exhausted to notice.

That morning, when she crawled out of bed, she felt so sick she could barely force any breakfast down. Nor-mally the hearty slabs of bread and margarine were just what was needed to fuel a morning's work, but she was finding it difficult to eat anything. She only managed to nibble at the edge of a piece of bread, which settled her stomach a bit with a cup of tea.

Her placement on A3 was almost over and they would be back in the Training School for a few weeks after that.

It felt like a relief. She was fast beginning to feel that she could no longer cope on the ward. All the time she was full of doubt. She was the worst nurse there had ever been – and to think she had wanted to be the best! Maybe she had aimed too high and it was not for her. She had failed.

When Melly walked on to the ward that morning she was feeling especially low. She thought every patient was looking at her and thinking, she shouldn't be here, she can't do the job. She's an impostor!

Even the simplest tasks such as emptying bedpans and serving out cups of tea filled her with nervousness, as if she was bound to do something terribly wrong – scald a patient with a cup of tea, drop the contents of the bedpans all over the place. As for writing down results of urinary and other tests, she kept checking over and over again. It made her very slow.

She was asked to go back to the kitchen when the tea trolley was going round. Melly walked along to the kitchen. She stood in the middle of the floor looking around, at a loss. Why was she here? Someone had sent her for something but she could not for the life of her remember what. She just stood there, helpless.

Nurse Jenkins came striding along looking very irritated.

'The sugar! I sent you ages ago. Oh, for goodness' sake – I might as well get it myself.'

'Sorry,' Melly said. Sugar – of course. What felt like several hours ago, someone had asked her to bring sugar.

It was later that morning, as she battled on, that Sister Anderson asked her to assist her while she removed the IV drip from the arm of a patient called Mr Brzezinski.

Mr Brzezinski had arrived from Poland after the war. He was in his forties, had a pale, chiselled face and spoke heavily accented English in which he had, with apparent zest, mastered the words for gratitude.

'Thank you, thank you!' he addressed them before they had even started.

'I'm going to remove this –' Sister pointed, speaking slowly. 'Take it out of your arm.'

'Ah, very good – thank you!' Mr Brzezinski beamed at her.

Melly stood beside Sister Anderson. Her head felt as though it was swimming. She would have liked to sit down but that was not a possibility.

Sister Anderson pressed gently on the cannula and slid it from the man's muscular arm. He made a small sound, an intake of breath between his lips.

'All right?' Sister looked at him.

'Oh, yes, thank you – very good!'

It was then, in those seconds when Sister Anderson went to press a small dressing on the wound, that Melly saw the bead of blood. It was welling slowly bigger. Panic exploded in her. She heard herself gasp and the next thing she knew she was tearing along the ward in utter panic, desperate to get away before the surge and flood of blood submerged them all.

Forty-Two

Nervous breakdown, they said at the hospital.

That day, after Mr Brzezinski, after the bead of blood which had turned into a spouting deluge in her mind, Sister Anderson had come back into the sluice, after the first ticking off, and found Melly crouched in the same spot in the corner, curled in on herself, her limbs quivering.

'Nurse?' Her tone was outraged at first. 'Nurse?' She came closer. Now there was caution, concern growing in her voice. Melly watched her shoes come closer, the sturdy ankles, the hem of her navy uniform.

'Nurse Booker.' Her voice had become chilly and professional, as if Melly was another patient. 'What are you doing?'

Melly began to tremble even more. She shook her head, kept shaking it, too many times to be normal; she knew but she could not stop doing it.

Sister Anderson bent down and Melly caught a whiff of her, a tang of sweat, lavender water, carbolic, so strong it made her stomach heave.

'Are you unwell?' She spoke very quietly now. They must not let the patients have any idea of this. They were professionals.

'I . . . I don't know,' Melly managed to say.

'Nurse – would you please stand up and continue your

duties?' Sister Anderson clearly decided to adopt the firm, no-nonsense approach.

Melly climbed shakily to her feet. A moment later she had thrown herself, retching, over one of the sluice sinks.

Sister Anderson waited, hands on hips now.

'Right, Student Nurse Booker, you had better call in sick.'

She turned and walked out. Melly heard the squeak of her shoes on the floor.

The next morning she could not get out of bed.

The bus crawled along the outer circle route away from Selly Oak.

Melly had climbed to the top deck and walked right to the front seat as far away from everybody as she could. The bus was not full but it was still fuggy with cigarette smoke and the stale smell of crammed-in bodies from the busier time of the morning. The window was steamed up and smeary.

She put her bag down on the floor beside her and sat holding her hands clasped together to try and stop them shaking.

It took barely twenty minutes to get to Harborne. She wished it was much longer, that she had got on the number eleven going round the other way so that she could spend half the morning just sitting here.

Twenty minutes for her to transfer herself back from one life – the only life she had really wanted – to another, which held nothing for her.

*

'What're you doing here?'

Her mother's face, after the initial shock, looked stern and guarded. She stood blocking the doorway.

'Let me in, Mom,' Melly said.

In silence they went into the back. Alan was playing on the kitchen floor. Rachel folded her arms across her pink blouse, her apron.

'You look like a widow. What's going on?'

Even then, Melly could not reach the tears which she knew must come. She felt queasy all the time, and wired tight inside, so tight that she still could not sleep. But she could not cry either.

She shrugged. 'They sent me home.'

'Why?' Her mother looked even more grim. 'What've you done?'

'Done? Nothing. It's not . . .' She looked down at the floor, the familiar well-worn quarry tiles. She had thought she was so encased in misery that nothing could affect her. But the way Mom was looking at her, her question, made Melly feel overwhelmed with shame and guilt.

'They said I'm not very well. That I needed to go home.'

Rachel softened a fraction. 'You don't look well, babby.'

Tears swam into her eyes then and she could not look up. 'Oh, Mom,' she said. 'I don't know what's happening to me.'

'You'll have to sleep in with Sandra,' Rachel said. Melly could hear a sigh in her voice. Even though Mom had not been keen on her going into nursing, she didn't seem any more enthusiastic about her coming home again. She'd got used to things the way they were. Having thought she'd got one child off her hands, here she was back again and not apparently fit for anything.

'You look as if you just need a good night's sleep,' she observed. Her worry made her sharp-tempered. 'Nervous breakdown indeed. I don't know what your father'll say about all this. Are they still paying you?'

'No – I don't suppose so.' Melly felt herself shrinking inside. She wasn't sure about the nervous-breakdown bit either, but Mom was acting as if she was putting it all on and just being a nuisance.

'But you'll be going back, will you – they'll take you?'

'I don't know.' Melly sat hunched at the table. She was finding this interrogation, as well as Alan's whirring about the room, very difficult to bear. She was close to screaming, and clutched her arms tight round herself to keep the scream inside.

Matron hadn't said that she couldn't go back. She said it depended on her recovery and then they would see.

It went quiet and after a moment Melly looked up, to find her mother staring at her with a worried expression.

'You look all in. Come on,' she said. 'Let's get you a bed ready.'

In the face of this kindness, as she took her bag and followed her mother upstairs, for the first time, Melly burst into tears.

Forty-Three

May 1961

'Back later!' Rachel called up the stairs. 'Don't forget to fetch Alan, will you?'

She heard a faint reply from upstairs.

'Well, I s'pose she heard me,' Rachel muttered, heading out of the front door. There was no time to go up and make sure. She was running late. 'At least one of us is out earning our living, any road,' she added huffily.

Soon after Melly arrived back home, Rachel had decided she might just as well go out to work. It was no good both of them mooning about at home. Ricky and Sandra's school, where Alan would soon be going as well, had been asking for more dinner ladies. It was only a couple of hours a day, supervising the dinners and outside playtime, and Rachel jumped at it. She had let her volunteering at Carlson House go when she had Sandra and then Alan and was yearning to have her own little job to go to again.

She was worried about the state Melly was in, but at least this gave her the chance to get out and earn a bit of money for a change. The work suited her and she signed up for three days to begin with. Once Alan started at Michaelmas, she thought, maybe she'd work there every day. She was already making friends with some of the other women, especially a lively, dark-haired mother called Gina who also had two children in the school.

She had said to Melly, 'Well, if you're around the house, you can mind Alan while I go out, can't you? Take your mind off things.'

After all, it was no good her just moping about. Rachel wasn't sure what all this nervous-breakdown talk was supposed to mean exactly, but she could see there was something up with Melly. She'd been most peculiar.

'It's as if the wench has been turned to stone,' Gladys remarked, when she came round and saw her. 'She can hardly seem to put one foot in front of the other.'

'She's just worn out, that's all,' Rachel had said. 'She says she hasn't been sleeping.'

Finally, Melly did sleep; she barely seemed to do anything else for a fortnight. When she was awake she was permanently in tears. The other kids didn't know what to make of it. Tommy tried to talk to her. Rachel was grateful to the lad because she had no idea what to say herself. Kev and Ricky mostly ignored it all, but five-year-old Sandra would go up and put her head in Melly's lap, her little arms round her sister's waist.

'Don't you go blarting, Melly,' she'd say. 'There, there – s'all right.'

It had been sweet, and Melly sometimes managed a little smile and stroked Sandra's hair.

Rachel didn't know what to do about any of it. It was as if going in for all that nursing had been too much for Melly. Best thing was for her to have a good rest. Rachel tried to make sure she had enough to eat and good food too. Beyond that she just left her be. She'd soon pick up and then she could look for a job.

Danny didn't have a clue either.

'Tell you what, wench,' he said when he saw Melly

was home. 'If you've packed in the hospital you can come and help me. I'm getting busy on the market and I can always use another pair of hands.'

Melly said she would one day, but not yet.

Now, after two months, it was frankly beginning to get on Rachel's nerves. It was time the wench pulled herself together. She was looking a bit better, less peaky in the face. She'd stopped crying all the time. And she was helping out with repairs to the coats for Danny and other stuff for the market.

That was the best thing, Rachel thought, as she turned in at the school gates. You had to keep busy and not mope. They hadn't got through the war years by moping, had they? It was bad enough having Tommy with a long face, without adding Melly as well. She didn't know what was wrong with her children sometimes. At their age she was weighed down by war and babies, with Danny away and not knowing if he'd ever come back. What did this lot have to put up with? Nothing, when you compared them. They didn't know they were born.

'I knew you were aiming too high with that nursing,' she'd said to Melly the other day. 'I never could see what you wanted to go and do that for – but now you've found out for yourself.'

'Like your mother says –' Danny supported her – 'it's not for the likes of us. Stick to what you know best, that's my way of looking at it. And in this family what we know best is trading and selling – buy for a shilling, sell for one and six – Bob's your uncle.'

Melly didn't say anything to that; she just gave them both that blank look she had these days and disappeared upstairs.

But they were right, she and Danny, Rachel thought. They should know, shouldn't they? They'd come through far more than Melly could ever know about. Whatever had happened in that hospital to send her running home, it obviously wasn't right for her. But at least she was on the mend now and she could start all over again.

Melly set out to collect Alan from a lady's house a few streets away. She had a little boy the same age and the two of them often played together.

As she stepped outside, the sunlight stroked her face. It's a nice day, she thought. And in that moment she knew something had shifted. For the past two months she had scarcely noticed the weather because a constant pall like heavy grey cloud had been hanging over her.

She felt as if she had passed through a terrible ordeal.

When she came home she had felt as if she was losing her mind. For the first few nights she still could not sleep, her pulse pounding, her nerves all a-jangle. She could not bear anyone near her, could not hold her thoughts together.

One night, at last, she slept. After that she could not seem to stop sleeping. Then she started crying and could not stop doing that either.

Mom and Dad tiptoed round her. Gladys, rather to her surprise, came over to visit a number of times and was the kindest of the three. She seemed to have some idea how Melly felt.

'It'll pass, bab,' she'd say sometimes. 'It always does, in the end.'

What was more comforting than anything was that Gladys had come; she just sat there, solid and reassuring beside her.

Melly felt useless. She tried not to take in any of their comments about nursing or to think about the hospital at all. Any time it came into her head – the wards, those patients who were there at the end – she was immediately flooded with panic. If she thought of Raimundo Alexander, instead of panic came an aching grief.

Gradually, as she spent time at home, the whirling inside her began to slow and settle. Recently she had begun to notice what was going on around her. Especially Tommy, her unhappy brother.

Tommy never complained but she could feel an air of permanent misery coming from him. She had managed to get a conversation with him last Saturday when they were alone – a rare thing in the house.

'What is it, Tommy? Is it the money, or what?'

'No – money's – all right.'

She had thought so – he was earning nearly six bob a week which did not seem too bad.

'What is it, then? I've never seen you look so browned off in your life. Come on – I'll make us a cuppa and you can tell me.' She wanted to be his big sis again, for him to need her as he always had.

He seemed reluctant at first, but he didn't push her away this time. Once she had filled the pot and sat with him, with a packet of Bourbons, really showing she wanted to listen, he began to open up.

Tommy was employed in the Suppliers' Accounts department. He had been handling invoices – Melly remembered this and asked him about it.

'They – took me – off that,' he said.

That was when he was supposed to staple invoices together – goods in and goods out – and put them in alphabetical order, to get through three hundred a day. But Tommy was working more-or-less one-armed and he couldn't keep up. Anyway, the others often fibbed about what they'd done.

'I never – thought to – tell him a – lie,' Tommy said. 'So I was – the – one – always in – trouble.'

Now, he said, they had taken him off that and put him on filing. 'Dead filing,' he said, all the non-urgent stuff.

As the story emerged, Melly's heart ached for him. Tommy could see himself spending his whole life in the same place, despite his O-levels, with everyone thinking him simple because of the way he talked. Around him, other people with no qualifications like he had would be getting promotions and pay rises.

'They think – I'm – stupid. But if – they want to – know – something – they – ask me,' he finished bitterly.

Melly felt sad and angry for him. It was a relief to think about someone else and their troubles. Every bit of her wanted to reach out and protect him.

'Oh, Tommy,' she said. 'Could you get another job somewhere?'

'It'd be – the same,' he said, staring down at the table-top. 'And – Dad – has to – keep – driving – me.'

'What about . . . ? Aren't they getting you a car – a three-wheeler?'

'Soon – I've – been to – the – doctor. He said – I – could.'

'That'll be nice. You'll be able to get about, won't you?'

Tommy nodded bleakly.

Melly left him, wishing there was something she could do.

Now, approaching the house where she had to pick up Alan, she was filled with dread at the thought of having to talk to anyone. But it had to be done. She knocked on the door and was able to go through the motions of thanking the lady.

'Come on, Alan,' she said to her sturdy little brother.

He had seemed pleased to see her which made her happy. In some ways it was nice to be at home. 'We'll go out to the park later, shall we?'

Alan took her hand and trotted along beside her.

As she drew close to the house, she saw a bus pull up at the stop along the road. When it had moved on, from among the few people who got off, two figures emerged. Seconds later she recognized them with a shock. It was as if two worlds were colliding.

It was Berni and Margaret, both in summery outfits. Margaret's top was bright yellow and made Melly think of a sunflower. For a second she felt like running away. And then she was overjoyed to see them. She raised her hand and waved. She saw them look at each other, then wave back.

'What're you two doing here?' she asked, trying to cover up the fact that she felt suddenly like crying. She swallowed hard and forced a smile.

'Come to see you – what d'you think?' Berni replied. She wore a navy blue dress, a rather austere-looking thing, and flat brown shoes. 'We got days off at the same time for once.'

They both looked relieved by the sight of her. They had sent a card in the early days, signed by a few of the girls in their year group. Melly wondered what they had expected to find. It was a good thing they had not come earlier, though, she thought – she would not have managed to hold herself together.

They did not stay too long – a couple of hours – both seeming to understand that she would not be able to cope with more. But they had a drink and took Alan out to the park. The three girls sat on the grass which still had a breath of damp about it.

'So are you getting better?' Margaret said. 'When we asked Sister what was wrong, she said you were sick. You had some sort of breakdown that morning, by the look of it.'

Margaret was more able to talk seriously than Berni, whose usual way was to tease and joke.

'Things just got on top of me,' Melly said. She had been thinking about it. There had been one thing after another – Mr Stafford's haemorrhage, then Mr Alexander. Deaths were a shock. Mr Palmer dying was a shock too. Nurses acted as if death was normal – which it was, of course – but not when you weren't used to it. It had all built up in her.

'I never felt I could say,' she added.

Berni was staring down at the grass.

'We've been back in class,' she said, seeming to want to change the subject. The two of them talked about the classes and their new wards and the gossip of the other girls, laughing together. As the conversation turned back to their day-to-day concerns they seemed more comfortable.

Melly felt herself shrinking inside. All of it was so familiar, yet it seemed so far away now, a world she could not be part of. It was desolate, like watching a train steam out of the station and knowing that the doors were closed and you could not get on.

Berni got up and started to run about with Alan. They had brought a ball and she kicked it about with him. Berni had younger brothers, Melly knew. How she must miss her family, she thought. But Berni never showed her emotions.

Margaret sat back, resting on her hands behind her, her

brown, shapely legs crossed in front of her. She looked neat, as usual. Her skirt was lime green, her tan leather shoes flat.

'You coming back, Melly?' she asked. 'What you going to do?' Her face was serious, but she asked as if this was quite possible and Melly had not missed the train after all.

Melly looked at her, grateful for her directness, but feeling suddenly full of anguish and close to tears. Her emotions confused her these days. She would be numb for ages, feeling nothing, only to be ambushed by a rush of overpowering feeling – anger or frustration or grief.

'I don't know. Mom and Dad keep telling me that all this shows it wasn't for me and I should go and get another job. I'll have to soon – I can't just sit around not earning my keep.'

'Matron – she said you could come back?'

She inclined her head. 'Maybe.'

Margaret was silent for a few moments, her eyes following Alan's movements. Melly thought the conversation was over, but then Margaret said:

'My mom had a breakdown – back home. I suppose that's what it was.'

Melly waited.

'After she had my brother. There are five of us. My sister and me – we looked after the house and the others, the baby.'

'Did she go to hospital?'

Margaret looked incredulously at her. She burst out laughing. 'Hospital? There's no hospital – not for that. No – she got a strong faith and she recovered from it in her way.' She leaned back and altered the position of her legs. 'It's just the way of things sometimes.'

Forty-Four

'That's it – squeeze, hard as you can. Good – now the other hand – ah, yes, that's your good hand all right! Good lad!'

The technical officer who was dealing with Tommy, a bird-like, black-haired man, kept up a breezy patter throughout the tests – eyesight, hearing, his reaction times and now the strength of his grip. They were in the Artificial Limb and Appliance Centre at Selly Oak, finding out if Tommy could have his disability three-wheeler and seeing what kind of controls he would need.

'You're going to have to do all the work with your right hand, but then you're used to that. We'll see what we can do. That's all we need for now.'

Tommy sat still, staring at the floor.

'It's all right – you can go now,' the man said. 'Don't worry – we'll be able to fix something up for you.'

'Oh.' Tommy stirred himself, reaching for his stick. 'Thanks.'

'Using the wheelchair most of the time, are you?'

'Mostly,' Tommy said. Never at work though. However slowly he walked, lurching on the stick, however tiring it was, he was not going in there in a cripple's chair.

'Are you all right, Tommy?'

All right – was he? The putty-coloured pall covering his life, his feelings, had become normal to him so that now he no longer knew.

He struggled to his feet. 'Yes. Thanks.'

'Buck up, lad! This is going to give you a new lease of life – freedom. The open road. So long as you're careful.' He patted Tommy on the back as he crossed the bare, clinical room. 'Someone waiting for you, is there?'

'Yes,' Tommy said. 'My – father.' At the door, again, he said, 'Thank you . . . sir.'

'Cheerio, lad. Good luck.'

'It's here, Tommy – they brought it this morning!'

Rachel ran to the front door the moment Danny brought Tommy back after work that day.

'I know. Dad said.'

'It's along at Mr and Mrs Turner's for the moment. The man's coming on Saturday, to train you.'

Mr Turner, round the corner, had a shed which he said Tommy could keep the three-wheeler in. They had been dismayed at first, when they found out that one of the conditions of having an invalid car was being able to keep it under cover. The house had no garage and they couldn't get it round the back, but the Turners had come to their rescue.

'Just think, Tommy,' Rachel chattered to him, as she stirred a pot of steak-and-kidney on the stove. 'You'll be able to go out by yourself. That's nice, isn't it?'

He nodded. She handed him a cup of tea.

Melly appeared downstairs. Tommy exchanged looks with her. There was a silent understanding between them. They didn't talk much but each knew the other was sad and suffering. It was no good talking to Mom and Dad. All they ever said was that you just had to buck up and not mope.

Tommy sipped his tea, still dragged down by his day.

He did talk to people at work sometimes, but his speech was just too slow for them. It felt as if they were putting up with him rather than ever being friends or treating him seriously. And they didn't always bear with him all that patiently. 'All right – never mind, I'll ask someone else,' he often heard when he'd been asked a question.

And that girl, Con, gave him such pitying, scornful looks.

In the dinner break, when the others went off in chattering groups, Tommy stayed at the desk, alone with his sandwiches.

Though he was glad to be issued with the three-wheeler, or Invacar as it was called, all it meant was that he could get to work by himself. It didn't change anything else. Looking ahead at his life, all he could see was this lonely toil, nothing interesting or demanding. Just a grey nothing-muchness, forever.

When could he ever get a better job or have any of the normal life the others looked forward to? To friends and marriage – even a family? These were things he never really dared to hope for.

When he did see the trike – in fact it was more like a little car – he felt more excited. This little blue, almost triangular vehicle was made especially for him! The controls were arranged so that he could do everything with his right hand.

When the technical officer arrived on Saturday morning to train him, Tommy was afraid that all the family would come out and watch. That was the last thing he wanted. He was grateful that Mom made them all go back inside.

'Come on,' she said. 'Kids – get in. Tommy doesn't need you gawping at him.'

The man was jolly and gingery, with freckles. He slid the door open.

'Here's your carriage, sir – all the way from Benfleet in Essex. You get in and try it.'

He showed Tommy the controls, and walked alongside him as he learned to use the little machine. As Tommy sat in the seat and the three-wheeler crawled noisily along the street and round the corner, he felt his spirits lift. It was true – it felt good to be on the road. And there was only room for him inside. It was all his and no one else could muscle in or beg rides off him!

'You'll soon get the hang of it,' the man said, smiling at him. 'The examiner'll be along next week to put you through your paces and then – off you go! And you know they have rallies and outings, don't you? I went down to Hendon to one last year – a mate of mine drove all the way down in his car like this. It's a nice day out. All very jolly. You could go this year – it's somewhere in Manchester. And there'll be things going on close to home.'

Tommy felt his face crease into a grin. It was an unusual feeling for him.

'Sounds – nice,' he said. He felt something lighten, like the clouds thinning, letting rays of light into his life. Suddenly something felt possible. New places – maybe even new friends!

The next week he did everything he had to do for the test: reversing, an emergency stop – he noticed the examiner got well out of his way when they were doing that one – three-point turn, indicators . . . After that he was on his own, though the man said he could leave his L-plates on for as long as he wanted to.

'Are you pleased?' Melly asked him that evening. She had been helping Dad and Gladys on the Rag Market that day. The rest of the family were all milling about. Tommy was at the table in his wheelchair.

'Yeah,' he said. He could feel that smile sneaking out again. Pleased? Oh, he was pleased all right!

'Go on, you lot,' Rachel shouted to the younger children. 'Out from under my feet or you won't get your tea.' There was a delicious smell of frying bacon in the room.

Tommy could feel his sister's eyes on him. Her pale, strained face was beginning to look a little bit better now as well, though her hair was long and straggly. She looked exhausted. She'd helped out at the market a couple of times now, but a day there really seemed to take it out of her. He wished he could help her but he did not know how to.

'Shame I – can't – give you – a ride,' he said.

Melly forced a smile, carrying the tea over to the table, and sat with him. 'That'd be nice. Couldn't I squeeze in? Where'd we go, eh?'

'France?' he said. 'South of – France.'

'Ooh,' Melly said. 'Bit of sun . . . But they can't go that far, can they?'

'Course. It's a – bike. Can – go any – where.'

He told her what the man had said about the day at Manchester. He was excited. He didn't know how far Manchester was but he liked the idea that he might go there.

'Well,' Melly said. 'You've got to get to work first – that's far enough. D'you think you can?'

His stomach twisted with dread. It was frightening enough to drive all the way into Birmingham.

'You gonna – just – stay home – now?' he asked.

Melly looked up at him over her cup, seeming startled. 'Stay home? You mean – not work? No! Mrs Pearce says I can work in her shop three days a week – and there's the market.'

He wondered if she was going to cry because she looked down suddenly and he saw her swallow hard, even when she hadn't taken a mouthful of tea.

'But – what about – you – being – a nurse? Don't you – want to?'

It took her a moment before she could look up and there were tears in her eyes. 'Yes.' She wiped the tears away. 'I'm not . . . I don't know any more.'

Tommy sat helplessly.

'Let's put – a – record on,' he said. His little collection of records was growing, week by week.

Melly brightened and got up. '"Little White Bull"? I'll do it.'

Hearing the music, Ricky, Sandra and Alan came charging back in singing 'Little White Bull!' at the tops of their voices.

'Flipping hell, Melly – did you have to?' Rachel said, seizing the handle of the frying pan as the kids danced about. 'Just keep out of my way, you lot.'

Forty-Five

For a few weeks, Melly kept going in to help on the Rag Market. She didn't want to, not at all. She'd liked the market as a child, all the bustle and excitement and things for sale. But now, having to go out and spend all day among crowds of people, having to smile and be helpful, cost her more effort than anyone else could have imagined. She wanted to like it, but she didn't.

She knew what Dad was after. He didn't want to be there on Saturday afternoons because he was really yearning to be at the Villa ground watching the game. So he'd much prefer her to be there instead.

When they set off to pick up Gladys that morning Melly was not in the best of moods, full of a sudden anger. It was as if her emotions, when they arose, were heightened, stirred up in a way she had never known before.

Got me right where you want me now, haven't you? she raged inwardly at her father as they drove off. But it's not what I want! That's not my life – it's yours! She didn't say a word as they drove across town, she was seething so much.

'Go in and get her, will you?' Danny said, pulling up outside.

Melly slammed the car door as hard as she could and stormed along the entry. Ethel Jackman was hanging washing in the yard. She turned, unsmiling.

'Oh, you're back, are you?' she said. 'Not that that'll do any good.' She jerked her head towards Gladys's house.

'Morning, Mrs Jackman,' Melly said, trying not to sound too sarcastic. She didn't realize what Mrs Jackman meant at first. 'Nice to see you too,' she muttered.

Instead of finding Gladys bustling and ready, she was sitting at the table, leaning her head on her hand. Melly could see at once that all was not well. There was a nasty, damp, musty smell in the house and she had never seen Gladys looking this way before. She was unwell and there was a sagging, defeated look to her which chased away Melly's anger.

'Auntie? What's happened? You look bad. And what's that pong . . . ?'

'Upstairs,' Gladys said. Her tone was flat, resigned.

Melly hurried upstairs. It took only a moment to see what had happened. Gladys slept in the bigger bedroom on the middle floor and the door was open. A huge section of the attic floor – her ceiling – had collapsed, right on to her bed. Parts of it were still hanging, a mess of plaster and flimsy batons. The floor and bed were covered with muck, all stinking of damp. She ran back downstairs.

'God, Auntie – when did that happen?'

'Yesterday. After that shower of rain.' Gladys leaned forward and coughed until her eyes watered. 'The roof's leaking – bad. I came and slept down here. If the bed had still been up there . . .' She didn't finish but they exchanged looks.

'You can't stay here, Auntie. I'm going to get Dad. This house is a wreck. You'll have to come and stay with us.'

*

371

For once Gladys didn't argue. She brought a bundle of her things and Melly sat behind her in the car. But she was adamant that she was coming to the market even though she sounded as if she should be in bed. Though she had spread in her later years into an imposing matron, Gladys seemed shrunken today. Melly looked at the back of her head as they drove, the faded hair pinned up roughly and held with combs, and, with a pang, suddenly saw her as an old woman.

Gladys perked up a bit when they reached the market.

'Better get weaving,' she said, before a bout of coughing bent her double.

Melly helped both of them set up. Now that she was home, she had learned the new routines of the business. Danny had expanded, taken to the road, not just getting clothes from jumble sales and working men's clubs. Now that Tommy had his own car, Danny could set off before dawn to his suppliers.

Tonight, after market day, there'd be a pint or two in one of the pubs nearby, the Drover's Arms or the Adam and Eve in Bradford Street. Gladys always went for a tipple as well. Tomorrow, Sunday, was a day off. Monday was the day for doing the accounts, Tuesdays – a trip out for stock, often to London now. On Wednesdays Danny set off by five in the morning to Somerset for sheepskins from the companies he traded with – Morland's and Bailey's and Draper's. Thursdays and Fridays were spent mending and preparing stock.

Business was going well, with occasional setbacks. Last Tuesday when he got home Danny had erupted, fuming, into the house. He had struck a deal on a whole lot of 'cabbage' as the seconds were called, with a manufacturer in the East End, stowed it in the car and walked round the corner to another firm. When he came back from the second place, the car was empty. Someone had broken in and pinched the lot.

'They must've been watching me,' he raged. 'I'd locked the flaming doors. That's London for you – it'd never happen in Somerset. *Bastards.*'

They had a double pitch in the Rag Market now with a big sign over it: *DANNY BOOKER, SHEEPSKINS AND LEATHERS, SLIGHT SECONDS AT BARGAIN PRICES*. The leather and sheepskin coats hung on hangers from rails. Danny surrounded the racks with netting to stop customers coming in through the sides, slipping on a coat and making off with it. Each coat had a label telling the customer what was wrong with it – a small but mended tear, a stain, a patch of slightly mismatched leather . . .

Melly glanced across every so often to see if Gladys was all right. She seemed to be getting along as usual, in between bouts of coughing.

Melly worked automatically, hanging the clothes, recognizing most of them because they had needed some repair – a button sewn on here, a rough hem trimmed with the Stanley knife and re-stitched. Some of the coats were returns from Rackham's department store. The manufacturer would make fifty-five or sixty coats for an order of fifty, to cover the number which had mistakes and problems – the 'cabbage'. Danny bought these up to sell them on. He had both gents' and ladies' coats to sell, and Gladys was selling more secondhand men's clothes again now.

They were soon busy. Melly dealt with the ladies who came in. She found she could tell, just by looking at someone, what size they were. She was good at finding them something to suit and complimenting them.

Despite wishing she was somewhere else, Melly was

not having a bad day. They had one sheepskin coat that had been left on hot pipes in a plastic bag, back in the winter. It had so much plastic impregnated into the leather that they thought no one would buy it. But one of the other market traders came in for a chat and spotted it.

'You can't be serious – who's gonna buy that? Look at the state of it, Danny!'

Melly saw her father sizing up the lad, who was in his late twenties and worked on a hardware stall across the market.

'Well,' Danny shrugged. 'It'll keep you as warm as any coat we've got here. And it's a fraction of the price – best bargain you'll find. It's no good waiting 'til next winter, mate – someone else'll've had it by then.'

The man held it against him. 'The worst of it's on the back – so it ain't me who'd see it, is it?'

Melly could see he was tempted. He was a bony lad, no flesh on him.

'You look as though you'd feel the cold,' she cajoled him.

'I *do*,' he said. 'How much?'

'A tenner to most people – but for you . . . Melly – go over to your auntie and see if 'er's got any ten-bob notes, will you?'

'All right.' She was quite glad of an errand. It wasn't a cold day, but she still got chilly standing about.

The smell of frying onions drifted across the market, making her feel that her morsel of toast at breakfast had been a long while back. Her tummy gurgled. She could hear the man selling china in full voice as she went over to Gladys's pitch at the back. In spite of her bad mood, she smiled. He was one for entertaining – juggling the crocks and doing tricks with them up his arms. There was a knot of people gathered around him and his baskets of sets of crockery, one of which he was holding up in front of the crowd.

'Right – who'll give me six pound for the lot? Eh – all this in 'ere – look at it! It's a bargain!'

'I bet them cups've got no handles on 'em!' someone shouted from the crowd.

'What? This is the best, this is – willow pattern. Look – straight from the works. Beautiful, that is! No one give me six for it? No? What about five pound ten? Come on – I'm robbing meself 'ere – taking the bread out of my children's mouths!'

No one took up this offer, either.

The moment came that everyone had been waiting for.

'All right – my last offer – a fiver? Just a fiver?' There was a pause as he looked round with persuading eyes. 'What – no one'll give me a fiver! Aaaagh!'

Swinging the basket round, he hurled it with full force against the wall. There was a great smashing and tinkling as the contents crashed to the floor and gasps and laughter came from the crowd.

Melly smiled. Anyone who'd been around the market any time knew that he always made up a basket or two out of all the broken crocks for this very purpose. It was just a shock to anyone who *didn't* know.

There were a few people round Gladys's stall. She saw two Indian men, both very young looking, trying on suit jackets.

Gladys found she did a good trade with men who had come over from India and Pakistan, having to kit themselves out with clothes to go to work. The men always tried on jackets by thrusting their arms right up in the air into the sleeves. Gladys said it was because they were used to putting clothes on over their heads.

'Auntie,' she said. Gladys left the men for a moment

and came over. 'Dad says have you got any ten-bob notes?'

Gladys fished in the purse at her waist where she kept her takings and brought out four ten-shilling notes. 'These do?'

'Here.' Melly handed her two pound notes in exchange. She lingered, in no hurry to go back. She knew the market man would come back for his coat. 'I had that lady from Sutton Coldfield come again today. "Oh – price is no object,"' she mimicked.

Gladys chuckled, chestily. 'Right. That's why she's here shopping on the Rag Market!'

'She's got a right smell under her nose! Dad's just flogging that coat with all the plastic in it, I think.' She saw Gladys blowing her nose, one eye on her customers. 'You all right, Auntie?'

'I'll be all right. While you're here though, bab, fetch me a cup of tea, will you? Hang on – let me see to these two.' She went over to the two Indian men who seemed about to buy the jackets.

Melly stood waiting, lapsing into the hazy, empty-headed state that often seemed to come over her these days. Nearby, a man was selling belts and watches, talcum powder and towels. She drifted off in her mind, thinking about the routine in the hospital, on A3. The thought did not fill her with panic any more. It just made her feel sad.

She was miles away and jumped as she heard Gladys's voice.

'Look who's here!' She sounded much cheered up. 'I can't remember the last time I set eyes on you, bab! Back in Brum for a bit, are you? Come and say hello to our Melly. She was at the hospital – being a nurse. But she's had to jack it in . . .'

Melly felt her stomach tighten and her pulse race. She hated anyone else talking about her and what had happened. Cheeks burning, she looked round and found she was staring into a pair of blue, familiar eyes. Reggie Morrison.

For a second she was thrown completely. She was twelve years old again and in love. Her legs went weak.

'All right, Melly?' he said.

He was still walking with a stick, but he looked strong and upstanding, his blonde hair clipped short. He had on a pair of denim jeans and a white shirt, the sleeves rolled up to show muscular forearms. He looked nice, she thought. But then he always looked nice in her eyes, with his broad shoulders and kindly face.

'All right, Reggie?' She made herself smile. It wasn't that she was pleased or not pleased to see him, she told herself. It just didn't matter either way. He must be twenty-six now, she thought. She was twenty. It didn't seem nearly such an enormous gap as when she was twelve and he had already reached the impossibly grown-up age of eighteen.

'Yeah, I'm all right,' he said. He smiled, looking at her and away. To her surprise she saw that he was nervous. She had always been the nervous one before.

'You still gardening?' She wanted to keep things light, to talk about him and not about herself.

Reggie nodded. 'Just started at the college – at Worcester. They're training me.' At this, he looked happy, and proud. 'I'm just back for a few days, that's all.'

'You like it then?'

'Yeah. I do,' he said. 'Suits me fine – best thing that could've happened. And you, Melly . . .' He looked more closely at her. His eyes seemed to drink her in. For a second a pulse of excitement passed through her, before she forced it away. For heaven's sake. But she saw how manly Reggie's face was these days, the jaw more pronounced. There was shyness in his eyes, but also concern. 'Our mom said you left the hospital – that you had a bit of a . . . Well, that you weren't well.'

Again she felt her cheeks burn red. Why did it feel so shameful to admit that you hadn't been well? At least, that kind of not well – when it was in your head.

'I, er . . .' She hesitated, looking across at the lady selling her bottles of pungent perfume, *Cologne de Paris*. 'I was a bit poorly. I'm all right now, though.'

She folded her arms across her, as if to protect herself. Reggie was looking intently at her, listening carefully. For a moment she felt tears prickle in her eyes at seeing this old, familiar face, his slightly lopsided smile. But she made herself smile.

'I'm back here for the moment, any road,' she said, putting on a cheery tone. 'Listen, Reggie – it's nice seeing you but I've got to take Dad his money. He's waiting . . .'

'All right,' he said, with seeming reluctance. 'Ta-ra then.'

She walked fast back across the market with her head down and did not turn back.

Forty-Six

They did not go for a drink that evening. By closing time
Gladys was close to collapse so they all went straight
home. Given the state of her house, it was clear that
Gladys was going to have to live with them.

'She'll have to have Tommy's room,' Rachel said, obviously put out by Gladys's appearance. 'You can go on
the put-you-up down here for a few days, can't you,
Tommy?'

Gladys, to everyone's astonishment, went to bed like a
lamb.

'She must be bad,' Rachel said, once she was settled up
there. She closed the kitchen door and turned to Danny.
'I s'pose she'll have to stay here for a bit, the state she's
in.'

'She can't go back there,' Danny said. 'The whole ceiling's fallen in. It's an absolute bloody mess. She'll have to
stop with us.'

Melly saw her mother digest this. She knew Mom was
not keen on living with Gladys again.

'Danny.' Rachel stood with her hands on her hips. 'We
haven't the room any more. I don't want us to live like
beans in a can again. She'll have to find somewhere else.
Soon as she's better. Are you listening to me?'

Danny was leaning over the table, eyeing the paper.
'Yeah – all right, wench. Yeah.'

*

On the Monday afternoon, Melly drifted along Harborne High Street, gathering bits of shopping: more bread, a pot of jam, buns, potatoes. A household of eight always seemed to need something from the shops.

She was glad to get out of the house. Sometimes when it was fine she went out and caught a bus, sat in a park where it was peaceful, just to get away.

It was bad enough sharing a room with Sandra again, who was always on at her for something. But Melly was the one who usually ended up chivvying Kev, Ricky and Sandra to get ready for school and walking the two youngest ones there as well. Sandra was a chatterbox and seldom stopped rattling on and Ricky was just dreamy and never got going in time. Most days he was dragging along the street still doing up his clothes.

She had also been looking after Gladys, who was feverish and had a bad chesty cough. And Mom and Dad had been having more of their ding-dongs since Gladys arrived.

Last night, Dad had been on about getting another stall – in London.

'Are you *mad*, Danny?' Rachel was off straight away. 'What the hell're you on about? We can only just manage the one you've got here – all that running about to Somerset and down to London. What d'you want to go piling it on for – eh? We've got enough coming in.'

'You have to diversify. That's business!' Her father stood in the kitchen, shirt hanging out of his trousers, waving his arms around so he nearly took Kev's head off.

'Apart from anything,' Rachel said, 'it's all owned by them Jewish lads down there. That time you went down and everything was shut, remember? Jewish holiday. Says it all, doesn't it.'

'They're all right, those lads,' Danny said. 'I do business with 'em all the time.'

'They'd run rings round you, Danny. You don't believe me, I know – but they would. Closed shop, they are – they look after their own. You're best off where you are.'

Rachel moved away to cook his fry-up, as if the argument was already closed. Which in a way it was because they'd never agree and Mom was usually right.

But it wasn't over because then she turned from the spitting frying pan and said, 'And anyway – I was thinking, it's time I learned to drive.'

It wasn't just Dad – everyone in the room looked startled.

'*You?*' Danny said. 'Drive?' He sank on to a chair as if the very idea had floored him and grinned at her.

'What d'you mean *you?*' Rachel was on her high horse immediately. She wielded a spatula in his direction. 'What's wrong with that? Even our Tommy's driving so why the hell shouldn't I?'

Tommy was still getting the hang of his three-wheeler. He had been very nervous at first, but Melly could see he was enjoying the freedom of it.

Danny shook his head. 'Lady drivers . . .' He was half serious, half teasing, but Rachel didn't see it that way.

'Ladies don't drive cars,' Ricky announced, not especially helpfully.

Mom was off. 'Oh, don't they? For heaven's sake, Danny, what about Cissy? That baby sister of mine's been swanning about in a car for ages. And Mrs Hipkiss along the road drives the car all the time – and that Mrs Robb – she's got her *own* car.'

'Well, she's a widow,' Danny pointed out, 'so there ain't no one to stop her.'

'For God's sake!' Rachel erupted. 'Of course ladies drive – what about all that lot in the war?'

Sometimes, even in this house which was a palace compared to the yard in Aston, it still felt as if there were too many people in it. Melly found herself aching for the peace of her room in the nurses' home.

She went home, carrying her few bits of shopping. Outside the house was parked a smart red car. She frowned. Whose could that be?

She could hear Gladys coughing upstairs and voices from the back. Mom was home from the school, but who else was here? She shouldered the kitchen door open.

'Mom, whose is that—?'

Sitting with Mom at the table was Reggie Morrison.

'Oh!' Melly stalled, startled.

'Look who's here,' Rachel said. 'Put the kettle on again, will you, wench. He's only just arrived. He went to see Auntie – didn't you, bab? – and found she was over here. That's nice of you, Reggie.'

'All right, Reggie,' Melly said, taking refuge in filling the kettle and unpacking the shopping.

'I thought I'd call on her before I go,' Reggie said. He seemed flustered.

'To the college?' Melly said. She found herself very conscious of her clothes, the same boring old rags: grey skirt, white blouse, black shoes. She had her hair just scraped up anyhow. She wished it didn't matter but she felt plain and drab.

'Yes – I'm going back on Thursday,' he said.

Melly nodded, not looking at him.

'Your mother all right?' Rachel asked. 'And Mo?'

'Yeah – they're all right,' Reggie said. 'Jonny's home –

nose in a book all the time as usual. Mom says you can't get a word out of him and when you do you can't understand it!'

Gladys laughed. After Jonny had done his National Service, he had gone to Birmingham University to study history. He was now completing his training to be a teacher.

'He's got his exams any day now, 'Reggie said.

'Rather him than me,' Rachel said. Melly felt a prickle of irritation. Why was Mom so down on anyone who tried to do anything different?

'Good for him,' Melly said, getting the teapot ready. She was glad to have something to be in charge of. It made her feel less awkward with Reggie being there. After all, it was Auntie he had come to see. Gladys was 'auntie' to all the Morrison kids as well as to her.

'Someone had to get the brains,' Reggie said.

'Have a cake with your tea, Reggie?' Rachel asked. 'Did you get buns, Melly?'

'Chelseas,' Melly said. 'And Auntie's cream horn.'

'Oh, no – you're all right,' Reggie said. 'I'm not hungry, ta.'

'I don't think Auntie'll be up to eating that,' Rachel said. 'You have it, love – keep you going.'

'Oh – all right then, if you're sure.'

They drank their tea and talked about the families. Reggie was very interested in Tommy's car.

'Fancy him getting one of them,' he said. 'That's nice for him.'

'He'll be back soon – you can see it,' Rachel said. 'You could have one, couldn't you?'

Reggie blushed. Melly felt very annoyed with Mom – she could see he didn't like being put in the same camp as Tommy.

'Don't need one,' he said. 'I can drive an ordinary car.' He jerked his head with a shy grin. 'It's parked out there.'

'Oh,' Rachel said. 'Yes. Course. I was thinking you'd come on the bus.'

So that was Reggie's! Melly thought. It was hard even now to remember how much money Mo and Dolly had going spare. They had been very careful with it.

'You've got a nice bit of garden here, haven't you?' Reggie said. 'You can grow your own stuff. Our dad's gone mad on it with that big patch they've got. He reckons he's grown the biggest swedes in the whole street this year.'

Melly wrinkled her nose. She was not keen on swede. Mom and Dad had never got round to planting anything in their strip of back garden. But she was intrigued. Reggie had changed.

'Nothing by halves, our Mo,' Rachel said. She pushed herself up from the table. ''Scuse me a tick.'

Melly felt herself tense as her mother left the room. She and Reggie were silent for a moment. She became acutely aware of his physical presence at the end of the table, the shape of his shoulders, the hairs on his arm below his rolled sleeve, as it rested on the table.

'I, er . . .' Reggie said. He glanced at the door. She could see he wanted to speak quickly, before Mom came back. 'I'm off on Thursday, as I say.' As he spoke he was looking at the tablecloth's red-and-white checks. 'I've got a couple of days free. I was thinking, as you're . . . Well, you know, you're at home, like – whether you'd fancy a day out somewhere?'

Melly's heart slammed into panicky thudding.

'I . . .' she began. 'I . . . That's nice of you, Reggie. But I can't. I'm at work the next three days – at Pearce's shop. Those are the days I do.'

'Oh.' He looked disillusioned. She realized that not only had she said she couldn't come with him, she had also sounded as if she didn't want to. In fact she was not at all sure that she *did* want to, but she felt terrible for hurting his feelings.

'Well . . .' Reggie was red-faced now. She was touched. 'What about today? Now, like? Have you got anything else on?'

'No,' she had to admit. A pain went through her. She could not make sense of it, how it felt. It was a long time since she had felt anything much. 'No, I haven't.' She looked across at him. Even though a part of her was desperate to run and hide, he was being kind and she couldn't turn him down. 'All right, then.'

Forty-Seven

'Fancy going out to the Lickeys?' Reggie said as they stepped out of the house. He lit a cigarette. Now that they were alone he seemed nervous again.

'All right.'

'Here we are then.'

She looked more closely at his red sports car – a sleek, low-slung creation with headlamps like peeping eyes – and a chuckle burst out of her.

'What's so funny?' Reggie sounded rather wounded. He was opening the passenger door for her.

'It's just – you know, any of us having a car like this. Is it a Daimler?'

'Austin-Healey – it's called a Bugeye Sprite,' he said. 'Dad gave me most of the money for it.'

Melly giggled, settling herself in the car's tight little space. 'It's like Cissy's. Hers is a Daimler, I think she said – and it's white.'

'Cissy's got a car like this?' Reggie said, astonished.

'Her husband bought it for her, if you please – they're rolling in it.'

Reggie laughed then, as he slammed the door and started up the throbbing engine. 'Blimey – trust Cissy. She always had an eye for the main chance, that one.'

Melly looked at him in surprise. It was news to her that he had ever even noticed Cissy.

She felt lighter at heart as Reggie turned towards Selly

Oak and then out along the Bristol Road towards the Lickey Hills. It was nice to get out – and to do it with some company for a change instead of sitting in parks alone, locked into her own moods.

They didn't talk a lot. It was too much effort against the force of the wind with the car roof down. She had tied her hair up, but even in the low seat, the force of the wind billowed bits of it round her face and her cheeks felt battered by it. She felt freer and suddenly more alive than she had in ages. It was a relief to feel something good, after the numbness that had taken her over.

Now and then, as they roared along, Reggie glanced at her. When she looked back, they smiled. Out of the corner of her eye she could see the movement of Reggie's thighs as he worked the pedals. He felt at once foreign to her and overwhelmingly familiar. It was all very strange. But she began to relax.

Once they had parked, he said, 'Well – how about a walk? Then I'll take you to the tea rooms, if there's time.'

'Yes,' she said. 'All right. But . . .' She looked at him, awkward now.

'It's all right,' he said, dignified. 'I can walk. Just not as fast as some.'

She was sorry for asking then.

They set off along the green paths of the hills, Reggie with his stick. Melly found the pace soothing. She kept thinking how odd it felt to be here with Reggie of all people. She imagined how she would have felt if she was twelve. Oh, how she had worshipped him! She thought he was the be-all and end-all. All that hanging about in the yard, waiting for him to put in an appearance. She smiled at the thought of herself.

They stopped at the top of the high hill. A haze hung over the city, which looked like a model in the distance.

'Doesn't look real, does it?' Reggie said.

'I can't believe that's really where we live,' she said. She glanced at Reggie. He was staring into the far distance. 'D'you remember that time you took me out on the bike?'

Again, she wanted to bite her tongue out – fancy coming out with that after what had happened to Wally! But Reggie didn't appear to be offended. He seemed glad that she'd brought it up and made an amused sound.

'Why did you?'

'Dunno.' He pushed his left hand down into his pocket. 'Probably felt sorry for you. You were always hanging about on your own.'

'Is that why you brought me out today? Cos you feel sorry for me?'

Her tone was sharper than she intended and Reggie looked uncomfortable. Straight away she felt drab and severe-looking again and wished she hadn't said anything.

'No,' he said. 'Well, maybe – a bit. But it wasn't just that.' He paused. 'I thought you'd like it.'

'I do.' She relented. She liked it more than she had expected. It felt good to be out, to be high up. She could breathe more easily. But she didn't want to feel pathetic, like some charity case.

After a moment she realized Reggie was looking at her, closely, seeming to search her with his eyes.

'Auntie said you'd been having a rough time – that's all.'

'Oh, *did* she?' Now she sounded really irritable and didn't mean that either. 'Come on – let's get going.'

They strolled along hardly noticing where they were going between the trees, talking more lightly. Reggie told her about the family, how his brothers were getting along, about his job.

'I never expected to do anything like this,' he said. He seemed to come fully alive talking about it. 'Growing up where we did – I hardly knew what a blade of grass looked like, never mind all the stuff I know now! I s'pose I've got the accident to thank for it. If that hadn't happened, I'd've just stayed on where I was, at GEC, even after the army. I know Mom and Dad got that money – that made a difference in a way. But it was smashing my leg up that did it really. It changed everything.'

'You've had a rough time as well,' she said.

There was a silence.

'I think about him every day.' Reggie sounded awkward, but as if he needed to say it. 'Wal. I wonder what he'd be doing. If we hadn't . . . You know.'

'Having adventures, I expect. Like he always did.' She didn't know what made her say that. Truly, she'd barely known Wally Morrison, as he was even older than Reggie. But he had been such a lively, good-looking man. Reggie gave a little laugh.

'Yeah. You bet.' He seemed pleased by what she said. 'There's not that many people remember him, except the family.'

'Oh,' she said, and added, because it would please him, 'I remember him.'

'He was the one with the looks,' he said, teasing a little.

'Not just him,' she said, teasing him back as he fished for compliments. 'Freddie's a looker as well. Cissy used to like him – remember?'

'I'd forgotten that. Well, Freddie's going about with a girl called Sal now – she's all right. Doesn't take any of his nonsense.'

They walked in single file for a moment along a narrow part of the path. Melly watched Reggie as he stepped ahead of her, supported by the stick. His injured hip still made his tread uneven but the sight of him walking moved her with tenderness. He had always been wiry, but the outdoor life had made him much broader and stronger than the pale lad she remembered.

As she rejoined him at his side, to walk down a wooded slope, he said almost casually, 'So, what happened to you, Melly?'

'Happened?' Her heart started thudding unpleasantly.

'At the hospital. You wanted to be a nurse, didn't you?'

Wanted. Past tense.

'I . . .' Abruptly, with no warning, she was sweating, her heart pounding. It was like going right back into it, the panic, the stifling sense of horror.

'Hey . . .' Reggie turned and saw that his question had stirred her up. 'Sorry, Melly. I dain't mean to . . . Shall we sit down for a bit – here.'

He led her to a grassy lip beside the path. She sank down, grateful, feeling the cool of grass stems at the backs of her legs. Without knowing it was going to happen she was heaving with deep, wrenching sobs. She heard the rough, distraught sounds as if they were coming from someone else. Her chest heaved and she gasped for each breath.

'Hey,' Reggie said. 'There now. It's all right. I dain't mean to make you cry . . .'

She felt his arm round her shoulders, his solid strength beside her as she screwed her eyes shut, falling into a dark place of scattered images – Mr Alexander on the floor; blood, so much blood; and above all terror and panic. For a few moments she knew nothing except this place where there was no base, nothing to catch her, just a sense of falling, of darkness and fear. Only when she began to

390

surface, to let cracks of light between her wet lids, did she realize she was shaking all over, her knees jerking up and down.

'Melly,' Reggie was saying. Then louder, 'Melly! Open your eyes. It's all right. Don't, don't – it's all right.'

Only then did she realize that what had held her and stopped her from falling endlessly was Reggie's arm and his voice, talking, making reassuring noises.

He didn't ask her anything until she was calmer and the shaking had almost stopped. She sat for a time, stunned, as if all she wanted to do was sink into sleep, there on the path. He was gentle and didn't push her, or say anything. He kept his arm about her back to steady her and he waited. Of all the things anyone had ever done for her, she was grateful for this, his sitting there, waiting.

Eventually, she pulled her hands over her eyes to dry her tears. She found herself yawning.

'Sorry,' she said, very quietly, embarrassed now. 'I never meant for that to happen.'

She turned to Reggie. In his eyes she could see bewilderment, but also that she had not frightened him away. He was here.

'It's all right,' he said.

They sat for a few more moments and then he said:

'What the hell happened, Melly – in that hospital?'

As they walked on, she tried to explain.

'I s'pose it was all a build-up of things,' she said. She felt limp and exhausted, but cleansed as well. 'No one tells you what it's going to be like. They can't, really. It's – well, it's life and death. Only it's one thing to say that but when you're there . . . The only death I really knew about before was Wally. And I don't know if I really took

391

that in. Not exactly. Anyway, there were other deaths before, on other wards. And it wasn't just *death*, exactly – it was . . . I don't know.'

She walked along, struggling still to understand it for herself.

'When you're working there, they're very strict about not getting close to patients, and if anything happens no one wants to talk about it. It's the professional thing. The patients think we're all angels and we have to behave as if nothing affects us.'

'Sounds like the army,' Reggie said. 'Well, except for the angels bit. It's more, you know, fighting men – made of stone.'

She looked at him. 'Yes, I suppose so. I hadn't thought of it like that. And you can't go blarting all over the patients, can you? Or running about in a panic. That's no help. But I don't know how you're supposed to . . . Anyway, there was Mr Palmer – he was a black man . . .'

She told him about Mr Palmer and Mr Stafford and finally Mr Alexander, that image she could not shake from her head of looking along the ward, seeing his body prone in the doorway. The body of a young, good-looking man who moments before had been walking along, getting better . . .

'God,' Reggie said.

'One minute he's talking to me about poetry and all sorts – the next . . .'

She stopped, shaking her head. 'It's . . . you feel you can't control *anything*. It's all slipping away and . . . and . . .' She couldn't say it, not to him – *Whenever I love someone, something terrible happens.*

'Yeah,' was all Reggie said. But he said it as if he had some idea what she was talking about.

She looked at him again. He smiled, shyly, then looked away.

'How about we go and get a cup of tea?' he said. 'I could do with one, I don't know about you.'

They had tea and scones in the Lickey Hills tea rooms just before they closed.

Once they got there, Melly felt wrung out and distant again, even though he had been kind and helped her. She couldn't help it; she seemed to shut down inside. By the time they got back to Harborne she was wiped out and needing to sleep.

'So – you're at work tomorrow?' he said as they drew up at the house.

'Yes,' she said.

'Shame.' He helped her out of the car. A real gent, she thought later but at the time she was desperate to go and lie down. She hardly knew what she was saying.

'It's been really nice, Reggie, thanks. And I hope everything goes well for you when you get back to Worcester.'

'Right – thanks.' He seemed deflated. As if he was disappointed but trying not to show it. 'Nice to see you, Melly.'

She waved him off from the front. Going into the house, she went straight up to her room. The rest of the family were watching telly. Canned laughter floated up the stairs. She lay straight down on her bed and fell asleep.

Forty-Eight

How long am I going to go on feeling like this? Melly thought as she walked home from work the next afternoon. I'm like an old lady.

A day in the sweet shop was not difficult but it still wore her out. Her feet ached. She could not clear her muzzy head. All she wanted was to go home and lie down.

As she was nearing the house, her heartbeat picked up speed at the sight of two people standing outside, talking. Tommy's blue three-wheeler was parked and in front of it, the red sports car. By the three-wheeler was Tommy, leaning on his stick, talking to Reggie Morrison who was leaning on his. Like two old men, she thought sadly. But what was Reggie doing here again? She thought she had said a final goodbye to him yesterday.

Surely Reggie was not interested in her – especially after all her carry-on yesterday? She realized she still saw Reggie as someone much older, more superior than herself. But a little, remembered pulse of excitement began to beat in her again. *Reggie . . . Reggie Morrison . . .*

The two of them were bent over the Invacar, Tommy showing Reggie the controls. Melly was tempted to slip past into the house but they both looked up as she came along.

'Reggie's here!' Tommy announced happily.

'Yeah,' Melly said. 'I can see. All right, Reggie?'

She turned away but Reggie hurried after her.

'Melly?' He touched her arm to stop her. 'I just came over to see if you . . . Well, if you was feeling better. You . . . We . . .' He seemed flustered. In the afternoon light she saw a scattering of stubble in his chin, like salt. He spoke fast as if he was afraid she might reject him before he had finished.

'We never said goodbye proper, like. And I wanted to see if Auntie's any better and . . .' He was almost gabbling. 'Today – I was going to go over to Wally's grave and I thought you might come with me and Mom and Dad said to bring you in to say hello – they haven't seen you in ages.'

This was true. But why on earth did Reggie want her company when she was so miserable and drab? He must feel sorry for her, that was what it was. She shrugged.

'All right. If you want.' She kept her voice flat. 'I could do with a cup of tea first, though. Come in and see Auntie. She's a bit better.'

'All right,' he said. 'Afterwards?'

'Yeah. I *said* – yes.' She heard her own sharpness again. She could not understand herself.

Tommy went to stow his car away. Reggie went up to see Gladys and after a quick cuppa with the family, they set out in the car again.

Melly told herself grumpily that whatever Reggie wanted it wasn't her. It might just have been company of any kind. She sat back in the cramped car seat, telling herself that none of it mattered anyway.

'Auntie's not looking too good,' Reggie remarked.

'She's got a bit of a chest,' Melly said. 'But she is better. You should've seen her the other night.'

'She knows she can't go back there, doesn't she?'

'Did she say that? Dad says she can't – the place is in a

395

right state.' They swung towards town. Wally was buried the other side, in Witton cemetery. 'She was going to have to get out sooner or later.'

'Stubborn old bird she is. She doesn't like being forced into it.' He shook his head. 'Funny, isn't it – the old end. Mom and Dad always say there was nowhere like it, even though where they live now's like a palace to that.'

'Mo's still going back to the Salutation, isn't he? It's not as if everyone was nice, though,' Melly said. She couldn't look at the shabby, broken-down yard through rose-tinted spectacles. 'Lil was always nice – she's still hanging on. But some of them . . .'

'Old Jackman and his missis – miserable pair of sods. And d'you remember that lot at number four – the blonde?'

'Irene Sutton. Oh, God,' Melly said, laughing at the memory of her. 'And poor little Evie. Auntie said she saw her – a while back – in town. Said she was ever so pretty.'

'She always was sweet looking from what I remember.'

'That terrible mother of hers . . .'

'D'you want the roof down?'

'Not if you want to hear yourself think,' Melly said.

Reggie glanced at her. 'No. All right then.'

'Have you got any flowers?'

'What for?'

'Wally's grave, of course.'

'Oh – no. I never thought.' He gave a laugh. 'Never mind – he'd've called me a right cissy turning up with a bunch of flowers. Mom comes every week with some.'

Leaving the car, they walked amid the quiet stones to the grave of Walter James Morrison, the dates 1933–1954 telling the story of a life cut short far too young. There were already fresh yellow chrysanths on the grave in a stone vase. From the corner of her eye Melly saw Reggie lower his head for a moment, then look away. She wondered if he would cry; if he ever did cry.

She thought about Wally, a big, grown-up man to her, when she was young. Now she realized that when he died, he had been less than two years older than she was now. The thought tore at her heart. Hardly thinking, she reached for Reggie's hand. He glanced at her, startled, then gripped hers back. They stood there for several minutes, the warmth of their hands increasing in each other's. His hand felt big, very solid. When they turned to leave, they let go.

'I want to say I'm sorry, Reggie,' she said. 'That it happened and everything.' No words seemed the right ones, but some had to do. She was glad she had been a nurse even for a little while. It taught you that you can at least say something. 'It seems a bit late. And a bit . . . I mean, not much to say, that's all. I never said it then – you were in hospital and everything.'

'Thanks.' They walked back towards the gates. Reggie shook his head. 'It was the worst time I can remember. I wanted to die myself, I really did. But now – well, I don't feel that any more.'

'Good,' she said, though this seemed even more inadequate than what she had said before. She felt as if she might weep again, but she swallowed the feeling away.

Their eyes met for a moment and they both smiled shyly. Reggie's face, so familiar, so loved once, stirred something in her. A warmth spread through her, a gladness at being here with him.

Reggie looked at her, seeing the tears in her eyes. He seemed moved. He looked down, then back at her. 'Melly . . .' he began. But he could not seem to finish.

'Come on –' he started walking again – 'Mom and Dad want to see you.'

Even now, Melly was amazed by the house in Moseley. They swept into the elegant road of enormous, ornate Edwardian houses, set back from the road with front gardens. As they drew up she saw Mo straighten from where he was bending over a flower bed. He waved, a grin spreading across his face.

Melly beamed back at him, full of affection. Mo had always been in her life somewhere, like a good-natured rock. She remembered him saying, 'They dain't know what'd hit them in this street when we arrived. But I think they decided we don't bite.' It was certainly a posh street compared to what they were used to, and Mo and Dolly were immensely proud of their lovely house. They kept their garden neat and did their best to be neighbourly and respectable. Even though they did not mix naturally with their neighbours, they seemed to have settled in well enough.

'Dolly – look who's here!' Mo called through the front door.

Dolly appeared looking lovely as ever in a navy frock, daubed with bright colours – red, green and yellow – with a full, swinging skirt. She wore her hair shoulder length, parted on the left and curled up at the ends. As usual she had a cigarette in her hand.

'You look like a model!' Melly said as Dolly flung her arms round her, wreathing her in smoke.

'Hello, bab!' Dolly squeezed her tight. 'Ooh, it's lovely to see you! Gladys's told me all about how you've been getting on. She said you'd been poorly.' Dolly stepped back and her brown eyes searched Melly's face.

'How're you feeling, darlin'? You still look a bit pale and peaky to me.'

'I'm all right,' Melly said. 'She's the poorly one now.'

'Poor old Glad.' Dolly steered her, an arm round her shoulders, into the elegant, tiled hall and through into the back. Dolly and Mo still spent most of their time in the huge kitchen with its red quarry-tiled floor and a big table. It always felt cosy in there.

'I've made nice beef stew and you, my girl, are staying to have some tea with us.'

'She still cooks as though there's an army of us living at home,' Reggie said. 'No wonder our Donna's getting fat.'

'Don't talk so silly,' Dolly said. 'She's not.' She looked at them both, wide-eyed. 'Did you go? Are my flowers . . . ?'

'They still look nice, Mom,' Reggie said.

'Call your father in,' she said. 'It's all ready – Mo's picked some of the new spuds and they're lovely. Bit of mint in them. Freddie's out, Melly. There's just Donna here.'

Donna Morrison was now fifteen and not far off leaving school. Melly had not seen her in a good while and when Donna walked into the room she actually gasped. Black-haired and brown-eyed like her mother, she had always been pretty but now she had developed into a stunner. Fat she definitely was not. She had a beautiful, curving figure.

'Oh, Donna – you look lovely!'

Donna blushed. 'Thanks,' she said, shyly slipping on to a chair. They all sat round the table. 'You all right, Melly?'

'Yeah, ta.'

'Mom said you're not doing your nursing any more.'

Donna had a soft, husky voice. 'Have you given it up?' she asked.

Melly looked down, trying to think what to say. At home everyone just took it for granted that she was now going to keep working on the market and in some other job – any old thing. There would be no more nursing now. She hardly dared ask herself this question.

'I don't really know,' she said, blushing.

Luckily they were interrupted by Dolly bossing them to pass things and telling Mo to go and scrub his nails. Melly sank into the comfort and familiarity of it all.

The kitchen was lovely, with light sloping through the big window and all Dolly's pans on shelves and pots of herbs growing on the windowsill, a starched white cloth on the table. And everything was as it should be – Dolly ordering Mo about and him thriving on it. They were both so kind. They ate Dolly's delicious cooking and chatted and reminisced and Melly slowly began to feel better, as if something was unknotting itself inside her and she was growing back into a whole person, instead of the drab, half-alive thing she had been all this time. She found she was laughing more easily and with Mo about, there was always laughing to be done.

'So is Glad on the mend?' Dolly asked, leaning towards her, elbows on the table. 'I must get over there.'

'She's better, but she's none too happy,' Melly said.

'Oh, she'll come round,' Dolly said. 'Poor old Glad, she's been hanging on to that old place long after she should've gone. It's so run down and the neighbours aren't . . .'

'They aren't what they used to be, is that what you're saying, Doll?' Mo laughed, topping up his glass of ale. 'Not the class of person old Glad's used to, eh?'

'Well, they aren't!' Dolly laughed. 'It's not like it used

to be in the old days. We had to pull together – especially during the war. But those cramped old bug-ridden wrecks of houses! She can find herself a much better place to rent over your way.'

It was a lovely, relaxed evening and when Melly said she ought to be getting back, Dolly hugged her again.

'Now next time, I want to see you with more colour in your cheeks. And –' she picked up a strand of Melly's hair – 'we'll do summat about this. I can give it a cut for you – liven you up a bit, eh, bab?'

It was impossible to take offence at Dolly. 'All right,' Melly said, smiling. 'If you like.'

Reggie drove her home. Things felt friendlier than yesterday as they parted.

'Thanks, Reggie,' she said, when he dropped her off. 'I've had a lovely time. It was nice to see them.'

Reggie was quiet for a moment. He kept his hands on the steering wheel.

'Tell you what,' he said. He stared out through the windscreen. 'Tomorrow's my last night. Why don't you come over again? Our mom'd love it. She can cut your hair and we could go out somewhere.'

Melly looked at him with a sense of wonder. She realized he was afraid to look at her, in case she said no. She had a moment of acute awareness of him next to her, every line of him, the man she had known for so long. Who would have thought she could have ended up here, sitting beside him.

'Go on, say yes,' he said softly. 'After that I've got to go and I need to know . . .' He hesitated. 'Just say you'll come.' He turned to her. 'Little Melly.'

She looked into his eyes, moved by the tenderness in his voice. She saw an earnestness that meant he was not playing with her. And how lovely it had been today with him. But she mustn't expect anything more. She didn't want to go through all that again. Tomorrow would be the last time and then he would be gone. He would forget about her.

'All right then.' She kept her voice light, protecting herself, pushing the car door open. 'Ta, Reggie. See you tomorrow.'

Forty-Nine

By the time Reggie called at the house, Melly was pacing up and down in the kitchen, waiting jumpily for the knock at the door.

While her mind was sternly telling her one thing – Reggie would soon be gone and none of this meant anything – she had found herself dashing home from work to brush out her hair, tie it back in a swinging ponytail and put on her favourite clothes. Reggie had said something about going out and she wasn't going in that dismal old grey work skirt!

It was a warm evening and she wore a cornflower blue cotton skirt and a white blouse with three-quarter length sleeves. She had a navy cardigan to go over the top. It was the first time in a long time she had paid any attention to her appearance.

In the mirror her face still looked pale and pinched, but it suited her having her hair back and she saw a light in her own eyes that had not been there before. She did not dare to ask herself why she was taking so much trouble, why she felt so excited.

'Oh!' Rachel said when she went downstairs. Melly was taken aback by how surprised and pleased she seemed. 'You look better. Where're you off to?'

'Just going out with Reggie for a bit.' Her face covered in blushes, she lowered her head, pretending to adjust her hair.

'What – again?' Rachel's voice was full of meaning.

Melly flung her cardigan over her arm and hurried to the front door. As she stepped outside, Reggie's car was roaring along the road towards her. She found a shy smile spreading over her face.

'She's deadly serious! She said to come, didn't she?'

Reggie had announced that they were going over to Moseley so that his mom could wash and set Melly's hair.

'But she must be busy – and how does she know how to do it, anyway?'

'Oh, you know our mom – she can do anything like that.' Reggie was looking over his shoulder as he reversed the car. Turning, he pulled out and they roared away. 'If I don't take you, I'll never hear the end of it.'

Melly heard a giggle come from inside her. The speed of the car rushing along and the prospect of a hairdo from Dolly made her feel bubbly and happy.

Reggie glanced at her, then back out of the windscreen, a smile on his face.

'You all right?' he said.

She looked at him. She was surprised *how* all right she felt suddenly, as if at last she was emerging into the light. 'Yes.' She said happily. 'Ta.'

Within minutes of being inside the house, Dolly had led Melly up to the bathroom and had her leaning over the bath, tipping jugs of warm water over her head.

'There you go, bab. You'll feel better for a good new head of hair. That's it – give it a good rub. We'll do it in the kitchen – I can sweep up easier there.'

To Melly's surprise, Reggie did not make himself

scarce while this women's business was going on. He made a pot of tea, plonked it on the table and sat watching as Dolly combed out Melly's hair in between puffs on her Player's No. 6. The smoke smelt reassuring. It felt like home.

Dolly left the half-burned cigarette in an ashtray on the table, beside a bowl full of blue and pink mesh curlers with hairpins stuck through them. She had slipped her shoes off and Melly saw her neat stockinged feet, with just a hint of bunions appearing, moving round the chair she was sitting on. There was a lingering smell of onions in the kitchen as well as the curling warmth of something simmering on the stove. And there was Reggie watching her. She could feel him looking, all the while Dolly was working her way round her hair.

Melly felt Dolly's intent brown eyes on her as well, as she stooped, snipping at the ends of her hair. Dolly smelt of cigarettes and scent. Sometimes she put her hand on Melly's head as she worked. Its warmth was reassuring. Melly relaxed. She couldn't stop yawning. She felt suddenly safe and warm and loved. She wanted to curl up in a ball and sleep and sleep.

'Am I keeping you up, bab?' Another puff on the cigarette. 'How's Glad today?'

'Still coughing a lot,' Melly said, forcing her eyes to stay open. 'She's not been up much yet.'

Dolly stopped cutting, her dark brows pulled into a frown. 'That's not like her.'

Donna wandered in with a shy 'hello' and stopped to watch, smiling. She had a mysterious, exotic look to her.

'You'll look like a glamour queen when she's finished with you,' Mo said, passing through and out into the garden.

'Donna, stir the soup,' Dolly instructed. 'Now,' she

said to Melly. 'I've got it cut all neat – so let's get you looking lovely. We'll have another cuppa while you set. Donna – kettle.'

She went to work with the curlers, pulling out the ends of Melly's hair, rolling up to the bottom of her ears and pinning. The pins scraped Melly's scalp but she kept quiet. Dolly plugged in her hairdryer.

Melly walked out to the car with Reggie, proud of the bouncy swing of her hair. Dolly had sprayed the curled-up ends so that they hung, tacky and stiff to the touch, each side of her face, curling under. She thought it made her look older and rather mysterious. Dolly had also looked down at Melly's feet in her white sandals and handed her a bottle of cherry red nail varnish. 'Here you go – put a bit of that on.'

With her red toenails and sassy hair, Melly felt more glamorous than ever in her life before.

'You look nice,' Reggie said as he held the car door open for her. 'Come on – I want to take you somewhere. D'you like jazz? There's this bloke playing in town tonight – he's got the same name as you . . .'

Melly had no idea if she liked jazz or not, but she said, 'Yes.' At that moment she liked everything and was hungry to like more. She was beginning to feel that she did not mind where she went, so long as she was with Reggie. The quiet, astonishing realization that Reggie liked – more than liked – her was beginning to sink in. She got in the car and drew in a deep, contented breath. Life was opening out. She looked round and beamed at him.

'D'you go out a lot in Worcester?' she asked. She

wanted to know if he had a girl down there, if she was a stand-in.

'Now and then.' He glanced at her. 'We're not in Worcester town, you know – Pershore College is miles out in the sticks.'

'Oh,' she said. It was hard to imagine.

'It's not like Birmingham. It's very quiet.'

Trying to sound casual: 'Have you got a girlfriend then, Reggie?'

He shot her a startled look. 'I dunno,' he said quietly. 'Have I?'

She knew what he meant. His words pulsed through her. All she had seen in his eyes – was Reggie really keen on her? Was it her that was being slow to catch on? Her heart thumped. What if she were to let herself . . . An image flashed into her mind of Raimundo Alexander prone on the floor. She knew she would never have been Raimundo's girlfriend – not really. But he was someone she had cared so much about and become attached to and look what happened . . .

'There's another place I'll take you sometime.' Reggie started chatting, as if to cover up her silence, her not answering. 'The Woodman pub – they do good music there, an' all.'

They parked in a side street off Digbeth. There was a concert on at the Institute, he said. He led her inside and offered her a drink.

'I'll have a Dubonnet and lemonade,' she said, trying to sound worldly and confident. But she was wondering if she had hurt his feelings. Reggie . . . I love Reggie . . . She kept trying it out in her mind, knowing there were all sorts of feelings growing between them and she could hardly keep up and was afraid . . .

Reggie had a pint and they stood in the crush of

people. She could hear a band warming up in the dance hall.

'This is going to be good,' Reggie said. 'Drink up – let's go in.'

The long room was filling up and some people were already dancing even though the band on stage was only warming up. The air was already stifling and full of smoke. Melly liked the place though. It was dark and cosy in a grand, old-fashioned way, a gallery halfway up round the walls, decorated with gilt swags. The band started playing and they were surrounded by people dancing and whooping to the music. Reggie took her arm and pulled her close to the wall at the side.

'Sorry.' His mouth was close to her ear. 'I'm not much of a one for dancing, not with this gammy leg.'

Melly was mainly relieved. She wasn't sure she was very good at dancing either, though she would not have minded giving it a try. She was drinking in the new experience, the wildly thrashing bodies, the rough smoke in her nostrils, the music going right through her. Her social life had never developed into anything exciting. People kept talking about all the things young people were getting up to these days, but for her, in the nurses' home it had just meant going out for a drink with other girls or chatting over cocoa in their rooms.

She liked the music, its wild edge. It made her feel adventurous. But above all she liked being here with Reggie. The discovery of this sent a thrill through her.

'It's all right,' she smiled up at him. His vulnerability moved her. She wanted to stay by his side, show that she didn't mind, that she was proud to be seen with him.

'This music's called "New Orleans Revival".' Again, he had to speak very close to her and his breath tickled her ear. 'I never knew about this kind of music 'til I was in the army. One of the lads there was mad about it. Chris Barber, Acker Bilk . . .'

She realized she knew almost nothing about his National Service years.

'This is him,' Reggie said later, as a tall man with a fleshy face and dark curling hair began to perform. She watched, fascinated. George Melly, Reggie said. She looked at him and grinned, tapping her feet.

'I'm a Ding Dong Daddy!' The music was fantastic! And she liked the way the man seemed to be chatting to them with his rich voice, relaxed in the music. She was full of life, full of . . . Standing at the edge of the heaving crowd, she looked at Reggie in wonder, her eyes drinking him in, falling, knowing in a floating way that she was falling and that this time she did not want to stop.

Reggie turned and held her gaze. He reached for her. They stood side by side, hand in hand, swaying to the music and she was twelve again, head over heels with Reggie Morrison. Only it was now – they were barely the same people they had been back then – and yet they were and he was familiar. *Reggie* . . .

As the next number ended and everyone cheered and clapped, Reggie put his arm round her shoulders, drew her to him and kissed her on the lips.

Fifty

Reggie turned off near Cannon Hill Park and switched off the engine. It was dark outside and quiet, but Melly still seemed to hear the pulse of the music in her head. Their clothes smelt of smoke and both of them were heady from a few drinks. But now that they were out of the heated atmosphere of the Institute where everyone was dancing and kissing, and they had kissed and swayed together, they had suddenly grown shy and had hardly spoken on the way back.

There was an atmosphere between them of someone needing to make the first move. After a few seconds, Reggie turned to her.

'Melly? Come 'ere.'

She leaned into his arms and his lips met hers again, kissing her hungrily, more forcefully than he had inside the Institute. She kissed him back, eyes closed, holding him close, the way she had embraced him on the bike all those years ago. And it was so different from how it had been with other boys. Now, she was full of tender, longing feelings. She stroked Reggie's hair, his neck and chest. She felt his caress on her back, then one hand edging round to explore her breast. But it grew uncomfortable in the tight space, as they twisted to face each other. Reggie drew back and let out a sharp sigh.

'I've got to go back tomorrow.'

Melly didn't say anything.

He turned his head. 'I don't want to. Well – I do and I don't.' He reached across and gently took her chin between his fingers, tilting her face towards him. 'I don't want to go away from you.' He released her and sat back, smiling. 'Funny, isn't it? There you were – all the time.'

She smiled shyly at him.

'That day I saw you, on the market . . . You dain't look very happy. But I hadn't seen you in ages and it was – well, I looked at you and I thought, she's lovely, she is. It hit me, just like that. I've never said this to anyone before – I honestly haven't – but I love you, Melly.'

Joy coursed through her. She laughed, full of astonished happiness. He loved her!

'I love you too, Reggie. Did you know I was madly in love with you when I was twelve years old?'

'No.' He looked truly surprised.

'I used to stand there in the yard waiting for you. When you came, my heart'd be going like mad and I stood there trying to look as if I was just, you know, hanging about.'

'Well, I thought you *were* just hanging about.' They laughed.

'I don't s'pose you thought about me at all. You seemed like a big grown-up man then. I used to watch you and Wally always messing about with the bike. And I'd stand there and think, just look up, just for a minute – look at me!'

Someone came along the street on the pavement next to them, a young man, walking with fast, purposeful steps. They waited until he had passed into the darkness.

'You never did look at me, not really. And then that one night, you took me off on the bike and I thought all my dreams had come true.'

Reggie smiled, then his face sobered and he looked

411

down. 'That ruddy bike. If it hadn't been for that . . . It was Wal's really. He was the one that was really keen. I never want to ride another one in my life.'

'I'm glad to hear it,' Melly said.

After a few seconds he said, half teasing, 'So – have you always been in love with me?'

Yes, she wanted to say.

'No. Not always. Not when I was two and you were eight and in short trousers! I think I fell for you that day you rescued Tommy – d'you remember? But when I saw you at Wal's funeral, and after that, I thought you'd never be interested in me. It was as if you'd gone somewhere far away. I could never think what to say to you after it. And anyway, when you all moved away . . . I just thought you'd have a girl – lots of girls.'

'Some girls're all right,' he said. 'A lot of them take one look at my leg . . .'

'But what difference does that make?' she said. 'You're just you – you're working, you're strong, good looking.'

'They just see me as a cripple. Like Tommy. But you don't.' He looked at her. 'You're kind and nice. You always were, Melly. The way you looked after Tommy and stuck up for him.'

Melly was gratified by his praise, but an uncomfortable feeling was nagging at her. If Reggie hadn't had a bad leg, would he ever have even looked at her? Was that what he was saying?

'Thing is,' he went on, 'it makes you see what's good and what matters – *who* matters.' Gently, he laid his palm against her cheek. 'You're lovely, Melly.' Humbly, he added, 'Will you be my girl?'

She felt a moment of resistance after what he had said about his leg. 'But you're going away. I don't even know when I'll see you again.'

'Course you'll see me,' he said. 'It's not all that far away and I've got the car, thanks to Dad. He got it for me because of my leg – and Mom said I'd never come home otherwise. I can come over . . . Thing is, Melly, why wait? I'm going to be thirty in a few years. I want to get married, have a wife and kids. I don't want to spend my life on my own, like some sad old cripple. I want *you*, Melly – I want to be with you.'

Melly felt a rushing sensation, as if she had been scooped up abruptly by a speeding train and carried along through life so fast she could hardly see the scenery. And yet what he was saying, the way he spoke that made her feel so loved and wanted; all that he was trying to rush her into – safety and family and children – were these not all things she yearned for? She felt washed in happiness and excitement. Her own mind raced forward. What if she and Reggie got married? She would have Dolly as her mother-in-law and Mo and Donna and the others and that lovely big house to visit – live in even. It would be paradise!

'Oh!' she said. 'Reggie – I love you. I do. But slow down a bit. You're making my head spin!'

'All I'm saying is –' he sounded deeply earnest – 'life's short. You can go –' he snapped his fingers – 'like that. Any minute. There was this bloke I saw, when I was in Germany. It'd snowed and he was on the roof, just across from us, knocking the snow off. One minute he was up there, sweeping – the next he was on the ground with his neck broken.'

'And Wally,' she said, thinking, and Raimundo Alexander. The thought wrung her heart. Reggie was right. They should live while they had life. They should get married – now, tomorrow, before it was too late.

'Once I've finished college I can get a good job,' he

said. 'But we don't need to wait. We could get married before I've finished. We could find a way . . .'

'Reggie, slow down a bit,' she teased him. 'This is the first time we've ever been out together!' But even as she said it, she was glowing inside. Everything was happening so fast, but wasn't Reggie, Reggie loving her, all she'd ever dreamt of? And didn't she love him too? She did – of course she did!

'Come on.' He turned the key and the car roared into action again. 'I'll take you home. We can tell them.'

'Who?' she said, startled.

'Your mom and dad – who else?'

'Reggie, no! Not yet.' Laughing, she put a hand on his arm. 'This is crazy! Just let me get used to things. We can't get married, just like that! Why're you in such a rush?'

'But – I love you!' He spoke with fervour. 'I want you, Melly. I want us to have a home together, be Mr and Mrs Morrison – you know, all the things people do.'

She looked into his face, with its longing eyes. He leaned to her and kissed her on each cheek. 'I love you. God – I love you, Melly.'

'All right,' she said, touched by him. 'But don't say anything – not yet. I haven't even said I'm going to marry you. This is all too fast!'

'Sorry.' He looked abashed. 'Sorry, Melly. Only sometimes when you know something's right . . . I knew when I saw you that day. It hit me. It was like coming home, just the sight of your little face there in the Rag Market. You're my girl – that's all there is to it.'

And she smiled back at him, caught up and swept along by the miraculous whirlwind of his feelings and hers together.

Melly managed to persuade Reggie not to say anything

414

to anyone, not for a while. They said tender goodbyes when he reached their house, kissing and holding each other in the car until she said she really had better go in.

'I'll have Mom after me. It's already well gone eleven,' she said.

'I'll be over soon,' Reggie said. He kissed her again. 'God,' he said, 'I love you, wench.'

Standing in the street between the lamps, she watched him drive away. She was brimful of happiness, the imprint of his love on her lips, her cheeks. She hugged herself. Reggie – *Reggie!* – loved her. And she loved him.

But it was like a dream, everything moving so fast that she was confused, needing to catch up. His hurry and desperation gave her a nagging sense of unease which puzzled her. Hadn't she always loved Reggie? Wasn't it what she wanted, in the end, a husband and children to love and who would love her back, the way Reggie had realized that was what he needed?

She shook her head as if to organize her thoughts and walked to the door. She found herself feeling relieved that Reggie had gone away. This was confusing, given the fact that since the moment he left she had been longing for him to come back. I'll sleep on it, she thought. Maybe things will make more sense in the morning.

Fifty-One

'Auntie?'

Melly tapped on the door of Gladys's bedroom the next morning. When there was no answer she tensed with alarm. Opening the door, she tiptoed in, grateful for the strip of carpet on the floor which muffled her footsteps.

All the time, even when she was doing something else, her mind had an extra pulse of *Reggie, Reggie* and all they had said the night before.

She slid the cup and saucer she was carrying on to the chair by the bed, pushing aside Gladys's black stockings that were lying there. Melly could hear the light rattle of her breath.

Looking down at her she saw the face of an elderly, sick lady. Gladys's hair had turned, rapidly, in the last months, from a dark chestnut threaded with white, to a greyish white like dirty snow. The flesh sagged on her big-boned face, there was a downward pull to her mouth. Even in sleep her brows were clenched in a frown and her eyes, those startling blue lights in her face, were closed.

The sight of her shocked Melly with tenderness. Gladys had been so strong, like an impregnable fortress, all through Melly's life. In Alma Street she had been the gaffer, queen of the yard. In Aston, she was someone. Now, here in Harborne, away from the old end and the neighbours who had drifted away, she was just another old lady, faded and unknown.

Thank goodness she's still got the Rag Market, Melly thought. But she had an ominous feeling, looking at Gladys. She had a bad chest – but was that all? Was there something really wrong? The idea of Gladys fading out of the world was shattering.

'Auntie?' She spoke a little more loudly.

Gladys opened one eye, then the other. Immediately she looked more in possession of herself.

'Uh? Oh! What, bab? Is everything all right?'

'Yes. Mom's out and the others've gone to work.' It was Melly's day off from the sweet shop. 'It's late – gone half past nine. I've brought you some tea. How're you feeling?'

Gladys, trying to sit up, fell into such a bad fit of coughing that she couldn't speak for quite a time. Melly helped her, but it felt very strange. Gladys had always been an intensely private person, her bedroom her kingdom where no one dare set foot. She had always been the same Gladys, downstairs in her dark clothes and shawls, her hair twisted up and pinned at the back. Melly was not used to dealing so intimately with her. She was aware, up close like this, of the slackness of the skin on Gladys's arms, the spreading weight of her in her pale blue nightie. She was not a small woman. To make it easier, Melly pretended to herself that she was nursing again, as if Gladys was a stranger.

'Oh,' Gladys groaned, once she was upright. 'Ta, bab. Ooh, I do feel bad. My head's spinning. Give us a bit of that tea, will you?'

Melly perched on the bed. She knew that Mom reckoned Gladys was putting it on now; was just after attention. But she felt sorry for Auntie. She'd been uprooted. She seemed lost and sad. Gladys took a sip of

417

the tea and closed her eyes for a moment. Then she opened them and gave Melly a wink.

'Ah, nectar!'

She was well enough to joke, Melly noted. Perhaps she wasn't so very bad after all.

'How many sugars d'you put in?'

'Three.'

Gladys nodded. She took a few more sips, and seemingly restored, fixed Melly with a shrewd look.

'You'll have to take over for me, Sat'd'y,' she said. 'I'm not going to be up to it.' Without waiting for Melly to consent to this, she was off, giving orders about how much stock she had for the stall in the house in town where some of the market traders stored it, and about the money she'd need to take in and what she was going to have to do.

'I know all this, Auntie,' Melly laughed. 'Mother's milk. You don't need to tell me.'

'Oh, ar.' Gladys peered at her over the rim of the teacup. 'All right, then.' She gave Melly a knowing look. 'Where were you last night then?'

'Out,' Melly said, blushing.

'With Dolly's lad?'

Melly nodded, looking down at the little flowers on Gladys's eiderdown.

'And?'

Melly looked up, half smiling. 'What d'you mean, *and*?'

'Dolly do your hair?' Gladys changed tack. 'Looks all right.' The style had held, to some extent, overnight. Melly nodded.

'You could do a lot worse,' Gladys said. She looked pleased, Melly thought. The Morrisons were like family already.

'Auntie!' She stood up. 'I've only been out with him a couple of times!'

She wasn't going to tell anyone that Reggie was behind her like a steamroller wanting to get married.

Melly was about to suggest breakfast when she saw that Gladys was looking solemnly at her.

'Your father thinks I should move in here, doesn't he? For good?' She seemed in need of reassurance.

Melly took a moment to answer, weighing her words. 'You can't go and live back there, can you?' she said gently. 'The place is falling to bits. But if you stop here a while you could find somewhere else. Somewhere you like?'

Gladys gave a little belch, fist to her lips. 'Well, if I'm going to go, the sooner I fetch the rest of my things out of there, the better.' She seemed already to have made up her mind.

Tommy had asked her to take a letter to the post for him and she went to buy him a stamp.

On the envelope, in his painstaking handwriting, Melly read, '*Invalid Tricycle Association*'.

Some club he was joining, he'd said to her as he got ready for work this morning.

'Costs a pound – a year,' he told her. 'But they – have socials.' He shrugged. 'Might as well. Make – a change.'

He seemed a fraction brighter, she thought. Getting his little car had definitely cheered him up. These concerns soon left her and she wandered along the road lost in thoughts about Reggie; how it had felt to be in his arms, his lips on hers.

'I'll come back and see you, soon as I can,' Reggie had

419

assured her as they kissed goodbye. 'I don't want to be away from you.'

Melly had to admit to herself that she was quite glad he was away for a while. Everything felt so new and fast. She was still trying to catch up. As if none of it was quite real, like a dream or in the pictures.

When she got home after posting Tommy's letter, her mother had just got back from work.

'She all right?' Rachel raised her eyes to the ceiling in an exasperated way.

'I don't know,' Melly said, filling the kettle. 'She sat up and had her tea and a bit of bread and butter. But her chest sounds terrible. And she's asked me to do her stall on Saturday.'

Rachel turned. '*Has* she?' This was a sign that Gladys must actually be ill.

'She says she wants Dad to fetch the rest of her things.'

Rachel stared at her. 'What – not go back?' Melly knew Mom did not really want Gladys here. She tutted and tightened her lips for a moment. Looking up again, she said, 'What time d'you come in last night?'

'Oh,' Melly said vaguely. 'I can't remember.'

She felt her mother looking at her. 'You and Reggie – are you . . . ?'

God, Melly thought, can't anyone mind their own flaming business round here for one minute?

She forced a laugh. 'Mom! We've just been out a couple of times – and he's not even here any more. He was just passing the time. You sound like one of those old matchmakers!'

'Huh,' Rachel said. 'Well, you were out very late for someone just passing time.'

Fifty-Two

It was a beautiful July day. The markets were thrumming with life. In the Rag Market everyone was setting up, paying the Toby Man, laughing and joking. In the warm air the scents seemed intensified: cigarette smoke, the mustiness of old clothing, a whiff of perfume, chips frying somewhere in the distance. Soon it would be time for the punters to come in but for the moment the huge gates were closed.

People kept asking her what she had done with Gladys. Everyone missed her. Melly had enjoyed setting up the stall the way she wanted. Gladys now sold a variety of things as well as second-hand clothes: a rack of skirt lengths, remnants for curtains, cards of poppas and safety pins and skeins of zips, spools of cotton, of bias binding and lace, of ribbons and elastic of varying widths. Melly set it all out to make it as attractive as possible, hanging things from the rails at the ends.

Maybe I could do this, Melly thought, leaning her hands on her stall, checking everything was in order. In the distance she could see her father, his stall already set up, the leathers and sheepskins all hanging in neat rows and now a rack of second-hand furs. He was always on to the next thing. She smiled to herself, enjoying being in charge.

Just as the gates were opening and the surge of shoppers burst inside, Danny came running over.

'Here, kid – you'll need these.' He thrust some change into her hand and rushed back again.

'Ta, Dad!' she called. She stowed it in the purse she had tucked into her waistband.

And then she was busy, with no time to think about anything except the crowds, keeping a sharp eye out for any light fingers round her stall, watching, chatting, selling. The warm weather brought a lot of people out for a mooch around 'rag alley' and soon the place was heaving and trade was brisk. Melly felt herself settle into her stride. The business came easily to her. Gladys would be pleased, she thought.

She spent a long time with a lady who said she was making clothes for her daughter's wedding.

'There you are,' Melly said, handing her a paper bag full of sewing things. 'I hope she has a lovely day!'

'Thanks, bab.' The woman smiled. She was a straggle-haired, beaten-down-looking person who counted out every penny very carefully. Melly followed the woman with her eyes as she moved away into the crowd, dressed in a shabby grey raincoat on this hottest of summer days. As she looked she became aware, at the side of her vision, of someone watching her.

'Hello.'

Reggie. Just standing there, with his stick.

'Oh!' She was startled, her heart speeding up. 'What're you doing here?'

'Well, that's nice.' He hobbled towards her. She liked the way he was dressed – jeans again, a blue-and-white checked shirt, the sleeves rolled. 'I wanted to see you. I went to the house and they said you was over here.'

He came close and kissed her cheek. 'Ooh's and other comments – 'Aren't you a lucky girl?' and 'Ooh, he's a good-looking feller!' – came from the cluster of women at the stall.

Melly blushed. She was suddenly very pleased to see him.

'Sorry,' she said. 'I'm working all day now. Auntie's poorly.'

'Yeah – your mom said. Never mind. I'll come behind and give you a hand, shall I?'

'You're a natural at this,' she said after he had sold a suit each to two Indian lads, both thin and bashful about their purchases. Reggie had talked to them nicely and helped them find a good fit.

'Well,' he said. 'Can't be easy for 'em, can it?'

The afternoon flew by. Danny popped over again at one point and greeted Reggie, surprised and pleased.

'Come for a drink with us after, won't you, Reg? We always go – the Adam and Eve. I'll stand you a pint.'

'Thanks, Mr Booker,' Reggie said. He smiled at Melly. 'Wouldn't miss it.'

In all the marketing and packing up, she worked in a haze of happiness. It was lovely working with Reggie. He was good with customers and it was such a help to have another person there, who went off and bought her a cup of tea, somehow managing to carry the two cups in one hand as he moved his stick with the other. She even imagined the two of them making this their business. How would that be? But she was also relieved that they were out among the crowds, that this was not the time to talk about the future or what it might mean.

After they'd packed up again and wheeled the remaining stock to the house nearby where they now stored it, they went up Bradford Street to the pub. The three of them stood amid the smoke and loud chat and laughter. Danny reminisced about the market and he and Reggie swapped army stories and Melly was happy seeing them together. She didn't say much. It was an effort to shout at the top of your voice over all the racket and she was feeling weary.

'Right,' Danny said, draining his glass. 'Better get back or there'll be trouble.' He rolled his eyes and Reggie laughed. Danny liked to give the idea that Rachel was a dragon who policed his every move. They all knew it wasn't really true. 'Want a lift, you two?' he asked, when they got out into the street.

They hesitated.

'Shall we stay in town for a bit?' Reggie said.

Melly nodded. If they went home there'd just be all the kids and no privacy.

'All right, then. Nice seeing you, Reggie.' Her father set off down Bradford Street with his energetic stride.

'He's all right, your dad,' Reggie remarked.

He said it in a certain way, a way that made her think, he's talking about his father-in-law. She felt herself tighten up inside, almost as if she was afraid.

'Fancy something to eat?' Reggie said.

'Ooh, yes.' Melly was starving hungry.

'Come on then – I'll show you a nice place. D'you like curry?'

'I'm not sure. I've never had it.' She'd heard her dad being rude about curry. It wasn't exactly a favourite of his from his time in India.

'It's nice – come and give it a try. There's a place just down here.'

He took her arm and they strolled along, cutting through to Bristol Street. It felt funny to her, walking into the dark restaurant with its foreign smells. But Reggie said the food was really good. He seemed to know all about it.

They settled at a small table and the waiters, all young men, fussed around them. One of them laid a napkin across Melly's knees. She smiled and thanked him. There was a strange, perfumed aroma mixed with the spicy smells of the food.

'This place opened last year,' Reggie said. 'Pete, one of the lads I did my training with in Kings Heath – he told me about it. The food's . . . Well, I really like it.' He leaned over as she peered, bemused, at the menu. 'I can tell you some nice things if you like.'

She felt the age gap again suddenly, Reggie much older and more experienced. He had learned to do all sorts of new things. And he had money. He ate in restaurants sometimes, something she had scarcely ever done, except for a couple of times before Christmas when business had gone especially well and Dad treated them.

'The chicken's nice,' he said. 'Go on – order what you like. It's all on me.'

He seemed excited, she thought. When she glanced up from the menu his eyes were drinking her in as if trying to memorize her, or as if – she realized afterwards – he was about to spring a surprise on her.

'I don't really know,' she said. She chose something that sounded fairly safe and Reggie ordered. He asked for lagers to drink.

'D'you know why they serve lager in Indian restaurants?' he asked, sitting back once the waiter had dissolved away like a shadow. 'There's this big restaurant in London called Veeraswamy's, been open for years. And sometime before the war the Prince of Denmark went there for a meal. He liked it so much that he gave them a present of a whole lot of lager. I suppose they must have found it went well with the food.' He laughed. 'Pete told me that as well. He knows all sorts of odd things, like a walking encyclopaedia.'

Melly laughed. She looked around her. There were a few other people in the restaurant, but it was only half past six – early as yet. She realized that today had made her feel less like drab little Melly. She had run the stall – run it well, she knew – and now she was sitting here, in a restaurant, with Reggie. She felt more grown up, her thoughts expanding wider.

'You'll have to tell me about Germany,' she said. 'You never said anything about your National Service.'

'I will.' Reggie took a drink of his lager. 'Thing is though, Melly. I want to say summat first.'

She saw that he was now full of some emotion that she could not read. He lit a cigarette and she noticed that his hands were not steady. He took a drag on it and set it down in the ashtray, his right hand reaching into his pocket.

'Before they bring the food I want to . . .' He had brought out a little blue box and, watching her, he opened it. Against a dark bed of velvet, she saw jewels winking – one at the centre a deep green, nestled between clear, glassy diamonds like tiny dots of light.

'I know it's been quick, Melly. But I've never been so sure of anything in my life. Not since I saw you again. Being away from you is terrible. I love you with all my heart and I want to ask you to be my wife.'

Fifty-Three

Tommy had woken that Saturday morning with his heart pounding hard. He opened his eyes and looked round, startled. He was still in the back room downstairs on the put-you-up – of course he was. Auntie was in his old room.

Usually he woke in a sweat about getting to work – still, after all this time. But there was no work today. As he sat up, he remembered that the reason for his pounding blood was excitement as much as nerves.

'*Dear Mr Booker . . .*' The letter had arrived by return of post from an address in West Bromwich. '*Thank you for your subscription to the Invalid Tricycle Association.*' The letter went on to give him information about events and socials that were planned.

'*You may be interested in an event that is coming up shortly . . .*' There was to be an outing to Cannock Chase; a picnic and social with games. Times and meeting places followed. Today – it was today. And he had decided to go. He had dared himself. What else would he be doing, stuck at home? It looked dry and bright outside. He had no exact idea where he was going, but what the heck? He and his little car would find the way together.

'I thought I'd better get over to Hay Mills and see your nan later,' his mother said as she drifted into the kitchen.

'D'you want to come with me? You could go on your Invacar thing now.' She peered at him. 'What're you doing?'

'Making a sandwich.' He was bent over, the loaf pinned with his left arm, sawing erratically at it.

'Here – let me.' She came over to him; her nylon dressing gown swished a faint smell of sweat and sandalwood talc. On her feet were little slippers with a strip of pink fluff across to keep them on.

'No – s'all right. I can – do it.'

'Well, what d'you want a sandwich for this time in the morning?'

'I'm going – for a picnic.' He explained about the ITA, the social. As he spoke, she immediately looked worried.

'But, love – Cannock? That's miles away, up Wolverhampton way, isn't it?' She had never been there. She scarcely knew. 'I mean, it's one thing going over to work in that thing, but all the way out there? Look – just let me do that.' She elbowed him out of the way. Spreading the marge was harder than cutting a slice.

Tommy gave in and asked her for cheese and pickle.

'There's a – group – going,' he said, sitting by the table as she parcelled up his food. 'All together. I want – to – go places.'

'Course you do, bab.' But she looked uncertain, her long habits of protectiveness warring with her longing for freedom – for both him and herself. 'Here – I'll cut you a piece of cake. And there's some apples. Want a flask of tea?'

'Yeah. Go on – then.'

'I hope you're going to be all right,' she said, heating the Thermos, swirling it in her hands.

'I'll be – OK,' he said. He smiled to reassure her.

*

428

He loved his three-wheeler, now he'd got the hang of it. Once he was inside this vehicle – built especially for him! – he felt equal to everyone else. He could roar along the roads – it was very noisy – the fact of his bad arm, his weakly functioning legs, for the moment irrelevant. He was part of the traffic, going places like anyone else.

And when he turned up at the meeting place for the social, half sick with nerves, he was amazed to see more and more invalid carriages arriving, of varying ages and styles. Driving them he could see people of varying ages and styles as well. An older man who he parked next to leaned over and called to him through his window.

'All right, lad? New, are yer? Don't you worry – just follow on. We'll all stick together.'

Tommy nodded and smiled back. He kept looking to see if he could spot anyone of his age in the cars but it was hard to tell from where he was. He had not met many people for any kind of social life up until now, except at the clubs organized by Carlson House. He still had a couple of pals from the school, but now he wanted something new, to prove to himself that he could do things outside just the Spastic Association.

No friendships had come out of being at work. No one was interested in waiting long enough for him to get out of the building, let alone to do anything else like help him go to the pictures with them. He was too slow. He didn't fit in. It made him feel as though he wanted to hide away again, away from people's harsh staring eyes and unkind comments, like, *Why don't you go to Remploy, hopalong?*

For years he had not let himself want any more, the things that able-bodied people took for granted like friends and social lives and love affairs. It hurt too much to want and know you were never going to get anything. It was better not to feel anything.

But now, even just being here felt exciting – with a whole new set of people who were something like him. He didn't care how young or old people were really. It was just nice to have a chat, do things with other people who knew what it was like. And – he allowed himself the thought – surely somewhere in all this lot there might be someone he could call a friend? That was his biggest dream. If only he could have a true friend.

They headed north, the sun out, the warm air coming in through his open windows; he thought he might burst with excitement. As they set off the man in the next car called to him again, 'Just follow me, son, if you don't know the way.'

So that was what he was doing, not needing to worry about reading a map or whether he might get lost and instead feeling as proud of his little vehicle as he might have been of the fastest racing car. He had wheels! He was off to see the world. He was amazed by the open space of Cannock Chase, the gently rolling hills, the woods all around and all the three-wheelers arriving. He looked round as all the little vehicles parked on a flat area, in a semicircle.

As he was getting ready to haul himself out, he saw that as well as the invalid cars, quite a number of ordinary cars had rolled up which must have been behind them. There were people with no disabilities walking about: friends or family of others in the three-wheelers. He saw wheelchairs being taken out of cars, people spreading rugs and carrying picnic baskets.

Tommy felt a pang of disappointment. He had hoped

it was just going to be other disabled drivers. He had no one with him. Now he was going to face a day sitting on the edge of things again, all on his own as everyone met up with their families in tow. He felt like starting up the engine and driving home again, only he didn't know the way. And he had wanted something of today, of joining the ITA. Wanted it so much.

He sat for a moment, his right hand gripping the steering bar.

Oh, well, he thought. Better get on with it. At least I've got a rug to sit on. A little rug that had come with the car.

He climbed out, put the strap of his canvas bag with his sandwiches and flask in over his head, reached down for his stick and tucked the rug under his right arm. This made walking very awkward. He could not hold the stick properly as he had to keep his arm clenched close to his body. He shuffled along a few steps feeling hungry and defeated and fed up before he had even started. The place where everyone was gathering for the picnic was about twenty yards away. It seemed like miles. He put his head down and resigned himself to shuffling along.

'All right, lad?' a voice said, approaching behind him. Tommy bristled for a second but the voice sounded friendly enough. 'Need a hand?'

A balding, middle-aged man had come up behind him, a wicker basket in one hand and a cloth draped over one shoulder. He was wearing sporty brown tweed trousers, a putty-coloured shirt and spectacles clamped on his bulbous pink nose.

'Let me carry the rug for you,' he said. 'It's cramping your style, I can see.'

Tommy allowed him to take the rug and the man walked slowly, as if keeping Tommy company.

'I've not seen you on one of these outings before, young man. Is this your first?'

'Yes,' Tommy said. 'I've just joined.'

'Good, very good.' The man spoke in the brisk way that Tommy often found people did to him. He expected him to stop talking and move away as soon as he could, but he said. 'We've been to a few – just over the last year, since my daughter had her car.'

They talked cars: the man's daughter's was a Tippen Delta, made in Coventry. Tommy told the man his was an Invacar.

'Marvellous, aren't they?' the man said. 'I'd never've thought there could be such a thing. Course there used to be the old bath chairs but these – marvellous.'

As they approached the place where everyone was laying out their rugs and food, the man said, 'Right – where d'you want to be?' He looked at Tommy and then back behind him. 'Isn't there anyone with you?'

'No,' Tommy had to admit.

'Oh, dear, oh, dear, well, that won't do. Can't have you sitting all on your own. I'm sure you've already done far too much of that if I know anything about it – eh?' He gave a little laugh. 'Come and sit with us – over there, look, that's my wife and family.' Tommy saw a small group of people sitting together, one, a dark-haired woman, had her arm raised, waving in her husband's direction.

'All right. Thank – you.' Tommy felt relieved but also a bit silly, like a charity case and a nuisance. It was still better than just sitting there on his own, but then he had to worry about eating in front of strangers. He tensed up, wondering what he was in for.

When they reached the spot, the woman got to her feet. Beside her was someone in a wheelchair, her back to

432

Tommy, and a boy who looked a few years younger than he was.

'Hello,' the woman said, a kind but enquiring look on her face.

'This is Tommy,' her husband told her. 'This is his first time – and he's come all on his own.'

'Oh, dear – well, we can't have that,' she said. Her dark hair was shoulder length and curled under at the ends. She had a fresh complexion and a smiley way of talking. 'Come and join us. Here we are, Jo-Ann,' she added to the person in the wheelchair. 'We've got some company!'

The boy, who must have been about fourteen and looked obviously very like his mother, got to his feet.

'This is Tommy,' his mother said. And to Tommy, 'This is Philip.'

''Lo,' Philip said. He seemed shy, but not unfriendly.

'And this is our daughter Jo-Ann.'

She was trying to turn in the chair to see who was there and her mother went to help. Tommy saw a girl of about his own age with long, straight brown hair and a shy smile which brought a deep dimple into her right cheek.

'Hello,' she said.

Tommy smiled back, squirming inwardly with shyness. The girl was lovely. Lovely in a way that made something cartwheel inside him.

'Come on – let's have something to eat,' the mother was saying. 'I don't know about you but I'm famished. Come and sit here, Tommy – are you all right down on the ground? Good – sit by Jo-Ann, she'd love to talk to you. Oh, I forgot to say, I'm Mrs Halstead – Marjorie. And this is my husband Roy. You've brought something to eat? Oh, good – but there's plenty here as well.'

Tommy sank to the ground, close to Jo-Ann's wheel-chair. He made a to-do about getting settled and getting out his sandwiches, because he was overcome with shy-ness and had no idea what to say. Just because Jo-Ann's mother said she would want to talk to him did not mean it was true.

But he had only just reached in his bag for his brown paper bag of sandwiches, when her voice came to him:

'What's the matter with you, Tommy?'

He looked up, startled.

'I mean – sorry,' she laughed, 'I wondered if you had polio like me. I could walk before that. Now my legs are hopeless. Arms are all right though, luckily.'

'No,' he said. He liked her frankness. He hoped she wouldn't mind the halting way he talked since she spoke normally, with the smiling speed of her mother. 'I was – born – like this. Cerebral – palsy. They didn't think I'd – walk – or talk. I had – help . . .'

'Oh, I see,' she said. 'D'you have a wheelchair?'

'Some – times. I can – walk – a short – way.'

'I was all right before I had polio. It was when I was eight – ten years ago. I went swimming one hot day and –' She shrugged. 'One afternoon splashing in the pool . . . The next, months in hospital. Once they realized what it was.'

She was the same age as him, he realized.

'That sounds – very frighten – ing,' he said.

'Yes, it was. But when you're quite young you just . . .' She thought about it. 'I'd be more frightened now. I didn't know what was going on then. I just knew I felt poorly. It was worse for Mom and Dad.'

'And me,' Philip said. He flashed a grin at his sister. 'No one took any notice of me – not for ages.'

'Why would anyone take any notice of you, tadpole?' his sister retorted.

'Where do you live, Tommy?' Mr Halstead said, half-way through a sausage roll.

'Harborne,' he said. 'There's a – special – school. Called – Carlson – House.'

'Ah,' Mr Halstead said. 'Yes, very good, very good.' Tommy could tell he did not know how to talk to him. He kept up a breezy tone all the time.

'I went to a special school as well,' Jo-Ann said. 'They tried to get my legs working. I had physiotherapy and exercises and everything for ages.' Her face clouded for a second. 'But they just wouldn't.'

'Are you working, lad?' Mr Halstead said. 'Remploy or somewhere take you on?'

'Not Remploy,' Tommy said. He wanted them to know he was in a place that was not for disabled people only. 'At Lucas's.'

'Lucas's? Ah – in Hockley?' Mr Halstead sounded surprised. 'Good firm that. What have they put *you* on then?' Tommy didn't miss the stress Mr Halstead put on the word 'you'.

He told them. He didn't say he didn't like it but Jo-Ann said:

'You don't sound very happy about it.'

'No.' He hunched his shoulders. 'It's boring.'

'I work for Dad,' Jo-Ann said. 'We live in Wolverhampton – he sells furniture. Halstead's? I don't know if you've heard of it. It's quite a big store.' Tommy hadn't. 'So I work as his secretary. Mom helped me.'

'I was a secretary before I married, you see,' Mrs Halstead said.

'Everything's all right with my hands,' Jo-Ann said.

435

'So I learned to type and do that sort of thing in an office.'

'That sounds – nice,' Tommy said. 'Not being – treated – like an – idiot.'

He saw Mr Halstead look startled at this and Mrs Halstead sad and faintly embarrassed.

Tommy decided he didn't care.

Jo-Ann put her head on one side; her eyes were sympathetic. 'Is it because of how you talk? I suppose it is.'

'There's nothing – wrong – with – my – mind,' he said, crossly.

'Oh, no – I can tell that. But people don't know – think all sorts of silly things.'

He frowned. 'I've – got five – O-levels. By the – way.'

Mr Halstead made a surprised noise as he bit into an apple.

'Golly – have you? That's more than I have. You're a brainy one.' Jo-Ann laughed.

Tommy looked up at her. She seemed to him like a goddess.

Fifty-Four

Melly didn't say a word to anyone about Reggie's proposal. But she told Reggie she could not see him the next day. She could tell he was bitterly disappointed.

'I promised I'd help Auntie move,' she said. And before Reggie could offer to bring his car to help as well, she added firmly, 'Dad and me have got it all organized, thanks.'

Gladys, having made up her mind, decreed that Danny was to drive her over to Aston to fetch as many things of hers as they could fit into the car. Reggie could have helped, of course, but Melly knew she wanted time to think, to take in the enormity of what had happened. She sat in the car behind Gladys who was bundled up in her coat although it was a warm day.

Driving there felt, once again, like going back in time. All the streets around were almost as familiar as her own skin, but each time she went back, it seemed more cramped, shabby and poor. And, people knew, it would only be so much longer before the bulldozers moved in. The city engineer, Herbert Manzoni, was working his way round the 'slums' as their neighbourhoods were now called. Development areas being razed to build new roads and blocks of flats.

Gladys had been one of the ones trying not to face up to it. But now she had reached the end of the line.

They parked in Alma Street. As they walked along the

entry, all the smells hit Melly again – the frowsty stink of the houses, the lavs at the end shared by eight families, the whiff from the bins. The yard seemed smaller and filthier even than last time she had come. Number four, the Davies's place, had the downstairs window boarded up. Gladys said the children there ran wild. They must have smashed the window while they were at it, Melly thought.

A girl with straggly red hair and a mucky little frock stood near the lamp, forcing a yo-yo up and down on a frayed string. Melly had never seen her before. She looked at them warily and ran into number five – Lil and Stanley's old house. Lil had moved out, unable to stand the place now Stanley was gone. She had a couple of rooms in Erdington.

The child must be one of the O'Hallorans. Gladys had mentioned them taking over the house. 'More Irish,' was all she said. Irish to Gladys – in most cases – meant foreign feckless Catholics breeding like rabbits. It was just another of the things changing and shifting about her ears.

When they walked into the house, Melly saw Gladys finally admit defeat. Perhaps she had hoped the place was not as bad as she remembered, but the stink of it hit them as soon as they got through the door.

'Look, you sit down, Auntie,' Danny said. 'You're not up to this. Melly and I'll bring out everything we can.'

'I'll make you a cup of tea,' she said stubbornly.

It felt very sad, carrying Gladys's possessions – very few really – out of the house. None of the furniture was worth salvaging and Melly was relieved that Gladys said nothing about it. The neighbours nosed as they took the wireless and its accumulator, her clothes and personal bits. She possessed nothing in the way of a suitcase – they had to drape everything over their arms. There were a few items from the kitchen, trinkets from the mantelpiece above the range, her photographs and mementos. A life with very little, soon transferred.

They were finished within an hour. Melly walked back to the house with her father, after carrying the last load. Gladys was still sitting at the table as if waiting to go to a funeral.

'You ready, Auntie?' Danny asked. The gentleness in his voice brought tears to Melly's eyes. They all owed Auntie everything – but Dad especially. 'You all right?'

'I'll do,' Gladys said.

When Danny suggested she go and say her goodbyes, Gladys struggled to her feet, coughing. She had to lean on Danny to walk outside.

'You're feverish still!' Danny exclaimed. 'I'll get you back in the car.'

'Oh, stop keeping on,' Gladys said. 'Let's get it over with. There's only the Jackmans to see anyway.'

Mr and Mrs Jackman were the only remaining neighbours with whom Gladys had come through the war. They could not have been said to be close, but there was something precious about their familiarity. While Gladys was saying goodbye, Melly looked out and caught a glimpse of Ethel Jackman. She was shocked at her shrunken appearance, her face small and lined. Gladys made it clear she wasn't bothering with the rest of the yard.

'Right,' she said, once that was over. She walked back to the door of the house and jerked her head at them. 'Off you go, you two. I'll be out in a tick.'

Melly exchanged glances with Danny. They walked towards the entry and stopped to wait for her. The red-headed girl had appeared again and was scuffing at the wall of her house, near the door, with her rubber shoes. The sole was half hanging off one of them.

There was a long pause while Gladys took her leave of the house where she had lived for the last thirty years. Danny lit a cigarette. Melly stood with him, both of them looking round, involved in their own memories. In her mind's eye, Melly saw Reggie and the other Morrison lads, all tearing up and down the yard, their blonde hair shining in the sun, and her lips curved up for a moment.

After a time, Gladys slowly came out of the house. It was hot, but as well as her coat she had on her winter boots, to save packing them. Turning, she pulled the door shut and stood, head down, with her hand flat against it.

'It's a rathole, Auntie,' Danny called to her. 'You're best off with us.'

Gladys raised her head, as if she was going to make a retort to this. But she looked back at Danny, saying nothing, her hand still on the chipped green paint.

'Come on then,' he said, turning away.

She didn't move immediately. Melly waited as her father turned down the entry. Gladys slowly removed her hand; her head bowed and she came along to Melly.

'All right, then,' she said. 'You lead the way, bab.'

Fifty-Five

'Is anyone listening to me?' Rachel stood by the table as her children all scrambled for their breakfast. 'I feel as if I'm talking to myself in this house,' she grumbled, feeling her temper rising to bursting point. Everything was getting on top of her today, the racket, the mess, the endless list of things needing doing. 'Alan – pack that in, you'll spill it! Come on, you lot, get moving. You'll be late for school.'

Kev, Ricky and Sandra wrangled their way noisily out of the door to school. Alan sat dabbling in a little pool of milk spilt on the table.

'*Alan!*' Rachel swept down on him and smacked his hand. 'I've told you – pack it in.'

Alan slithered down from the chair, bawling.

'Oh, God Almighty,' Rachel said, rolling her eyes. 'Don't flaming start.'

Alan bawled even harder when he found Tommy standing in the way when he wanted to get out through the door.

'What're you looking at, Tommy?' Rachel demanded. What was wrong with him these days? 'Anyone'd think there was a ghost in the hall the amount of time you spend looking out there. Just get out of the road.'

Tommy stood back and they heard Alan go thumping up the stairs.

'And as for you two,' Rachel turned on her two eldest

children as she gathered plates and knives from the table. 'You're the worst of the lot, I can't get any flaming sense out of anyone! Go on – out of my way.'

As they drifted from the kitchen Rachel looked at the wreckage of milk and crumbs on the table and slammed round the room clearing up.

'No one else lifts a finger, I notice,' she grumbled to herself, throwing cutlery into the washing-up bowl. She decided to ignore the fact that she was the one who had told them to go away. 'Idle bloody lot. Now I'm going to have to take *her* a cup of tea, I suppose.'

She slammed the kettle down on the gas, feeling put out but guilty that she was so resentful of Gladys being here. She knew how much she owed Danny's auntie; they had been through such a lot together and now it was Gladys who needed something from her. She knew that really she wanted to give it, to repay her and help. All the same, having Gladys living with them made it feel as if everything was closing in again, hemming her in with endless work.

Back to square one, she grumbled in her mind. It was bad enough Tommy mooning around with a face like a wet Wednesday, but she already knew that he would always be here. She'd realized that since he was very small. He wouldn't be leaving home and getting married the way the rest of them would. That was just how it was.

But what with Melly coming back home in a state and now Gladys here needing looking after as well . . . She sank on to a chair for a moment, waiting for the kettle.

'I could've done without all this,' she complained to the empty room. 'I really flaming well could.'

*

442

Melly walked to work in a daze. She had been in the same state more or less since Saturday night when Reggie sat across the table from her in the Indian restaurant and produced the glittering engagement ring, an emerald in a nest of tiny diamonds.

It was so beautiful and precious – she gazed at it in astonishment. Never in her life had she thought anyone would offer her such a thing!

Reggie had leaned across the table, holding the little box with its velvet insides. Melly could not look up at him for a time. His eyes were there, waiting. All of him was waiting for her reply. She sat, trying to remember to breathe, aware of nothing around her except the ring in its luxurious bed and what it meant. He was asking her to marry him. It was an engagement ring. She had seen a tremor in the hand that held the little box.

'Melly?'

She dragged her eyes up to meet his. Though he was smiling, she could see how nervous he was and she was touched. Reggie put the ring down on the table, beside the brass ashtray. He left the lid open so that she could still see it.

'I know it's all a bit soon,' he said quietly. 'But I said to you, didn't I, when you know something, when you're so sure, there doesn't seem any point in waiting. I just . . .' He sounded emotional. 'I want us to be together – to be Mr and Mrs. I love you, Melly. Will you – say you will?'

She could feel that her face had set in a solemn expression as she looked back at him. She could not reason. There was no time to think things through. He had gone out and bought a ring – such a beautiful ring. Looking deep into his eyes, she saw his left eyelid twitch. He looked shy as she gazed at him. His eyes pleaded with her. She believed that he loved her. And she loved him. . .

'Yes.'

'What?' He leaned closer. 'Say it a bit louder.'

'Yes,' she said. 'I will, Reggie.' She held a hand up to slow him down. 'I want to marry you. I love you – I do. But Reggie, it's all so fast. Can we wait a bit?'

Reggie was grinning. 'Oh, Melly! Will you? Will you really?' He was overjoyed. She saw his whole body relax into relief. 'You'll be my girl – my wife? Oh, Melly. Oh, Mom and Dad're going to be *so happy*. They'll be over the moon!'

She found a smile spreading across her face and a rush of warmth and joy inside her. Dolly and Mo: family, happiness, Melanie Booker and Reggie Morrison! And she would be Melanie Morrison! Of course it was what she wanted . . . But it was still so fast and he didn't seem to have heard the bit about waiting. He was in such a hurry!

'There's no rush, is there?' She felt like a sober old matron, trying to be sensible and calm him down. 'How about we wait – I don't know, a year or so.'

'A *year*?' His face fell. 'Why? What's the point?'

''Til the spring then.' She added inventively, 'I've always wanted to get married in the spring.'

'Have you?' He still seemed disappointed. 'It's such a long time away, that's all. What – March?'

'April or May would be nicer,' she said. 'It'd be warmer – wouldn't it? And all the flowers.' She reached for his hands across the table. 'I do love you, Reggie. I do. Only – I've been in a bit of a state. I want to make sure I'm better and get myself sorted out. Let's not rush things – we can look forward to it. And I want to make sure . . .'

She couldn't finish the sentence. Make sure of what? She lowered her gaze to the table, at the astonishing, the terrifying ring. Make sure it's safe, she might have said.

444

That nothing bad will happen. Not like before, with you and Wally, with Raimundo Alexander.

'But you will?' he insisted.

Melly looked up at him again and smiled. Excitement filled her. 'I will,' she said. 'Yes, Reggie. I want to be Mrs Morrison.'

Walking to the sweet shop now, she knew that soon they would have to tell everyone. As they sat in the restaurant Reggie had slid the ring on to her finger, so pleased and proud. Once home she had taken it off again and hidden it away in its box. It had sat there, in her drawer, wrapped in a camisole vest, all the time she was helping Gladys fetch her things. It was still there . . .

She had not had the heart to ask Reggie not to say anything to his parents. He would, she knew. And surely telling everyone would make it all seem more real? But she had said nothing so far. She wanted time to get used to the idea that her life had changed in this magical way for the better.

'I'm going to marry Reggie,' she practised in a whisper. Or, 'Mom, Dad – Reggie's got something he wants to say to you,' or, 'Yes, my name's Mrs Morrison.'

Tommy could not keep still.

Monday morning and he was back and forth to look at the front door no matter how many times he told himself not to be so daft. Nothing was going to come this soon, was it? This thought would be followed by another, heart-sinking one: if anything ever did come. Maybe it wouldn't. There would be no letters, ever. His excitement was all a wasted dream.

He had sat all the afternoon with Jo-Ann and her family on Saturday. They had kindly listened to him, patient as he formed his sentences. And he and Jo-Ann had talked just to each other – these were the times he had loved the most, him and her talking like friends. The day had gone by like a wondrous dream. And he was completely, in-over-his-head, in love with Jo-Ann Halstead.

He had sat on the rug at her feet, only eating a few morsels of his sandwiches. He did not like eating in front of strangers anyway but now eating just felt like a waste of time.

The family were kind to him, in a polite way. He realized they were glad to have someone to keep Jo-Ann company. After they had polished off their sandwiches and coffee out of a Thermos and some fruit cake which they offered him as well and he had politely refused, Philip asked his mom and dad to come and play with him.

'Just hold on a few minutes, lad, while we let our food go down,' Mr Halstead said.

To Tommy's surprise, both Mr and Mrs Halstead got up and kicked a football back and forth, without much energy or skill, in the hot afternoon. A few others were up and about playing games.

'Philip's mad about football,' Jo-Ann told him. She did not have to say that she could no longer play with her brother, that her parents felt obliged to instead. 'Are you keen on it, Tommy?'

'Not – very,' Tommy said, squinting up at her. 'I've never – played it.'

'No, you wouldn't have, I s'pose,' she said. She gestured at the ground to her left. 'Why don't you move round here so that you're not facing the sun? No – hang on,' she corrected. 'I can shift myself.'

She started to move her chair forward, pushing on the wheels. It was difficult on the uneven ground.

'Oh, Roy, look – help Jo-Ann, will you?' Her mother's voice, edged with worry, floated to them.

'Jo-Ann – steady there!' Mr Halstead came over half running, the worry in his face stretching to a little smile as he came up close as if to cover his panic.

'It's all right, Dad,' Jo-Ann said. She was very patient but Tommy could sense her frustration. 'I'm only moving so that Tommy doesn't have to have the sun in his eyes. I can do it myself – I really can.'

'Well, I might as well help now I'm here, mightn't I?' Mr Halstead said in jolly tones. Tommy recognized this – the endless cheerfulness and pretending everything was normal. Mom was like that a lot of the time.

Mr Halstead manoeuvred the chair to the other side of Tommy.

'All right, pet?' He leaned over her.

'Yes. Thanks, Dad.' She sat facing the front, not looking round at him.

'Warm enough? And you, Tommy lad?'

'Yes, thanks,' they both said. It was hot as anything.

'Well, I'll just finish off with Philip . . .' He moved away, almost guiltily.

Jo-Ann shook her head apologetically.

'Are they – always – like that?' Tommy asked.

'Yes,' she said. 'Always, always.'

She looked down at him. He loved her face with the kind grey eyes, the mane of thick brown hair, her calm voice. He loved everything about her. Above all he loved the attention with which she listened to him.

'Nice – for – you to – work,' he said.

'Yes, I'm very lucky.' She hesitated, looking away and across the green in front of them, trees in the distance. 'I feel ungrateful saying this. I'm very lucky that I can work for Dad the way I do. But . . .' Again, she stopped. He could see she was fighting a sense of disloyalty and he knew how she felt. He knew he was a burden to his own family, stopping them doing things for so many years, making extra work and worry. But how he yearned to get out, just to lead his own life.

'I sometimes wonder, though,' she said softly, turning to him again. 'If . . . I mean, it's no good thinking about the things I used to do. Tennis and – well, I wanted to be a teacher. But I think I could work somewhere else, maybe. Somewhere not at home, always under Mom and Dad's feet.'

She spoke the last words lightly, almost like a joke. Tommy was bewildered to find that his chest had gone tight, that he was fighting back tears. He swallowed hard, looking down to cover it for a moment. When he looked up at her again, into those kind eyes, it was even more of an effort to speak because of the lump in his throat.

'But you – were – born – normal. It must – be – worse. I never – had – anything else.'

'Yes,' she said.

The light went out in her eyes. It was the first time he had seen that. When her mother and father were there, she always seemed to be smiling. 'I suppose so. I know two other polios. There's Micky, who's on crutches. His legs are getting a bit better. And Lucy – she's almost completely better now.'

'No one – like you?' he said. Hope flickered in his heart. He almost wanted her to be lonely, to need to be his friend.

'No one exactly the same, not nearby anyway. What about you?'

He explained about Carlson House, that he had

known some people for years. That everyone was differ-ent. He tried to convey that he had no one who was very close. Jo-Ann listened. It was bliss, Tommy thought as the sun beat down around them and the shadows of leaves riffled by an occasional warm breeze danced on their faces. Sitting here with her was like going to heaven. It came to him suddenly that she looked a bit like Melly, was kind like Melly.

'This is so nice,' she said, speaking his thoughts. 'Talking to someone who understands. Where is it you live again, Tommy?'

'Harborne – Birmingham.'

She looked downcast. 'That's a good way away.'

'I've got – my – three-wheeler,' he said, daring to hope. 'I can – go anywhere. We could – meet . . .'

'The trouble is –' She eyed her parents. Mrs Halstead was walking over to fetch the ball again, in her neat white slacks. 'They won't let me go anywhere without them. They don't think it's safe so they follow on in the car. Course, if I stop I can't get out and walk. I tell you what, though!' Her face brightened. 'We could be pen-pals.' She looked stricken for a moment. 'You can write, can't you?'

'Five – O-levels – remember?' He grinned.

'Oh, yes – sorry! Well, let's swap addresses – would you do that? Will you write to me, Tommy? I promise I'll write back. I've got a pen-pal in France who I've never met, but I'd love to have a proper friend nearby to write to. Look – see my little bag over there? If you pass it, I've got a notebook.'

Tommy reached for the black leather bag, his heart overflowing. They managed to exchange addresses before Mr and Mrs Halstead came back with a red-cheeked, sweating Philip – and this felt like a small victory.

He knew she would write. He trusted her as a person who would keep her word. But even if she had written a letter the moment she got home, which he knew was not likely, and got it into the post on Saturday night which was even less likely, it still would not have got here by Monday. He would have to wait and he had started writing a letter himself.

Even so, when he was at work the next day, he could not stop thinking about the postman, all day long.

Fifty-Six

Melly had asked Reggie to wait, at least until the next weekend, to tell the families about their engagement, even though she knew Reggie was sore that she did not want to shout it from the rooftops. She told him she just wanted to get used to the idea.

'It'll be our secret this week,' she said, smiling up at him. 'It's exciting!'

Once again, she ended up working in the Rag Market. Gladys seemed to be on the mend – her chest was clearer and she was not coughing. But progress was very slow and still she hardly left her bed.

'I don't know what's got into her,' Rachel said, one morning that week, coming down with an armful of washing for the single tub they had now in the kitchen. It had its own mangle fixed to the top. 'There's nothing the matter with her now so far as I can see. Lying about up there like Lady Muck and rest of us run ragged . . .'

Melly eyed her mother. Both of them knew this was not the point. Mom didn't much want Gladys around downstairs either. She thought Gladys ought to be getting on and looking for somewhere else to live. And she was grouchy because it was the school summer holiday and there was no job for her to go to until September. She had lost both her earnings and the company it gave her outside the house.

Unlike her mother, Melly enjoyed caring for Gladys. But she was worried about her.

'It's not that she's poorly so much I don't think,' she said. 'She's . . .' She hesitated. 'It's as if she's turned her face to the wall, you know, like they say.'

Rachel made an impatient sound. 'Well, she'd better flaming well turn it back again. She can't go on lying about up there forever. She didn't even go to church, Sunday.'

'She says they're stuck up,' Melly said.

She had been along to the parish church in Harborne with Gladys a time or two and she could see what Auntie meant. Gladys had been going to her church in Aston for years. It was home from home and everyone knew her. It wasn't that anyone said anything bad to her. They just didn't say much at all. They were not her sort, in their smart clothes and hats, and she thought they were looking down their noses at her, even if this was mainly in her mind and not true at all.

'Maybe she should go to the Methodists,' Melly said.

Rachel looked up, tutting. She had no time for religion. 'You'll have to work her stall again,' she said. 'If she's not going to shift herself.'

Reggie arrived at the Bookers' house on Saturday evening, once they had got home after the market and a drink in the pub. Melly hadn't said he was coming. When he arrived, the family had had tea and were watching *The Avengers*.

Melly heard the knock at the front and ran to let him in. Part of her mind was still in the story on the TV which involved a ghost train and a hypnotist.

452

'Shhh,' she said, beckoning Reggie. 'You'll have to wait 'til it's finished. It's nearly over.'

Reggie looked rather hurt. But when he had kissed her and followed her into the front room, he could see what she meant. The entire family was silent and gripped, the pale light from the TV flickering on their rapt faces – even Gladys. She loved telly programmes.

There'd be no sense from any of them now. Melly and Reggie stood by the door.

As soon as the credits were rolling, everyone surfaced.

'Oh – hello, Reggie!' Rachel said.

'Hello, Mrs Booker,' Reggie nodded. 'Auntie.'

'Didn't see you there,' Rachel said. 'Go and stick the kettle on, Melly. And bring us in some crisps, will you?' Crisps were a Saturday-night treat.

'All right, lad?' Danny lit a cigarette and held the packet out for Reggie to take one.

Reggie accepted and gave Melly a significant look.

'Hang on, Mom,' Melly said. 'Dad – Reggie'd like a word with you.'

Danny looked baffled.

'In private, like?' Reggie said.

'Here'll do, won't it?' Danny said, reluctant to leave his chair.

'Danny!' Rachel said. 'Get up and go out the back. Reggie's got something to say to you!' Her tone was full of meaning and Melly could feel her mother looking hard at her but she kept her gaze on her father.

'All right, then,' Danny said, looking bemused.

They disappeared out to the kitchen. For about half a minute. Reggie came back, red in the face and excited looking as his eyes met Melly's. Melly thought her father looked bashful. He kept his cigarette in his mouth and stuffed his hands into his pockets.

'We've got summat to tell you all,' Reggie said.

Melly found her heart pounding. At the same time it all felt like a dream.

'Are you getting married?' Sandra piped up.

Everyone laughed.

'Well,' Reggie said, blushing even more and reaching for Melly's hand. 'Yes – we are.'

The pair of them were surrounded then by the family all exclaiming and asking questions. To Melly's surprise, Rachel pushed through all the others. Melly found herself pressed against her mother's warm, fleshy body, Mom's arms tightly round her. She couldn't remember the last time this had happened and it felt nice. Tears filled her eyes.

'Oh, I'm so glad!' Rachel said, sounding really emotional. She drew back and looked into Melly's face and through her own wet eyes she saw the tears in her mother's eyes and the care-lines on her forehead and round her mouth.

'You're doing the right thing, kid. Much better than all that nursing carry-on. I never liked you doing that. If you're going to look after anyone it might as well be your own family. And Reggie – have you told Dolly yet? Oh – she'll be over the moon!'

'Tomorrow,' Reggie said. 'When Melly comes over. If I can keep my trap shut long enough.'

Melly could see how happy he looked, his eyes bright with excitement. And Gladys came up to them looking all emotional as well.

'I never thought I'd live to see this – little Reggie,' she said in wonder. 'Oh, I can't wait to hear what Dolly and Mo have to say – we'll be all one family!'

Dad looked pleased and Sandra was prancing around the room singing, 'Here comes the bride!'

'All fat and wide!' Ricky boomed out and Sandra told him to shut up, he was spoiling it.

The younger boys were less interested but Melly saw Tommy smiling at her from his chair. She pulled away from Mom and Gladys and went over to him.

'Good – for you – sis,' Tommy said. She could see he really was happy for her.

'Thanks, Tommy.' She perched on the arm of a chair next to him. A pang of sadness went through her. When would her sweet brother ever be able to announce something like this? Just as she was thinking despairing thoughts about Tommy never having any sort of life, he twinkled up at her.

'C'm'ere.' He beckoned her closer. In her ear she heard him say, 'I – met some – one. Her – name's – Jo-Ann.'

She drew back and looked at him in amazement. Tommy's right hand shot to his lips. Then it moved to pull something from under his jumper – an envelope. He looked ecstatic.

'Don't – say – anything.'

Still astonished, she patted his shoulder and winked. 'Tell me later, OK?'

'Right – this calls for a celebration,' Danny was saying. 'Kev, you can get yourself down to the Outdoor for me and get some more ale in. Go on, lad!'

Reggie came over and took Melly's hand. He pulled her towards him and laid his arm round her shoulders, beaming.

'Well,' he said. 'Here's to the new Mrs Morrison to be.'

A cheer went up. Mom was pink-cheeked and smiling and Gladys was wiping her eyes with the end of her sleeve. It was lovely to have made her family so happy. And soon everyone would know. Tomorrow they would tell Dolly and Mo and the boys and Donna. And she'd have to tell Nanna Peggy – and write to Cissy. Cissy would be over the moon! It was a warm feeling.

Melly looked round at her family. Everything about them, their happiness, the celebration, told her she was doing the right thing.

Everyone insisted on coming to Moseley the next day, piling into the car. Reggie came over to fetch Melly and Tommy went with them in his car.

'What on earth's Dolly going to say when we all roll up?' Rachel said before they set off. 'I don't think Reggie's said we're coming.'

Dolly was happy as anything when Reggie made his announcement as they all stood round the kitchen table. Jonny had a teaching job now and lived on the outer edge of town and Freddie was out, but Donna was there.

'Oh, love!' Dolly cried, coming over and hugging each of them. 'Little Melly – another daughter. Hear that, Donna? You're going to have a new sister!'

''Bout time,' Donna said with her mysterious smile. She came and kissed Melly, looking really happy.

'More women,' Mo said with mock despair.

'Well, you'll just have to put up with me, Mo,' Melly said. She realized how happy she was at that moment, to have Mo and Dolly as her in-laws. How could that be any better?

'Oh, come 'ere, wench, and give us a kiss,' Mo said, holding his arms out.

Melly found herself bear-hugged against Mo's sizeable tummy, her face rasped by his stubble.

'Lovely news,' he said, misty-eyed. 'The best news, wench.' Releasing her, he patted her back. 'You've always been a good'un, you.'

She saw Reggie watching them, proud and affectionate.

'This is the best news we've had in ages,' Dolly said, tears running down her cheeks.

For the first time Melly felt her own eyes fill. She loved Mo and Dolly as if they were already family. She had seen them suffer and now she and Reggie were making them happy. As Mo said, how could things be any better? She had a lovely man to marry, into the best family she could think of, who all wanted to welcome her and celebrate. Her future spread out before her, full of family, security and happiness. She was doing the right thing and everyone was happy and celebrating. What more could she possibly want?

Fifty-Seven

Tommy lay on the put-you-up in the middle room, hearing the murmur of the television from the front room. His dad was still up watching something.

The light on overhead, he pulled the envelope from under his pillow. It must have been the thousandth time that week he had done the same thing, since the miracle of that white rectangle had appeared on Wednesday, waiting for him on the table when he got home. He had almost yelled with delight when he saw it.

Alone at night, or sitting in the Invacar or at his desk at dinner time when he was at work and everyone was out – even sometimes in the lavatory – he would nip the edge of the envelope between his teeth to draw the letter out with his right hand. Every time, he felt the same thrill of excitement. He already knew her blue, careful copperplate handwriting as well as he knew his own, the long J of her signature.

Beneath the Wolverhampton address she had written:

Dear Tommy,

    It was ever so nice to meet you on Saturday. I can hardly believe I've now got a pen-pal who speaks the same language as me because it's not the same with French which I'm very bad at. I missed so much school. So I hope you get this and that you'll be able to write back.

I've been trying to think of something to tell you, which is hard because my life is much the same every day. I suppose I'd better tell you about that! Mom helps me get up in the morning and then we have breakfast (so far, so fascinating!). We get up pretty early because I need to go to work with Dad in the car and getting me in and out of the wheelchair takes such a time. I can tell he finds it a bind although he tries not to show it. He's arranged things so that once I'm through the door of the shop I can get to the office at the back and there are no steps. I know I'm lucky.

We sell furniture and carpets and rugs and things. In the office there's me and Mrs Andrews who's a nice lady who does the books though she's getting on a bit and is quite deaf. She's got (I feel unkind saying this but it helps you imagine) some big warts on her face with hairs growing out of them and it makes me think of witches in the fairy stories. Especially as she wears her hair in a hairnet thing. Though I suppose witches don't really have hairnets or smell of lavender water the way she does – or of stew. She must eat stew every single night. She's worked there since the dawn of time. Oh, dear, I must stop. She's all right really.

Tommy smiled every time he read this, hearing her voice and picturing 'Mrs Andrews'. Jo-Ann wrote as she talked. In private, away from her parents who she felt she had to appease and not alarm, he could see she was funny and spirited and like him, desperately in need of someone to talk to in an honest way.

Jo-Ann went on to tell him about the rest of her day working in the shop, with a wry humour about how boring it all was really but what else did she have to say?

Sometimes, she said, very rarely, her mother and father took her and Philip out to see a picture. The last one she had seen was *The Greengage Summer*.

> It was lovely – very exciting – and it was all in
> France. I'd love to go to France one day. D'you think
> our three-wheelers could go all the way there?

Of all the things she said, it was this that thrilled Tommy the most. She was thinking of schemes, of adventures which might never happen, but that didn't really matter – what mattered was that she was including him in them.

She ended the letter by saying:

> Please write back soon, won't you? It would really
> make my day to get a letter.

He had thought about nothing else. On the Wednesday night when everyone else was in bed, he sat down at the table at the back. He had a board now and some big bull-dog clips to fix his paper to. He was up very late but he didn't care how tired he might feel the next day. He sat for ages after he had written the words, '*Dear Jo-Ann . . .*'

All his misgivings about not wanting to seem too keen had vanished. All he wanted was to talk to her and hear her talking back as often as possible. He could easily have written to her every day, several times a day. '*It was a real treat to get your letter*,' he wrote. His handwriting was smooth and fast so long as the paper was held down.

> It was waiting for me when I got home from work. I
> parked up the three-wheeler – I keep it in a
> neighbour's shed round the corner – and walked into

the house without expecting anything much of this evening. When my mother said there was a letter for me I knew straight away it must be from you. I was hoping and praying it wasn't a boring little note from the ITA instead! And there it was, on the table.

I've never had any sort of pen-pal before. And I suppose it's also not the same as a pen-pal you've never even met. At least I can picture you when I write.

He thought about asking her to send a photograph of herself but this seemed rather forward.

He went on to tell her about his day, also joking about how boring it was:

Driving across Birmingham, sitting in the same old office with the same old people who have not one interesting thing to say all day and don't talk to me anyway because they think I'm a half-wit. Well, until they actually need to know something and then they do ask me.

He fed his bitterness into humour, telling stories about a couple of his work mates. He did not describe what he actually did – it seemed so lowly and tedious.

When I get home I have my pesky brothers and sister running around and hogging the telly watching kids' stuff. My big sister Melly is living back with us again – she's all right – and then below me there's Kev, who's a brainbox, Ricky and Sandra (very bossy) and Alan, who's four and a menace. Other than them there's Mom and Dad and my auntie who lives with us at the moment. She's my great-auntie, in fact.'

461

> I like going to the pictures too though I hardly
> ever do as it's so difficult where there are stairs. But I
> like adventures as well – and Westerns. Maybe one
> day, somehow, we could go together?

He felt very daring writing the last sentence and had no
real notion that it would ever happen. It was a way of
trying to say, *I want to see you – somewhere, anywhere.*

He thought of a lot of things he would like to say to
her. He wanted to pour his heart out – his lonely, longing
heart. But he did not want to make a fool of himself or to
scare her. He finished with:

> Well. Better go up the wooden hill to Bedfordshire.
> Except I'm sleeping on the ground floor – which is a
> good thing as I'm the last up tonight.

Danny had clumped off upstairs as he was writing.

He wanted to end by saying, please write back soon –
please!

> I hope this has reached you all right. And to hear
> from you before too long.
>   With regards,
>   Tommy Booker

He sealed the envelope, wrote her address and turned the
light off, before shuffling his way over and into bed. He
lay for a long time, wide awake, thinking of all the things
he might have said. He'd ask Melly to post it for him in
the morning.

The letter was posted on Thursday and quite early. So
it might have arrived Thursday second post or Friday. If

Jo-Ann wrote back the same day he might have a letter on Saturday. . .

But none came. He made do with keeping that first letter always close to him, relishing it until its happy novelty had worn off and now needed another one in answer to his.

That Monday after Melly and Reggie announced to the families that they were engaged, Tommy spent the day at work in a fidget of impatience to get home and see if another white envelope might be there, waiting, full of *her*. At the thought, every time, his heart beat harder in his chest.

He sat in the Invacar on the way home, the engine roaring in his ears, breathing in the fumes of other traffic as they crawled through the mashed-up waste lands of the city's inner ring, past Five Ways and south-west towards Harborne. Let there be a letter, please let there . . .

It was easier to feel more like other people when he was sitting in his little car. And it came to him suddenly; a moment of amazed realization, that he was a man now. Of course he knew this really. His own father had been away at war at his age. But now something had happened that he had never dared to expect: he could feel like any other man, a man hurrying home with a girl on his mind, dying to hear from her.

Fifty-Eight

That Sunday morning after they had announced their engagement, Melly walked with Gladys to the church.

'Come on, Auntie,' she'd coaxed her. 'Let's go together. It'll do you good to get out – sing a few hymns. And it's lovely out.'

Melly knew her next task was to coax Gladys back to the Rag Market. At the moment she was running her stall for her every Saturday. Mom was at her wits' end having Gladys – of all people – in this state.

Gladys agreed almost wordlessly. Very slowly, she dressed herself and came downstairs, putting on her big brown coat.

'It's quite warm, you know,' Melly said. But Gladys took no notice. She looked heavier and bowed down.

Melly kept having to slow her pace so as not to stride on ahead. It wrung her heart to see Gladys like this. With her faded hair and stiff gait she really did seem like an old lady, when until now she had always been full of vigour, always been the boss of the family.

In the ancient parish church, Gladys stared ahead at the mellow-coloured windows behind the altar. But she did not join in the service or sing the hymns. Melly quite enjoyed singing and wished Gladys would join in as she had always done in Aston. It bucked you up, a good singsong. While the vicar was talking Melly sat thinking about Reggie. Soon, she would stand beside him and make her marriage vows. It seemed very distant at the moment and not quite real.

Once the service was over and the organ playing them out, they shuffled along amid the congregation.

No wonder no one speaks to Auntie, Melly thought. She just sticks her head down and never looks at anyone. She, instead, looked round, smiling, saying good morning. She knew a few people vaguely and they greeted her.

'I say,' a voice said behind her. Melly turned, to see a middle-aged, toothy woman in a white straw hat and pale green suit, her hand held up tentatively. 'Yes – you, dear. Sorry – can't quite remember the name?'

'Melanie.'

'Ah, yes, that's right.' Appearing to think that Melly should remember hers she did not disclose it, but drew her aside at the back of the church. Gladys showed no sign of hearing all this and continued on outside.

'I just wanted a word, dear – you being the age you are. I'm worried about Mrs Hughes.'

Melly waited and gave what she hoped was an obliging smile. She hadn't the remotest idea who Mrs Hughes was.

'She attends here usually – off and on. A young mother – little boy called Peter?'

Melly vaguely recalled a lady of about thirty, with a solemn, brown-haired little boy, so she nodded.

'Well, of course she's not been here lately because of having the second one – a girl, I believe. The thing is, dear . . .' She seized the top of Melly's arm and pulled her even further into the side aisle to whisper to her. 'She's not very well. By that I mean . . . You know, some women, after the baby . . .'

'A bit low in herself?' Melly suggested, thankful once again for the nursing conversations she had heard.

'Exactly, dear, yes. She's looking to employ someone

and I did wonder . . . Someone said you had done some nursing – or perhaps you might know somebody? She really is in desperate need of help with the children.'

Gladys was waiting for her in the churchyard, near the gravestones with their slanting shadows. She had closed her eyes and tilted her face up to the sun. Sensing that someone was standing close to her, she opened them again.

'What did that one want?' she asked.

'I *think*,' Melly said, starting to walk, 'she's just offered me a job.'

Mrs Hughes was a sallow-skinned lady with bushy brown hair, cropped startlingly short in a bob round her ears. She opened the door to Melly, the baby in her arms, looking out with anxious, grey eyes. She was wearing a straight, shapeless, steel grey dress.

She conducted a brief interview in the front parlour, holding the restless baby on her lap, wrapped in a gauzy thin blanket. Even that, Melly thought, looked too warm for the weather. The room, shrouded by net curtains, was furnished with solid, boxy armchairs upholstered in sage green. There was a black-and-white patterned rug by the fender and a leaded fireplace. Against the back wall was a piano, the lid open and music on the stand.

'This is Ann,' Mrs Hughes told her, nodding down at the baby. 'I can't seem to get her to settle very well . . .' Her eyes filled with tears. 'Oh, dear . . . I just . . . It wasn't too bad with Peter. He's two and a half now – he's with my friend at the moment. I thought it would be easier . . . He was a placid child . . . I just seem to let things get on top of me.'

The baby squawked and Mrs Hughes hefted her up against her shoulder. 'Oh dear . . . I should be asking you questions.' She got up and jiggled the baby. 'Why don't you tell me about yourself – Melanie?'

'Melly, usually.' She decided she might as well be honest. After all, she already had a job. It wouldn't be the end of the world if Mrs Hughes did not want her. 'The thing is, I'm not a children's nanny or anything. I was training as a nurse – at Selly Oak. I was . . .' She hesitated. 'I was ill. So I had to stop. I've been getting over that. But I'm the eldest of six – I'm used to little ones. I could help you for a time, if you like.'

Her words seemed to catch Mrs Hughes's interest. 'You were nursing? I see.' She paced back and forth, which seemed to settle the baby a little. 'Are you not going back?'

'I . . .' Melly hesitated again. 'No. Well, I can't really. I'm getting married.'

'Really? Goodness, I see.' Mrs Hughes seemed to see her with new eyes. 'You look so young! How old are you, if you don't mind?'

'I'm about to turn twenty – in a couple of weeks. D'you think,' she dared to suggest, as the baby's wailing took off again, 'she might be a bit hot?'

'Oh – is that what it is?' She peered down at the child in consternation. 'I expect you're right. Look – why don't you hold her for a moment and get to know each other?'

She thrust the moist, squeaking bundle at Melly. The baby was pink with whatever annoyance she was feeling but had a sweet, round face. Melly lay her on the chair, unwrapped the blanket and picked her up, looking into her eyes.

'Hello, little Ann,' she said.

Baby Ann seemed to find this turn of events so astonishing that she stopped crying immediately.

'Oh, my goodness,' Mrs Hughes said, slumping on to another chair opposite. 'How soon can you start?'

'I thought I might as well,' Melly told Reggie the next weekend as they walked round the park. 'I've told her I won't be here forever. She's just a bit mithered at the moment – but she only wants help in the week anyway so I can do the market with Auntie on a Saturday. And the boy, Peter, is all right – quite quiet really and sweet. It's better than standing in that sweet shop all day long. I can bring them here for walks – get out of the house.'

It felt, in fact, more what she was made for – looking after people – though she didn't say that to Reggie. They were walking hand in hand. It was a dry, sleepy August day.

'Good practice for when we have our own,' he teased, drawing her close to kiss her.

Melly looked back at him, trying not to show her alarm. Children – already? God, she hardly felt more than a child herself, as Mrs Hughes had said. She was startled to realize that the thought of having her own children had hardly crossed her mind.

'What – straight away?' she said. 'Reggie – you haven't even finished at college yet.'

'Well – it'll be all right. That's what married people usually do, isn't it? And you'll be living with Mom and Dad. Mom'll love it – you know what she's like. Can't get enough of babbies.'

'Oh, flipping heck, Reggie!' She took his arm, trying not to show that she felt as if the walls were closing in, that he was asking her to end her life before it had really begun. It was all part of the dream that Reggie had led her into. But it was one that would mean the end of her other dreams. Having a baby would surely mean she could never, ever be a nurse – didn't it? She hardly dared think about whether she had fully closed the door on that. But she didn't mention these misgivings to Reggie.

'One thing at a time,' she said, laughing. 'We haven't even got married yet!'

Fifty-Nine

'There's another letter for Tommy.' Rachel frowned at the handwriting and felt the good-quality envelope. 'Nice. He's the only one ever gets any letters in this house.'

Melly was on her way out to work with Mrs Hughes and Tommy had already left.

'Know who it's from?' her mother asked.

'No. Unless it's the people about the three-wheeler. He had a few letters about that.' She opened the front door. She knew perfectly well who it was from.

'This is different writing,' Rachel mused, squinting down at it.

'See you later,' Melly called.

Melly set off to Mrs Hughes's neat terraced house. It was almost the end of her second week there and life felt good. Reggie had taken her out last Saturday for another curry to celebrate her birthday, and the days with Mrs Hughes were already taking on a rhythm. She was enjoying the job, especially as it was the summer and that meant she could take the children outside.

Mrs Hughes insisted that Melly call her by her first name, Dorothy.

'It makes me feel so old being called Mrs Hughes all the time,' she said. 'I can't get used to it.'

Sometimes when she arrived, she found Dorothy

470

Hughes playing the piano. It helped to lull baby Ann back to sleep after her morning feed, she said, and she wanted her children to grow up with the piano as one of their earliest memories. Peter would be playing on the floor behind her with his tin fire engine or a row of soldiers. Melly saw that Mrs Hughes adored playing the piano. She rushed to it whenever she had the chance. Whenever Melly took the children out, Ann in the pram and Peter walking along holding on at the side, she would come back into the house to the sound of music.

Melly had quickly come to the conclusion that there was not much wrong with Dorothy Hughes that a bit of company and time to herself would not cure. She soon came to like her very much. Dorothy told Melly that before she married her Victor – who worked in technical drawing and was *very busy* – she had trained in secretarial skills. 'Shorthand and typing and all that,' she added. Melly wasn't sure what 'all that' meant except that it was to do with offices. She worked in the offices of the LMS Railways. Her real passion, though, was for music.

'I should have liked to be so much better at it,' she sighed. 'Then I could have been a teacher.'

'You sound very good to me,' Melly said.

'Well, that's nice of you. But I'm very run-of-the-mill. And Victor doesn't like me playing in the evenings. It gets on his nerves. But it's such bliss to have time to play in the day now you're here. I was beginning to think I would go mad. One child is difficult enough . . . No one ever really tells you what it's like.'

Melly did not find the two Hughes children difficult. They were just like any other children so far as she could see and she became fond of them. Her week was spent moving to the beat of their routines. On Saturdays she was at the Rag Market and on Sundays, Reggie was always there. The summer was rushing past.

Everyone was excited and full of plans about the wedding, for which Melly and Reggie still needed to set a date. On Sundays when they went round to see Dolly and Mo, as they almost always did, Gladys and Rachel often with them as well, it was all everyone wanted to talk about. Sometimes Freddie was there too with his new girlfriend, Sal, a plump, cheerful girl with waves of blonde hair round her cheeks, and the four of them got along well. Despite the fact that they had been engaged for months they had still not set a date.

'Seems like you're gonna get there first, Reg,' Freddie said. 'Still – it's only right, you being older than me, I s'pose!'

Melly and Reggie had decided to get married at St Mary's in Moseley.

'It's ever so pretty,' Dolly said one afternoon as they were all sitting round with cups of tea and fruit cake. 'I mean, I know there's some in my family'll have summat to say about it.' Dolly's family were all Catholics. She eyed Gladys.

'I don't recall you ever taking your lot to church,' Gladys said. 'Except for . . .' She trailed to a halt. Everyone knew what she meant. Going to Mass had meant mostly bad times: her mother's funeral, Wally's funeral. Though there had been her sisters' weddings.

'Well, Melly's not a Catholic,' Dolly said. 'And Reggie's hardly . . . You don't go to Mass, do you, Reg?' She looked round at him. Reggie shook his head.

'Filthy little heathen,' Dolly said fondly. 'Anyway –

Melly does go to church with you, Glad, so it only seems right. Don't you think, Melly?'

Melly nodded. It all just felt unreal to her still, as if she was at the pictures, watching herself. In a few months she'd be married. In a year she might be like Mrs Hughes, if Reggie had his way. At home with a baby. Here in fact, most likely, with Dolly, in this lovely big house.

'She'd have to move over here for a bit, Doll,' Gladys said. 'A month or so before. So they can read the banns.'

'Well, that's all right, isn't it?' Dolly said happily. 'You can come and stop with us before the wedding. You'd like that, wouldn't you, Donna? We can get you all ready – do your hair and . . .' She stopped, suddenly realizing she was taking over. 'I mean – Rach, you could come over here whenever you like as well. We could all do it together.'

Melly saw her mother smile. Rachel didn't seem resentful. Melly felt a pang of hurt at this. But then she looked at Donna and Dolly and thought, Donna's going to be my sister-in-law. She was so sweet and beautiful, and Mo and Dolly were so kind, she felt a swell of excitement. How lucky she was! She reached for Reggie's hand and squeezed it. Their eyes met.

Love you, he mouthed silently and she beamed back at him.

'Ooh, you look so pretty these days, Melly,' Dolly said, 'Doesn't she, Mo?'

'Yeah.' Mo looked at her. 'She always was, though.' Which made Melly blush.

'Nice to see you up and about again, Glad,' Dolly said. She stubbed her cigarette out in a grey-stained saucer on the table and stood up. 'You back on the market then, are you? You don't want to let this one take over your stall for too long – you might never get it back!' She reached for the teapot. 'I'll go and top this up.'

After tea they all saw Rachel and Gladys off in the car. Rachel had to get back to cook for everyone. She was the one driving now – with her L-plates on. Melly had come over in the back of the car, clenching her jaw as Rachel rasped the gears setting off. She was used to Reggie's smooth driving.

'Dear God,' Gladys muttered, one hand clasping the side of the seat.

'There's no need to be like that,' Rachel had snapped. 'I'm getting the hang of it. It always takes me a while to get going. You just keep quiet, both of you.'

If Tommy could drive, she kept saying, then surely to God she could as well.

They had got there without major disaster, though there was one nasty moment as she stalled turning right across the Pershore Road. Melly was relieved not to be driven back home by her as well. She said Reggie would bring her later.

She and Reggie went to the little park down behind the house and strolled round the lake, hand in hand in the serene afternoon.

'I wish I didn't have to go back,' Reggie said, his warm hand squeezing hers. 'I just want to stay here with you.'

'It'll soon go,' she said. 'And I'll be here with your mom.'

She didn't like to admit that it was a relief to her that he was away some of the time. She loved him and missed him but she just wasn't sure she was ready to live with him day in and day out yet. Every time she thought about it she had an uncomfortable, shameful feeling, that this was the end of the line. It seemed so wrong to feel that about the man she loved.

'Melly.' He stopped her, in the shade of a tree close to the water. Moorhens drifted nearby. 'You're so pretty and so . . . Well, nice. You're my girl. I love you – I do.'

He pulled her tight into his arms and she wrapped her arms round his waist. She hugged him, her face turned to nestle against his shoulder.

'Reggie,' she murmured, feeling the beat of his blood under his warm shirt, smelling his man smell of cotton, sweat, salt. She swelled with love for him. 'My Reggie.'

'Won't you mind?' he asked. 'When we're wed, like – being here with my mom instead of with your husband? It seems wrong.'

Melly knew she had to be careful what she replied. She didn't want to hurt Reggie's feelings by saying she really didn't mind – which was the truth.

'It's not nearly as bad as my mom had to put up with, is it?' she said, looking up at him. 'In the war. Our dad was away for *years*. And she never even knew if he was coming back.'

Reggie gazed deeply at her and kissed her briefly on the lips. But he looked troubled.

She reached up and stroked his cheek. 'And you're only down the road and I know you're coming back – or I hope you are!'

'Oh, I am.' He grinned then. 'You can bet I am.'

It wasn't until Melly had been working for Dorothy Hughes for three weeks that she met Victor Hughes, her husband. That Friday evening she stayed a bit later than usual, listening to Dorothy play the piano after they had fed the children. As they sat in the front room, they heard his voice from the back of the house.

'*Dorothy!*'

He sounded peevish, as if he had called before and not been heard.

Dorothy's hands sprang from the piano as though it had given her an electric shock. A moment later a man's head appeared round the door of the front room. Mr Hughes was a tall, long-faced man with thin brown hair and a solemn expression. His brow was moist and there were rings of sweat round his armpits from his cycle home from where he worked in Smethwick.

He looked about to say something abrupt, but he spotted Melly sitting on a chair with Ann on her lap.

'Er . . .' He gave a terse nod. 'Hello?'

'This is Melanie, dear,' Dorothy said. Melly could see she was nervous. 'The girl who comes to help with the children.'

Melly thought she had better stand up and she struggled to her feet, still holding Ann.

'I see,' he said, looking her up and down. 'Did we get references for her, Dotty?'

Melly felt chilled by the way he was looking at her.

'Well, no, dear, but . . .'

He looked at her disparagingly. 'You didn't get *references*? You've just handed *our children* over to some . . . Some child who we've never seen before?'

Melly shrank inside. She was insulted and appalled in equal measure. For a moment she felt like crying, but then she thought, he's not very nice. I don't like him. If he wants me to leave, I'll leave. Sod him.

'She's very good,' Dorothy Hughes said, giving Melly a stricken, apologetic glance. 'She's been here three weeks already, Vic, and I've no complaints at all. The children love her. Look how happy Ann is with her. And you did *say* it would be all right . . . We talked about it.'

Melly looked at little Peter. She could see where he got his solemn looks from, but he also seemed quite scared by the sight of his father.

'Huh,' Mr Hughes said. 'Well . . .' He looked Melly up and down. 'We'll be keeping an eye.'

Will you? Melly thought. You're never here.

'I'm going up to clean up.'

'I'm sorry,' Dorothy said as they heard his feet on the stairs. She went to the piano and in a flustered way cleared her music into the piano stool as if it was a dirty secret. 'He's never at his best when he gets home. Hungry, I suppose. I keep saying why don't you take something to eat before you come home . . . ? He's very stubborn.' She turned to Melly, her eyes wide and anxious. 'I'm sure everything will settle down, dear, and will be all right.'

Sixty

'Melly?' Tommy spoke to her softly, through the Saturday-morning mayhem in the house. 'Can I – talk to – you?'

Melly looked at the eager, anxious expression on her brother's face. Ricky and Alan were roaring about the place, Sandra was singing to herself, Danny and Gladys – who had at last gone back to the market – were getting ready to go out and Mom was clearing the table with one hand and eating toast with the other. Why on earth was Tommy asking her now, she thought?

'Knock it *off*, you two!' Danny turned on the boys. 'Get out of here – upstairs if you're gonna carry on like that in here.'

'They'll only fight,' Rachel said through a mouthful of toast.

The boys thundered up the stairs. Sandra carried on with her singing, tuneful but irritating nevertheless.

'We'll have to build a cowing wall between 'em,' Danny muttered, leaning over the table to look at his accounts book. 'Like that one they've put up in Germany. That'd sort 'em out.'

'What – now?' Melly said to Tommy, in between all this.

He nodded. He seemed emotional, desperate in some way. Another of those letters had arrived this morning. From his friend, his pen-pal, he had told them. Someone he met on the picnic when he went in his three-wheeler.

All the family had started being nosy about the white envelopes that kept arriving over the past few weeks – as often as every other day sometimes. Melly was the only one who knew they were from someone called Jo-Ann Halstead, because she was the one he asked to post his frequent replies. It was so much easier for Melly to get about, and he liked involving her, enjoyed her knowing that Jo-Ann Halstead, whoever she was, had captured her brother's tender heart. They shared the secret between them.

'All right.' In truth she was relieved. Gladys wanted her help on the market. Now that Gladys had been back at work for a couple of weeks, building up the stock again and running her stall, she still expected Melly to come and help.

'Auntie – you go on with Dad,' she said. 'I'll be in a bit later, on the bus.'

They went outside to get out of the way of Mom and the others and had to keep telling Sandra to go back in and mind her own. Sandra pouted and slammed the back door.

Tommy sat himself in his wheelchair, which Melly pushed out for him, and she perched on the wall at the end of the little lawn. It felt nice, that Tommy wanted something from her.

'What's up?' she asked, once they had got shot of Sandra. 'Is this about the letters?'

Tommy put his head on one side. Melly saw that her little brother was blushing. A smile broke out over his face.

'Tom – who is she?' Melly laughed.

Tommy looked down, blushing even more. 'I like –
her – a lot.'

'Well?' Melly said, though her mind was jumping with
questions. None of them had ever thought about Tommy
having a girlfriend, doing the things other boys did. She
found a blush moving thickly through her own blood
as she wondered exactly what Tommy was capable of.
Tommy, a man? This was a new thought. And this girl –
was she like him? Or was she . . . Normal? She felt sorry,
for not thinking of these things before. And awkward.
How were you supposed to talk about this?

'Why don't you tell me a bit about her?' she said,
hoping this was a safe way to begin. Already her big-
sister protectiveness was taking her over again. Was this
girl nice? Would she hurt Tommy's feelings?

'She's – called – Jo-Ann.'

'Yes, you said before. Is she your age, Tommy?'

'Yes. Eighteen – like me. She – had – polio,' he said.
Gradually he explained – about the swimming, the hospital and wheelchair. About Jo-Ann's family, her job in
the shop.

'Well, that's good,' Melly said carefully. 'Nice that her
dad has a business she can work in.' She was still wondering what the problem was. 'So what's up, Tommy?' she
repeated.

He gave her a look of naked longing. 'I – want to – see
her. And – she – wants – to see – me.' He was worked up,
almost tearful.

'Careful – deep breaths,' Melly said. 'I suppose Wolverhampton is a bit of a way away.'

Tommy was shaking his head. 'She said . . . She wrote
. . . She'd – come down here. In – her three-wheeler.'

But, he explained, her mom and dad had said he
couldn't see her. That she was not to see him.

480

'Why not?' Melly's fear for him, her protectiveness, made her instantly angry on his behalf. 'Why shouldn't you see each other?'

'They – don't let her – do – anything,' he said. 'And they – don't – want – me.'

His face was working, his left arm going more into spasm, as it did when he was mithered.

'It's – not – right.' Melly had never heard such passion in his voice before. 'She – wants – me. She wants – to run – away. And I – love – her.'

'Oh, Tommy.' Tears rose in Melly's eyes at the sight of his anguished emotion, at the unfairness of all of it. That he and Jo-Ann were so incapacitated at all; that other people were ruling their lives.

Tommy explained about Mr and Mrs Halstead, that he had met them, that they hadn't been nasty to him, not then. They were nice people really, he thought, but they were so worried about Jo-Ann and what had happened to her, that she was wrapped in cotton wool at all times.

'Look,' he said. From his pocket he took out one of the white envelopes, folded in half, and pulled the letter from it. 'Read the – last – bit.'

Melly looked at the tidy blue handwriting.

I feel so down, Tommy. Ever since polio I've been here like a child, feeling as if I'll never be anything else. Writing to you is the best thing in my life now. It's made all the difference, us getting to know each other, because for once I can say what I actually feel. I wish so much that you lived nearer. Even then, Mom and Dad would be a problem. All I asked is to go and see you or for you to come here. They were so against it, it was . . . Well, it's just silly. I know they're just frightened about me doing anything – but they're more frightened than I am! When I said I'd go on my own, in my three-wheeler, whatever they said, they had a pink fit. But we've got to find a way, Tommy. You're my friend. Do they think they're just going to keep me locked up forever, as if polio has taken away any other feelings I might have? I'll talk them round – I will. And if that doesn't work, I'll run away – run on my little wheels!'

'She sounds nice,' Melly admitted, handing the letter back, with its signature, '*Love Jo-Ann*', at the bottom. She sounded genuine and brave.

'Look, they can't just stop her, can they?' she said. 'Not forever. I expect they're just worried for her.' She thought for a moment. Dad could take Tommy up there . . . But that didn't seem right and she couldn't see him agreeing to do it anyway.

'How about if I come with you? We can find a way, somehow, can't we?'

'Would you, sis?' Tommy said desperately. But he did start to look a little more hopeful.

Sitting on the bus into town, Melly thought about the strength of feeling in her brother and remembered herself, young and silly and head over heels in love with Reggie. How painful it all was. How full of awkwardness and longing. But Jo-Ann sounded as if she really cared for Tommy. Whereas when she was young, Reggie barely even noticed her. He did now, though. A warm, affectionate feeling filled her. She sat thinking of Reggie, his smiling face, the love in his eyes. By the time she reached the Rag Market she was ready to deal with grumpy Gladys and be ordered about all day.

On the way in she stopped to see her father but he was already busy. He gave her a wave.

'Tell Auntie – the Adam and Eve after. A drink'll cheer her up!'

'All right.' Melly knew Dad looked forward to his pints in the Adam and Eve once trading was over and he could chew the fat with some of the other traders from round the markets.

She settled into the day, managing a smile at the man – even more grumpy than Gladys – who sold toys some distance away from them, and at the antics of the crockery seller. She spent a while talking to a lady who sold tatty knick-knacks, glass vases, brass ashtrays, candlesticks and suchlike.

Gladys had paid the Toby Man and was doing a brisk trade. Melly looked around her. It was all so familiar. A rush of fondness came over her. Maybe, once she was married to Reggie, this really could be her life. She could take over from Gladys. After all, she knew the trade back to front. And Dad was branching out – selling furs as well now. She could do a lot worse, she told herself.

Once the Rag Market was cleared and they had stowed away their remaining stock, Danny drove them the short distance up Bradford Street.

'No Reggie today?' he said, as they parked near the pub.

'I'm seeing him later,' Melly said. Sometimes Reggie came to help on the market, but not always. 'So I'll not stop long.'

'All right . . .' The three of them pushed their way into the heaving pub, the air full of smoke and ale and loud talk and laughter. 'Dubonnet for you, Melly?'

She nodded. 'You want to learn to drink pints, wench,' he grumbled. 'Auntie – your usual?'

Gladys, without fail, had a glass of stout. She looked round to see if there was anywhere to sit but the place was so full they could barely move.

As they were sipping their drinks, Melly enjoying the sweet, heady taste of hers, she saw a face through the crowd – Freddie Morrison. She pushed through and went to talk to him.

'All right, Melly?' he greeted her. 'How's the family? What about Cissy?'

He grinned, as if remembering his flirtations with Cissy.

'Oh, you know Ciss,' Melly laughed. They had to talk very loudly, heads close together, to hear each other over the racket. 'Always falls on her feet. Living the life of Riley out near Coventry. She's got a little boy – Andrew. Dear little lad – we hardly ever see her, though.'

Freddie laughed. 'Good old Cissy. And you and Reggie – eh? You'll soon be my sister-in-law.'

'So I will!' Melly laughed. 'Who'd have thought, eh?'

'Got a date yet?'

'Not for sure. April probably. How's your . . . Sal, isn't it?'

A happy smile came over Freddie's face. 'Yeah. She's all right.'

They chatted about the family a bit more, Jonny with his teaching job and Freddie at one of the foundries nearby. He downed the last of his pint. 'Wait there. I'm going back for another – get you one?'

'I'm all right, ta, Freddie.' Her glass was still half full.

She was enjoying talking to him, especially with the added thought that they were to be family. Freddie had always been all right. All the Morrisons were all right, she thought, a warmth spreading through her. She was very lucky. It was as if family was wrapping itself around her in a safe cocoon that she need never leave.

Freddie came back, shouldering through the crowd with his pint.

'Who's that Auntie's talking to?'

Melly turned. 'Where?'

'She's there – behind that big bloke.' Since she left Gladys, she had moved further towards the bar. 'Talking to the tall one. He's a size – must be six foot four!'

Melly could make out a man who was at least a half-head taller than most people in the room and a whole head taller than some. He had very short, grizzled hair and a strong, comical-looking face which, as she watched, she saw break into a smile. She presumed he was smiling at Gladys, though she could not see her.

'I dunno,' she said. 'Never seen him before. He's a wopper.'

'Straight as a ramrod an' all – look at him. Must be a soldier.'

They carried on with their chat until Melly had finished her drink.

'Got to go, Fred,' she said. 'I'm meeting Reggie.'

Freddie grinned. 'Nice seeing yer, Melly. Ta-ra.'

She noticed then that Gladys was still with the very tall man. Working her way to her father, who was talking in a gaggle of men, she touched his arm and said, 'I'm off now, Dad. Meeting Reggie in town.'

Danny blew out a whorl of smoke. 'All right. See ya later, wench.'

'Who's that Auntie's with?' she asked.

'I dunno.' Danny turned, found Gladys with his eyes and narrowed them, suddenly attentive. 'I dunno who he is – but whoever he is, he's put her in a good mood.'

Melly moved her head so that she could see Gladys. It took her a moment to recognize her. Her face was alight, smiling, like a new, suddenly younger woman.

Sixty-One

'What's this about Auntie and some guardsman?' Rachel said the next morning.

She was standing resting against the stove, clad in her pink nylon dressing gown, a cup of tea held close to her face. Sandra and Alan were already downstairs, rattling about in the passage. Melly poured herself a cup and pulled out a chair at the table.

'Guardsman?' She had got home quite late last night, after her evening with Reggie. Her head was full of him. He was so keen on her, so amorous and in need of affection that she wondered how she was going to keep him at bay until they were married. In fact, she was pretty sure she wouldn't be able to resist for much longer. But she'd missed any follow-up on what happened in the Adam and Eve.

'That tall feller, you mean?'

'Your dad said he nigh-on had to prise them apart!'

Melly laughed. 'What – *Auntie*?' But she had seen Gladys's face, all lit up. 'I s'pose they were talking for quite a bit. I didn't see 'til I left – I was talking to Freddie.'

'What – Dolly's Freddie?'

'Yeah. He's doing all right. I reckon he'll be getting wed to that Sal girl he's with.'

'He'll be your brother-in-law soon.' Rachel lit the gas and reached for the frying pan.

Her words sent another thrill through Melly – of both excitement and misgiving.

'Melly! Are you there? I said, d'you fancy an egg butty?'

'Take the lads out of here, for heaven's sake,' Rachel said later to Danny. 'They're driving me round the bend. Kev's got a face as long as Livery Street and the other two are like bloody ants.'

'C'mon –' Danny hustled Kev, Ricky and Alan along – 'we'll go and have a kick-about – bring your ball, Kev.'

'Can I come?' Sandra whined.

'No!' they all said in chorus.

'You can help me,' Rachel told her. 'You can shell me some peas for a start.'

'I don't wanna stay in the house and help you!' Sandra roared.

Under cover of this, Tommy said, 'Sis – come – outside – a tick . . .'

Melly could see he was in a state, pale, and as if he had not got much sleep. They went into the garden and both perched on the low wall.

'Can – we ask – if – we can – visit?' he said with no preamble. 'Mom – maybe?'

'Mom?' Melly rolled her eyes. 'Heaven help us!'

'But can't – we – ask?' Tommy pleaded. His speech was more laboured because he was worked up. 'How're – we – gonna – g-go?'

'If we ask Mom she'll have a fit,' Melly said. 'Can't you imagine the state she'd be in if she had to drive to Wolverhampton? She's never even been there and her driving's . . . Well, anyway. She'd say "over my dead body" – I can hear her saying it. But –' She held a hand out to stop Tommy interrupting. 'There's Dad – but even better, what about Reggie? He can drive anywhere. We could go – the three of us. Why don't you write to her and see if we could go next Sunday?'

A look of utter joy filled Tommy's face.

'Would he?' He was squirming with delight. 'Would – Reggie – do that – for me?'

'Course he would.'

Their eyes met, full of fond, happy light. It was like old times, Melly thought. Her helping Tommy and him not minding, actually wanting her.

'I'll ask him,' she said. 'Later.'

Melly spent most of the day with Reggie, who of course happily agreed to drive them to Wolverhampton.

They went for a walk round the park in Kings Heath. The trees were lit by mellow, late-summer light. Reggie held her hand, his stick in the other. Melly felt bubbly. Everything in her life was so happy these days. Even Gladys was suddenly lit up like a beacon.

'I think Auntie's in love,' she told Reggie.

'No!' He laughed. 'Auntie? You're having me on!'

'I didn't take much notice – I saw Freddie, in the Adam and Eve last night.'

'How is the little bugger? He's hardly ever at home.'

'He's all right. Anyway, Auntie was nattering away to this bloke – he's ever so tall. I could barely see her there was such a crush but you could see him. This big . . .' She stretched her arm up. 'Mom says he was a guardsman, Welsh Guards – in the first war.'

'They've taken a shine to each other, have they?'

'Dad says they never stopped talking all evening. And she looks like a cat with the cream.'

Reggie stopped in order to laugh thoroughly. 'God – never say die. How old is she?'

'She must be – sixty-six – nearly.'

They walked on, chatting and laughing. Every so often, Reggie stopped and drew her close to kiss her.

'Oh, Mel,' he said, after drawing back from a long kiss, under a spreading beech tree, 'I know it's the right thing to wait 'til we're wed and all . . . But I don't know as I can.'

She looked into his eyes, her own desire meeting his. She knew she was supposed to prefer to wait – but she didn't. She loved the way he wanted her and she desired him back with a force that surprised her. It wasn't difficult to find time to be alone in Mo and Dolly's house. Unlike the cramped dwellings of their childhoods, the Moseley house sprawled upwards – seven bedrooms, including an attic, like an eyrie looking out over the garden. Since only Donna and Freddie were still living at home, not all of the rooms had occupants.

They had a cup of tea with Dolly and Mo. All the time, desire hummed between them in the sultry afternoon, a sound that only they could hear. Sometimes their eyes met, as if making a date for later, as they talked about mutual friends and the day-to-day things of Dolly and Mo's lives.

Afterwards, almost as if under a spell, they climbed the stairs hand in hand. Dolly was cooking, Mo outside. The house was quiet, a region they could explore in almost guaranteed peace.

Reggie's room was not in the attic but on the first floor, looking out over the road. As Melly followed him upstairs, his warm hand in hers, she did not question or resist. She wanted Reggie as much as he wanted her. She had felt his desire for her, his body pressed against hers so often now that she no longer knew how to resist. Did not want to resist.

As soon as they closed the door, they were kissing, half frantic for each other, removing clothes with their mouths locked on each other's.

His bed was under the window and he led her, laid her down and she felt the soft pillow under her head, and Reggie's weight, the salt sprinkle of his blonde stubble. Reggie, her Reggie now, so close, in her arms.

Afterwards, she explored him with her fingertips: the white scar worms on his body, the long mauve zip-fastener from the operation down his right thigh. All the smashing up and rearrangement had left that leg at odds with itself and a fraction shorter than the other.

'Not pretty, is it?' he said. He seemed bashful at her seeing it.

'No – but it's all right. It works.' She thought of the hospital, all that it had taken to restore him to life and mobility. None of that possible for Wally. She kissed him. 'And it doesn't matter. I love you. And you're here.'

They both knew what she was talking about. She saw a shadow cross Reggie's face. They lay back together, cuddled close. After a silence, Reggie seemed to think of something. He moved to look into her face.

'It won't . . . Mean anything – will it?'

'How d'you mean?'

'You won't have a baby?'

She stared at him. She knew the facts, sort of. In a vague way.

'No,' she said. 'Course not. Not from just one time. People try to have babies for ages, don't they?'

That's what Mrs Hughes had said. She and her husband

had taken a good while to have Peter. But she felt foolish. In the heat of it she had not given it a thought. Why was she so ignorant? She had been training as a nurse but she still didn't know much. She left before they got to 'Human Reproduction'. She promised herself that in the week, sometime, she would go into Harborne Library and look it up.

'If you did,' he said, sounding as if he was trying to convince himself, 'it wouldn't be the end of the world. It'd be . . . Lovely. It would.'

'No,' she said. 'Not yet. I don't think that would be right. We need to be married at least.'

He rolled over and cuddled her tight. 'We'd best get up in a tick. Don't want Mom coming in, do we?'

Sixty-Two

'*The human race has been kept within reasonable limits in the past by famine, pestilence and war.*'

Melly sat in a corner of Harborne Library a couple of days later, looking up often to see if anyone was near her because she felt so self-conscious about the medical book she was reading. Even though there were not many people in the library, her cheeks were hot with blushes. She had managed to get away from Mrs Hughes's house early and slipped into the library.

'*Pregnancy is the state of being with child . . .*'

She kept looking for new headings that might help. If you were already expecting a child it was rather too late for famine, pestilence or war to remedy the situation. The book said that the first sign that you were having a baby was the stoppage of monthly periods.

'*. . . the child's birth may be expected nine months and a fortnight from the first day of the last period.*'

The next symptom that would apparently show itself was '*morning sickness*'. She remembered this from when her mother was having Sandra and Alan. Immediately she started to feel queasy. Now she was not in Reggie's arms she was worried sick. This book was all very well but how were you supposed to know how likely it might be that *you* had caught for a baby?

Earlier, when Mrs Hughes had passed a comment

about the time when she was carrying Ann, Melly had jumped in with, 'How did you know – at first, I mean?'

'Oh,' Dorothy Hughes said, taking Ann from her to give her a feed. 'You don't know to start with. You just have to wait and see. Some women catch a lot more easily than others.'

Melly shut the heavy book and slid it back on the shelf. A fat lot of good that was. The sense of utter dread that had come over her at the possibility of a baby was almost puzzling. She didn't want to be caught pregnant before she was married. But she loved Reggie, didn't she? She didn't want to stay working with Mrs Hughes forever, nor would Dorothy need her forever. Marriage, family – it was all good. It was what she wanted.

But not yet, the thought throbbed through her. Oh, please, not just yet . . . Give me a bit more time . . .

She walked home in a sober state, calculating on her fingers the date of her last period and when the next one was due. Nothing was all that regular. And she was going to have to wait at least two weeks to find out. That felt like forever.

At home, she found that an enormous man was sitting in the front room. His legs reached halfway across the floor. Seeing her, he drew them to him and stood up, straight as a telegraph pole in a spruce black suit.

'Hello there, my dear.' Smiling, he greeted her, one hand outstretched, towering over her. Her hand disappeared into his palm. His face was craggy and kind looking, the grizzled hair that she remembered clipped very short. He reminded her of a big, crumple-faced dog that looked sad until he smiled, as he was doing now, and all the lines pointed suddenly up instead of down.

'You must be Melly.' The voice was deep and big, like a tuba. 'I'm Dudley Rainer.'

'I saw you in the pub,' Melly said, in some confusion. What was he doing sitting here on his own in the front room? What was he doing here at all?

'I've come to visit your, er – aunt? Gladys Poulter.' He was full of old-world courtesy and there was a light in his eyes that seemed to hold humour, or at least a fondness for life in general. She warmed to him straight away. 'She's just making us a cup of tea.'

'Melly?' She heard Gladys call. 'That you?'

'Yes,' she called back. Dudley Rainer released her hand. 'Nice to meet you,' she said to him, and meant it.

Gladys was bustling about in the kitchen. The kettle was boiling and there was a tray on the table with a little embroidered cloth on it that to Melly's bemusement she had never seen before. The best cups were laid out and a vast, sticky fruit cake on a plate. The kitchen smelt of baking. Gladys had evidently been busy.

Gladys was also dressed up, in a black skirt and scarlet blouse with black piping at the edges. Her hair was dolled up, with tortoiseshell combs pressed into it. There was a new, quick purpose to her movements. Melly watched, amazed. The old Gladys she remembered was back.

'Goodness,' Melly said. 'Where's Mom?'

'What d'you mean, "goodness"?' Gladys said huffily. But her glance darted at Melly. She could not conceal her excitement. 'Your mother's gone round to see one of her pals – she took the three young'uns.'

Melly grinned at her. 'He looks nice, Auntie.'

A sunset blush crept across Gladys's face. She looked down and picked up the tray. 'Oh, I know he is,' she said, sweeping out of the room.

495

'Shall I start cooking tea, Auntie?' she asked her departing back. No one else seemed about to do it.

'Ar – go on, then.' Gladys was already gone.

Turning, Melly saw that on the table from where Gladys had picked up the tray, was another letter for Tommy.

As soon as he came home, Tommy grabbed the envelope and went outside. A bit later, with the tea simmering on the stove, Melly went out to find him. As she cooked a stew for tea she had been fretting endlessly about herself. Could she be having a baby? Every time she thought of it she felt a bit sick. But as soon as she caught sight of Tommy, all her own problems left her mind.

She could see straight away that there was something terribly wrong. Tommy was sitting on the wall, his head bowed, the letter in his hands. He must have been sitting in just the same spot for ages.

'Tommy?'

He didn't even move. She went to him and bent to touch his arm gently and look into his face. It was already wet with tears. As his body began to shake with silent sobs, he handed her the letter.

She could see immediately that the blue handwriting, normally so neat and careful, was bigger, hurried and agitated, and that there were smudges on the page as if Jo-Ann had touched it with wet fingers.

Oh, Tommy, I don't know what to do. I've had a
terrible row with Dad and he's been so horrible I can
hardly look at him. Your letter came and it was nice
and a good idea but when Mom and I asked him
about it he just flew off the handle and said straight

496

away that he didn't want you or anyone coming here. And then he said he doesn't want me writing to you or seeing you ever again.

I don't know what to do, Tommy. He was so angry because he didn't know about all the letters. Mom did and she thought it was all right. I never said anything to him because he keeps on so about everything and I wanted something to be mine for once without having to ask him. Why shouldn't I at my age? You and I are grown up almost. When are we ever going to have a life of our own?

I'll think of something. I'm determined he's not going to stop us seeing each other – but how? I can't even get out of the house on my own even though he's talking about putting a ramp in at the front but he hasn't done it and sometimes I think it's because he doesn't want me to go out, ever. I don't feel like a proper person.

You're the only one who understands what it's like. I love your letters. We should be able to see each other – it's not fair of him.

I think I love you, Tommy. I know I've never said it before but now this has happened, I know it. Oh, what are we going to do?

I'll write again soon – somehow I'll get it posted again.

With my love,
Jo-Ann xxxx

Melly looked up at her brother, tears in her own eyes.

'God, Tommy – she sounds a lovely girl. Oh, I'm sorry for you – I really am. But he can't just stop her seeing you, can he?'

Tommy rubbed his right arm fiercely across his face.

'I dunno,' he said miserably. 'But I – don't . . .' He kept having to stop for breaths. 'Want to – push in if – I'm not – wanted.'

'But you *are* wanted. By her.' Melly sat on the wall beside him. 'She wants to see you. It's just that – if only she wasn't . . .' She tailed off.

'A c-cripple?'

'No. Well – it'd make life a lot easier,' she admitted.

'If – she wasn't a – cripple, she – wouldn't – want – me,' Tommy said bleakly.

'Oh, Tommy.' She slung her arm round his shoulders. 'How could anyone not want you – eh?'

He stayed silent, staring at the blue bricks at their feet.

'She says she's going to think of something,' she suggested.

'I – ought to – go. Just – drive – there . . .' He sounded angry now, mutinous. 'Who – cares – what *he* – says?'

'Are you going to tell Mom?'

They looked at each other. Tommy shrugged. 'Not – yet. I – want to – write – back first. He can't – bloody – stop me – doing that.'

Rachel walked in about half an hour later. Melly, in the kitchen, heard Ricky and the other two come in noisily. It went abruptly quiet as the front door banged shut. The sight of Dudley Rainer and a vast fruit cake together in the same place seemed to have silenced the children. She heard her mother's voice, followed by laughter and the sound of Dudley in the hall as if he was taking his leave. A moment later Rachel came into the kitchen.

She looked round, still all smiles. She always seemed happy when she'd been with Gina. They were best friends and the kids played together.

'Oh – you've done the tea then, have you? Ta, Melly.' Humming, she went to the stove and lifted the pan lid. 'Gina's such a laugh – she really is. D'you put plenty of onion in?'

Melly nodded. She's got me just where she wants me, Melly thought. In the kitchen, getting married – all just like her. Nothing new. Nothing different. She was surprised by the force of resentment that came to her out of nowhere.

'Mom – Tommy's upset.'

Rachel looked round, though Melly could tell she was only half listening.

She explained about the letter and what Jo-Ann had said.

'Oh, dear,' Rachel said. 'Here – let's lay up. The spuds are nearly done.'

'*Mom!*'

Rachel put her hand on her waist. 'Well, what d'you want me to say? I don't know who these people are. They're miles away. He'll get over it.'

Melly got up and went over to her. Her intent face finally got Rachel's full attention.

'Mom – he's up in my room writing a letter to her now. I've never seen him so heartbroken. He was outside crying his eyes out. Why shouldn't they see each other? They're friends – and they're not kids any longer, are they?'

Rachel folded her arms and looked away, thinking. She sighed and looked back at Melly.

'I don't know. If they don't want him there . . .'

The door opened and Gladys came in with a smile nearly as wide as the door, bringing the conversation to an end.

*

499

Melly posted Tommy's letter for him the next morning before going to Dorothy Hughes's house. Tommy looked white and upset.

'I feel – like – driving – over – there,' he said. She could see all the pent-up emotion in him.

'Don't do anything rash, Tom,' Melly said. 'Maybe she can talk her mom and dad round – give it a bit of time.'

'She – shouldn't – *have* – to,' he said, as he limped with his stick to the front door.

Walking through Harborne she thought of her brother, knowing he was in for a truly miserable day.

Her own was not much better. She felt distracted by her own worries – about Tommy and about herself. Was she carrying a baby – *was* she? Her head ached with tiredness from not sleeping well. Both children seemed to sense her mood and were fractious.

'Oh, dear,' Dorothy Hughes said. 'I do hope they're not sickening for something. Victor does so hate it if the children wake at night and disturb his sleep. It's always worse if they're ill.'

'It must be difficult for him,' Melly said, thinking in fact that Victor Hughes was a selfish old stick who had no idea about looking after the children he had produced with little cost to himself.

'I tell you what.' Dorothy perked up. 'Shall we have a little sing-song?' She lifted the lid of the piano.

Melly held Ann and sat beside Peter while their mother played some nursery rhymes. Half her mind was on the singing, the other half thinking of the night before, Gladys's radiant face, Tommy's pale, distraught one. Then Ann started off crying again, a sound which grated on her nerves more than usual.

Don't let me be having a baby, she kept thinking. The idea of it made her want to cry herself. Please, no – not yet.

Sixty-Three

'What'm I going to do with him?'

Rachel stood at the sink in her yellow Marigolds and pale blue spotty apron. She wrinkled her nose as the smell of bleach came up to meet her.

'Who – Danny?' Gladys said. She was at the table, sewing up the hem of a slinky frock in coppery colours.

'No – for once. Tommy.'

Gladys shook her head. Rachel had already explained.

'I don't know, bab. Can't really interfere, can you? We don't know these people.'

Rachel stood with one hand in the water, the other pushing her hair out of her eyes. She felt reassured by this. She wanted to be told there was nothing she could do.

'He's nice, your Dudley,' she said, watching Gladys with sudden fondness.

'*My* Dudley?' Gladys looked round at her. She spoke harshly but Rachel could see it was because she was shy about it all.

'He's mad on you,' Rachel laughed. 'He was round here like a dose of salts.'

'Well . . .' Gladys looked down at her sewing again. She held it further away from her. 'I need my eyes seeing to . . .'

'He is, isn't he?'

Gladys turned to her again, blushing. Rachel saw that

her handsome face looked firmer again, lifted and as beautiful, in its tough way, as it once had been.

'We'll see,' Gladys said. 'Hark at that – was that the front door?'

There was another tap, timid, but definite.

'Who the heck's that?' Rachel pulled her apron off as she went, still holding it in her hand.

Outside she found an attractive woman with stylish dark hair curled under at her collar. There was a smile in her dark eyes, but she looked very nervous. They regarded each other for a moment.

'Yes?' Rachel said. 'Was there something you wanted?'

'I . . . yes,' the woman said. Rachel realized she looked more than nervous – she was suddenly close to tears. 'I'm sorry . . . Are you Mrs Booker – the mother of Tommy Booker?'

'Yes.' Rachel folded her arms. She didn't mean to sound aggressive, but she felt immediately worried and defensive. She thought the woman must be from Tommy's work. 'Is he all right? What's happened?'

'It's all right,' the woman said. She really was nice looking, Rachel thought. She was pretty and seemed pleasant. 'It's not that. I'm – I've come from Wolver-hampton. My husband doesn't know I'm here . . .' The tears started to take over her voice.

Rachel stood back, beginning to grasp who she was. 'You'd better come in.'

In the kitchen, Rachel said, 'I'm Tommy's mother. This is my husband's aunt – Mrs Poulter.'

The woman greeted Gladys politely. She seemed so ill at ease that Rachel felt sorry for her.

'I'm Mrs Halstead – Marjorie.' She kept wringing her hands as she spoke. 'I have a daughter called Jo-Ann. I don't know whether you know, but she met your son,

Tommy, at one of the picnics for the . . . The people with the special invalid cars.'

'I've heard a bit about it,' Rachel said, starting to wish she had paid more attention.

'Have a seat,' Gladys said, pulling a chair out. 'You've come all that way?'

'Yes.' Marjorie Halstead eased herself on to a chair as if being polite to it. 'On the bus – well, two buses. It's taken me a while.'

'Get the lady a cup of tea,' Gladys said.

'Oh – thank you.' As Rachel filled the kettle she spoke to Gladys. 'My daughter, Jo-Ann, caught polio – ten years ago, you remember when it all happened . . . Anyway, we're lucky to have her with us still. She's eighteen now, but she lost the use of her legs. And she and Tommy seemed to get along well – Jo is very attached to him, in fact. But there's been the most dreadful difficulty with my husband. He's so very protective of her. It broke his heart when she fell ill. I've never seen him in such a state, before or since. He's a very organized sort of man, likes things to be – you know – just so.'

She looked round at Rachel, trying to include her in the conversation.

'Unfortunately, polio is not something you can organize out of the way. He really does try hard. We both do. Jo-Ann's a good girl. She works for him, you see. All he wants is to make sure she's safe and looked after. But I know she's getting very fed up – she's growing up.'

Rachel brought cups to the table. 'I know they've written a lot of letters,' she said. 'What's the harm in that?'

'None at all – I couldn't agree with you more,' Mrs Halstead said fervently. 'Your Tommy's a lovely boy. I could see that when we met him. And clever too.'

Rachel smiled at last and sat down.

'Jo-Ann has been terribly upset ever since her father forbade her to see Tommy or even to write to him. She's . . . Well, I think she and your Tommy have become quite close, from writing letters. And . . .' She drew in a deep, emotional breath. 'What Roy doesn't understand, or won't let himself think about, is that the two of them are just like anyone else. They want . . . Well, you know . . .' She blushed then and looked down at the tabletop. 'Sorry – I'm probably saying too much.'

Rachel felt a blush spread over her own face. Lord above – was this woman talking about . . . ? About her Tommy as a man and this woman's daughter as a woman, in a relationship together as man and woman? She sat, feeling outraged for a few moments, with nothing to say. Had she ever really thought of Tommy like that? She knew she had pushed it out of her mind, just the way she had never thought, once upon a time, that he would ever go to school.

'It just doesn't seem fair, does it, for them not to be able to see each other?' Mrs Halstead was saying, the pent-up words rushing out. 'How are they supposed to make friends or have any sort of life? I keep saying to Roy, she's not your baby girl any more. You have to let her grow up. Even if she can't walk, she's not your puppet, for you to arrange her whole life for her. If only he'd *listen*.'

'I s'pose he can't just wrap her up in cotton wool forever,' Gladys said.

'Exactly, Mrs Poulter – that's what I keep telling him.' She sat back and looked from Rachel to Gladys and back again. 'I just wondered . . . You may not like the idea, but now I've met you – and if Roy was to see that Tommy has a family and that everyone is supporting them . . . At least they could be friends – it doesn't seem too much to ask, does it?'

Rachel nodded. With every word she had heard she was warming more to Mrs Halstead. She had had to be on her daughter's side the way Rachel had had to struggle and root for Tommy.

'You've come all the way over here,' Rachel marvelled, her voice gentler now.

'I didn't know what else to do,' Mrs Halstead said. 'I don't drive, you see. Do you drive, Mrs Booker?'

'I'm just learning,' Rachel said, proud of herself. 'The car's not here, but my husband will be back soon. He'll give you a lift home.' Firmly, she quelled Mrs Halstead's protests. 'Oh, yes, he will. It's ever so good of you to come. Now – we'll have that tea. Will you have a piece of cake?'

Rachel and Melly were in the kitchen when Tommy came in from work. They heard the front door and exchanged glances.

'Come in here, Tommy!' Rachel called to him. 'I've got something to say to you.'

They heard him stumbling along the hall, the tap of his stick. He came into the kitchen with his head bowed, pale and silent with misery.

'Sit down, bab,' Rachel said.

Tommy slid his skinny body on to the chair and looked up at them guardedly. Melly was opposite him.

'We had a visitor today, love,' Rachel said gently. She sat down.

Tommy immediately looked even more apprehensive.

'It's all right.' She touched his hand. 'It was a Mrs Halstead.'

Tommy's eyebrows puckered for a second, before it dawned on him who she meant.

'What – you mean . . .?'

'Your friend Jo-Ann's mother, yes. A nice lady, isn't she? Any road, she's worried about her Jo-Ann – about the both of you.' She chose her words carefully, not wanting to raise his hopes too much just in case.

'She thinks her husband is . . . Well, taking things a bit far. So she came to see me. She's going to see if she can get him to meet us and have a chat – see where we go from there.'

'You and – Dad?'

'I think so, yes.'

Tommy looked across the table. 'I want – Melly to – come. They'll – like – her. She's good – with – people.'

His words sank into Melly like the seeds of beautiful flowers. Tears rose in her eyes. Tommy wanted her!

'Course I'll come, Tom,' she said. 'If that's what you want.'

Sixty-Four

She was excited – she was free.

A week ago, she woke one morning and realized. She burst into tears of relief in the lavatory. Her period had started. Until she found herself crouched, doubled over, sobbing with relief, she had not realized just how worried she had been. Pregnancy did not seem real to her, but all the same she had kept on feeling sick, having odd little pains in her body and was frightened to death that this was what it meant. It must have been all in her mind, though.

She walked round all that day in a haze of joy, like someone let off a prison sentence. Her mother had had her at sixteen and she was now twenty – but she was still not ready. She loved Reggie, wanted to be with him – but not that. Not yet. She wanted them to have a life together first.

All week she had been fizzing like a bottle of pop with excitement at her sudden sense of freedom. But there was still the nagging worry. Even though she and Reggie did not manage to be alone very often, she knew that when they did, he would want to make love again. Even though she wanted it too, she was going to have to stop him . . . or find a way of taking precautions, using those *things* she had heard that men could put on. It made her blush to think about it, but think about it she would have to.

And as well as this, now she had regained her freedom,

she began to realize that she had barely asked herself the question: freedom for what?

And, the Sunday afternoon before, the four of them – Mom and Dad, Tommy and her – had piled into the car and driven to Wolverhampton to see Mr and Mrs Halstead and Jo-Ann. She had seen that Tommy was almost sick with nerves. She nudged him on the back seat.

'It'll be all right – Mrs Halstead was nice, Mom said.' She didn't know if it would be all right or not but she wanted to try and make him feel better.

Tommy nodded, tight-lipped. He turned away to look out of the window.

The Halsteads lived in a solid brick villa in Wolverhampton.

'God,' Melly heard her mother say to Dad as they climbed out of the car, 'my knees are knocking.'

Danny drew himself upright. 'No call for that, wench. If these people think they're too good for us, p'raps we're too good for them.' But Melly could see he was nervous as well.

They both looked nice, Melly thought, eyeing her parents. Dad was in a suit and Mom a navy dress with white flowers on it and a belted waist. Her hair was sleek and cut stylishly so that it hung just above her shoulders. Melly had put on her favourite cornflower blue skirt. We look all right, she thought. We *are* all right.

With a pang she had watched her brother's slow, dragging walk up the path behind their father and prayed things would work out well for him.

Mrs Halstead opened the door. Melly thought she looked terrified, but she could see at once that she was a nice lady with a welcoming smile.

'Come on into the front,' she rattled on nervously. 'I

hope you had a good journey. Now – here's Jo-Ann. My husband's just coming.'

They'd trooped into a very tidy front room, with a powder pink carpet and deep, rose-pink curtains. In a wheelchair, between two of the light-green armchairs, she saw Jo-Ann Halstead, a pale girl with a long thin face and long, straight brown hair. When she saw Tommy her face broke into a joyful, dimply smile. They all said hello and Melly thought how nice Jo-Ann seemed.

Danny walked towards the window and looked out, hands thrust into his pockets. Rachel stood close to Jo-Ann as if to walk away would be rude and Mrs Halstead kept insisting her husband was on his way. After a moment she went out and called up the stairs:

'Roy, dear – our visitors are here.'

He was stiff with them at first, came hurrying in as if from some urgent business meeting, Melly thought, when he had most likely been in the lavatory or something. But he was polite enough, shook each of their hands and gave each of them a little nod.

'I've got tea ready,' Mrs Halstead said, looking round as if wondering whether they were all safe to be left while she fetched it. 'Sit down, won't you?'

Danny and Mr Halstead, in one corner, started talking about cars.

Melly turned to Jo-Ann. 'I've heard a lot about you.' She smiled. Tommy looked bashful. Without making a big to-do about it, she said, 'Tommy said you had polio?'

'Yes,' Jo-Ann said. 'When I was eight.'

'Terrible, that,' Rachel said. 'I remember, lads we had living near us, and everyone trying to stop them going off swimming. But Tommy –' she glanced at him – 'I didn't have to stop him. He wasn't going anywhere, were you, Tommy?'

Tommy shook his head, blushing.

Jo-Ann seemed to be hanging on Rachel's every word, as if anything to do with Tommy was fascinating to her, Melly thought. Or perhaps because she just did not see many people. But whatever the reason, Melly could see she was a pleasant girl.

They all made polite conversation and once Mrs Halstead had handed round cups of tea and Melly had made sure Tommy had somewhere to put his saucer down so that he could hold the cup and they had plates with slices of Victoria sandwich cake on them, they did at last get to the point.

In a pause which arose, Mr Halstead cleared his throat.

'Roy has something he'd like to say,' Mrs Halstead prompted.

Her husband laid his cup on the little table beside him and sat up straight.

'I, er . . . As you know, our Jo-Ann is in a delicate sort of state. As is, er . . . Tommy, of course. Very difficult for all of us. I'm ever watchful, you see – don't want any more sort of trouble or difficulty for her.' He cleared his throat again. 'But Marjorie says – and I agree – that I've been a bit hasty.'

Marjorie Halstead was nodding at each of these phrases, her eyes fixed on her husband's flushed face as if this was a speech they had rehearsed and he was getting through it line by line.

'Our Jo-Ann's getting older and, well, she has to have some life. It's not easy for me to remember that. We're doing our best . . .'

'I'm sure you are, Mr Halstead,' Rachel said. Her tone was warm and Melly looked at her in surprise.

'Can't just wrap her up and . . . Anyway. Tommy's a good lad, I know. Bright feller, aren't you, Tommy?'

The humouring tone raised Melly's hackles. She looked at Tommy. He kept his face blank, listening.

'All right for them to write to each other, of course.' Mr Halstead emitted a little chuckle. 'What's wrong with that, after all?'

'Dad,' Jo-Ann said. She spoke calmly and clearly, looking at him directly. Melly was moved to see she had tears in her eyes. 'I want to see Tommy as well. Not just write. I don't want you to decide for me. I'm eighteen. When Mom was eighteen she was helping to shoot down German aeroplanes.'

Everyone looked at Mrs Halstead.

'I was on a predictor,' she said, blushing at the sudden attention. 'Ack-ack battery.'

'Good for you,' Rachel said. She looked back at Tommy. 'And you'd like to see Jo-Ann sometimes, wouldn't you?'

Tommy nodded, a smile beginning to break over his face. He was looking at Jo-Ann and she was beaming back at him, through eyes full of tears.

You could hear the fairground and smell it from streets away.

Reggie parked close to the big Jacobean Hall in Aston and as Melly got out of the car, she could immediately hear the fair's distant turmoil, the shrieks and drone of engines. The smells of diesel and fried onions and the sickly whiff of candyfloss reached them on the breeze.

'Come on then, kid,' Reggie said, once he had fished his stick out of the car. He was as excited as a child. Mo and Dolly had taken their kids to Pat Collins's Onion Fair on the Serpentine Grounds most years. Reggie looked surprised when Melly said she had never been.

'Tommy couldn't go so the rest of us didn't either. Dad took Kev and Ricky once or twice, I think, but I never went.'

'Well – you're in for a treat then, aren't you?' he laughed. 'I'll buy you some candyfloss!'

Melly was excited but she started to wish she had worn a coat. It was four in the afternoon and the autumn chill of late September was settling in. But as soon as they reached the fairground, the pungent smells of it all, the strings of coloured lights, the roar of all the rides and blare of music through loudspeakers, everyone laughing and shrieking or filling their faces with hot pork sandwiches or faggots and peas or candyfloss, she forgot completely about being cold. The atmosphere was fantastic.

'Kev said there was a ghost train,' she said to Reggie, gripping his arm. 'Let's go on there!'

Reggie was looking round. 'They've got rid of all the steam engines,' he said, wistfully. 'T'ain't really the same without them. There used to be a great big bugger called *Goliath*. And *Queen Mary* was another – they put strings of onions on them.'

Melly found herself wishing she had been able to come as a child. How magical it would have been! But still – it was magical now, with Reggie at her side, both of them ready for some fun, like kids again.

'Dodgems first,' he said, steering her over.

'But you've got a real car!' she protested, seeing white, sparking lights issuing from the clashing cars. It all looked a bit rough.

'Go on – one go. Then we'll go on the ghost train.' He gave her a boyish grin and leaned down to kiss her. 'You have to do the dodgems.'

She climbed into the car with him, tucking her skirt round her knees, and squeezed her eyes shut.

'You do all the driving,' she said, giggling. 'Tell me when it's over!'

'My legs feel all rubbery,' Melly complained as they climbed out of the car afterwards. 'That was *horrible*!'

'No, it wasn't – it was bostin!' Reggie teased her.

'Ghost train now,' she insisted.

Melly screamed with laughter and hid her face in his shoulder all through the ride. They went on the carousel and the big wheel, so high, swooping up and round so that you could see all over the fairground and the city around, the lights and swirling movement of it all. She gripped Reggie's arm in terror and felt even shakier when she came off there.

'No more rides – not for a bit!' she pleaded. 'It scares the pants off me.'

'Ah – that's cos you never came as a kid,' he said. 'You're never scared when you're that age.'

'Let's go and see if we can win ourselves a coconut, eh? I love coconut.'

The light was beginning to fade now and the fairground lights glowed in the dusk. They were walking through the smells of hot oil, the sickly whiff of candy-floss, the sea of laughing, shouting bodies nudging at them, the slap of the belts turning the rides. In the crowd, Melly caught sight of a familiar face. She had to look twice, turning to make sure.

'Reggie – that was Lil, wasn't it? Lil Gittins?'

By the time Reggie turned, the woman had stopped at a stall nearby where you could win a goldfish. They could see her face in profile in the light from the stall. Her pale hair was piled on her head.

'Is it?' he said doubtfully.

'It *is* her, surely?' Melly said, tugging on his arm. 'Oh, let's go and say hello. She looks better, if it's her.'

The closer they drew to the woman the more sure Melly was that it was Lil, looking, in an aged, shadowy way, a little bit more like the Lil of the past. Melly tapped her gently on the arm.

'Oh, Mrs Gittins, it *is* you,' Melly said. 'It's nice to see you!'

'Oh!' Lil beamed at her, delighted, showing a row of bright new dentures. 'Little Melly – and Reggie as well. Fancy – ooh, I haven't seen you in ages. How are you?'

'We're all right,' Melly said. 'We're . . .' She looked at Reggie.

'Getting married, us two are,' he said, full of pride.

'Oh!' Lil put her hands to her cheeks. 'I hadn't heard. Oh, how lovely, bab – I'm ever so pleased for you.'

Melly saw that Lil's hair was bleached blonde and she was well made up. Nothing could take away the lines that years of worry and strain had written on her face, but she had gained some weight and lost the scrawny look she had worn for so many years after the war. It looked as if life was treating her better.

'How's Stanley?' Melly asked, feeling she must, even though she dreaded the answer.

'Oh, well,' Lil said, with the practised evenness of someone who has come through hell and become accustomed to it. 'He's going along, you know, in there. I still feel – well, I always will until my dying day – that I should've kept him at home. But I just couldn't handle him any more. He . . .' She looked down, then up at them again. 'I s'pose you heard. He went for me – more than once. The last time, he put me in hospital.'

'Oh, Lil,' Melly said. 'I'm ever so sorry. But it was all such a strain on you – he's in the best place.'

'I don't know about that,' Lil said with a wan expression. 'But I do know I couldn't go on. And now – I'm here with a gentleman friend.' She looked back through the crowd. 'My Jimmy. He's gone to fetch us some potatoes.' She smiled at Melly and Reggie. 'We'll never marry, of course, but . . .' She shrugged. 'Life's been good to me, lately.'

'I'm glad for you, Mrs Gittins,' Melly said.

'And you – you were always a good girl,' Lil said fondly. 'Our little nurse we used to call you. Didn't you go to be a nurse?'

'I did,' Melly said. 'For a while.'

'Ah, here he is!' Lil said. 'This is Jimmy.'

A man with a thin, kindly face appeared, holding two hot potatoes. They were introduced, but soon made their goodbyes.

'You two will be very happy, I'm sure,' Lil said, as they parted. She touched Melly's arm. 'Bless you, love.'

Melly linked arms with Reggie.

'Course we will,' he said. 'Won't we?'

She smiled up at him. Reggie was always so optimistic.

'Fancy a spud?' he said. 'I caught the smell of them. My mouth's watering.'

They made their way back towards the barrow selling hot potatoes. They had to pass the big wheel again and the ride had just stopped to let everyone off, seat by seat, the bloke unlocking the bar across the front.

A man was getting down from the ride with a young girl beside him. Father and daughter, I suppose, Melly thought. Nice that, him taking her on the ride. They slipped to the ground and started to walk away. But within a few paces, something was wrong. The man stopped abruptly a few yards in front of them. There was a moment when he was leaning back, clutching at himself.

The girl started shouting, 'Dad – Dad! What's up with you?'

The man pitched sideways and fell unconscious to the ground. Everyone around screamed, leaping back so that there was a ring around him.

'Oh, my God,' Reggie said. 'He must be having a heart attack.'

Melly froze. Her mind was racing. Mr Alexander. What did the nurse do? You were supposed to do mouth-to-mouth or something – she had never been taught to do it but she had seen it done – maybe she should at least go and try . . .

But amid the shouts and consternation people were running, people in uniform rushing to kneel over the man and work on him. Melly let out a breath of relief. Of course, the St John's Ambulance Brigade. She and Reggie stood in the crowd, everyone watching, willing the man to come to consciousness as his daughter knelt wailing and crying beside him.

Melly watched them as they worked, knowing what to do, competent, calm: there to help people. In that moment certainty reawoke in her. Her pulse raced. That was her, there, helping. That was what she should be doing! Over this dream of a summer, she had tried to forget that this was what she was made for.

The man was carried away on a stretcher and they watched until he was out of sight. All the time, Melly's heart was hammering, her blood pulsing hard.

'Come on,' Reggie said. 'We can't do anything. Let's get that spud.'

'Reggie.' She seized his arm. Now. She had to say it now, this minute. 'Wait. I need to talk to you. Come over here.'

She led him to a quieter spot at the edge, where the

fairground machines gave out to the darkness and a light mist was rising to mix with the fumes.

'What's got into you?' Reggie complained, limping along with her. 'I thought you was hungry?'

'Reggie.' She faced him and put her arms around him. 'I love you, but – no, don't say anything. Just listen. I can't marry you – not quite yet. I want to marry you and be your wife – I *do*. But all my life I've wanted to be a nurse and if I get married now, they won't let me finish my training. I want to finish it, Reggie, my love. I love you with all my heart, but that's what I've got to do.'

Sixty-Five

March 1962

Melly stood in the road outside St Paul's church and kept looking along the Moseley Road. Her mother came to join her, smart in a soft brown coat and hat, her hair pinned up in a stylish pleat.

'Any sign of him yet?' They both peered in the direction of town, eyes narrowed in the chill wind. 'The bride'll be here before him if he's not quick.'

The rest of the congregation, who had been standing in shivering, smoking, chatting clusters outside, pressed their cigarettes out and made their way into the church.

'He knows how to get here, doesn't he?' Rachel said.

'Course he does,' Melly said.

'Who'd have thought, eh?' Rachel said, her eyes still on the road.

'What?'

'This – all of it. And Tommy . . .'

Melly could hear the pride in her mother's voice and was about to answer when she caught sight of an unmistakeable shape along the road.

'Here he comes!' She was on tiptoe. 'Look!'

Amid the other cars and vans they saw the little blue three-wheeler move bravely closer and turn into St Paul's Road. Tommy saw them waving and soon he was parked by the kerb.

'You made it!' Melly slid the door open for him, noticing immediately how cheerful he looked.

'You all right, love?' Rachel said. She was still not used to Tommy living away from home. It had only been three weeks so far. 'You look thin,' she said, eyeing him as he climbed out, brushing down his black suit. 'You are eating, aren't you?'

'Yes, Mom.' He laughed her off. 'Mrs – Lane's – trying – to – fatten me – up.'

'I'm glad to hear it. You look nice, love,' she added, sounding almost tearful. 'Come on – we'd best go in. Look – Dolly's waiting for us with the rest of 'em.'

Dolly, lavishly dressed in a bright royal blue suit and hat, was standing with Kev, looking self-conscious in a suit, and Sandra, Ricky and Alan. Her own boys were there too, including Reggie. Reggie reached for Melly's hand.

'Right,' Rachel lectured her own children. 'Behave yourselves. Ooh – look at Dudley. He's really done himself up! Doesn't he look smart?'

They greeted Dudley, shaking his enormous hand. He was tall and imposing in his top hat and tails; a fine figure of a man and, they had learned, a competent and kindly one as well. He had been a widower for five years and now had a light of new happiness in his eyes.

'I hope that husband of yours is on his way,' he said to Rachel with joking anxiety. 'Taking care of my girl.'

Rachel laughed. 'They'll be here on the dot, Dudley, don't you fret. In fact, you'd best get yourself down to the front – look, the vicar's after you.'

A robed figure stood beckoning anxiously at the church door.

They shuffled into pews near the front of the church which, despite the candles, seemed dark on this spring day. Dudley lived in Balsall Heath and Gladys was to join him: this would be her new parish. Dolly and Rachel got into one pew with Mo and all the younger children. Melly and Reggie moved into the next one, to sit behind Dolly and Rachel. Jonny and Freddie came to join them and Tommy squeezed in at the end, by the side aisle.

'Oh, he's a nice man,' she heard Dolly say. 'I couldn't be happier for her.'

'He is.' Melly could hear her mother's whispers. 'And no fool.' Dudley had been a sales manager for a firm selling weighing machinery after leaving the guards. 'He'll be good for her – look after her.'

'She could do with a bit of that after all this time, bless her,' Dolly said.

They both kept turning as the organ played softly, to see if Gladys was arriving and to give little waves to people coming in.

'Ooh – there's Lil,' Melly said, tapping her mother's shoulder. They all waved and smiled.

'Old Ma Jackman,' Dolly said with a slight grimace. More waving. 'Nice to see the rest of the old end here.'

The neighbours took seats a bit further back.

'Here's Cissy!' Rachel said. She raised her arm, mouthing, *Come here, Ciss!* 'No husband with her, I see,' she added to Dolly. 'She's brought the little lad, though. Oh, look at him, bless his heart.'

Andrew, Cissy's son, now a plump and endearing toddler of eighteen months, was all togged up in a smart sailor suit. He stared round him with wide blue eyes.

'Looks to be another on the way too,' Dolly observed.

Melly sat up straighter to look as she waved at Cissy. Cissy, dressed to kill in pale yellow frills and a buttercup-coloured hat, was well out at the front. Melly, giving

Cissy a broad smile, found herself wondering exactly whose child it was.

'I can't fit in there with all of you,' Cissy hissed to Melly, looking at the crowded pew. 'We'll go behind. Come on, Andrew, take Mommy's hand.'

Melly would have liked to talk to Tommy but he was on the far end of her pew. That would have to wait. With them both being away from home now, she had hardly seem him since Christmas.

A few weeks ago, Mr Halstead had written to ask Tommy whether he would be prepared to come and train as the bookkeeper for his business. Mrs Andrews, who had been there for years, wanted to retire and, having seen something of Tommy and got to know him, he thought he would be well capable of it. Tommy was now living with a landlady, Mrs Lane, in Wolverhampton and working at Halstead's. Melly looked along at him; he met her eye and they exchanged smiles.

Melly felt a tap on the shoulder and then Cissy's breath in her ear. 'You all right, Melly?'

'Fine,' Melly whispered. 'I'll catch up with you after. I see you're keeping well.' She eyed Cissy's swollen belly.

'Oh, yes – Teddy's so pleased!' Cissy beamed at her and gave a sizeable wink.

'The bride!'

A hiss went through the church. The sound of the organ changed and the wedding march boomed out. Melly saw Dudley standing at the front. They all turned, agog to see Gladys walking, on Danny's arm, up the aisle.

She was wearing a straight navy dress and matching navy jacket over the top, navy shoes with a strap and a little circular dark blue hat just resting on the top of her coiled, pinned, snowy hair which stood out strikingly against her dark clothes. Her face was solemn. She seemed tremulous, shy of all the attention. But, Melly thought, she had never seen Gladys look more smart and handsome or more happy. Beside her, their father walked tall and proud in his suit, to support the woman to whom he owed so very much in his life.

They stood up to sing the first hymn and Melly found tears on her cheeks. She wiped her face and glanced up at Reggie. She knew he was still sore about her postponing the wedding for another two whole years. And there were the other things they would have to get used to. As well as not being able to see each other as often as they would like ... 'I'm not going to have a baby along the way,' she had told him. 'So none of that – not unless you do something very clever about it!'

The nursing school had suggested she rejoin her training in February and repeat the second year. She had already done her weeks in the training school and was now overjoyed to be back on the wards. She had been nervous at first, fearful of a repetition of her problems when she left. But there had been no trouble and her worries soon disappeared. Even with the tiredness and hard work and sore feet, she felt useful and truly herself. She was loving it even more than before. She saw Reggie as and when they could manage it. But he was still in Worcester and once he had got over his disappointment, he had become used to it and could see the sense in them both finishing their training before they settled down.

'I know where you are,' he said. 'And –' it had taken him some time to admit this – 'I know you'll be good at it, nursing.' He had had to adapt, gradually, to the fact that she had something else in her life as well as him – and he could see that his girl was even more glowingly happy.

But as they watched Gladys and Dudley make their solemn vows to each other, they did look at each other, each knowing that if things had been different, they would soon have been making their vows as well. As Gladys spoke her final 'I do', Melly laid her hand on Reggie's thigh for a second. *I do*, her hand said. *I'm here, and I love you.*

They all showered Gladys and Dudley with rice and confetti outside, amid cheering and whistles and laughter.

The photographer got them all lined up. Melly found herself next to Tommy.

'You all right?' she asked as they shuffled into place on the church steps.

'Yeah,' he said. She could see he looked happy. 'It's nice.'

'Jo-Ann all right?'

'Yeah. She's – all – right.' He reached out with his good arm and touched her hand for a second. 'Ta, sis.'

The photographs which they saw later had caught Tommy's face in a lopsided smile of utter joy.

The next morning, Melly was back at Selly Oak hospital: an early shift on a women's medical ward. Getting up that morning did not feel any hardship. Despite all the excitement of the celebrations yesterday, the drinks and sandwiches in the pub afterwards, she did not feel tired.

As she dressed in her uniform – the stockings, dress, apron with its crossed straps, her cap – she was conscious of every piece of it, loved every piece of it, aware that this meant she could be a nurse. She was sad that her other trainee friends had gone on without her, but she was back now and the new group were all nice enough.

When she said goodbye to Reggie the day before, after the wedding, they had held each other close. She looked up at him, with solemn intent.

'You know I love you, don't you?'

'Oh – and I love you an' all.' And he followed it with something he had never said before. 'I love you – and I'm proud of you, wench.'

Walking into the long corridor of the hospital, Melly thought of this and held it close to her, feeling in it all the warmth of his love. And then she walked into the ward to begin her work.

Acknowledgements

Thanks for particular help with the research for this story are due to: Adam Siviter, David Barnsley and Anthony Lunney of Cerebral Palsy Midlands for their generosity in giving time, information and insights; once again, Iris and Gordon Parker for their hospitality and for talking to me about life on the Rag Market – it was such a pleasure meeting you both; Anne Howell-Jones and Professor Paula McGee for information about nursing in the early 1960s; and Jim Rawlins of Disabled Motoring UK who was invaluable in answering questions, as was Stuart Cyphus of the Invalid Carriage Register. Others who helped were Debbie Carter and Maureen and Fred Hyde.

The Birmingham History Forum is always a valuable resource. I used a wide variety of books, but of particular help this time were: Mary Joyce Baxter's *The Past Recaptured;* Judith Smart's *I'll Never Walk Alone*; *Out of Sight* by Steve Humphries and Pamela Gordon; *A Fifties Childhood* by Paul Feeney; and, as ever, the collected works of Professor Carl Chinn.

A very big thank-you also to the staff at Pan Macmillan, especially Natasha Harding and Kate Bullows, and all the others working hard in the background in so many ways. Also to my agent Darley Anderson and all the staff at the agency. I couldn't ask for a better team.

Q & A Annie Murray

How does it feel to be publishing your twentieth novel?
It feels rather astonishing. Writing a novel is like being in a dream state which you can re-enter if you read the books again (which in the main I don't – I'd rather be reading someone else's!). So it's strange to look back at all those books, all those dreams, and think, did I actually write those? And where did all that time go?

How did you come to choose Birmingham as the setting for your novels?
It was my home at the time so it was what was all around me. I had gone there for my first job and ended up staying and having all my four children there. It's a city that often seems to get ignored. Not many people were writing about the city and its experiences at the time – at least not in the form of fiction, though there were a number of personal accounts. I was – and still am – a very interested outsider.

Can you tell us how you research historical settings?
When I began, in the early 1990s, there was no Internet. That has its uses now, certainly. But I've always done my research by a mixture of listening to people's stories, using personal written accounts and history books, looking at the many photographs of old Birmingham and, very importantly, drawing on old maps because the place

has changed a good deal and keeps changing. I always go and walk around the areas I'm writing about, even though some of the inner-city wards have changed almost beyond recognition over the past fifty years. Apart from that, like anyone else writing stories, I draw on my own experience or imagination about how things would feel.

How long does it take you to write a novel?
There is an expectation of producing one book each year. I write the first draft in about six or seven months.

Do you have a favourite novel that you particularly enjoyed writing?
I think at the time of writing I often have a love/hate relationship with each one – I have chosen to write it because I love the idea but also hate each one at times, because of the difficulties it presents. But in terms of subject matter, I remember particularly enjoying researching and writing the two books about canals, *The Narrowboat Girl* and *Water Gypsies*. For one reason or another I liked all the others as well, though.

Now the War is Over *revisits the characters of* **War Babies.** *How does it feel to return to characters from a previous book?*
It's a good feeling. You already know them, quite deep down, and what has happened to them, so you are not starting from nothing. You can live on with them and see what happens in their lives and how it affects them.

Your characters go through some very difficult and emotional experiences – does this affect you while you're writing?
Yes – especially once I have got past the first draft, which

entails working out what's going to happen. There are so many details to worry about at that stage that the emotion is slightly secondary. After that, when you are reading it back to rewrite it and following the thread of it like a reader, that's when it hits you. In fact the older I get, the more unbearable it seems to become to imagine your way into the things some people have suffered.

Do you have a particular place you like to write?
I have a work room at the back of the house, one wall of which is formed by glass doors looking out at the garden, and where I have a lot of the books I need. I love light rooms and it is quite cheerful even in winter. It feels right. However, sometimes I just take off with a notebook and sit outside or in some odd place in the house and write by hand. It's important to have a change now and again. For some reason it helps 'creativity' – though I'm still trying to work out exactly what that is.

What inspires you to write?
I find life and the world and people so very interesting and that is always the way I have responded to it – by wanting to make stories out of it. It honours life and makes it meaningful. It's what makes sense to me.

What advice do you have for aspiring authors?
If you want to write, you'll write. I suppose 'aspiring author' means unpublished author? In that case, I'd say, keep writing, keep working at understanding the process and improving and find some other writers who you feel a kinship with and share your writing with each other. It's always really good to get constructive feedback from other people who you trust. It is also a way to find encouragement in what is otherwise a very solitary activity.

Who are your favourite authors? Do you feel they have influenced your writing?

Everything you read influences you one way or another, I think, though you feel much more drawn to some writers. I have different kinds of favourite authors. I love world literature which shows me people and places and experiences I would not ordinarily see. There are so many, but for example, Rohinton Mistry and Andre Makine would be two. And then there are the long-term favourites that you read when you are growing up and they teach you about stories and always stay with you – like Dickens and Charlotte Brontë and Anna Sewell who wrote *Black Beauty* and Helen Forrester's books about her family in Liverpool. I am a fairly conventional writer in that I enjoy narrative storytelling in the way it has mostly been written for the past 150 years or so. I'm more interested, in the end, in people, than in experimenting widely with form.

How has the publishing process changed since you published your first book in 1995?

The main thing, of course, is that everything is done on computers. This has, among other things, speeded everything up. Twenty years ago there was a lot more paper. I wrote my first few novels by hand and then typed them up, before I felt compelled by the demands of speed to learn to write more on the keyboard. And back then there were parcels of thick typescripts to be sent in the post, when now you can submit your book as an email attachment. Actually it feels much less of an occasion doing it at the press of a button instead of carting it along to the post office and queuing with the other people with dripping umbrellas. This has also meant a more print-on-demand approach to publishing, rather than the old discussion of how large a print run there should be. And now a lot of it does not even get printed because so many people are reading books electronically.

How are you going to celebrate the publication of your twentieth novel?
With a nice glass of something red, I hope.

Do you have an idea for your next book?
Yes – and the one after that!

Keep in touch

Are you on Facebook? If so it would be good to hear from you. You can follow my author page on Facebook at **www.facebook.com/Annie.Murray.Author** or search for 'Annie Murray Writer' on Facebook. You may also like my website **www.anniemurray.co.uk**.

War Babies

BY ANNIE MURRAY

She'll have to fight to keep her family together . . .

Rachel Booker has had a difficult start in life. When her father dies, deep in gambling debt, it's up to her mother to make ends meet. Hardened by the daily struggle, she has little time left for affection or warmth. Mother and daughter work together at Birmingham's Rag Market, selling second-hand clothes to put a little food on the table.

There is a silver lining as Rachel makes her first childhood friend, Danny, at the market. As they grow older, friendship blossoms into something more. But at the tender age of sixteen, Rachel falls pregnant just as World War Two breaks out. The young couple marry in haste but it isn't long before Danny is called up.

Left on the home front with a new baby, Rachel must scrape by with the other residents of Aston. If Danny ever makes it back, will he be the same boy she loved so fiercely?

FOR MORE ON

ANNIE MURRAY

sign up to receive our

SAGA NEWSLETTER

Packed with **features, competitions, authors'
and readers' letters** and **news of exclusive events**,
it's a must-read for every Annie Murray fan!

Simply fill in your details below and tick to confirm that you would
like to receive saga-related news and promotions and return to us at
Pan Macmillan, Saga Newsletter, 20 New Wharf Road, London, N1 9RR.

NAME _____

ADDRESS _____

_____ POSTCODE _____

EMAIL _____

☐ *I would like to receive saga-related news and promotions (please tick)*

*You can unsubscribe at any time in writing or through our website where you can also see
our privacy policy which explains how we will store and use your data.*

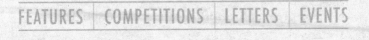